BOUND

SANDSTARR PUBLICATIONS
Dallas - Chicago
USA

SandStarr Publications
a division of SandStarr Entertainment
www.sandstarr.com

ISBN: 978-0-9826697-6-1

Cover art by: BLDGtheBoutique/BLDGtheBrand

THE ART OF SEDUCTION HAS LITTLE TO DO WITH SEX, CONTRARY TO POPULAR BELIEF...

As my clothes came off,
He proceeded to turn me on.

OTHER FACTORS COME INTO PLAY, SUCH AS TEASING, TRUST, AND A MUTUAL SENSE FOR EROTIC ADVENTURE...

As my eyes filled with hope,
He bound my hands with rope.

SHE WAS EMOTIONALLY WOUNDED BY THE BETRAYAL OF HER EX-BOYFRIEND...

As I begged him, "Please,"
He shoved me to my knees.

HE WAS A MULTIMEDIA MOGUL WHO DIDN'T BELIEVE IN LOVE...

As my will to serve rose up,
His adoration came raining down.

BUT SOON, BOTH OF THEM WILL REALIZE THAT SHE IS HIS DESTINY...

BOUND

SHILOH STARR

1

Destiny Richards placed a tray of pastries in a large, industrial oven and drew an arm across her brow. After closing the oven door, she efficiently cleared the area she'd rolled and molded the pastries in. Once her working area was cleared, she called out to her co-workers that she was going on break.

Standing at 5'7" with full lips and a rich, toffee brown skin tone, Destiny was a pretty girl of African-American descent. Although she was slender in the waist, she had a curvy frame.

Before exiting the Employees Only area, she untied her apron and removed the disposable polypropylene gloves covering her hands.

The back door of Eli's Bakery opened into a small parking area. A sidewalk bordered the parking lot and beyond that, a narrow street where cars lined up at a red stoplight. She tilted her head back and welcomed the feel of the fresh, Washington D.C. air.

The atmosphere was significantly different from her warm, colorful hometown of Tempe, Arizona, but she'd wanted to attend Howard University ever since she was in junior high school. She was proud of her heritage, loved her people, and loved what Howard University stood for.

There was no denying that Tempe, Arizona, was a beautiful city. While a special place in her heart would always be reserved for it, she'd felt like a caged bird when she was there. As beautiful as the city was, career options were limited for her preferred field. Since that was the case, it had felt like her fate was bigger than Tempe. Journalism was her passion and she wanted to travel the world. It was her desire to experience other cultures so she could share those cultures - and her own - *with* the world.

Once she'd gained admission into Howard University, she'd felt that she was well on her way. Fast-forward a few years, and she had internships with two small local publications under her belt. Now that she was in her fourth year, it seemed that there weren't enough hours in the day. When she wasn't working at the bakery or spending time with friends, she wrote and edited articles for *The Hilltop,* the university newspaper. Even though it often felt like she never had a minute to sit and catch her breath, she wouldn't trade her experiences for anything in the world. This was what she wanted; this was what she lived for.

The sound of a door closing registered to her, and that sound was soon followed by a relatively high-pitched male voice.

"Hey, are you okay over there?"

She turned her head and flashed a cursory smile at the naturally tan young man with dark curls pulled back in a ponytail.

Carlos Villegas, her flamboyant Latino co-worker, leaned against the brick wall of the bakery with one leg raised. A cigarette dangled between the index and middle fingers of his left hand. He tapped the cigarette lightly, causing a small flurry of ash to drift to the ground. "You look deep in thought over there," he observed, bringing the skinny cigarette back up to his lips.

Digging her hands into the pockets of her khakis, she walked over to join him. "I was just thinking about home."

"Home," Carlos echoed, blowing out a puff of smoke. "There are definitely days when I miss home."

"Venezuela, right?" she asked, leaning back against the wall.

He nodded, squinting off into the distance. "Caracas. There were…major political issues going on when my family and I lived there. Many of those issues are still going on, actually."

"What made you decide to move here?"

He took another puff of his cigarette before answering. "My siblings and I were born here. My mother is a citizen of the United States. About a year after I was born, my grandmother - my mother's mother - got really sick. None of my aunts or uncles were willing to step in and take care of my *abuela*, even though they only lived a short distance away from her. Being the dutiful daughter, my mother decided that my father should stay behind in the U.S. to earn money for us while we moved to Venezuela. My *abuela*…she fought for a long time. For *years*, she held on." A pained expression crossed his face as he stared at the flaming end of the cigarette. "After holding on for five or six years, her body just…gave out. She couldn't hold on anymore. At that point, my mother had to make a decision. Stay there and live in my grandmother's house, or move back to the United States, where my father was still working. We missed Papa so much and told her that. Because of that and because she felt that there were more opportunities for us here, she picked up our family again and moved us back here."

"Wow," Destiny remarked, shaking her head.

He laughed wryly and dropped the butt of his cigarette on the ground. After crushing it with a dark brown work boot, he asked her, "Heavy, right?"

"A bit," she said with raised brows.

He shrugged his shoulders. "I know so many Latinos with stories like mine. When you were thinking of home, where were you thinking of?"

"Tempe, Arizona," she replied.

"I have friends from Arizona," he said. "I hear… mixed reviews about it."

"It has good and bad areas, like most other places," she admitted. "There are other areas that are just...very rural, without much going on. The heat is too much for some, but I always liked the weather there. It was a beautiful place to grow up in."

"But no ocean," Carlos whined, twisting his mouth into a frown.

"There's no ocean around here either, unless you're willing to make a forty-five-minute drive," she pointed out, laughing.

"Touché, but I do not intend to live here for forever," he said, raising an index finger. "This is a pit stop."

She withdrew her cell phone from her pants pocket to check the time. There were only a few minutes left of her break. "Where are you planning on moving, if this is only a pit stop?" she asked, returning the cell phone to her pants pocket.

"California," he replied readily with a grin on his face.

"Expensive," she commented.

"Worth it," he sang with a sparkle in his dark brown eyes.

His optimism was infectious. He hadn't worked at the bakery for long, but she could tell she was going to like him. She followed him back into the bakery, but only after casting one more glance at the streets of D.C. On her first day working here, her manager had told her, *All you need to know about working here is that this is the land of politicians and professionals, and executives tip big. If you are courteous, professional, and approachable, it is quite possible for you to earn enough to live on tips alone.*

By no means was Destiny living a lavish life, but those words had proven to be true. She'd managed to make a decent living.

For the rest of her shift, she'd work the register, taking orders. One employee would assist her with taking orders, and another employee would assist Carlos in the back while he prepared breakfast orders.

On school days, she worked from 5:00am to 9:00am. That gave her an hour to get home, shower, dress, and make it to class. Extra work hours were often available if she ever had any downtime to spare.

After logging into the cash register with her employee ID, she gave the bakery a once-over. The front counter faced the entrance of the establishment. Booths lined the walls and tables filled in some of the floorspace. Politicians and business executives were seated at the tables, eating and conversing.

Eli's Bakery was well-known for making great quality breakfast food, lunch food, pastries, and coffee. The bakery was founded decades ago, and the customers who frequented the place always spoke of feeling a sense of nostalgia whenever they walked through the door.

The bell above the entrance tinkled as the door opened.

Destiny's attention was drawn to the tall, well-built, well-dressed man approaching the counter. It didn't take long for her to recognize him: a thirty-year-old actor-turned-rapper/singer-turned-multimedia mogul. He had a complexion the color of an iced vanilla latte, thick, dark brows, chocolate brown eyes fringed by thick lashes, and some of the fullest lips she had ever seen on a man. The low fade his hair was cut into looked fresh, the hair on top of his head forming what was becoming a trademark wave pattern. His shoulders were broad and his body, encased in the finest of Italian suits, was lean. He smoothed down his tie as he approached the counter and licked his lips as he scanned over the menu.

Remembering that it was rude to stare and bordering on #creeplife status, she tore her gaze away from him. "How can I help you today?" she greeted after finding her voice.

His gaze lowered and settled on her face.

He didn't speak right away, and she wondered what he was thinking. When he saw her, what did he see? Just an average-looking Black girl with long, dark hair pulled back into a ponytail? Did he think she was attractive? Or at this point, was he wondering why she was staring at him for so long? She blinked and looked away again.

His lips stretched into a smile. "I'll take a number seven," he said in a deep, velvety smooth voice, reaching his hand into the pocket of his dark blue dress pants. There was the faintest hint of an unfamiliar accent in his voice. When he withdrew his hand from his pants pocket, he was holding a compact money clip with a black carbon fiber design.

Eager to do something other than gawk at him, she punched his order into the cash register. "Did you want anything to drink with that?" she asked, trying to keep her voice level.

"Coffee. Sugar. Cream." He withdrew several twenty-dollar bills from the money clip. Then he tipped his head towards the tip jar located near the cash register. "When customers tip you, do you actually get that money?"

She finished entering his order into the register. "We remove our tips when we log out of the register. Tips that go into the jar while I'm on the register go to me."

With a nod of acknowledgement, he smoothed out the twenty dollar bills he held in his hands. One of the bills, he handed her to cover his order. Then he proceeded to fold the remaining two. The lines in the bills were sharp and precise, which helped the bills to fit into the small slot at the top of the tip jar.

"Thank you," she told him earnestly.

"Now that I think about it, can you add a cherry Danish to my order?" he asked. "Suddenly, I feel like tasting something sweet."

2

After work, Destiny rushed to her apartment. She had to quickly shower and change into an outfit that was more appropriate for class. Her khaki pants and white button-down shirt had specks of flour all over them. She chose a pair of jeans, a simple lavender top, sneakers, and a black bomber jacket that matched her backpack.

Candace Patterson, her roommate, poked her head out of her room just as Destiny was evaluating her reflection in the living room floor-length mirror. "Are you headed to class?"

"Yeah," Destiny replied, slinging her backpack over one shoulder. "Did you need me to pick up anything on the way back?"

Candace, a pretty, brown-skinned girl with eyebrows arched to perfection, shook her head firmly. "No, but you might want to call Jordan back," she suggested. "He's calling the landline like crazy. I finally picked up so the boy would stop calling. He knows you're ignoring his calls to your cell."

"And I'm going to continue to ignore his calls to my cell," Destiny stated, rummaging around the front pocket of her backpack and withdrawing a tube of lip gloss.

"You're going to have to talk to him at some point," Candace insisted, opening her bedroom door wider and planting a hand on her hips. Her shoulder-length hair was pulled up into a sleek bun. She wore a white tank top and red plaid shorts. By the loungewear she had on alone, Destiny could tell Candace didn't have classes today.

Destiny mulled over her friend's words. For sophomore and junior year of college, she and Jordan Beckford had been couple goals for a lot of the student population. The moment she had walked into Jordan's apartment and seen his lips locked with another girl's, an internal switch had flipped. There was no telling how far Jordan would have taken it if she hadn't walked in when she did. Her feelings for him had died that day.

In addition to being a show of disrespect, cheating was completely avoidable. Why was it so difficult for men *and* women to have a conversation and suggest taking a break to see other people?

Shaking out of her own thoughts, Destiny zipped up her jacket.

"Even if you call him back to tell him to fuck off, that would be better than ignoring his calls at this point," Candace said with her arms outstretched. "I just want the boy to stop calling. You delaying this conversation is why he still has a shred of hope that you'll take him back. That is why you need to talk to him…so you can kill that last shred of hope he has left."

"Maybe," Destiny allowed.

After finding him hugged up with another girl, she had screamed at him that she never wanted to see him again. That was still how she felt. What more needed to be said? Her expectation had been that over time, he would stop calling. There were obviously other women waiting in the wings for him. She figured that he would have moved on with one of them. So far, that hadn't been the case.

Candace is right, she decided. *At some point, I need to have a conversation with him.*

As she left her apartment building and got into her modest blue sedan, her thoughts drifted elsewhere. She pictured a certain powerful man she'd met earlier that morning. That powerful man went by the name of André Damian Gaines.

André had grabbed a booth near the window. For the better part of his stay, he had done a lot of typing into his phone. A businessman as prominent as he was may have been texting business associates or replying to business emails. His phone rang a couple of times, but he silenced the ringer both times. He ate his food slowly while gazing out of the window. A few customers recognized him and approached him. He'd been polite but not chatty; his answers to questions were brief, one-word responses. While eating, he'd cut into his food in a very precise manner. None of his movements, or words, ever seemed to be wasted.

Watching him had fascinated her. Quiet, reserved, with a regal poise that she hadn't personally seen anyone else possess. He exuded an understated confidence that quite drastically contradicted the attitude he'd possessed in his days of being a rapper. Back in those days, his lyrics had boasted to the world how justifiably cocky he was. It was possible that the cockiness he'd displayed earlier in his career was a part of an act or celebrity persona.

Or maybe he's simply grown up, Destiny had thought while observing him. Either way, now he gave off an elegance, a classiness, that she had never associated with him before. There was also an air of mystery about him. Mystery packaged that beautifully was just begging to be solved.

At one point, he'd turned away from the window and stared straight ahead. Then, he'd turned his head further and looked at her, as if he'd felt her eyes on him. Her breath had caught in her throat, and she had temporarily forgotten how to breathe. Attempting to look busy, she had randomly started wiping down the counters.

There was no point in standing around and watching his every move, no point in daydreaming about him. When he looked at her, he didn't see a future award-winning journalist. When he looked at her, he saw a lowly barista, a girl who tendered his cash, took his order, and poured his coffee. They lived in two completely different worlds.

While wiping the counters, she'd snuck another look at him. He was still staring at her thoughtfully and without shame. Then he'd finished his breakfast and carefully collected the remnants of his meal. Smoothing his tie again, he rose to his feet and carried his trash to the nearest trash bin. He reached in his suit jacket pocket, removed a small packet, and opened it. After extracting a moist towelette out of the packet, he wiped his hands and tossed the towelette (and its wrapper) into the trash bin. The screen on his cell phone lit up as he collected it from the table. Another call was coming in, but he ignored the call and instead nodded in her direction before leaving.

She could still see him once he exited the bakery, via one of the large picture windows. Only once he was outside of the bakery did he lift the cell phone to his ear and start speaking into it. That was the last image of him she'd seen before he strolled out of sight.

The memory faded. Realizing that she was sitting in her car with the key in the ignition, she blinked her eyes and started the car. *How is a girl supposed to focus on classes after an encounter like that?* she wondered as she drove through the streets of D.C.

He had looked downright delectable in that suit. His deep voice had rolled across her skin, as effective as a gentle caress. And those eyes...hands down her favorite feature on him. Downturned at the corners, filled with intensity, and the color of Godiva chocolate. He didn't use a lot of words when he spoke, and his movements were calculated. But everything anyone had to know about him resided in those beautifully shaped brown eyes.

Howard University's campus consisted of a mixture of both classic and modern-looking tall, brick structures. Both Destiny's classes and the *Hilltop* newsroom were located in an area referred to as "Main Campus, Section 2." The buildings in this area had classic styles of architecture and sported tall, white column posts at their entrances.

The Howard University School of Communications offered multiple concentration options. The option Destiny selected was Media, Journalism, and Film. Her college professors had her full attention on most days. On this *particular* day, focusing on her studies was damned near impossible. She was plagued by daydreams of a certain former rapper. When an image of him didn't fill her head, then one of his melodic tunes would. He was one of several rap artists who'd popularized incorporating melody into hip hop. His music focused more on emotions and relationships than his hip hop artist counterparts, and that was something that his fans had come to love about him. His experiences were relatable and his words were catchy.

Somehow, Destiny managed to make it through her two classes for the day. After her classes were finished, she headed to the *The Hilltop* newsroom. The newsroom was located on the upper level of the building.

Enter a major publication newsroom in your choice of any major city in the United States, and you would most likely see chaos. College newsrooms only experienced that level of chaos occasionally, but today seemed to be one of those days. Everyone ran around like chickens with their heads cut off, shouting over each other and into their cell phones.

An attractive, dark-skinned girl wearing wire-framed glasses walked past Destiny with a stack of papers in her hands.

Destiny reached out and touched her arm. "Jasmine... what the hell is going on in here?"

Jasmine Brown, dressed to perfection in a button-down blouse and pencil skirt, arched a look at Destiny over the top of her glasses. "Girl," she said, shifting the stack of papers. "Everyone has flipped their shit. Dré Gaines is in town working on some hush-hush project. No one knows if the project is relating to a new artist he is working with, or if he's releasing new music. Ever since he started working behind the scenes, everyone has bent over backwards trying to get an interview with him. But he has completely shut out the media, meaning he refuses to do interviews. Now that he's in town, everyone from our paper to the *Post* is trying to get a word with him."

Destiny's eyebrows shot up. "That's insane," she said. "He stopped into Eli's today. I rung up his order."

All the noise in the room stopped, and Destiny could almost hear the wind resulting from everyone whipping their heads around at once.

Jasmine slid her glasses down her nose and looked at Destiny over the wire frames. "Say what?"

Destiny looked around the room. "What?"

Everyone in the room clamored around her. They wanted to know whether or not a woman had been with him, what he'd ordered, what he'd said, what he was wearing, how he'd seemed - was he polite or in a rush? She held her hands up in a defensive gesture.

Jasmine, who ran the advice column for the paper in addition to serving as the publication's editor, raised both hands and tried to help settle down the excited journalists. "Calm the hell down!" she shouted. "Let the girl breathe."

"The man came in, got breakfast, and left," Destiny told them. "Nothing important happened."

"Is he coming back tomorrow?" someone in the room asked.

"He's probably coming back tomorrow," someone else predicted.

Destiny shrugged. "I don't know."

"If he comes in tomorrow, you should ask him for an interview," Chad Matteson suggested. Standing at 6'4", he towered over the rest of the crowd. He had been something of a college football phenom, until he suffered a torn ACL. Now, he served as the sports editor for *The Hilltop*, a role he never imagined pursuing. He didn't give himself enough credit; he was a very talented writer.

Destiny shook her head at his suggestion. "I'm not going to hound the man for an interview," she said flatly.

Everyone protested her response.

Jasmine held a hand up. She turned to Destiny. "You don't have to *hound* him, but it's worth asking."

"I doubt he's even coming back to the bakery," Destiny said. "It was probably a one-time thing. At his level, he probably travels with his own personal chef."

"*Now* you're just talking crazy," Jasmine admonished, laughing. "Just casually ask him if he'd be willing to give you an interview. If he says no, then back off. You never know. He *could* say yes. Think about how much of a jumpstart that would be for your career."

"*If* he even comes back in," Destiny added. "Which is a huge *if*."

Jasmine tilted her head forward in agreement. "You could be right."

"She's not even going to ask him." One of the newer journalists shoved her way to the front of the crowd of writers and editors. She was a girl with short, salon-styled hair and a chip on her shoulder. "I'll go to Eli's tomorrow and ask."

"Easy, grasshopper," Jasmine cautioned. "Destiny got the chance to talk to him. She has already established a rapport with him, so she has dibs on this." She turned and leveled a glance at Destiny.

Destiny relented. "Fine. I'll ask him."

The crowd of journalists dispersed and went about their business, but Destiny was now the talk of the office.

That evening, Destiny had a hard time falling asleep. Her anxiety levels were through the roof as she'd tossed and turned, fretting about whether or not André would return to the bakery. The feeling was foreign to her. She wasn't easily intimidated, a result of growing up in a family where everyone spoke their minds freely. Facts weren't often sugarcoated in her household. Being raised that way instilled in her the ability to freely communicate her opinions without fear of judgment, and yet...there was something about André that *did* intimidate her. The thought of asking him for an interview made her nervous. The fantasies she'd had about him only added to that feeling of anxiety.

The next morning, she was running late. She showered and dressed quickly, but took a little extra time fixing her hair in the mirror. While she wanted to make it to work on time, that didn't mean she had to show up looking like a street urchin - *especially* considering the gentleman who might be in attendance.

Evaluating her reflection, she smoothed down her plain white button-down shirt and khakis. After taking a deep breath, she grabbed her purse and keys.

When she showed up to the bakery, she immediately recognized a few of her fellow journalists staking out the place. One of the journalists was seated in his car outside of the bakery. He was most likely looking for anyone who halfway fit André's physical description. A few other journalists were seated at tables in the bakery, casually sipping their coffee, but with eyes that were unusually sharp for that time of morning.

They're probably making sure that I stick to my vow of asking for an interview, she thought, greeting them before heading to the back area of the bakery. *If I don't, any one of them will. Hell, they may even ask him before I get the chance to.* She clocked in for work, placed her purse in her assigned locker, and tied an apron around her waist.

Carlos was hard at work, molding pastries.

She peered over his shoulder to inspect his work. "Good job," she commended, clapping him on the shoulder.

"Aren't you the talk of the place today?" Carlos asked nonchalantly as he rolled a croissant.

"What do you mean?" she asked, having a feeling she knew exactly what he meant.

Carlos turned to face her, arching a perfectly tweezed brow. "Dré came in this morning."

Her face flushed. "What does that have to do with me?" she asked, busying herself with retying an apron that didn't need to be retied.

"He asked for you," Carlos said, smiling and crossing his arms over his chest.

"Why would he ask for me?"

"You tell me," he said with raised brows.

"I don't know. He placed an order, just like any other customer."

"Well he likes *something* about you, *mami*," Carlos insisted, "because when I told him you weren't here, he turned right around and walked out the door. He didn't want anything to do with Eli's if you weren't here."

Her heart pounded in her chest as Carlos turned his attention back to his pastries. *Why would he ask for me?* she wondered. *I didn't do anything special yesterday. I definitely didn't* look *special yesterday. I looked a hot mess.* Lost in her thoughts, she returned to the front of the bakery and positioned herself behind the cash register.

Eventually, the journalists who were staking out the place left. She felt better once they were gone. During their time there, she could feel their eyes on her. She knew that they were wondering why, out of all of them, *she* was the one to have gotten the chance to meet Dré Gaines.

Her workday was uneventful. André didn't return to the bakery, and she didn't catch any other *Hilltop* columnists casing the joint. She finished her shift, attended her classes, made a quick stop by the newsroom, and headed home.

The first thing she did after stepping into her bedroom was collapse face-first on her bed, still exhausted from the lack of sleep the evening before. Her eyes fluttered closed and the last thought on her mind was, *Will I ever get to see André Gaines in person again?*

3

"Suddenly, I feel like tasting something sweet... sweet...sweet..."

Destiny was seated on the counter of Eli's Bakery. André stood in the space between her thighs, caressing the side of her face and trailing his hand from her jawline to the slope of her neck. From there, he traced the lines of her collarbone with just his fingertips, causing shivers to run down her spine. Her back arched ever so subtly.

His gaze remained locked on her profile for several moments before dragging down the length of her body. Then his arms circled around her waist. He pulled her closer to him, until there was no separation between them. *"I want you so close to me that I can't tell where I end and you begin,"* he murmured, his voice deep and raspy.

She lifted her hands to his shoulders and peeled the suit jacket off of him as if it were the outer layer of an onion. Her slender fingers attacked the buttons of his button-down shirt next. And then his face was buried in her neck, pressing hot kisses where her pulse throbbed.

He pressed his body into her, and she wrapped her legs around his back, using body language to echo the sentiment that she wanted to be as close to him as possible. He dug his hands into her hair as he kissed his way to her cheek. When his mouth found hers, he groaned against her lips.

She slid his dress shirt down well-toned arms while sucking on his bottom lip...

A sharp knock sounded on the door. Destiny bolted upward into a sitting position with her eyes narrowed into slits. The knock sounded again, and she swiveled her head around in the direction of her bedroom door. Her room was dark. She'd slept through the afternoon and into the evening. Rubbing her eyes, she stood from her bed and padded to the door.

Upon opening the door, she was greeted with the sight of Candace, who gave her a long look before asking, "Did you just wake up?"

"What's up?" Destiny croaked, still trying in vain to rub the sleep out of her eyes.

"You have a visitor," Candace announced, hooking a thumb over her shoulder. She stepped to the side of the doorway.

A tall, brown-skinned young man with short, curly hair stood in the living room. Even though he was watching the television with his back to her, Destiny knew exactly who it was.

With a heavy sigh, Destiny looked down at herself. Her rumpled work clothes were still on. *Then again, the last thing I want is to look good, if he's the one who's looking,* she reasoned with herself. With a newfound confidence, she breezed past Candace and entered the living room. With her arms crossed over her chest, she went to stand in front of her ex-boyfriend.

He was dressed nicely, in a forest green dress shirt, black dress pants, and shiny black dress shoes. The scent of the rose bouquet in his hands blended with his cologne. The bouquet smelled good...*he* smelled good. "Hi, Des," he greeted, flashing a smile the minute his eyes landed on her.

"What are you doing here?" she asked tiredly.

"You weren't returning my calls," he explained. "So, I wanted to come here in person and talk to you."

Candace disappeared down the hall and into her room.

Destiny waited for the telltale sound of her roommate's door closing before looking Jordan in the eyes. "What is there to talk about?"

"I wanted to apologize. Again."

"You've already apologized." Impatiently tapping her foot on the floor, she tilted her head in the direction of the flowers. "Are those for me?"

He nodded and extended them to her.

She sighed and accepted them. "Thank you for these. You didn't have to do this, Jordan." Raising the flowers to sniff them, she turned and headed into the kitchen. There, she set the bouquet on the counter and stood on tiptoe so she could open the cabinet doors above the stove.

Jordan followed her into the kitchen and moved to help her open the cabinet. "I know I messed up. It was just a kiss though, and I can promise that it will never happen again. I want you to take me back." With ease, he pulled a tall, clear vase out of the cabinet and handed it to her.

She accepted the vase from him, unnerved by how close he was standing to her. "We all want a lot of things in this life," she told him while watching him close the cabinet. "But we don't get everything we want."

He frowned. "You're really just done with me over that one mistake?"

"What do you want me to say?" she demanded, moving around him and returning to the kitchen counter. "When we *first* started dating, I told you that cheating was the one thing that I can't forgive someone for. I told you that if you wanted to see other people, or if you were attracted to someone else, to man up and *tell* me, Jordan. What did you turn around and do, though?"

He hung his head in shame, having no response for that.

"If I give you another chance and you cheat on me a second time, then I'm as much to blame as you," she said as she carefully placed the roses in the vase, avoiding the thorns jutting out from the stems. "I'm not going to set myself up like that."

"But I'm promising you that it won't happen again."

She picked up the vase full of flowers and turned her back to him, flipping up the faucet above the kitchen sink. *He's being sweet to you now but if you give him the chance to hurt you again, he will, girl. Stay strong.* After briefly closing her eyes, she lowered the vase into the sink and turned the faucet so that it hovered over the vase. "Jordan…"

"Do you remember the weekend we spent in Miami?" he asked before she could get the sentence out.

If Jasmine were eavesdropping on this conversation, she'd tell me that he was bringing up good memories to manipulate me into remembering him in a positive light, she thought as she watched the water filling up the vase. "Yes, I remember the trip to Miami."

"That was the best weekend of my life," he said earnestly, seating himself on the stool in front of the counter.

"It was a fun weekend," she admitted, turning to face him.

"We should take another trip," he suggested, the tone of his voice lighter. "Not Miami, since we've been there, but maybe Vegas. Or San Diego."

She slowly shook her head, looking at him intently. The desperation she saw in his eyes was heartbreaking. A part of her wanted to forgive him, because she could see that he really wanted another chance. But if she gave him another chance, she would become one of those crazy girlfriends, one of those girlfriends who timed how long it took for him to get home from school or work. One of those girlfriends who snuck peeks at his cell phone screen to see who he was texting. She didn't want a life like that for herself. She wanted someone she could truly love, someone she could have absolute trust in. And right now, that man was not him. How did she tell him that? How did she say all of that to him without hurting his feelings? And more importantly, why did she still care about his feelings when he'd stomped all over hers by kissing another girl?

On Thursdays, Destiny didn't have any classes. That resulted in a longer shift at the bakery and more time for Carlos to delve into her personal business. She didn't mind it. He was hilarious, overdramatic, and entertaining. He worked the cash register while she stocked pastries on the shelves behind the register.

"So...let me get this straight," Carlos said, turning around to face her as the bell over the door rang. "He cheated on you. You broke up with him and ignored him. Instead of moving on with his life, he shows up to your apartment...for what?"

"He wanted to apologize and patch things up," she answered, sliding a tray of pastries onto a mid-level shelf. "He brought flowers and everything."

Carlos rolled his eyes. "Ugh. Why buy flowers when staying faithful is free?" He proceeded to assist the patron who'd entered the shop.

"Right?" Destiny asked him after the customer's order was entered into the register. "My roommate, who used to *hate* him, is practically siding with him now. She thinks I should consider taking him back."

"Oh, no, honey," Carlos said, snapping his fingers in the air.

"I know. I'm not taking him back," she told him. "I could hardly even stand to look at him. I just hate that he does me dirty, and then has the nerve to make me feel like the bad guy. *He's* the one who cheated."

Carlos shook his head firmly just as the bell over the entrance door tinkled again. "You don't have anything to feel bad about. You're standing up for yourself, letting him know you won't put up with bullshit. You deserve better than some jerk who's going to cheat on you and come crawling back with his tail between his legs."

"Amen," Destiny called over her shoulder, squatting down to load a pastry tray to one of the lower shelves.

Carlos watched her work as he said, "If you take him back, I'm disowning you."

She laughed. "Disowning me as what?"

"As…as…my co-worker and friend," he stammered.

"You don't have to worry about that," she assured him, clapping her hands to shake the flour from them. "I'm not taking him back."

"You should come with me to Crave tomorrow night," Carlos suggested.

Destiny finished loading the final tray of pastries and straightened, rubbing her hands together and flipping her hair over her shoulder. "Why should I come to Crave with you?" she asked. "So you can get me drunk and help me hook up with some random stranger?"

Carlos shrugged, a small smile curving his lips. "The best way to fall out of love with someone is to fall into bed with someone else," he theorized, turning to face the register and the customer waiting to be serviced. His eyes widened and his mouth dropped open.

"Thank you for the tip, Dr. Phil," she joked. "But I don't need to fall into bed with someone to get over Jordan. I fell out of love with him when I walked in and saw him kissing someone else." She turned around because she had more to say, but her voice caught in her throat at the sight of a very familiar business executive.

André's eyes were on her and they were filled with curiosity. "Your boyfriend cheated on you?" he asked softly.

Carlos answered for her since she couldn't find the words. "Her *ex*-boyfriend," he clarified readily.

André seemed to notice Carlos for the first time. "I'd like a number seven," he said, handing over a twenty-dollar bill. "Cream. Sugar. Keep the change."

Destiny lowered her gaze to the floor, feeling her cheeks burning with embarrassment.

"Do you have a break coming up?" André asked her.

She started to shake her head, but again Carlos answered for her. "Actually, she was just about to start her lunch break."

Destiny glared at Carlos. "My lunch break isn't for another two hours," she said, giving André an apologetic look. "I'm sorry."

"You can take your lunch now," Carlos encouraged, nudging her. "I can cover you."

"Are you sure?"

Carlos nodded and dismissively waved his hand at her.

She walked around the counter and went to stand beside André. The suit he wore today was a shimmering charcoal gray color. It was fitted perfectly to his frame. He most likely had his suits tailored. Suits rarely came off the rack fitting quite that perfectly.

He placed a guiding hand at her back as they walked to a table in the corner of the shop, away from most of the other patrons. As he seated himself, he smoothed down his tie.

At a complete loss for words and wondering whether or not this was really even happening to her, she claimed the seat on the opposite side of the table.

"Your ex-boyfriend cheated on you?" he questioned as soon as she was settled in her seat.

He doesn't waste time with ice breakers, she thought. "He did, yes," she replied aloud.

"And now he wants you back?"

She nodded. "He showed up at my apartment last night, since I wasn't taking his calls."

André's brows furrowed. "You're not going to take him back, are you?" he asked.

Carlos approached their table carrying a tray. He set the tray down in front of André. "Were you needing anything else?"

André shook his head, with his eyes still on Destiny. "No, thank you." He waited for Carlos to leave before repeating, "You're not going to take him back, are you?"

"I'm not planning on taking him back, no."

"Good. You shouldn't." André surveyed the food that was laid out in front of him.

She tilted her head to the side. "Can I ask something?"

Something about her question made him smile. "Yes, you can."

"Why did you want me to sit with you?"

A hint of a smile touched his lips. "You fascinate me."

"*I* fascinate *you*?" she asked incredulously, laughing. "Why? I'm boring. Especially compared to you."

He looked up at her. "How would you know?"

"Because…you're *you*," she said, gesturing to him. "I mean, everyone knows you. When the staff at my school newspaper heard that you came here, they begged me to ask you for an interview. They said that newspapers and media outlets all around the city want to interview you, but you refuse."

Mirth danced in his eyes. "You write for your college newspaper?"

"Yes," she said.

"And you told your newspaper staff about meeting me?" he asked.

"When I walked in, they were talking about you. And I just mentioned that you were here."

He nodded in understanding and proceeded to inspect the silverware that Carlos had given him. "I don't often participate in interviews," he confirmed. "In that regard, the rumors are correct."

"Why not?" she asked him bluntly. "Interviews can serve as marketing or PR for upcoming projects. You run one of the most successful multimedia companies in the world. Wouldn't you want that continued exposure?"

He smiled. "Yes, I've considered that. What I've found out, throughout my career, is that the majority of the media is full of shit."

Her eyes widened at his choice of language.

"The media makes a habit of trash-talking a public figure until said public figure walks through their doors for an interview. At that point, they promptly begin to kiss ass. It's disgusting. It's phony." He sectioned off a piece of crêpe with a fork. Then, he gestured to his plate. "Do you want any of this?"

Knowing herself, she'd hold an entire conversation with pieces of food on her face after taking just one bite. "No, thank you."

"In the beginning of my career, I played the media game and tolerated it. I kind of had to. I was new to the industry, and the media was an important tool to introduce me to the public. But the more established I became, the less I put up with disrespect from…anyone, really. Over time, I started to have fun with the whole interview bit. I started lightly poking fun at whoever was interviewing me, and over time, that poking fun became…less light. Media personalities would watch the interviews before airing them and realize that I used wit to make them look completely idiotic." He popped the piece of crêpe into his mouth.

"There has to be at least a few journalists you've come across who had good intentions," she said, her faith in her own dream occupation faltering.

He looked at her for a moment while chewing. "You're correct. There are two, *maybe* three journalists that I trust to write ethically and without bias. Emmett Winslow of RapScope Connect is one of them." Pausing, he studied her face. "I don't want this in any way to discourage you from becoming a journalist. I do want to emphasize that if you become a journalist or media personality of any kind, make sure that you remain ethical. Make sure that you report honestly, and without malice."

"I intend to."

He nodded and looked down at his plate.

"What fascinates you about me?"

"You're beautiful, for one," he said without hesitation. "You're also a walking contradiction. You have a certain confidence about you, but at the same time you have this…shyness. This naïveté. You have this sexiness, this sensuality about you. You're sexy without even trying to be. And yet…you also have a certain innocence. You manage to juggle qualities that are at opposite ends of the spectrum."

Her cheeks were growing hot again, a trend whenever she was around him.

He looked up at her and smiled the widest he had since the first day he'd come into the bakery. "That's exactly what I'm talking about. Unintentional sexiness. Adorable to a fault. You've been on my mind since the first day I saw you."

Her heart pounded in her chest, because she knew the next words that were coming without him having to say them.

He said them anyway. "You're the only reason I came back."

Those words caused a shiver to run down her spine.

He smoothly changed the subject. He asked about her schooling, asked which college she attended. He asked what intrigued her about the field of journalism. She told him about her interest in other cultures, her desire to travel the world. He confessed that one of his favorite aspects of his former life as a music artist was traveling.

"I work behind the scenes now and I still do quite a bit of traveling - just not as much as I used to," he told her. "Back when I made music, I got to see different countries and cultures all the time. I would travel on my own time, and a week later, I would get another music artist texting and asking if I wanted to join them for a video shoot in Turks and Caicos, Maldives, Jamaica, Africa, or the

Dominican Republic. I was on the go all the time back then, and I tried my best to introduce those cultures to the rest of the world with my music. Of course, that resulted in people labeling me a culture vulture...but the exposure that the artists from these other countries were able to get was worth substantially more to me than whatever haters felt like labeling me on any given day."

This would be amazing content for an article, was the first thought that occurred to her. For how intimidating he was, he was surprisingly easy to speak to. *Or maybe it's easier to talk to someone once you know they find you attractive and sexy,* she thought as she watched him eat the final bites of food on his plate. It was difficult for her to believe that a public figure of his caliber would find her interesting. She found him incredibly attractive, and the more she talked to him, the more of a mystery he became to her.

As an entertainer, he'd seemed extremely outgoing and extroverted, but sitting before her, he was reserved. He would lapse into silence and just sit, looking at her. It made her uncomfortable at times, which seemed to amuse him. He was a tough person to read.

She glanced at the clock hanging behind the front counter area. Her break was nearly over.

"Is our time almost up?" he asked her with an arched brow.

She nodded.

"Do you have plans tonight?"

She shook her head.

"What time do you get off of work?"

"Seven o' clock."

He looked at the expensive-looking watch looped around his wrist. "That's perfect, actually. I will pick you up from work."

Is this really happening? she thought. *Is he really asking me out? Nah, I must be dreaming.* She'd already had several dreams about him. Images from those dreams

27

played behind her eyes. In one of those dreams, she'd sat on the counter just twenty feet away from where they were sitting right now. He'd stood between her thighs and...

"What are you thinking about right now?" he asked.

Alarmed, she snapped out of her reverie. "Nothing," she replied quickly, running a nervous hand through her hair. Embarrassed and in a hurry to put distance between them, she stood from the table a little too quickly and stumbled in the process.

He reached out and grabbed her wrist to help steady her. "Are you all right?"

Her wrist tingled in the spot where he touched her, but she managed to bob her head up and down. "Yeah, I'm fine. I do have to get back to work, though."

"Seven o' clock?"

"I'll be ready."

She returned to the counter, where Carlos gave her a satisfied look.

"*Mmmhm*," was all he said.

André threw away the remnants of his meal and just as he had the first day she'd met him, wiped his hands with a moist towelette. He smiled at her before leaving. It was quite possible that a smile as bright and charming as his could cure cancer, solve world hunger *and* help heal the global warming issues.

The sound of Carlos's voice behind her prevented her from melting into a puddle on the floor. "Well?"

"He's picking me up at seven," she said dazedly.

Carlos squealed and gave her a high-five. "Oh my God, oh my God!"

"I know," she said, shaking her head. "He could have anyone he wants. Look at me. I mean... *seriously*, look at me." She stepped back and stretched out her arms.

Carlos looked her over.

"Boring white shirt, boring khakis. Sneakers. My nails aren't even done." She lifted her hand to inspect her nails and frowned in disgust. "I probably have flour in my hair. I look crazy."

"He sees past all of that," Carlos said in wonder, examining his own manicured nails. "Wow."

Destiny laughed and shook her head. She logged into the cash register next to Carlos's.

"So…where is he taking you?"

"I don't know."

"A little surprise factor, okay, I like it." He crossed his arms over his chest. "You're so lucky. I wonder if I show up to Crave tomorrow with khakis on and flour in *my* hair, will I meet my prince charming?"

She lightly slapped his arm. "Time will tell if he's any kind of prince charming."

"I saw you blushing like a junior high schooler over there," Carlos quipped. "So, he's *something*."

He's definitely something, she agreed, smiling to herself.

After Destiny finished her shift, she released her hair from its ponytail and brushed it out. Her next mission was reapplying her eyeliner and lip gloss.

Seven o'clock rolled around. True to his word, André rolled up to the sidewalk in a sleek, black chauffeured Bentley. To say that Destiny felt underdressed would have been the understatement of the year.

He stepped outside of the car holding a sleek, black garment bag. "Let's go inside," he urged.

She led him into the bakery and there was his hand again, light and gentle on her lower back as he followed her inside.

Carlos was closing up the shop and looked up as they entered.

"I want you to try this on," André announced, extending the garment bag to her.

She blinked as she accepted the heavy offering. "Okay," she said, albeit a bit stiffly.

"If it fits, there are matching shoes in the car."

The employee bathrooms were adjacent to the lockers. Feeling jittery, she entered the Women's bathroom and closed the door behind her. Her thoughts were all over the place as she flipped on the light switch and set her purse on top of the sink.

Her attention shifted from her mirrored reflection to the garment bag he'd handed her. What awaited her inside of that bag? What kind of dress would he have picked out for her, and what size would he have guessed her to be? She tugged on the garment bag zipper and peered inside. A gasp escaped her lips as she hurriedly continued to unzip the bag. The garment bag contained a beautiful, royal purple halter style dress. The material was silky between her fingers. The dress was long and elegant.

She hung the garment bag on the bathroom door and quickly removed her shoes, pants and work shirt. Once she pulled the slinky fabric up over her curves, her eyes widened. *He knew what size to buy you,* she thought as she tried to fasten the portion of the dress that secured around her neck. The hooks were being a bit stubborn, but she held the straps up to get an idea of what the dress would look like. It fit her perfectly. The material clung tight to her skin and it flattered her every curve.

Lip gloss wasn't enough for this dress; she wanted a bolder lip. She dug around her purse, bypassing her usual lip gloss for a tube of lipstick. Then, she smoothed a hand over her hair, wishing she had a curling iron. After giving her reflection one more glance, she pulled the garment bag down from the door, collected her purse, and exited the bathroom. Almost as an afterthought, she stopped by her employee locker so she could grab the peacoat she'd worn into work today.

When she returned to the front of the bakery, André was standing between two tables. He appeared to be staring out of the window with his hands in the pockets of his dress pants. She admired the sight of him for a few moments before clearing her throat.

He turned and looked at her. The grin he wore as he approached her was very telling. No compliments were necessary; that grin and the look in his eyes said it all.

"I couldn't close the top part in the back," she said, turning around and sweeping her hair over one shoulder. His dress shoes clicked across the tiles as he moved closer to her. A minute later, she felt the back of his hand brushing against the nape of her neck. His hand lingered there before pulling on the straps and securing them.

"How does that feel?" he asked her. "Too tight at all?"

"I like the way it feels. Does it look okay?" She turned around in a circle, barefoot, causing the flowy hem of the dress to swirl around her legs.

A twinkle lit up his eyes as he said, "Breathtaking."

Carlos flashed two thumbs up signs, barely able to contain his squeals as he waved them out of the bakery.

Moments later, Sade's voice serenaded André and Destiny through the speakers of the chauffeured vehicle. As the dark Bentley cruised through D.C., she smoothed down the skirt of her dress, loving the feel of the dark satin material beneath her fingertips.

"Do you like the dress?" he queried. It had seemed odd to her that he'd insisted on sitting across her instead of beside her. With the way he was looking at her though, she was beginning to understand why he may have made that request. From where he sat, he got an eyeful of her in the dress that he'd bought for her.

She returned his frank perusal, for the first time noticing that he wasn't wearing the same suit he'd worn earlier that day. He was wearing a more formal suit. At first glance, the suit looked to be black in color, but when light shined on it in just the right way, a shimmery blue undertone was visible. "I love the dress," she said.

He smiled and sipped from a long-stemmed glass of champagne. Champagne was known to be his signature drink, and it seemed that was not false advertisement. His fingers traveled up and down the stem of the glass in a manner that looked sexual in nature. "It looks amazing on you," he complimented softly.

Determined not to blush at his flattery, she said, "You clean up pretty well yourself."

His smile widened.

"Where are you taking me? We've been on the road for quite a while."

"We're almost there," was his vague reply.

She slanted her mouth in disapproval, but instead of pointing out that he'd evaded the question, she looked out of the window. They were driving along the Potomac River and passed several landmarks along the way. Many well-known, highly rated restaurants lined the river.

The car slowed down and turned into the parking lot of a tall, white non-descript looking structure. Destiny had seen it before, a countless number of times, but had never paid attention to what the building was. As the car pulled up to the front doors, she could clearly see a sign stating that the building was the John F. Kennedy Center for the Performing Arts. Elegantly dressed men and women exited their cars and entered the building. She marveled at the beautiful dresses she saw on the women of all ages that lined the sidewalk, some mingling and smoking.

The door to the Bentley popped open and André stood out of the car. He leaned in and offered his arm. Destiny grabbed onto his arm as she rose out of the car, clutching her coat with her free hand. He was quick to remove the coat from her hand and drape it across her shoulders, to help shield her from the cold. The autumn wind rolled over her, lightly playing with strands of her hair.

André shook hands with the driver and glanced at his watch as he advised what time the driver should return.

Then, with a warm hand placed at Destiny's lower back, he guided her to the front doors of the Kennedy Center.

She felt like a tourist but couldn't help looking in every direction once they entered. The carpeting was red and lush beneath her heeled feet (she couldn't help but wonder how many women a man had to sleep with, in order to be able to accurately guess their dress and shoe sizes based on sight alone). The walls were adorned with abstract art and ornate lighting fixtures hung from the ceiling. People were gathered in the large lobby and their voices echoed off of the walls. She could hear faint music seeping through multiple sets of closed double-doors.

Amused at her excitement, he withdrew two tickets from his suit jacket pocket as he steered her in the direction of the ticket counter. He presented the two golden rectangular pieces of paper to the ticket agent. Then, he escorted her past the double-doors and towards a staircase that was a blend of white marble and glass.

She twisted around and looked behind them, blindly following his lead.

"I take it you've never been here before," he guessed.

"How could you tell?" she asked, still staring behind them.

"Just a guess," he said, grinning.

She looked at him and rolled her eyes. "It's a beautiful building," she said in her own defense. "And no, I've never been here before. Are we coming to see a play?"

"Yes. In my down time, I frequently attend plays and operas."

Was it customary for former rappers to attend plays and the opera? He spoke the words so casually, as if attending the opera was second nature for him.

"The play we're seeing tonight is one of my favorites." He leaned towards her as they climbed the stairs. "You're going to love it, I promise."

Two tall doors swung open and a laughing Caucasian couple emerged. They held the doors open for André and Destiny.

Destiny tilted her head forward to them. "Thank you," she said graciously.

André smiled down at her as they moved through the doorway.

The sight that stretched before them took her breath away. They were standing in the upper level of a large auditorium that buzzed with excited voices. Balcony seats were located to their left and right. Destiny disengaged her arm from his and moved forward to the railing that kept attendees on the upper level from falling on an unsuspecting attendee seated below. She held onto the railing and looked down upon a sea of red, plush seats. People below who saw familiar faces called out to each other.

She raised her gaze and looked towards the stage. Thick, heavy curtains were pulled together. She turned and angled a look over her shoulder at André, who had his hands clasped in front of him while he waited for her to return to his side.

Her steps were slow and deliberate as she returned to him. "Thank you for bringing me here," she told him.

His eyes crinkled at the corners when he smiled. He lifted a hand to her cheek and held it there for a moment before offering her his arm. She accepted it gladly and he escorted her to their box seats.

They took their seats and Destiny leaned forward immediately, clinging to the railing in front of them. The lights died down and the hand that André had at her back began to move up and down in a caressing, comforting motion.

Her spine tingled at his touch. Surges of electricity crackled beneath the surface of her skin. Anticipation built up within her as the overhead lights dimmed and colorful lights lit up the stage. In this moment, she could feel it. She could feel that after tonight, nothing would be the same.

4

André handed Destiny stylish Swarovski binoculars so she could clearly see the actors move around the stage.

Unable to contain her excitement, she turned to him. "This is amazing."

"I told you that you would enjoy it. Shhh." He held a finger up to his lips and pointed that same finger forward, signaling for her to pay attention.

She turned back to face the stage and watched the scene play out before her. The actors on the stage were performing *Phantom of the Opera,* a play she'd long since heard about but had never had the chance to see for herself.

The male lead character ached with longing, and his voice was rich and deep. She leaned back in her seat as she continued watching. André's hand shifted from her back to her thigh, but she barely noticed. She was held captivated by the performance of the cast. The story was a haunting tale about how far a disfigured loner of a man was willing to go on his quest to experience love.

When the curtains closed for intermission and the auditorium lights flashed on, she had tears in her eyes.

André frowned in concern as he wiped away her tears. "I wasn't expecting the performance to have that much of an effect on you."

"It's sad," she said, sniffling and dabbing at her eyes. She'd neglected to bring her purse in, because it hadn't matched the dress she was wearing. There had been tissues in her purse, tissues that would have come in handy right about now. She was probably making a mess of her eyeliner.

Wordlessly, he withdrew a silk handkerchief from the pocket of his suit jacket and held it up to her face.

She shook her head and grabbed his wrist. "Wiping will ruin it."

"Let me," he commanded, his voice gentle but firm.

Lapsing into silence, she angled her face so he could dab at her tears with his handkerchief. Her grip on his wrist weakened and after a moment her hand fell away altogether.

"Look up," he instructed.

She did as she was told, and he continued to dab the napkin beneath her lower eyelids.

"All done." He refolded the napkin precisely as it had been folded originally and inserted it back into his pocket.

She patted her cheeks lightly. "Do I look okay?"

"Beautiful, as always."

She looked at him, trying to gauge whether he was just placating her.

"What do you think of the production?" he asked.

"Very well done. What I can grasp of the story is very haunting and sad. I feel for him."

André's brows shot up. "You feel for the phantom?"

She nodded. "To go that long without love...it's no way to live."

He looked at her thoughtfully while stroking his jaw. "I don't want to spoil anything for you, so we can revisit this conversation after the play."

"I know that he kidnaps her," she told him. "I haven't seen the play before, but I'm familiar with the story."

"In response to your earlier statement, then," André said, "one could say that kidnapping women is no way to live."

"But if he was living underneath the opera house hearing all of these different plays and operas about love and he hears how amazing and life-changing it is, and *finally* gets the chance to experience a taste of it..." Destiny shrugged. "I can understand why he would want to desperately reach out for someone that could possibly love him. I mean…it's still wrong of him to kidnap a woman, yes, but you can understand why he did it, can't you?"

A glint sparkled in his eyes as he nodded. "I guess I can, yes."

She glanced around them. "It's amazing that we get this entire box to ourselves."

"I own this box during my stays here in D.C.," he told her, rolling up the sleeves to his suit jacket. The motion revealed a small birthmark on his right forearm.

Without thinking, she reached out and touched it.

His eyes fluttered closed as soon as her hand came into contact with the mark.

"André," she whispered.

He clamped his left hand down on hers and removed it from his arm, opening his eyes. His jaw clenched as his gaze met hers. The look in his eyes softened a bit and he lifted her hand to his lips and kissed it.

Feeling like she'd done something wrong, she settled back in her seat and patiently waited for the intermission to end. He kept her hand clasped in his, but that didn't stop her heart from hammering in her chest.

When the show ended, he remained seated and didn't look like he intended to move. "It's going to be a mad house while everyone leaves and tries to make it to their cars," he explained. "I take my time in leaving."

"So, do you come to these shows a lot?" she asked, and then mentally kicked herself for asking the question. *Earth to Destiny, he bought out the box for the entire time he's here.*

"I come here quite a bit, yes."

"What else do you do in your spare time?"

"I read. I enjoy watching movies when I have the time to. I still write music sometimes, even though I don't release it. I listen to a lot of music. I work out quite a bit."

"Do you…have any friends here?"

He draped an arm across the back of her seat. "Are you interviewing me?" he asked, narrowing his eyes at her. "Did you just slip into journalist mode right in front of my eyes?"

She shook her head and stared at her lap. "Just trying to get to know you better."

"No," he answered after a moment of thought. "My company has a small office here, so there are co-workers that I sometimes attend events with when I'm in town. There are politicians that I know, but I definitely wouldn't call them my friends."

She nodded in understanding and remained quiet.

He laughed. "Are you ever going to stop being nervous around me?"

"I was wondering the same thing," she admitted. "I don't usually feel nervous...*ever*, really."

"Why do you think you're nervous around me?"

She looked him in the eyes and the rest of the world fell away. "Because..."

His eyebrows lifted and his lips parted while he awaited her response.

Her eyes lowered to his lips and she remembered the fantasy she'd had about him. *That fantasy would be one of the reasons why I'm always jittery around him,* she thought as she struggled to find words, *any* words, to say so he didn't think she was a complete weirdo.

"Because...?" he prompted with a playful smile on his face.

"Because you're an intimidating person," she finished.

"What makes me an intimidating person?"

She shrugged. Now it was his turn to play the role of journalist, apparently. "Who you are...how you carry yourself..."

"How do I carry myself?" he pressed.

She tilted her head to the side. "Seriously?"

He laughed. "I'm curious. I want to know how you see me."

She shook her head and looked away from him. "You seem…very particular. About what you like, who you talk to. Even what you like to eat, and how you like to eat it. You seem very observant. You do a lot of watching. You're also kind of bossy."

His eyebrows shot up. *"Bossy?"* he repeated.

"Just a little bit," she said, holding her index finger and her thumb close together.

"I don't know if I like that description," he muttered, almost to himself.

"Then stop being so bossy," she told him simply.

A slow smile stretched across his face. He stood from his seat and offered an arm to assist her in standing. "What if it's in my nature?"

"Then, I guess I'm going to have to learn to live with it," she replied as she accepted his hand.

Upon André's and Destiny's return to the Bentley, he sat next to her instead of across from her. Then, he poured himself a glass of champagne. Sade's lilting voice could still be heard wafting from the speakers.

"Do you want a glass?" he asked her when he finished pouring.

"I don't turn twenty-one until next year," she told him. "And I'm fine, I don't need a glass."

"Sometimes, I forget about the difference in drinking ages between the U.S. and Canada," he murmured before taking a sip of his drink. Silence lapsed between the two of them as he turned to stare out of the window.

Seizing the opportunity, she reached out and touched his birthmark again.

He swiveled his gaze back to her. "What is it with you and my birthmark?"

"Why do you always react so strongly when I touch it?" she countered, not moving her hand.

He stared long and hard at her, swirling his drink around in the glass. Then he set his glass down on the minibar, his movements slow and calculated. Her fingers continued to dance lightly across his arm. He looked down at her hand, then back up at her face.

The look in her eyes dared him to grab her hand and move it, the way he had in the opera house.

"You think I'm bossy?" he asked quietly.

With her heart racing in her chest, she nodded.

"Come here," he said in a soft voice.

She scooted closer to him.

"Closer," he commanded.

Any closer and I would be on top of him, she thought. *And maybe that's what he wants.* She closed the final inch of distance between them.

His movements were slow and deliberate as he leaned over and kissed her on the lips.

She kissed him back without hesitation. Her hand fell away from his arm. All her thoughts flew from her mind as their kiss deepened. He hooked an arm around her waist and pulled her on top of his lap in a smooth, scooping motion. She briefly worried about the dress tearing, but soon that thought also escaped her.

He pressed feverish kisses to her lips and lowered his kisses from her mouth to her neck, to her collarbone. She tilted her head back, loving the feel of his lips on her skin. Her entire body was on fire for him. She'd never felt this way for anyone else, not even Jordan.

She cupped his chin and tilted his head back so she could kiss along his jawline. He groaned and tightened his grip on her waist. Her pulse quickened as she continued to kiss beneath his earlobe. Feeling daring, she caught his earlobe between her teeth and sucked on it.

"Ah," he gasped, sucking air between his teeth. His hands worked at lifting up the skirt of her dress.

She returned her attention to his lips and kissed him, wrapping her arms around his neck.

He opened his eyes mid-kiss and pulled away from her. "Destiny," he whispered.

"André," she whispered back, and started to kiss him again.

He pulled even farther back. "Destiny," he said again, his voice sounding a lot clearer.

She blinked. "Yes? What's wrong?"

"If we're going to take this any further, there's something I need to tell you."

She ran a hand through her hair. "O-okay," she said, confused. Now that she was sitting on his lap, he wanted to have a conversation? His timing was far from ideal.

He brushed a strand of hair out of her face. "I'm not looking for a committed relationship right now. If we continue like this, the arrangement would be strictly casual."

She sat back on his lap, frowning. "Casual?"

"Being who I am, with the interests that I have, a contract would also be involved. To ensure discretion."

Her brows knitted together as she tried to make sense of his words.

"I would give you an interview, if you wanted," he offered. "For your paper."

Those words sent her scrambling off his lap, hastening to adjust her dress. She felt hurt. Offended. Cheap. Tears burned the back of her eyelids while she straightened the bodice of her dress.

"I'm sorry if I gave you the wrong impression," he apologized quietly.

"Wrong impression?" she mimicked. "You took me on a date, André. *This* is a date. You bought me a dress and shoes. You took me to an amazing play. For what? Why do all of this, if you just want me to be some glorified booty call?"

He touched her shoulder gently. "I don't want you to be a booty call. That's not what this is."

She swiped his hand from her shoulder. "Then what is it?" she demanded.

"You were right about me earlier. I'm very particular. I have interests that are…out of the ordinary."

She shook her head. *I am an idiot. I should have known this was too good to be true.* A successful, gorgeous media mogul showing interest in her, a girl who was wrapping up her final year in college while working in a bakery? She'd had some modern-day *Cinderella* type of fantasy in her mind if she thought that she would skip off into the sunset with him for a lifetime of happily ever after. Of *course,* he was into strange shit. If she rejected his advances, he would probably troll the grocery store cashiers next to look for someone desperate enough to fulfill his weird fetishes.

"Look at me."

"You can't tell me what to do anymore," she said firmly, continuing to stare straight ahead. "Take me back to the bakery so I can pick up my car." She could feel him shifting in his seat but didn't dare look in his direction.

"All right."

The rest of the ride was quiet. When the car pulled up to the curb in front of Eli's Bakery, she couldn't get out of the car quickly enough. She slammed the car door shut and stormed down the sidewalk with her arms crossed over her chest. Her anger didn't allow her to hear the car door opening and closing a second time, but she did feel someone grab her elbow a moment later. Furious, she whirled around with angry tears in her eyes. "What do you want?"

"I want you to get back into the car with me," he told her.

Still refusing to look at him, she turned her head to the side.

"I'm sorry. Maybe I sprung this on you too soon."

"No, I'm glad you brought this up now. I almost made a *huge* mistake."

He searched her eyes and sighed. "Please come back to the car. We can talk about this, maybe over a nightcap in my hotel room."

She met his gaze head-on. "I'm not signing a contract. I'm not looking for a casual *arrangement* with someone. I want a real relationship. According to you, *you* can't give me that. There is no reason for me to get in that car with you. We just avoided one major mistake. We should part ways right here and now."

"If you come with me, you can interview me with no strings attached," he said, holding up his hands in a defensive gesture. "You don't have to do anything for me in return."

"I'm insulted that you thought I would enter into some weird arrangement with you for an *interview*," she spat at him. "Is that how lowly you think of me?"

"Of course not," he insisted.

"And now you're patronizing me." She turned on her heel and walked away from him.

He followed her around the corner of the building, to the parking lot at the back of the building. "I don't mean to patronize you. What do you want me to say?"

"I want you to apologize to me," she said, stopping and leveling a glare at him. "What you asked of me was very offensive and inappropriate."

He blinked. "I'm sorry," he said.

She shook her head, more at herself than at him. She was so angry at him, *so* angry, and yet looking at him, her anger was already dissolving. It was impossible to stay mad at him when he looked so apologetic. Frustrated, she tore her gaze away from him before her resolve vanished completely.

"Destiny," he said.

"Stop saying my name," she muttered.

"Okay." He stood there, looking completely helpless for several moments before asking, "Can I just do one thing?"

No. "Yes."

He stepped forward and grabbed her face in his hands. Her chest heaved as his face lowered close to hers. He kissed the tip of her nose, then lowered the kiss to her lips. She reached up, intending to pull his hands off of her face, but her hands remained limp on top of his as he kissed her. Any protests she had were muffled against his mouth. His arms lowered and snaked around her waist, pulling her closer to him.

A runaway tear rolled down her cheek as she kissed him. She liked him. A lot. They had come close to making love in a moving car. Even though she was a firm believer in waiting before becoming intimate with a guy, she'd almost thrown caution to the wind. One look from him, and she'd been ready to jump into the sack with him. She pulled away from him and turned blindly, her eyes filled with tears as she stumbled towards her car.

This time, he let her walk away.

Destiny most loved the newsroom late at night. She was usually one of the last writers to leave. The night hours tended to pull the best writing from her. Maybe it was the calm of night, or lack of distractions.

The only other writer/editor who kept late hours was Jasmine. When writers turned in their articles, she would spend the late hours editing the articles for content and placement in the news publication.

Destiny tapped the end of her pen on top of her desk. She'd stared at a blank word processing document for the past half-hour without typing one single word. As much as she tried to will thoughts of André from her mind, she couldn't. He dominated her thoughts. Spending time with him had been electrifying. Walking away from him hadn't been easy, but logic had prevailed last night.

I am not the casual encounter kind of girl, she told herself.

"You look like you're deep in thought over there," Jasmine observed, twirling a red pen between her fingers. Her desk was across the aisle from Destiny's. They were both working on a deadline and for that reason, they'd both been quiet for the majority of the night. "I didn't know articles about campus culture were that deep."

Destiny shook her head. "I *wish* I was thinking about an article," she muttered. "I've been trying to focus for the past half an hour."

Clucking her tongue in sympathy, Jasmine tilted her head to the side. "What is it? Jordan again?"

Destiny had nearly forgotten that Jordan existed, André had occupied her mind so much. With another shake of her head, she twisted her chair so that she was facing her friend. "Can I ask your opinion on something?"

Jasmine leaned back in her chair and crossed one leg over the other. In contrast to Destiny's casual jeans and t-shirt, she wore a beige and brown turtleneck, a beige skirt, and brown heels. "You know you can, go ahead."

Feeling an attack of self-consciousness, Destiny stared down at her hands. "What do you think about casual sex?"

A giggle burst from Jasmine's mouth. "Definitely not the question I was expecting," she said.

"I know, it's out of the blue."

Jasmine continued to twirl the pen in her hand. "I am a bit more open-minded than the average person," she started. "As long as two adults are up front about what they want and safe about it, I don't see anything wrong with it."

Destiny mulled over the response.

Jasmine watched her thoughtfully. "I guess the real question is, what do *you* think about casual sex?"

"I never thought it was for me," Destiny said slowly.

"Past tense," Jasmine commented. "So, your thoughts have changed?"

Images of André clouded Destiny's mind. "I don't know."

"Hmm." Jasmine turned from side to side in her chair as she thought. "The thing about casual relationships is that you have to be very sure that you're only interested in sex. What tends to make these setups fail is one person wanting more than the other. Did someone approach you wanting a sexual relationship?"

Destiny chewed on her bottom lip as she nodded.

Jasmine smiled. "And you're actually considering it? Juicy."

If you think that's juicy, you'd fall over if you knew who approached me with the proposition, Destiny thought. "I don't know...I *do* want more from the situation than just sex," Destiny said. "Or, at least, I'd like to explore the possibility of having something more. I associate sex with love."

"Many women do, if not most," Jasmine said, tilting her head forward. "You just have to handle this situation with care. Engaging in casual sex is an easy way to get your heart broken, if you go into this situation knowing you want more than he does."

Destiny lowered her eyes solemnly and turned back to stare at the monitor.

A knock sounded on the closed door of the newsroom.

Jasmine glanced at her cell phone to check the time. "It's past ten o' clock. Who would show up this late?" She stood from her seat and strode down the aisle of office desks.

Destiny attempted to return her focus to the article that had to be turned in by Monday morning. She positioned her fingers over the keyboard.

Jasmine pulled the door open.

"Hello. Is Destiny here?"

Destiny frowned at the sound of the deep, male voice. She rose from her chair, looking in the direction of the newsroom door. Her heart did backflips in her chest as

Jasmine stepped to the side, holding the door open for the visitor. With Jasmine standing out of the way, Destiny had a better view of the tall, light-skinned, well-dressed man who'd asked for her. She was staring directly into the face of André Gaines.

5

Destiny remained behind her desk. "What are you doing here?" she asked quietly.

"I'm here for my interview."

Jasmine's eyes grew wide with shock. Her eyes darted back and forth between the two of them. "Destiny?"

Destiny's eyes remained on André. "We didn't have an interview scheduled."

"But schedules *do* change," Jasmine declared, linking arms with André and escorting him to Destiny's desk.

André lowered his gaze to where Jasmine's arm was linked with his until she detached herself from him and returned to her desk. Then, he turned his attention to the petrified looking girl cowering in front of him. "I can't stop thinking about you," he told her. "Last night, things got pretty intense and we ended on a bad note. I don't feel right, leaving things that way."

Destiny had wondered if she'd ever get the chance to talk to him again, but she wasn't quite ready to have this conversation. She needed more time, but how could she tell him that after the trouble he'd gone through to find the newsroom? He was a busy man, and she couldn't help but feel flattered that he'd taken the time to track her down. "I don't have anything else to say," she told him.

"Is there a place where we can speak privately?"

"We have a conference room."

"Lead the way."

She locked eyes with him and hesitated only briefly before walking around her desk and gesturing for him to follow.

He trailed behind her.

She opened a heavy wooden door and flipped on the light switch. Fluorescent lights flickered on, shining down on a long cherrywood and glass table with black leather seats surrounding it.

He remained standing in the doorway, surveying the room.

She turned and gave him an expectant look. "Well?"

After a brief hesitation, he stepped inside the room and closed the door behind him.

Her heart thumped in anticipation as he turned and shifted his gaze to her. His dark eyes combed over every inch of her. "I'm not used to women running away from me," he confessed.

"I'm not used to having men proposition me like I'm some streetwalker," she said, meeting his gaze full-on.

One corner of his mouth lifted into a half-smile.

"I'm glad one of us is amused," she muttered, pulling back the chair at the head of the table and sitting in it. She folded her hands together and rested them on top of the table.

He removed his suit jacket and draped it over the back of the nearest chair. Then, he proceeded to loosen the striped tie at his neck. Releasing a weary sigh, he seated himself in the chair to the left of her. His movements were precise and fluid. There was a grace in his movements that she'd only seen in trained dancers. "I apologize for my unsolicited proposition."

"Does that approach ever work for you?" she asked, sounding more curious than angry.

"Yes."

Of course that approach works for him, dummy. He's him. *Women probably throw themselves at him without him having to say anything at all.* Visuals of him seducing other women entered her mind, causing her to frown. "So…instead of seeking out a real relationship, real love, you have casual relationships with women that are strictly sexual. That doesn't get old after a while?"

"It hasn't yet," he replied.

"You have no interest in finding love?"

He shrugged his shoulders and managed to make even that movement appear graceful. "I'm not sure I believe in love."

"Wow." Her expression turned to one of sympathy.

He gave a brief shake of his head and held up an index finger. "Don't."

"Don't what?"

"Don't pity me." His voice hardened. "There's no reason to feel sorry for me. I'm a successful man. I've experienced a lot of good things in my life and I plan on experiencing a lot more. Love isn't one of those things. I've come to accept that."

She exhaled deeply, stunned at his admission. "It's hard not to pity you," she said, leaning forward. "Love is one of the most sought-after things in this world, for good reason."

"For good reason? Have you ever looked at the relationships around you, including your own recent relationship? They're all train wrecks." He rolled up the sleeves of his dress shirt. "People may show the highlight reels of their relationships on social media, but they aren't as quick to show the drama that is going on behind closed doors. Rather than sign up for that type of drama, for the sake of conformity, I'd rather live by my own rules. The way I live has served me better than believing in love ever has. When I look around, I'm shown that believing in love usually just results in heartbreak."

"But that's a part of why it's so special," she insisted. "If love were easy to find, it would be taken for granted. No one would appreciate it."

His eyes sparkled as he smiled at her. "You have a very innocent, naïve way of viewing the world."

"And you have a very pessimistic way of viewing the world," she retorted. "This hasn't always been your view on love, unless all of your songs were bullshit."

He sighed and glanced around the room. "Listen. I'm here to grant you the interview that your fellow writers so desperately wanted you to get. Is there anything you want to ask me that can actually go to press? I don't think I need to tell you that everything we've said up until now cannot be included in an article of any kind."

"I would have prepared questions for you, if I'd had prior notice that you were coming," she said, sitting back in her chair.

"If I'd warned you, would you have agreed to see me?" he asked. It was now his turn to be curious.

"Probably not," she admitted.

He stared down at the table.

"Why are you here?" she asked him. "I mean, really?"

"I tried to let you walk away from me," he said slowly. "I know that I disappointed you, that you were unhappy with me. So, I tried to let you go. Only…I couldn't stop thinking about you."

She rolled her eyes. *Do not fall for this. He used to be an actor, and now he's a slick businessman who knows how to manipulate the people around him.*

When he finally lifted his gaze to her, his eyes were shimmering with emotion. "I tried so hard to stop thinking about you. I've never had to *try* to stop thinking about a woman before…not recently. If things ended, I was just done. It was systematic for me. When it comes to you…I don't know. I don't know, and I don't understand it."

"While I feel for you, I don't understand what you want from me."

"I want…you."

She stared at him without speaking.

"You're what I want," he repeated.

"You want me to enter into an arrangement with you where there are no commitments," she elaborated.

He nodded his head firmly. "Yes."

"You want me to sign a contract and have sex with you," she went on. "That's what you want."

"That's what I want, yes." He saw the unimpressed look on her face and hastened to explain. "Discretion is of utmost importance to me. I can't risk certain...interests of mine...being made public."

Oh, right. He's into weird shit. I was so hung up on him wanting a casual affair, I haven't even begun to unpack that part of the situation yet. Abruptly, she stood up from her chair and walked over to the window in the corner of the room. She stared out across the campus courtyard and wrapped her arms around herself. *Assuming that what he is into isn't* that *weird, could I handle what he's asking for? Could I handle a no-strings arrangement with a man that I'm wildly attracted to but would have no claim on? What happens when he approaches the next woman with a crazy proposition like this? Am I willing to share him with someone else? Could I ever handle something like that?* There were so many questions running through her mind, so many doubts, so many mixed feelings. When she turned to look at him, she could feel her heart melting beneath her chest.

What she saw was a beautiful man, a beautiful man who was broken. Since he was a public figure, there were intimate details of his life that she knew. She knew that his parents divorced when he was young. She knew that he spent his childhood volleying back and forth between Mississauga, Canada, and Houston, Texas. The one thing that she didn't know was at which point he had stopped believing in love. The man she looked at now was very poised, very articulate, and very coordinated – like a fine-tuned machine. He didn't express intense emotions often and whenever emotions did rise to the surface, even he seemed surprised at them. It was as if he wasn't used to them.

He waited patiently in silence, observing her just as she was observing him.

She sighed. "I cannot do this, André."

"The aspect that bothers you most about this, is the lack of commitment?" he asked.

"Yes."

He lowered his gaze and drummed short fingernails on the top of the conference table. "Well, I'm very sorry to hear that. The offer for the interview still stands."

She glanced at her watch. "It's getting pretty late, and I have plans with a friend tonight."

"Oh?" A single brow arched.

"I'm sorry...I know you're a busy man, and I know you've made an effort to give me this interview," she apologized. "It's just...not a good time."

To her surprise, he laughed. His laugh was a deep, rich, hearty sound that bounced off the walls in the room. "Are you dismissing me?"

Her lips formed into a small smile. "I guess I am."

One of his hands reached into the pocket of his dress pants. He withdrew a polished business card holder and flipped it open. He withdrew a thin, cream-colored business card with raised lettering on it. He slid the card across the table and clamped the business card holder shut. "Call me. We can reschedule the interview."

The thin card lay flat on the conference room table, but it may as well have been a brick wall erected between them. "I told you that I'm not interested in your offer. Why do you still want me to conduct the interview?"

He stood from his seat and grabbed the suit jacket he'd thrown across the back of the chair. "Maybe I believe in your talent as a journalist," he said as he drew the suit jacket across his shoulders.

"Or maybe you think you can change my mind about having casual sex with you," she guessed, narrowing her eyes at him in suspicion.

The grin he flashed her was mischievous. "Maybe."

After André left the newsroom, Jasmine descended upon Destiny's desk. "Girl, you have some explaining to do."

"There's not much to explain," Destiny said, sitting in her desk chair.

Jasmine shook her head and held up an index finger. "Uh-uh, honey that does *not* fly. You seriously just had André Gaines walk up in here checking for you? Talking about not leaving things the way they were last night? What happened last night?"

"Jas…"

"You're not getting out of this. I can't believe we sat in this office this entire time and you haven't said anything about seeing him last night."

Destiny logged back into her computer. "I saw him at the bakery again. We…had words."

"Words? What words? You are leaving so much out, and I hate you for it," Jasmine said, her mouth slanting into a frown. "And I know you didn't interview him that quickly. You guys weren't in the conference room long enough. It doesn't add up." She turned her back to Destiny and took a step towards her own desk. Then, she whirled around, her eyes round.

Destiny looked up at her, feeling the first needles of panic crawl up her forearms. *Discretion is of the utmost importance to him, but thanks to the questions I asked Jas earlier, she's about to blow the lid off this entire thing.*

"Oh my God!" Jasmine shrieked, covering her mouth with her hands. "*No.*"

"Jasmine, please leave this alone," Destiny begged.

Jasmine shook her head, pointing her finger at Destiny. "He's the guy," she sputtered. "He's the guy who wants to have a casual relationship with you."

Destiny's cell phone vibrated. She was relieved for the distraction.

"Oh my *God*," Jasmine exclaimed. "I'm right, aren't I?"

Destiny busied herself with replying to Carlos's text message. Earlier that day, he'd invited her to Crave. Her first inclination had been to brush him off, but she figured she could use a little bit of fun after two back-to-back love life disappointments.

"Don't think you can ignore me, missy," Jasmine said, planting her hands palm down on the desk.

"I don't have any comments on the theory you've come up with," Destiny said evasively, setting her phone down.

"Oh, cut the bullshit," Jasmine grumbled. "I would bet money he's the guy. It makes sense. You're against the concept of strictly sexual setups, but for some reason you are considering it. Why are you reconsidering? Because he is one of the hottest men in our country and for close to a decade, has been one of the most influential men in the *world*. Not to mention, he's extremely charming. It also explains why he came in talking about not wanting to leave things the way they were last night, because last night would have been when he approached you with this idea. You already admitted to seeing him again yesterday. Wow. Wow, wow, wow."

Destiny saved the word processing document on her flash drive and began to close the applications that were still open. "Are you done yet?"

Jasmine sighed. "Fine, don't tell me anything."

"There's nothing to tell," Destiny assured, withdrawing her flash drive from the USB port and dropping the small gadget into her purse. She shut down her computer and turned off the monitor. When these tasks were completed, she wheeled around to face Jasmine. "But I will let you know that arrangements without commitment aren't for me."

"Which would explain why he walked out of here looking like someone told him his dog died," Jasmine quipped.

A wave of concern washed over Destiny, but she fought to keep it from showing in her facial expression. "I'm leaving for the night, but I'll probably be in over the weekend."

"Are you going to interview him?" Jasmine asked. "I figure that question is safe to ask."

"I'm not sure," Destiny answered honestly.

"It would be a huge boost for your career, since every journalist in the country is trying to get an interview with him," Jasmine reminded her. "No matter what the two of you have going on, throwing away this opportunity would be absolute madness."

Which could be why he insists on giving me the interview, Destiny thought. *Maybe he really does feel bad about last night and wants to make it up to me by helping my career.* She slung her purse over her shoulder and headed to the door of the office.

"Just one more question," Jasmine said from behind her.

Destiny turned her head. "Yeah?"

"If you're not going to take him up on the no-strings attached deal, can I?"

Destiny erupted into laughter as she walked out of the newsroom.

A few hours later, Carlos was ushering her inside of Crave nightclub, shouting to her about how live the club was tonight. Destiny was wearing the shortest dress she owned, a crimson little number with short sleeves. The music blasted from strategically placed speakers. The dance floor was crowded with writhing bodies.

Initially, she hadn't wanted to come out tonight. Some of her friends entertained the eighteen and over club scene, but she'd never been much of a club person. She would have preferred to go home, but all that awaited her there were thoughts of André. Even now, his business card was burning a hole in her purse, just waiting to be used. She figured that if she joined Carlos at Crave, she'd be so busy dancing that she wouldn't have time to think about André.

Carlos hooked a skinny arm around her shoulders and steered her around the club. His lean body was encased in a pair of jeans, a suit jacket, plain white t-shirt, and dress shoes. Destiny also suspected he was wearing guyliner, but she couldn't quite tell. He whisked her over to the bar and ordered drinks for them. "You look like you've had the day from hell!" he shouted at her.

"It has been a tough day," she admitted.

"I'm going to make it all better!" he exclaimed as the drinks were served to him. Orange liquid sloshed around in the glass he handed to her.

Her brows furrowed as she accepted the glass from him. "What is in this?"

"Ingredients that will make all of your problems go away," he told her with a wave of his hand.

She used the small straw in the glass to stir the liquid. *I agreed to come to the club tonight because I wanted to get my mind off of André...but I wasn't planning on drinking.* She was still technically underage, after all. Images of André floated into her mind, and she remembered just how good he'd looked in the conference room of the newsroom. She remembered how good his lips had tasted the evening before.

Carlos watched her with a knowing smile on his face.

Whatever it takes for me to stop thinking about him, she thought, raising the glass to her lips. Tilting her head back, she downed the contents in the glass.

He threw his arms around her neck. "There you go, girl! By the end of tonight you'll be asking, 'André who?'"

Intent on showing her a good time, he proceeded to lead her around the nightclub. He seemed to know everyone that passed by. If people weren't coming up to him, he walked over to them and joked along with them. A cycle was born. Talk, introduce, dance, drink, repeat. Whenever they returned to the bar counter, more drinks would materialize in front of her.

Occasionally, Carlos would scamper off to dance with some equally attractive young man. During those times, thoughts of André would creep back into her head. Those thoughts resulted in her tipping back more glasses than she could count on one hand.

The minute she attempted to stand to go dance, the ground started moving and the world tilted. She reached out to grab something, anything, to keep from falling. That something wound up being someone's arm. She stared up into the face of Chad Matteson, athlete-turned-sportswriter for *The Hilltop*. He smiled at her, clearly unbothered that she was wrinkling the sleeve of his long-sleeved black shirt.

"Are you okay?" he queried, steadying her with both hands.

She shook her head. "The world is moving," she slurred, trying to walk back to the bar stool. She stumbled and fell against him.

He held her steady in his hands. "Maybe what you need is to sit down...here." He guided her to the nearest bar stool and helped her onto it. His hand lingered on her arm a few beats longer than it needed to. "I think you've had a bit too much to drink."

"Maybe a little bit," she mumbled, barely able to keep her eyes open. She grabbed the edge of the bar counter to help keep herself upright. "Carlos is here...somewhere."

"Is that who you came with?" Chad asked.

The bartender asked if Chad wanted to order a drink.

"A few waters, if you don't mind," Chad responded, looking down at Destiny.

"You don't have to worry about me," she said, her words running into each other. "I can see that you're worried, but you don't have to be."

"We're going to get some water into your system," he said, fishing out a few dollar bills from his wallet to tip the bartender once the two cups of water were placed in front of him.

She wrinkled her nose. "Water? I don't want water, I want..." Her brows furrowed and she stopped in mid-sentence. "I don't know what I want," she said finally, after some thought.

He shook his head. "I never took you for the type of girl that would get this wasted."

"Do you know what's funny?" she asked. "I'm *not* the type of girl that gets wasted. I'm really not, but there is someone... someone I'm trying to forget. Someone who wants to just... have sex with me. He wants to have sex with me, but he doesn't want a relationship with me. Do you know what he wants, what he *really* wants? He wants me to be his sex slave, is what he wants. Can you believe that? He wants me to be at his beck and call, just…fuck him whenever he wants."

Chad's eyebrows shot up. "Ummm..."

Carlos jogged up to them. "What did I miss?" He laid eyes on Destiny. "*Ohhhh*, honey. I shouldn't have left you by yourself."

"She's pretty wasted," Chad advised, rubbing the back of his head and looking quite flustered himself.

Carlos looked the brown-skinned former football player up and down. "Hello, and you are...?"

"Chad," he said, extending his hand.

"Carlos," Carlos greeted, accepting the offered hand.

"I gave her some water, but it will take some time for that to begin to help," Chad explained. "She's pretty far gone and might need something stronger, like coffee."

Destiny slid off of her stool. "I want to dance."

"Honey, I think it's best if you sit down for a while," Carlos suggested.

She shook her head firmly. "I don't want to sit down." Frowning, she searched her brain for the words she wanted to say. "I want André."

Carlos's eyes widened.

Chad scratched his head. "What did she just say?"

"Oh, nothing, she's out of it," Carlos said quickly with a nervous chuckle as he helped his friend and co-worker back onto the stool.

"I could have sworn she said-" Chad started.

Carlos peered at some point over Chad's shoulder. "Damn, that girl's ass is huge!"

Chad whipped his head around. "Who? Where?"

"Predictable." Carlos placed his hands on either side of Destiny's face. "You need to calm down, honey, okay? Chad got you some water. I suggest you start sipping."

"I want André to be my boyfriend, and he just wants to have sex with me," Destiny whined, her eyes shining with tears. "Like I'm some...cheap hoe or something."

Carlos brushed her hair back and hugged her. "I'm never giving you liquor again," he vowed, rolling his eyes heavenward.

She pulled out of the embrace and fumbled for the purse still dangling from her shoulder.

"What do you need, hon?"

She withdrew her cell phone and a small, thin card from her purse.

"Destiny...you should put the phone down," Carlos cautioned, reaching for her cell phone.

She moved the phone out of his reach, glaring at him. "You can't tell me what to do, Carlos!"

"Okay, okay. Just chill." Carlos turned, checking for Chad, but Chad had disappeared into the crowd...most likely in search for whatever large ass Carlos had claimed to see.

Destiny squinted at the card in her hands, trying to focus on the phone number listed on it. She would later swear on any Bible presented to her that the numbers were moving. And her fingers refused to move when she wanted them to. She groaned in frustration and after several attempts, finally got the number dialed in. She held the phone up to her ear.

The phone rang once, twice, and a third time before the call was answered. A deep, gravelly voice came on the line. "Hello?"

"André?"

There was a long pause. Then, "Destiny?"

She pushed her hair out of her face as she struggled to remember why she'd called him. "There was something I wanted to tell you," she mumbled, almost to herself, "but I forgot what it was."

"I can hardly hear you," he said. "Where are you? What is that noise in the background?"

"I'm at Crave, but it sucks here," she told him.

"You're at a club?" His voice was laced with worry. "How did you even get into the club? You're not twenty-one."

"Anyone eighteen or over gets in," she said, laying her head on the bar counter. "You just need ID to drink."

He paused again, and there were subtle noises in the background, quiet music and the sound of moving fabric. "Are you drunk right now?"

"I don't know. I can't tell. But there was something I wanted to tell you. Hold on, I'm trying to remember."

"I'm coming to get you."

Those words made her lift her head. For some reason, she didn't want him to come. Wait a minute, who was she even talking to again? "No, don't."

"I'm not going to let you drive yourself home in this condition. I'll be there in half an hour." He disconnected the call.

She pulled the phone away from her ear and stared at it.

Carlos stood beside her, silently watching her with fidgety hands. "What did he say?"

She looked up at him with a confused expression on her face. "He said...he's coming to get me," she said.

Carlos rubbed his temples. "Oh, dear."

André sat on the edge of his bed, waiting for the sleepiness to subside. He gripped the edge of the mattress to keep himself steady. He'd been suffering through a restless sleep when the phone call came in. Lately, he'd been plagued with nightmares of dying alone. It was a nightmare he couldn't shake; he'd been having them for years.

The discussion he'd had with Destiny in the newsroom office was fresh in his mind, and that scene had played out in his mind the minute his head hit the pillow. The look of disappointment on her face had broken his heart, and the look of anger she'd given him made him feel like a monster.

The night he'd taken her to the performing arts center, he hadn't intended on having sex. He preferred sexual relationships to happen over time. Even though he wasn't seeking a commitment, he still liked a bit of a chase. There was no experience quite like those first initial stages of flirtation, the not knowing whether a woman would shoot him down or respond positively to his advances. Women assumed that because he didn't care for monogamy, sex was all he wanted. That was a misconception that couldn't be further from the truth. He still liked to spend time with women that wasn't sexual in nature. He still liked to have deep and insightful conversations with them.

The first time Destiny had touched him, his body had responded in a way that he'd never experienced before. He was a wizard with words and still found it difficult to explain how her touch had made him feel.

He hadn't intended to touch her or kiss her, but once they *had* touched and kissed, he'd felt obligated to warn her that he was not seeking a relationship. His timing had been wrong, way wrong. He knew it and felt it as soon as the words had left his mouth. That initial expression of confusion had haunted him for the past twenty-four hours. The first time he met her, he'd sensed that there was something different about her. He hadn't been able to put his finger on it, but she'd managed to get under his skin in a way that was unprecedented. Many women in the past had tried to gain and maintain his attention; nearly all others had failed. She'd garnered his attention and held it without even having to try.

He stood from the bed and walked over to the window. There was a reason he'd chosen to take her to *The Phantom of the Opera*. Even though the male lead in the story believed in love and André did not, he still related to the character. He didn't believe in love, but he suspected that deep down, he wanted to. Taking her to that specific play had been a test of sorts to see if she would have empathy for the phantom. It was a test she'd passed with flying colors; he'd been both pleased and impressed. After the show was over, she'd laid her hand on his arm, and that had been the very undoing of him.

He was sensitive to touch in general and didn't allow many people to touch him. In past sexual relationships, women had touched him, but he'd always controlled the manner in which they had. If it had been anyone else setting their hand on his arm, he would have politely asked them to remove their hand. With her though, it had been different. He'd enjoyed her light touches. It seemed that he enjoyed everything about her.

He ran a hand over his head and released a deep sigh. She wanted nothing to do with him romantically, since they wanted different things in life. That was fine. It was disappointing, but fine. Even though they weren't seeing eye to eye, he would not allow her to mess up her life. Driving drunk had the potential to result in a ticket and/or arrest for driving while under the influence. It had the potential to result in someone being seriously hurt if an accident occurred. He wouldn't allow anything like that to happen.

He flipped on the light in the bedroom of his expensive, stylish hotel suite. The unmade bed was expansive with a dark brown leather headboard attached to the wall. A large, flat-screen television was mounted on the wall opposite the bed. The bedroom boasted a balcony, a large bathroom, and top of the line furnishing. Bare-chested and clad in white linen pajama pants, he collected articles of clothing from the walk-in closet.

Crave was only a short distance from his hotel. After dressing in dark designer jeans and a white button-down shirt he left untucked, he searched for the directions to the club. He grabbed his car keys from the bedroom desk and strode down a short hall, passing an additional bathroom and a doorway leading to a guest bedroom. As he moved through the living room of his hotel suite, he adjusted the collar of his shirt.

He stood in the dark for only a brief moment before leaving his hotel room and heading for the hotel garage. He hadn't wanted to disturb his driver at this time of night. This was a drive he would make himself.

André cruised the streets of Washington, D.C., in his sleek, dark luxury car. As he drove, he thought of Destiny.

"It's hard not to pity you. Love is one of the most sought-after things in this world, and for good reason," she'd told him earlier tonight. When she'd spoken the words, passion and fire lit up her eyes. She'd spoken with a conviction that many women even twice her age didn't possess.

He pulled up to the front of Crave and climbed out of the car. *I guess eighteen and over clubs don't bother to hire valet service,* he thought, surveying the long sidewalk that stretched in front of the club entrance. He used the key fob in his hand to engage the alarm on his car before walking through the front doors.

Frequenting dance clubs had been mandatory in his days as an entertainer, but these days he only made club appearances when it benefitted one of his music acts.

The music in the place made the walls shake. People surrounded him right away, clamoring to give him hugs and high-fives. Some wanted to know if he was there to perform. Young women stumbled past him wearing too-high-heels and barely any clothes, too drunk to recognize him. Young men followed behind them, always in close pursuit. André didn't miss the hint of desperation that lingered in these places. In clubs, women were often desperate to find love, while men were desperate to find their next lay.

He stopped walking and glanced at the line of young adults at the bar counter. There was no sign of her there. His gaze swiveled to the dance floor. That was where he found her, tossing her head back and forth with her arms in the air. Beautiful, wild, and carefree, dancing alone. The center of attention but not caring to be, in her own little world feeling the music.

As he drew nearer to her, he watched her hips sway to the repetitive, hypnotic beat playing over the speakers. He watched her move slowly while everyone else around her gyrated and thrusted in sharp, jerking movements. Her body was liquid flow, poured into a tight, crimson sheath of a dress. Her long hair, damp with perspiration, hung in her face. A fine sheen of sweat covered her arms and the top of her chest. Something was stirring within him, something that hadn't awakened in a long time. The feeling frightened him.

He took a few steps backwards. Had someone sucked all the air out of the room? It felt like he was being smothered. He couldn't tell if the sight of Destiny had brought it on, or if it was the fact that he hadn't been in a room this crowded with people in quite some time.

She pushed her hair back while dancing and her eyes landed on him. The minute she saw him, her movements halted. It appeared as if someone had pressed the Pause button on her only, she stood so still. Everyone around her continued dancing and mashing their bodies together on the dance floor. Her lips parted and she stared at him with wide eyes. Standing there, she looked the way he felt: naked and vulnerable.

6

André started to approach Destiny, his legs moving in a long, lean stride. He stopped just short of the dance floor, feeling a bit anxious at the sight of the dance crowd. He stared past flailing arms and curved hips, locking eyes with the most beautiful young woman on the dance floor. He wanted to walk over to her, wrap her up in his arms and never let her go. The unpredictable movements of the dancers, however, served to heighten his levels of anxiety.

She stared openly at him, breathing hard with her full lips parted.

He lifted his hand in one slow, smooth motion and crooked his index finger at her repeatedly, beckoning her over to him.

She lowered her eyes and remained in the center of the dance floor. The blue, purple, and red lights suspended above the dance floor shone on her, lighting up her hair and skin with color.

He waited patiently with the tips of his matte black designer boots just barely touching the edge of the dance floor. "Come to me," he whispered.

She lifted her gaze as if she'd heard him. That would have been impossible; the music was way too loud. And still, she started moving forward, walking through the sea of moving dancers. Her eyes were heavy-lidded, a side effect of inebriation. Despite her drunken state, she moved like a long-limbed gazelle. Her eyes remained on him until she came to stand before him. At that point, she looked him up and down. "I never thought I'd see you in jeans."

He could smell the liquor on her breath. "I never thought I'd see you completely intoxicated," he returned.

She tilted her face up at him and pouted. "You did this to me."

And there was that feeling again, the feeling of something stirring within him. He felt a strong urge to touch her or kiss her. He had to remind himself that she didn't want anything to do with him, no matter how much lust he saw in her eyes right now.

She lifted her hand to his shoulder and trailed it down the length of his arm, pausing at the rolled fabric at his elbow. Her gaze anchored to his arm for a long moment, then she peered up at him.

He knew what she was going to do before she did it. If he'd wanted to, he could have stopped it. Instead, he allowed her to satisfy her own curiosity.

Her fingers continued to trail down past his elbow and to his forearm. They lightly touched his birthmark. She took a step closer to him, closing the small distance that was between them. Still stroking his forearm, she raised her gaze to meet his.

He lowered his eyes from her face down to where the curve of her breast pressed into his chest. He wasn't a stranger to sexual tension; he rather enjoyed it. And he liked knowing that he could turn a woman on. If he wanted to be, he could be quite the tease. But standing here, now, with Destiny's body pressed against his, he was afraid to move. The thought of moving even one inch scared him to death. Her doe brown eyes were imploring, pleading for him to do something, to make a move, but he was frozen with fear.

She must have seen the battle that was going on behind his eyes, because as she continued stroking his arm, she rose on her tiptoes and touched her lips to his.

His arm shot out and he grabbed her wrist. It wasn't a planned move; it was just a reflex. His grasp on her wrist was quite tight. When he realized just how tight his grip was, he loosened it.

She didn't stop kissing him. If anything, her kiss only grew more intense and passionate.

The kisses he gave back to her were desperate and hungry. He released her wrist and grabbed her by the waist. The music pulsed around them as their tongues touched. She sucked on his bottom lip before ending the kiss.

When the kiss was over, he slowly opened his eyes. Without a word, he grabbed her hand and whirled around. A few club patrons shouted his name over the music, but he ignored them as he led the way outside.

Half-expecting to see a parking ticket tucked beneath one of his windshield wipers, he assisted her into the passenger side seat. After helping to secure the seatbelt across her chest, he raised to his full height and closed the passenger side door. He was pleasantly surprised to find no parking tickets on the windshield and breathed a sigh of relief as he walked around the car.

As soon as he lowered himself into the driver side seat, she leaned over the center console and kissed him again.

He groaned against her mouth and played with her hair while kissing her back. Using her own move against her, he sucked on her bottom lip. Hard. He relished the sound of her gasp when he did this. Pulling back and grabbing her hand, he said, "Just hold on for me, baby." Then he brought her hand up to his lips so he could give it a light kiss. He started the car and pulled the vehicle away from the curb.

During the drive, they couldn't keep their hands off of each other. She rubbed his thigh, which definitely got a rise out of him. It had become increasingly distracting, to the point where he covered her hand with his and moved it to rest in his lap.

When they reached the hotel, he parked the car in the hotel garage and removed his hand from hers. He opened his car door, exited the car, and went to open the passenger side door for her.

He offered his hand and assisted her out of the car, admiring the shape of her long, well-toned legs. She stood in front of him, slightly more sober than she'd been in the nightclub. But she had a look in her eyes, a look that said she was going to kiss him again if he stared at her for too long. Smiling, he shook his head at her. Keeping her hand tucked in his, he guided her to the elevator at the far end of the garage.

She stood close to him in the elevator, close enough for him to smell the vanilla scent of her perfume. Close enough that he could feel the slight tremor that ran through the length of her body. Close enough that he couldn't wait another minute without feeling her mouth on his again. He scooped her up in his arms and held her against the wall of the elevator. She cupped his face in her hands and wrapped her legs around his waist. Their lips met, but he wanted to taste more of her. He quickly moved his lips from her mouth to her cheek to her neck.

She breathed heavily and tilted her head back against the wall. "André," she gasped.

He angled a look up at her. "Yes?"

"I'm not signing a contract tonight."

He caressed her cheek with his hand and said, "The last thing on my mind is that fucking contract."

They kissed again, long and deep. A dinging sound indicated that they'd reached his floor. She started to lower her legs, but he held on tight to her waist. He proceeded to carry her out of the elevator and down the hall to his hotel suite, and all without interrupting the kiss.

Whenever she touched him, it sent a trigger reaction of shocks beneath his skin and throughout his entire body. He felt her and wanted to feel more of her, tasted her and wanted to taste more of her. Her lips were full and soft.

He held her in a death grip and didn't let go once they entered his hotel suite. They were bathed in darkness but didn't have to see each other to enjoy each other.

She slid both hands beneath his dress shirt and lightly touched the skin below his belly button. With his mouth planted firmly on hers, he carried her through the living room, down the hall, and into the master bedroom of the suite.

He didn't bother with lights. He didn't bother with words. There was only kissing, only touching, only exploring. Only his hands unzipping the back of her dress, only her hands unbuttoning his shirt. Only him setting her down on the bed like she was a delicate piece of glass and bending down to her so he could continue to press feverish kisses to her mouth.

A bright sliver of moonlight shone between the gap in the window curtains. Destiny peeled the shirt off of André's shoulders and felt an incredible sense of déja vu. The scene was similar to the fantasy she'd had about him. She drank in the sight of him: muscled, tattooed arms and chest, glistening skin, rock-hard abdomen and the sacred V-shape to his pelvic area.

In return, he stared at her long and hard. Her dress was falling off her shoulders and starting to sag down in the front, revealing the slope of her breasts. He parted her legs and positioned himself between them. Licking his lips, he touched her shoulders with the backs of both hands as he pulled down her dress. The fabric of the dress fell away from her skin and bunched at her waist.

She planted her hands on the bed and raised her hips, allowing him to slide the crimson material and matching lacy undergarments down her legs.

Naked, vulnerable, and drunk on lust, she watched him.

Holding her dress in his hands, he looked...almost afraid to touch her.

She tilted her head to the side, trying to read the look in those dark, beautiful eyes that turned down at the corners.

His movements were slow and deliberate as he stood up. He carefully draped her dress across the back of the bedroom desk chair, then returned to his spot between her legs. A growing bulge pressed at the front of his pants.

She ran a hand down the front of his jeans. Desire shone in his eyes as she unbuttoned the top of his jeans and tugged the zipper down. She leaned forward and kissed his stomach while pulling the jeans down the length of his muscular legs. Her teeth nipped at the waistband of his boxer briefs.

He tilted his head back and dug both hands in her hair. "Not yet," he said roughly. "I want you in the middle of the bed. Now."

She blinked in surprise but scooted backwards on the bed as she was told.

"Lie down," he ordered, removing his boxer briefs.

Her heart skipped at least three beats at the sight of him naked, but again she followed his orders.

"Close your eyes," he instructed softly.

Her brows furrowing, she stared up at the ceiling a moment before closing her eyes. She felt completely exposed, completely open to him. He had the freedom to look at her, but she couldn't do the same to him. Her pulse jumped when she felt him sliding his fingertips up her legs. The bed sank under his weight. Then she felt his lips on her kneecaps and on her thighs, and felt his hands gently parting her legs wider. Felt soft, fluttery kisses on her inner thigh, which caused her entire body to tremble.

He covered her hands with his while teasing her with his lips and with his tongue. He grazed her inner thighs with his teeth before turning his attention elsewhere.

Her breath caught in her throat. She desperately wanted to open her eyes and look at him as he tasted her. Spasms rocked her body, causing her to whimper and cry out as his tongue danced across her most sensitive area. A heady excitement built up within her, the longer he licked. Her past few boyfriends had always rushed foreplay, whereas

André was intent on taking his sweet time with her. He hooked his arms around her thighs, pulling her closer so his tongue could delve even deeper inside of her. Her entire body shuddered as she reached climax. Even as her climax subsided, his tongue did not stop. His tongue continued tracing the shape of her pussy before plunging back inside of her.

It was silly of her, really, to think that he would stop there. He licked his way up to her stomach and braced his arms on either side of her. A moment later, she felt his lips on the tip of her left breast. His kisses and gentle suckling sent tiny little shockwaves rippling beneath her skin.

"You can open your eyes now," he told her.

Her eyes fluttered open. He hovered over her, propped up by his arms, which were braced on either side of her. He ducked his head down and kissed her. She could taste herself on his lips, and for some reason that turned her on even more.

She wrapped her legs around him and locked her ankles behind his back. *I love the way he kisses me,* she thought dreamily. His kisses were either gentle and affectionate or demanding and hungry. He seamlessly alternated between the two different modes. It drove her crazy. Everything about him did.

He lowered on top of her while his tongue wrestled with hers. She thought that this would be it, the moment when he'd push into her, but she was wrong. He continued to tease her to the point where she was already near the brink of ecstasy by the time he finally did enter.

She gasped and clung to him, squeezing her eyes shut.

"Look at me," he commanded in a voice barely above the volume of a whisper.

Without hesitation, she obeyed the instruction. Their bodies moved together slowly at first. The pace gradually gained in speed. Small moans escaped her lips. The more he picked up the pace, the louder her moans became.

He brushed her hair back from her face as he moved on top of her, his muscles tensing.

She rose up on her elbows and kissed him passionately.

He snaked his arms around her waist and scooped her up onto his lap while groaning loudly and hoarsely into her neck. She gave herself to him completely. A wave of pleasure crashed unto them, and they were both caught in the undertow.

A faint buzzing sound roused André from sleep. When the sound persisted, he lifted his head and squinted into the darkness. Destiny slept peacefully in his arms with her back to him. He kissed her shoulder blade and, as gently as possible, removed his arm from beneath her. He rubbed his eyes and sat up in bed.

The buzzing sound stopped, and then started again a moment later.

He turned his head, frowning. Still feeling groggy, he swung his legs over the side of the bed and rose to his feet. A small rectangle of light glowed on the floor, saving the need to turn on the light. Kneeling, he lifted Destiny's mesh purse from where it rested on the floor near the bed.

He glanced at her sleeping figure and sat on the edge of the bed, removing the vibrating cell phone from her purse. He flipped the cell phone over in his hands. That simple action caused the bright screen to unlock, revealing an incoming text message:

TEXT FROM: Carlos Villegas
MESSAGE: *This isn't funny, Destiny. Where are you? At least text me back to let me know you're okay. I waited at the club for as long as I could, but they were starting to close down for the night. Text me or call me when you get this, PLEASE.*

There was an entire string of similar messages from Carlos, whom André vaguely remembered meeting at the bakery. *Destiny was probably too drunk to realize she was leaving a friend behind,* André thought. He glanced over his shoulder at her; she was still sound asleep.

He didn't want to wake her, and he also didn't want her poor friend to worry about her well-being throughout the wee hours of the night. He ran his thumb over the smooth glass screen of the phone and typed a response.

TEXT TO: Carlos Villegas
MESSAGE: *This is André. Destiny is fine, but she had a bit too much to drink. I'm sure she would apologize for not responding to your messages sooner. I'll make sure she knows that you messaged her to make sure she was okay.*

Destiny moaned softly and rolled over in her sleep.

André returned the cell phone to her purse and set the purse on the nightstand beside the bed. Then he brushed her hair back from her face and leaned down to press an affectionate kiss to her forehead. Releasing a long sigh, he moved away from the bed and crossed the room.

His emotions were beginning to run rampant within him. Music began filling his head. Humming a tune, he entered the walk-in closet and sourced a fresh pair of white linen pajama pants. He pulled them on and returned to the bedroom, throwing one more look in Destiny's direction before exiting the bedroom.

One of the many reasons why he always stayed at this hotel when he visited D.C., stood polished and regal in the living room, near the sliding balcony door: a gleaming black baby grand piano. He seated himself on the bench, smoothing his fingertips along the top of the hinged fallboard, the lid that covered the keys.

Although the piano was his reason for returning to this hotel, he hadn't yet touched it since he'd arrived in town. He hadn't had the time. His purpose for being in town was the launching of a music program for disadvantaged youth. The program would help to provide disadvantaged youth with work-study programs and scholarships for college. Even though he was working hard with a team of politicians, it was taking longer than he'd anticipated to get the program off of the ground. Politics were beginning to get in the way.

When he stopped and served himself a dose of honesty, even those extra hurdles weren't enough to explain why he hadn't yet laid a finger on the piano. Back when he consistently made music, he would sit at the piano for fun, even if he only had five minutes to spare. Time wasn't the only thing keeping him from music. He simply hadn't felt inspired enough to write or play music.

There was a time when I didn't need a reason to play or write music, he thought, lifting the fallboard and stroking the ivory keys wistfully. *A time when I wrote or sang or rapped because it was a part of who I was, how I expressed myself.*

Songwriting, rapping, singing, all made up a large part of his identity. He'd loved all three of those crafts, still did. Sadly, there were other elements that went hand in hand with being an artist at the forefront of the music industry…other necessary evils and means to uncertain ends. There was a lot of dishonesty, a lot of betrayal, a lot of negativity. He'd handled a lot of it well, especially in the beginning.

There had come a time, though, when it had all become too much for him. While he loved the craft, he didn't love the demons that came along with being a superstar. Much to the shock of his fans, he and his team strategized a plan for him to fade into the background of hip-hop. He made a seamless transition from being a rap/singing sensation to being a record label owner and mogul who helped to introduce other rap and singing sensations. He did his best to help cultivate them as artists, to warn about all that would come their way, positive *and* negative.

He closed his eyes and pressed a few piano keys, the first resonating chords of a melody. There were times when he missed writing music or performing for a crowd. He still received an outpouring of love from new and longtime fans, and that touched his heart. Many of his songs were still getting a fair amount of radio play, despite how old they were. As a result, new fans were born every day, only to discover that he no longer recorded music.

Since he quit recording music, his life had become a lot more peaceful. The paparazzi were still a pain, due to the curiosity surrounding his bachelor status. The media still contacted his former management team in hopes of being granted interviews. The mild level of attention he received now was a lot easier to handle than the fans sneaking onto his estate bordering L.A. or asking for his autograph while he was standing at a urinal.

These past few years, he'd very much become the hermit. He worked, visited his mother occasionally, and went on dates whenever it suited him. Lately, he hadn't come across many women with similar interests. For this reason, he kept in touch with women from his past who remained reliable. Despite the history he shared with these women, he didn't want more than friendship and sex from them. Granted, they were great women. They would make a great catch for *someone*. Just not him.

And then there was Destiny...

She drew him in without even trying. She was genuine, engaging, and direct. Although she'd made remarks about feeling nervous around him, she wasn't afraid to speak her mind to him, as many people were these days. The beauty she possessed was pure, the type of beauty that didn't need to be accompanied by a mask of makeup. She carried herself with a sense of self-respect that many other young women her age did not have.

His nimble fingers continued to move over the keys of the piano, effortlessly playing a slow, haunting tune. He abruptly stopped playing and opened his eyes. Emotions were bubbling up to the surface, insisting upon release. Feeling the thick layer of ice around his heart beginning to melt, he opened his mouth and started to sing. His voice was rich and ached with longing. He started to play the instrument again and tilted his head back. His voice grew stronger, louder, as he sang. One hand crossed over the other as he played.

"My heart had a layer of ice around it,
And then you walked into my life.
Hid my heart from the world but you found it,
Baby, continue to shine your light.
You've got me wishing I could be more open,
But I must warn you that I'm scarred,
As much as I want to let you in, I'm broken.
Why must all of this be so damned hard?
How do I even begin to fix my trauma?
Without causing you more drama?
How do I erase a past that's catching up to me?
So, I can be the man that you need me to be?"

After the last line, his hands hovered over the keys, trembling. He lifted his eyes and saw Destiny standing near the entrance to the hallway. She leaned against the wall, wearing nothing but his dress shirt from earlier this evening. Raw admiration filled her eyes.

As she moved further into the room, the darkness gave the appearance that she was gliding. She resembled an Egyptian goddess with her tousled, dark hair flowing over her shoulders and her rich, brown skin. His dress shirt slid down one of her shoulders. She hadn't bothered to button it, revealing quite the spectacular view of her torso.

He remained completely still as she made her seductive approach. His eyes lowered to the ivory keys as she sat beside him on the piano bench. "I must have been singing too loud. I'm sorry."

"I don't mind waking up to beautiful music," she said, lightly touching a few of the piano keys.

"Do you play?" he asked her.

She shook her head. "I always wanted to learn, but I never had the time. I was in a lot of school programs and advanced classes. I also had a babysitting job that kept me busy. I have a high respect for artists and musicians. Those are two talents I wasn't blessed with."

"Learning instruments can be time-consuming for sure. Becoming good at it takes practice." While stroking his jaw, he stood up and moved to stand behind her. "Here. Scoot to the middle of the bench."

She scooted over. "Are you going to try to teach me how to play the piano in one night?" she asked him, her forehead creasing with doubt.

He laughed. "That would definitely be a challenge. No, I don't expect for you to play Bach or Chopin well after a one-night tutorial." The sight of her bare shoulder, even in the dark, was enough for him to temporarily lose his focus. He cleared his throat and positioned himself so that he was sitting behind her on the bench with each of his legs on either side of her. Her back touched his chest, but he tried not to think about that. He slid his fingers down the length of both of her arms and covered her hands with his own. He adjusted her hands over the keys.

There was a long mirror mounted on the living room wall facing the large instrument. In that mirror, he could clearly see her facial expression reflected at him. Her eyes were heavy with sleepiness or lust, or both.

He guided her through a few piano playing basics as he moved her hands across the keys. "While it can take a long time to get the hang of complex piano playing, you can learn a lot of the basics fairly quickly," he explained as he used her hands to play a simple tune.

She stared down at his hands covering hers.

"Pay attention," he chided.

"I am," she said defensively. "I don't think I ever knew that you played the piano."

He smiled and resumed the piano lesson, speaking softly with his mouth next to her ear. After half an hour of coaching her through it, he removed his hands from hers and observed her playing. She stumbled through a simplified arrangement of the song "Someone Like You" by Adele. Her fingers stumbled over each other, but other than that, she was surprisingly decent for someone who'd only had a half hour of piano lessons.

He lowered his hands to her waist as she played and pulled her back against him so that her rear end was flush against his lap.

She stopped playing and slanted a look at him. Strands of dark hair hung over one eye. Her lips were parted.

"Did I tell you to stop playing?"

She lowered her eyes before turning back around to face the piano. A moment later, she started the song over while frowning in concentration.

Keeping his left hand on her waist, he lifted his right hand and brushed her hair off her neck. He lowered his head and kissed the top of her shoulder. She continued to play the song, but her breathing was becoming shallow. Another kiss to her shoulder, and then he was gently nibbling at her shoulder with his teeth.

She gasped, her fingers growing still on the piano keys.

"Keep playing," he whispered roughly into her ear, sliding the hand that was at her waist beneath the fabric of the dress shirt.

She sat still for a few moments before collecting herself and starting the song over. He moved his lips from her shoulder to the back of her neck, kissing and nipping with his teeth. He dug one hand into her hair while the other moved beneath the button-down shirt she was wearing, stroking the skin beneath her belly button. She moaned softly but continued to play the song.

"Good girl," he encouraged, lowering his hand to her pelvic area.

Another moan, soft and barely audible. He glanced over the piano, towards the mirror, and saw her bite her bottom lip as she focused on the piano keys. He lowered his hand even further, closely watching her reflection. She closed her eyes and tilted her head back, but he shook his head firmly. Sensing that he was near the point of chastising her, she started the song back up where she left off.

"Do you notice that every time you start back up, you play a little better than you did the previous time?" he asked, whispering in her ear.

She nodded, and it was at this point that she spotted the mirror on the wall. Her eyes met the eyes of his reflection as her fingers caressed the ivory keys of the piano.

He pressed his fingers into her while sucking on her earlobe. Then he used both hands to tease her beyond the brink of ecstasy while grinding against her rear end.

She pushed back into him, eliciting a low growl from him. This time when she finished the song, she didn't start over. Her hands gripped the edge of the piano while he worked his fingers inside of her. Their gazes locked in the reflection of the mirror. She started to massage his thighs as she moved against him.

"Stand," he instructed abruptly.

She slowly stood to her feet.

"Grip the edge of the piano, the way you were before," he told her.

She did as she was told while watching his reflection in the mirror.

He rose behind her and kicked the bench out of the way. Then he stood behind her, a tall, muscled, powerful force. Meeting her gaze in the mirror, he took a hand and trailed it along the length of her spine, starting at the top and working his way down. "Bend over," he said gently.

She glanced at him over her shoulder.

He looked back at her with a calm expression on his face.

She turned back around and bent at the waist, keeping her grip on the edge of the piano.

He lowered his pajama pants and lifted the dress shirt she was wearing. "Do you want me?" he asked her, his voice low and deep.

She nodded and he could feel her body quaking in anticipation. "Yes," she whispered.

"Yes, what?" he prompted, sliding one hand around her waist and teasing her with his hand again.

She leaned back into him and moaned. "Yes, I want you," she confessed.

When he pushed into her, she wasn't ready. She cried out in pleasure and held onto the piano's edge for dear life.

Destiny sprawled across the bed, naked, with her arm dangling over the edge.

André stretched out alongside her, tracing the curve of her jaw with his index finger.

She wondered what he was thinking. Was it possible for him to completely rock her world off its axis, and then lovingly stroke her face like this without having any sort of real feelings for her? If she agreed to his terms and signed the contract, is this what it would be like? Would he still be affectionate like this, or would that fade away as soon as she signed her name on the dotted line?

"Do you know how sexy you are?" he asked her, his question interrupting her train of thought.

A small smile curved her lips. "Do you know how sexy *you* are?" she returned.

He grinned and shrugged his shoulders.

"The things that you said to me while we were..." She paused, not even knowing what she wanted to ask him. "Where do you learn to say things like that?"

He brought both of his hands to rest behind his head and stared up at the ceiling. "Would you believe me if I told you that I don't remember where I picked it up?"

"No," she said, laughing.

"Well, my bossiness, as you call it, comes from a combination of things," he said. "Some of those things, I will fill you in on later. There have been women in my life and one in particular who got the ball rolling as far as my dominance is concerned. But I like playfulness and teasing. I always have. I like testing limits, to see what I can get away with and what you're able to withstand.

"That could actually be a part of why the concept of monogamous relationships turn me off," he said, the tone of his voice contemplative. "I notice that when you put a title on it, when you label it a relationship, the dynamics of the relationship often change. In the beginning, before you call it what it is, two people can be playful with each other. They can be each other's best friends, they can have crazy chemistry in bed, but the minute you start calling it a relationship, or the minute you put a wedding band on, something seems to change."

"Not always," she said, frowning. "I've seen plenty of couples who are playful and youthful into old age while married."

"Exceptions to the rule," he said wistfully.

"So, you think that if you get into a relationship, all of the fun will be sucked out of it?"

He sighed deeply. "I don't know. But I have seen it happen so many times, starting with my parents." Memories danced in his eyes and he laughed. "Oh, man. They were so funny together, you know? Very cute, very playful from what I can remember. Cracking jokes, so many laughs and fun times. But..." His voice trailed off and sadness touched his eyes.

The look in his eyes was heartbreaking. As a rapper, he had outlined some of the family drama he'd had to heal from. From the look in his eyes now, she could tell that he was still battling some of that trauma. Her heart broke a little for him.

Flashing a sad smile at her, he turned on his side. "Enough about that."

But I have so many questions, she thought. "So...to be involved with you, I need to sign a contract," she stated.

"We don't have to discuss that right now."

"I think we should," she insisted. "We need to know where we stand."

"All right. Yes, you would need to sign a contract."

"What does the contract say?"

"It outlines what my interests are and asks for you to specify your interests."

Her brows furrowed. "My interests?"

"Sexually. What you are willing to do and what you are not willing to do. What you expect of me, and what you would like me to do for you, and *to* you. It gets pretty specific."

"Oh."

"The contract details both your and my roles in the arrangement." He paused. "The contract also explains that the arrangement is non-exclusive."

"Meaning that both of us are free to date other people," she clarified.

A glint sparkled in his eye. He reached over and tamed a few strands of her tousled mane before saying, "We can talk about this another time. You need rest."

"How can I fall asleep with all of these unanswered questions running through my mind?" she muttered.

He chuckled and circled his arms around her, pulling her close to him.

Moments later, he snored peacefully while her mind was filled with questions. Without a doubt, they had amazing sexual chemistry. He ignited a passion within her that she'd never felt before. His reaction to the attention she gave him indicated that he was turned on by her as well. As much as she enjoyed making love to him, though, she couldn't help but wonder if she would be able to handle a strictly sexual arrangement.

The man who had his arms around her was charming, intelligent, affectionate, sexy, talented, and witty. He was as close to perfect as a man could get. Sure, he'd had more than his fair share of women. He had his pessimistic views regarding love and had industrial strength walls up to prevent himself from getting emotionally involved. She could live in a fantasy world and tell herself that she'd be able to scale those walls in a single bound, but she was sure that he'd left many a woman in his wake who'd thought the same thing. If Destiny was going to continue spending time with him, she had to be realistic with herself and ask herself if she was capable of being nothing more than his plaything.

Images from their lovemaking session at the piano flickered behind her eyes and she smiled in the dark. *If I have to be anyone's plaything, it should be someone as skilled and attentive as he is,* she thought, listening to the rhythmic sound of his breathing. *And I'm young, so maybe I shouldn't even be looking to settle down with someone right now. Maybe what I need after all of the bullshit I went through with Jordan is just something lighthearted and casual. Maybe an arrangement like this is just what the doctor ordered. This might turn out to be good for me.*

André groaned in his sleep, drawing her attention to him. His thick, long lashes fluttered, and his eyes moved restlessly beneath his eyelids. His arms tightened around her.

*If you enter into this arrangement, you can*not *fall in love with him,* she told herself. But looking up into his sweet, peaceful face, she didn't know how that was possible. Could you prevent yourself from falling after the moment you've stepped off of a cliff?

7

"A part of me wants to kill you for ditching me last night," Carlos declared threateningly, wagging an index finger in Destiny's face, "but the look on your face tells me that you've had an entire night filled with orgasms and I want to hear about it. So, I guess for the time being, I have to keep you alive."

Destiny laughed as she tied an apron around her waist. "I am *very* sorry about leaving you without telling you. I was...out of it."

"You were drunk off of your *ass*, honey!" he exclaimed as he used his employee key card to clock in for the day. "I made a vow to myself to *never* hand you a glass of alcohol again in this life."

She shook her head and prepared the ingredients she would need to make pastries for that day.

He was looking at her expectantly. "Well?"

She shrugged her shoulders, staring at the metal table in front of her. "*Well*," she repeated, carefully choosing her next words, "he was very kind and gentle. He made sure that I got home okay."

"Did he make sure you got home okay last night or this morning before work?" Carlos asked with a knowing glint in his eyes.

"A good girl doesn't kiss and tell, Carlos," she said, giving him a pointed look.

He returned the frank stare and said, "First of all, thank you for letting me know that kissing was involved. Now we're getting somewhere. And second of all, that glow you've got going on isn't a good girl's *glow,* honey, so something tells me that you'll be all right if you spill the deets."

Out of respect for André and his position as a well-known entertainment industry mogul, she couldn't talk about what had happened the previous evening. Not even with someone that she could trust, which was proving to be tougher than she'd anticipated.

Carlos soon gave up trying to get the details from her, but he didn't hide his disappointment.

They both got to work molding and baking pastries and bread that would be served for the day. Business trickled in, but it was noticeably slower than it had been all week.

Destiny tried her best to focus on work, but it was difficult with memories of André playing in her mind. The feel of him, the smell of him, the taste of him all burned fresh in her memory.

A phone call from her manager had come in early that morning. There were two call-offs for the day and Destiny's help was needed. She had cast a look at André, who hadn't roused when the phone rang. She would have loved to stay cuddled with him through the late hours of the morning. Eat breakfast with him. Have a long, drawn out, exaggerated kiss goodbye before leaving. But that didn't seem to be in the cards for them - not today, at least.

André had woken up as she was getting dressed. She explained the situation and apologized. He'd been understanding, had gotten up and dressed along with her. Since her car was still parked at Crave, he'd driven her back to the nightclub himself, holding her hand for the entire duration of the car ride. He'd advised that he would follow her home to make sure she got there safely. They had kissed goodbye, but it was short. She had to get home, shower, get changed, and head to work.

For the better part of her morning, he dominated her thoughts. Was he thinking about her? Each time she found herself glancing at the clock mounted on the wall of the bakery, she wondered what he was doing. That curiosity didn't have to fester for long. While she was on her lunch break, her cell phone buzzed in her pocket.

TEXT FROM: André Gaines
MESSAGE: *I can still smell you on my pillow.*

TEXT TO: André Gaines
MESSAGE: *Good morning, Mr. Gaines.*

TEXT FROM: André Gaines
MESSAGE: *Good morning. Dinner tonight? Pick you up from work?*

TEXT TO: André Gaines
MESSAGE: *I would need to change...*

TEXT FROM: André Gaines
MESSAGE: *Pick you up from home? Say, 8pm?*

TEXT TO: André Gaines
MESSAGE: *Sure. I'll see you then.*

TEXT FROM: André Gaines
MESSAGE: *I will text you when I'm on the way. Are you feeling any soreness at all?*

Destiny's eyes widened. She reread the message again, just to make sure she'd understood it correctly. Seated in her usual corner booth, she checked her surroundings to make sure no one was hovering over her. Giggling in disbelief, she began to type out a response.

TEXT TO: André Gaines
MESSAGE: *Yes. A lot of soreness, actually.*

She tapped her index finger on the side of her phone as she waited for his response. The response didn't come by the time her lunch break ended. About an hour later, her cell phone vibrated against her thigh. The sensation of the vibration against her thigh almost caused her to moan out loud. Checking to make sure her manager wasn't nearby, she withdrew her cell phone from her pocket and checked her text messages.

TEXT FROM: André Gaines
MESSAGE: *Good. And Destiny...*

TEXT TO: André Gaines
MESSAGE: *Yes?*

TEXT FROM: André Gaines
MESSAGE: *I didn't respond to your message right away, because I was counting on you to put your cell phone in your pocket before returning to work. Since you're at work, I was also counting on your phone being on vibrate. I'm not there to touch you the way I want to, so I used your phone to do the job for me. I'll see you at 8pm.*

Her heart hammered in her chest as she read the words. She returned her cell phone to her pocket, plastering a smile on her face as a customer approached the counter to put in an order. It was a miracle that she got through taking his order without spontaneously combusting from the last message she'd received. Just as the customer was walking away, her cell phone buzzed against her thigh. A tiny moan escaped her lips and her knees turned to jelly. She reached out to grab the edge of the counter as the cell phone continued to vibrate. This time, instead of checking her messages, she savored the feel of the small gadget. The little device was fast becoming a tool André used to give her pleasure, even when he wasn't in the same room with her.

Candace Patterson was one hundred percent certain that her roommate had been replaced by a pod person. What else would explain her rapid transition from mopey and depressed to bubbly and cheerful? She watched her roomie from the living room, where she sat perched on the couch eating out of a small pint of Cherry Garcia ice cream.

Destiny walked back and forth in varying states of dress. The poor girl even mumbled under her breath as she looked for random items, scouring the bathroom for makeup or jewelry she'd loaned Candace forever and a day ago. When she walked past in a flowy gold sheath of a dress, Candace perked up on the couch. "Now, wait a minute..."

Destiny stopped in mid-stride. "What?"

"You're not just going out to any old club, not looking like that," Candace accused, narrowing her eyes. "You're going on a *date*."

Destiny continued walking and disappeared down the hallway, heading towards the bathroom. "I don't have time for this conversation!" she called over her shoulder.

"Who is it with? Jordan?" Candace demanded, setting her pint of ice cream on the table and leaping off of the couch. "Inquiring minds want to know."

"Inquiring minds need to mind the business that pays them," Destiny quipped, eyeing Candace's reflection in the mirror.

"It's going to take more than that to shut me up," Candace muttered, crossing her arms over her chest. She looked her friend up and down, taking in the shimmery gold empire-waisted dress and the naturally curly hair. "What the fuck have you done with my roommate?"

Destiny smiled at Candace's reflection before putting finishing touches on her eyeliner.

A firm knock sounded on the door to their apartment. Candace backed out of the bathroom, eager to see who was at the door. *I wonder if it'll be Jordan at the door,* she thought. *Maybe she decided to give him another chance. That would explain why she seems so much happier. Or maybe she's met someone new and is already working on replacing Jordan.* The knocking persisted. "Yeah, yeah, I'm coming, I'm coming!" Candace shouted. "Keep your pants on." She unsecured the locks and pulled the door open.

A tall, light-skinned man with dark, downturned eyes stood in the hallway dressed in a perfectly fitted suit. And it wasn't just *any* man. "I might have the wrong place...is Destiny here?"

Candace nodded, her eyes wide and disbelieving. "Are you...Dré?" she asked him, already knowing the answer to the question.

A slow grin curved his lips. "I go by André now," he corrected, extending a hand. "And you are?"

Her eyes fluttered and she fell backwards, onto the floor.

Hearing the loud thud, Destiny darted out of the bathroom, panicked. "Candace, what's wrong?" She stopped in her tracks when she saw André lifting Candace and carrying her to the couch in the living room.

"She fainted," he explained, setting the pretty, brown-skinned girl down on the couch and kneeling beside her. "It happens more than I care to admit."

"Is she okay?" Destiny's voice was laced with concern as she drew closer to her roommate.

Candace's eyes fluttered before opening. She stared up into André's face, looking dazed. "Did I imagine you?"

Wearing a warm smile on his face, he touched the back of his hand to her forehead. "She should be fine - it was just a fainting spell." He paused before saying to Candace, "How very princess-like of you."

Candace started to sit up, holding a hand to her head. "So...I didn't eat too many Hot Cheetos and I'm not hallucinating? You're really in our living room right now?"

"I'm really here right now," he confirmed, rising to his full height. It was at this moment that he looked up at Destiny. He opened his mouth to speak, but no words came out.

She gave her curls a self-conscious pat. "Is it the hair? You don't like it?"

He blinked slowly. Then he walked around the couch and moved to stand in front of her. He cupped her face in his hands and gently kissed her on the forehead. "This is the most beautiful I've ever seen you," he commented, lightly touching her hair.

She beamed up at him as his arms slid around her waist. Instead of responding to him, she peered around him at her roommate, who was still looking a little disoriented. "How are you feeling?"

"I'm good," Candace replied, standing from the couch. She turned to face them and immediately her gaze shifted to the placement of André's arms around her roommate's waist. "You two are going out tonight? Like...on a date?"

"We are going to spend some time together tonight," Destiny said carefully.

"And you couldn't warn me about it so I could at least change outfits? Look presentable? *Not* faint when I go to answer the door?"

"You look fine to me," André said with a shrug.

Candace waved a hand at them and stalked out of the living room, heading towards her bedroom. "Don't forget to lock up on your way out," she called over her shoulder.

"Some friendship you two have," André remarked with a chuckle.

"I don't know what I can tell my friends since you're all non-disclosure about everything," Destiny told him pointedly.

That drew a burst of laughter from him. "You can tell your friends that you're spending time with me. They just don't need to hear about everything that I'm doing to you when you're with me."

"Good to know."

Still laughing, he lowered his head and kissed her hungrily. "I missed you," he growled in between kisses, pushing her against the nearest wall. He braced his arms on either side of her as their kiss deepened.

Her hands slid beneath the lapels of his black suit jacket, grabbing him by the waist. Lust threatened to take over, but reality hit her when his kisses began to lower to the tops of her breasts. "My friend is right down the hall," she reminded him, lifting his head up. "We can't do this right now."

"Or *can* we?" His tone made the words sound like a joke, but the devilish glint in his eyes said otherwise.

Laughing, she playfully shoved at his chest.

Licking his lips, he backed up a few steps and nodded in understanding.

"I'm going to check on Candace one more time before we leave," she told him. "Make sure she's okay. I'll just be a minute."

"I know better than that." He planted himself in one of the armchairs adjacent to the couch.

Before Destiny could make her way to Candace's room, a knock sounded at the door. There was a pause, and then another knock sounded.

Frowning, Destiny glanced towards the door.

André looked over at her. "Did you double-book tonight?"

She shook her head. "I'm not expecting anyone else. Maybe Candace is, though."

His gaze shifted to the pint of ice cream Candace left on the coffee table. "Something tells me that she wasn't expecting company."

If Candace really isn't expecting anyone, then there's only one person that could be on the other side of that door. Sure enough, it was her ex-boyfriend standing on the other side of the door.

"I was hoping to surprise you," Jordan said, holding up two plastic bags. "I brought takeout."

"Jordan...what are you doing here?"

"You look so beautiful," he said instead of answering her question.

"Jordan..."

Dressed in a nice polo shirt, pressed khaki slacks, and designer sneakers, he held up the two plastic bags in his hands. "I stopped by your favorite Thai place," he announced, brushing past her. He stopped short when he saw André seated in the living room.

André returned the frank perusal, arching an eyebrow.

"This...is not a good time," Destiny said awkwardly. "You should go, Jordan."

"Who is this?" Jordan asked, setting the bags on the kitchen counter. He swaggered into the living room and his eyes lit up with recognition. "You've got to be shitting me."

Here we go. "Jordan, you need to go," she urged, grabbing his arm and tugging on it.

He yanked his arm out of her grasp. "Yo...don't touch me." He stared down at her. "*Dré*, Des? Really?"

André remained seated, but when he spoke, his voice was firm and authoritative. "Watch the way you speak to her."

Jordan glared at him. "You think you can control what I do or what I say?" he demanded. "Watch the way I speak to her, or what? What are you going to do about it?"

"Are you the one who cheated on her?" André asked.

Jordan grabbed Destiny by the wrist and drew his face close to hers. "You're telling him shit about us? Huh? You're telling him shit about you and *me*? *Our* business?"

André sprang out of his chair and grabbed Jordan by the back of the neck. "If you don't let her go, you and I are going to have a *serious* problem."

Jordan released Destiny immediately. "Okay, okay," he said, holding his hands up defensively.

André steered him to the door of the apartment and swung the door open. He removed his hand from Jordan's neck once Jordan was on the other side of the threshold. "I don't think I need to tell you to leave Destiny alone."

"I get it, I get it," Jordan said, rubbing the back of his neck and wincing.

"I don't want to hear that you've shown up here ever again." André slammed the door and quickly strode to Destiny's side. "Are you all right?"

She nodded. "More surprised than anything," she said, gingerly touching her wrist.

Candace came padding into the living room, her brows furrowed in concern. "Did I miss something?" she asked. Shock morphed her face when she saw the anger burning in André's eyes. "What happened?"

"Jordan happened," was Destiny's response.

"I told him not to come here again," André advised them both. "If he does, let me know. I can take care of it."

"How very...mobstery of you," Candace said, tilting her head to the side.

"How are you feeling, after that fainting spell you took, princess?" André asked her.

Bristling at the word "princess," Candace dismissively waved André off with a flurrying motion of one hand. "I'm telling you both, I'm fine," she insisted. "I just can't believe I missed a Jordan tantrum. Please stop worrying about me and have a good time."

Destiny watched her roommate closely. "Jordan was pretty pissed off. He could try coming back."

"Girl, I'll be fine. All right? I *wish* Jordan would try me. Okay? I would like to see him try. I'm more worried about him following you guys to wherever you're going. I'm sure Dré can protect you, though. *Go*. Have fun. You deserve it. You *need* it, okay?" Candace smiled and looked up at André.

André smiled back at her. "If you need anything, just text Destiny. We can come right back."

Candace nodded.

Destiny leaned forward and hugged her.

"You're not going to wear a coat?" he asked, offering her his arm.

She shook her head. "I want to feel the breeze."

They left the apartment. She locked the door and followed André down a flight of concrete stairs. Her apartment complex was fairly new, built within the past five years. It was very well-kept, and the neighborhood was quiet. As they walked, they passed well-manicured lawns and a pool area that was closed off for the season.

"I'm sorry about...that," she apologized finally, after they'd walked in silence for several minutes.

"You don't have to apologize for him," he told her as he guided her towards his car. He opened the back door and gestured for her to get inside.

Making sure to lift the hem of her dress so it didn't drag on the ground, she ducked into the vehicle. She stuck her hand out to assist him into the car. Fear froze the blood in her veins as she noticed a shadowy figure looming behind him. "André!" she yelled.

He frowned and turned a few seconds too late.

Jordan landed a blow to André's face. André stumbled back against the car, losing his footing.

"Stop!" Destiny screamed, lurching out of the car. "Jordan, what the hell are you doing?"

"I'm teaching a lesson to someone who thinks they can tell me what to do," Jordan shouted, his dark eyes filled with rage. He lunged at André again. "Teaching a lesson to someone who thinks they can take my girl from me."

She pounded her fists on Jordan's back. Jordan drew his elbow back sharply, jabbing her hard in the cheek. She fell back and landed on the grass.

André saw her fall and jumped to action, grabbing Jordan by the collar of his polo shirt. He slammed Jordan into the car door and punched him hard in the stomach. The boy struggled against him, but André laid into him relentlessly, landing punches to his stomach and face until his own knuckles were bloodied. He positioned his face close to Jordan's and whispered harshly into his ear.

Jordan nodded, reduced to angry tears.

The driver hopped out of the car and ran around the vehicle. "Mr. Gaines?" the brown-skinned man addressed André.

"I'm good, you can get back in the car," André called to the driver. He tossed Jordan to the ground like a sack of potatoes. Seeing that Destiny was still on the ground with frightened tears in her eyes, he walked over to her. Leaning down, he gathered her up in his arms. He carried her to the vehicle and set her down on the backseat. She immediately moved to make room for him. He lowered himself into the car and closed the door.

"I'm sorry I didn't see what was happening until it was too late," the driver hastened to apologize. "Everything happened so fast."

"You don't owe me any apologies. You signed up to be my driver, not my muscle."

The driver started to pull off, but André told him to stop. He turned to Destiny. "After everything you've been through tonight, we don't have to go on this date. We can reschedule."

She shook her head. "I want to go," she insisted.

He stroked her cheek and tilted her face, inspecting the broken skin on her cheekbone.

She looked into his eyes and returned the gesture, lightly touching his cheek. "That's going to bruise," she said softly. "Does it hurt?"

He winced the second she touched his cheek, but in response to her question, he gave a slow shake of his head. "It doesn't hurt at all," he lied. "He punches like a little girl."

As the car cruised through D.C., Destiny touched a hand to her cheekbone and winced.

André's brows drew together as he watched her. He leaned forward and rummaged around the mini bar. When he settled back in his seat, he held a bottled water and an empty glass in his hands. He reached into his suit jacket pocket and withdrew a black silk handkerchief. Balancing the handkerchief and glass in his lap, he opened the bottled water. His movements were meticulous, as always. He poured water into the glass and screwed the top back on the bottle. Balancing the glass of water on his thigh, he placed the bottle at his feet and twisted in his seat to face her, giving her a long look.

Guilt bubbled up within her. The guilt threatened to overwhelm her whenever she saw his cheek, which was already beginning to darken. *An esteemed businessman with a bruise on his face, and it's all my fault,* she thought while bowing her head.

Releasing a heavy sigh, he tilted her head so he could get a good look at the cut marring her cheekbone. His eyes met hers. Wordlessly, he lifted the silk handkerchief from his lap and dipped its corner into the glass of water. As he went to work wiping the blood from the broken skin on her cheekbone, he attempted to make conversation. "So, this Jordan is quite a character."

For some reason, the gross understatement made her laugh.

He paused in wiping her cheek, waiting for her to be still.

Quieting her laughter, she sat regally with her hands clasped in her lap and her head held high. "I've never seen him that angry," she told him. "It really scared me."

"Has he ever hurt you in the past?" André asked as he dipped the corner of the handkerchief into the water glass again. "Physically, I mean."

"Never."

"Are you sure you don't want to go back home?"

"Candace was pretty determined to get me out of the apartment, so we don't need to go back. I will keep texting her to check in on her, though. I hate the idea of her being in that place alone, after what just happened." She reached for her purse and immediately cried out in pain.

He reached across her lap and lifted her arm. A two-inch gash now decorated her elbow. "He really roughed you up," he murmured, lowering her arm and dipping the handkerchief in the glass of water again. Then, he slid off the seat and moved into a kneeling position.

"All he did was knock me back, so I must've fallen on something," she muttered. "I was mainly worried about you. Everything happened so fast."

He parted her knees and positioned himself between them. The devilish grin he flashed her was enough to make her melt. Twisting her arm so he could evaluate the gash, he proceeded to dab the cut on her elbow with the wet corner of the handkerchief.

She watched him, in awe of how gentle he was with her. His eyes lowered and his forehead was creased with concentration. She didn't realize she had a dopey smile on her face until he looked up at her and laughed.

"What are you smiling about?"

She shook her head. "Nothing," she mumbled, turning to look out of the window.

He arched a brow at her and finished tending to her elbow. "Are there any other areas on your body that need my attention?"

Sensual visuals leapt to mind at the suggestive words he'd used.

There was the smallest hint of innuendo in the depths of his dark eyes.

She rolled her eyes. "You think you're so smooth," she said, snatching the handkerchief from him. "Now it's your turn. Sit." She gestured to the spot beside her on the car seat.

Amused at her daring to order him around, he rose from his kneeling position and reclaimed his seat beside her. She moved down to the floor and kneeled in between his parted knees. He drew in a sharp intake of breath at the sight of her kneeling before him.

She poured a new glass of water and used the opposite corner of the handkerchief that he'd used to prevent their blood from mingling. Then, as a form of payback for his arousing innuendo, she leaned over his lap so that her breasts brushed against his thighs. Raising her gaze to meet his, she dipped the handkerchief into the glass of water.

He arched against her in the slightest way. It was such a small action, but one that still garnered a strong reaction from her. Her eyes fluttered closed and she bit her bottom lip. Moistness gathered at the apex of her thighs.

Realizing that she was playing with fire and possibly attempting to tease and tempt the master of temptation, she straightened her posture and cupped one hand beneath his chin. Her eyes lingered on the shiner developing on his cheek and the cut that sliced into his eyebrow. With a deep sigh, she went to work dabbing at the drying blood on his face. "I'm so sorry about this."

"Look at me," he ordered.

Tears were filling her eyes and she tried to blink them away.

"I need you to understand that this isn't your fault. Stop blaming yourself. I mean it." He angled his face so she could continue tending to his cuts. When he next spoke, the tone in his voice was much gentler. "It felt good to hurt him, since he hurt you."

Her hand stilled, hovering above his cheek. "I don't understand you," she said with a shake of her head.

He blinked. "What don't you understand?"

"How you can be this affectionate, and charming, and caring, and romantic, but not want a real relationship."

For a while, he was quiet. "I'm not a heartless man," he said after several moments of silence. "I'm not looking for commitment, but that doesn't mean I wouldn't treat my companion well. It doesn't mean that I wouldn't care about you or your happiness."

She shook her head. His response was not good enough for her. "It's dangerous for you to be as charming as you are," she remarked, turning his face left and right, checking for any more scuff marks or blood smears.

"What makes me dangerous?" he asked, touching a fingertip to his eyebrow and sucking air between his teeth at the sting of pain.

"Don't *touch* it," she admonished, wiping at it again. "You want to keep it clean."

"What makes me dangerous?" he repeated.

She shrugged her shoulders. "Even if a girl agrees to an arrangement with you, one without commitment, and even if she intends to keep emotions out of it, your charm and...the way you are makes it too easy to fall in love with you."

One corner of his mouth lifted. "I disagree with that."

"How can you?"

"*If* love is real," he said slowly, "and I'm talking about true love, romantic love. If it exists, then you can only experience it with one person. What you are describing, the *easiness* of it, sounds more like infatuation than love. There are a lot of people I have known in my life who would swear up and down that they were in love, but all I ever saw was infatuation or unhealthy addictions for one or both parties. True love, if it exists, wouldn't bloom because someone is as charming as you claim me to be, or as beautiful as you are."

She lowered her gaze at the compliment.

"True love would come from peeling back the layers beneath the charm, and beneath the beauty. True love would come from seeing who the person is, beneath all of that, and still feeling like you would do anything for them." His face turned beet red and he appeared sheepish, as if he'd said more than he'd intended. "I mean...that's how I think about it, anyway."

"That makes perfect sense, actually," she said.

"That was something that always killed me when I was an entertainer, you know? Fans and women shouting to me that they loved me. I would always think to myself, if they *really* knew me, knew who I was beneath this public image...if I bared everything and showed them all facets of me, would they still feel like they loved me? My tongue was sharp with anyone who betrayed me. I was downright *mean* to some of them. I've done shit that I am not proud of, shit that I'm *ashamed* of. Shit that wouldn't fit into the cookie cutter image of the brokenhearted lonely boy the majority of my fans thought I was back then. If they knew how mean I was back then and the shit that I pulled, would they still love me? Would they judge me? Or would they realize that I was just a person, like them? And what if they *did* realize that I was just a flawed human being and not someone to be worshipped on this ridiculously high pedestal? How would they react? Would they still want to listen to my music? Would they still want to come to my performances? Or would their 'love' for me fade away once they realized that I'm not any different from them, any better than they are? These were questions I always used to ask myself after attending an awards show or after performing. The concept of love has been so bastardized these days. It's no longer held sacred. It's thrown around so casually." He stopped and ran a hand over his head, feeling sheepish. Feeling a bit embarrassed, he rolled his eyes heavenward. "And now, I'm rambling."

"You have...the most beautiful mind," she told him earnestly, wiping one final smudge of dirt, or blood, or both, from his jawline.

He tilted his head and studied her. With lowered eyes, he slowly leaned forward and claimed her lips with his.

The limousine came to a stop, but André didn't pull back. He continued to kiss her, caressing her upper arms. When they finally did pull away from each other, they were both gasping for air. He cleared his throat, smoothed down his dress shirt, and adjusted his suit jacket. After examining her face and elbow one more time, he pressed a kiss to her forehead just as the door was pulled open for them.

Destiny didn't know what to expect when she stepped outside of the long, black limousine. She never knew what to expect with him. He hadn't told her where he was taking her; he'd just told her to dress formally. As she stood outside of the car, she could understand why. They were standing in front of a tall, three-story building that had a row of thick white columns. The building had a very colonial look to it. Formally dressed couples gathered near the front entrance, talking and laughing.

Before they embarked on whatever adventure this was guaranteed to be, she texted Candace, checking to make sure she was all right.

André grabbed her hand right after she clicked Send. "Are you ready?"

"Despite the fact that we both look like we just survived a car wreck?" she fretted, checking her hair. "How does my face look?"

He chuckled and slid an arm around her waist. "You don't have anything to worry about. Now that the cut is cleaned up, you can barely tell it's there."

"I don't believe you," she muttered as he escorted her towards the front doors to the building. She took a deep, steadying breath, not knowing what to expect. Her phone chimed, a text message response from Candace telling her to stop worrying and have fun with her new man. While laughing, Destiny shook her head and leaned into André as they walked.

The event being held was a charity fundraiser for underprivileged youth. Politicians, celebrities, athletes, and unrecognizable faces alike mingled in the large banquet hall. Ice sculptures were scattered throughout the room and a contemporary jazz band played on the front stage. Dinner tables were lined up in front of the stage. There were several charity booths sprinkled throughout the large event hall.

As soon as they entered, people flocked over to André. They shook his hand, clapped him on the back, and spoke jovially. People from all walks of life commended him for coordinating a music program for underprivileged youth.

When they were alone, Destiny looked at him. "That's the project you're working on?" she asked him, unable to hide her shock. "That's why you're in D.C.?"

"If you'd taken my interview offer, you would have known," he said, grabbing a glass of champagne from the tray of a passing waiter. "Do you approve?"

"Are you kidding me? That's amazing."

He guided her through the room, tipping his head in greeting to those who acknowledged him. "The project means a lot to me," he confessed to her. "I thought by now everything would be up and running, but a few politicians are trying to stonewall me. It seems that some of them want to prevent the program from happening. At the very least, they're looking to delay it. I don't know. It's very frustrating."

"If you're having trouble getting the program off the ground, then you definitely should be out there doing interviews, André."

He shook his head firmly. "I told you about my views on that."

"You also said that you have one or two people you can trust," she reminded him.

He smiled, swirling the champagne in his glass. "You pay attention."

She blinked at him. "Of course, I do."

"None of the journalists I trust have the local clout it would take to get the program on track," he told her.

"So, what...you just let them steamroll you?" she demanded. "Exposing what is happening would be of national interest, if it's something involving you. It doesn't matter if the journalist is local or not, the story would pick up traction and gain enough steam to maybe get the program rolling."

His brows furrowed as he seemed to weigh her words. Before he could respond, a middle-aged Caucasian couple approached them. The wife, a tall, slender brunette, kissed André on both cheeks. The husband, average height and portly, echoed his wife's sentiment that it had been too long since they'd seen André last.

Destiny held on fast to André's arm while he spoke to them, but she had a ton of questions burning in her mind. The minute the couple left, she looked up at him again. "A program like this is too important for you to throw away just because a couple of politicians would rather pocket that money than invest it in a beneficial program."

André chuckled. "You sound just about as passionate about the program as I am."

"After school programs were a huge benefit to me when I was younger," she said defensively. "Music and other extracurricular activities are being cut from schools all over the country. Kids need programs like that to stay engaged, to help them discover what it is they want to do in life. Without programs like that, a lot of kids turn to gang affiliations and drug use to fill up their spare time."

"I agree wholeheartedly - and by the way, I never said I was *throwing away* anything to do with the program," he corrected her smoothly. "Never underestimate me. I have a few aces up my sleeve."

"You should be doing interviews," she maintained.

"With whom?" he asked, his eyebrow arching as he looked down at her. His eyes dared her to speak what she was thinking.

Taking on his dare, she said, "With me."

Mirth filled his eyes. Another couple approached them, but he didn't acknowledge their presence right away. He continued staring at Destiny, his lips curving into a satisfied smile. Only after a few awkward moments did he greet the couple.

A short female announcer wearing a black floor-length gown tapped the microphone at the center of the stage. "Thank you for joining us tonight. Now that everyone has had a chance to get acquainted or re-acquainted, dinner will be served. Throughout this dinner, we will be providing awards for stellar humanitarian achievements and announcing new philanthropic initiatives. Place cards with your name on them are set on each table. We have several booths set up with a number of causes that could use your support."

After inspecting a few of the tables, André said in a low voice, "The names on the place cards are arranged alphabetically. Our table will be up front somewhere, near the stage."

He was soon proven to be correct. They found their table rather quickly. André pulled out her chair for her, waited for her to sit, then helped to push her chair forward. "Tell me what you think an interview will do to help my cause," he urged as he seated himself. After setting his nearly empty champagne glass on the table, he folded his hands together and rested them on top of the table.

"It would inform people that your program is in the works, and it would put pressure on the politicians who are delaying the program from starting," she answered readily. "Once it's in print, they'd have to answer to the public as to why the program is taking longer than expected to get off the ground. At the very least, having that magnifying glass on them would nudge them into taking action. The public would be inspired to demand the program, so you wouldn't have to."

He leaned back in his chair, appearing to be impressed.

"You don't have to throw them under the bus or anything," she said hurriedly. "When asked how long you think it will take to get off the ground, you can just drop a subtle line about it taking longer than expected."

"Politicians are a very special breed of people. No matter how nicely I said the words, these men would take offense. Still, you make a good point." He stroked his jaw. "Would you allow me to read the article before you submit it for print?"

"Yes, of course," she said emphatically.

After a few moments of consideration, he nodded his head slowly. "Okay."

"Okay?" she repeated, her voice rising in pitch. "As in, yes?"

He smiled and took the last swig of his champagne. "As in yes," he confirmed. "I *do* owe you an interview."

She squealed and threw her arms around his neck.

"Shhh." Even while shushing her, he returned the embrace.

When she pulled away from him, she was grinning from ear to ear. "This will be the most important article I've ever written," she confessed. "I'm honored. Thank you."

He fingered the stem of the champagne glass, a gradual smile creeping onto his face. "Thank you for giving me the opportunity. Your advice was very valid. You have the potential to become a very powerful journalist."

His praise touched her, but she barely had time to bask in the positivity. The lights in the banquet hall dimmed and the event was officially under way.

Destiny tried her best to focus on the award ceremony, but that was difficult to do with André's thigh brushing against hers. The waiter stopped by their table, offering a much-appreciated distraction. The waiter dragged a huge cart with covered plates of food piled on top of it. He gave her the choices of eggplant Parmesan, Alfredo, salmon, or chicken. She chose the eggplant Parmesan and André selected the Alfredo. When he turned in his seat to accept his plate, his knee bumped into her thigh, causing shivers to run along her spine. To take her mind off of the reaction her body had to the slightest of his touches, she asked him, "What made you want to start a program like this?"

Another waiter approached their table, offering to refresh drinks. André lifted his champagne glass into the air expectantly and replied, "For the same reasons you're so passionate about it. Music is a creative way for kids to channel their frustration, angst, and anger without causing harm to themselves or anyone else. Taking it away from them, I feel, would be an injustice."

As expected, the waiter refilled his champagne glass before moving onto the next table.

"A lot of people would donate money, not spearhead a program as huge as this one sounds," she pointed out, raising her dinner fork.

"You're correct. When I donate money, however, I don't know exactly where it's going. For all I know, most of it could be going into the program directors' pockets. For obvious reasons, this cause is close to my heart. I want to know exactly where my money is going. By running the program and heading its campaign, I would control where the money goes."

"That's so...smart and noble of you," she gushed with a shake of her head.

"The next award we will be presenting is for the Humanitarian of the Year Award," the event emcee announced into the microphone.

André twirled his fork in the middle of the pasta dish and said, "I have no choice but to be smart. If I'm not, I'll be taken advantage of." He inserted the noodle-wrapped fork into his mouth and made a pleased sound at the taste of the pasta.

"...And the award goes to, André Gaines!" There was a smattering of applause. "André, or Dré as he was called throughout the duration of his music career, has been known throughout the humanitarian circuit for quite some time now. Initially, his contributions were anonymous, but lately he has placed himself more at the forefront of causes involving domestic violence, education, fighting homelessness, cancer research, and mental health. He has proven to be an iconic example of what it means to be a humanitarian. Please come to the stage, André."

André used the provided cloth napkin to wipe his mouth. "Well, that was unexpected," he said. "Usually I get notice that I'm being presented with an award prior to the event." He slid his chair back and stood. Just as a spotlight was aimed at him, he bent at the waist and pressed a kiss to Destiny's forehead before sauntering towards the stage.

A feeling of awe washed over her. The man making his way to the stage may not believe in true love, but he certainly possessed a heart of absolute gold, to speak on school programs as passionately as he did. He turned his head and looked at her as he walked up the stairs. A flurry of butterflies fluttered their wings in her stomach.

He gave the short, bubbly emcee a warm embrace and accepted the glimmering award from her. The applause he received drowned out the sound of his voice when he tried speaking into the microphone. Smiling charmingly, he used his hands to gesture for the audience to quiet down. "Thank you for that. I wasn't expecting to receive an award tonight." His eyes lowered to the engraved award in his hands as he waited for the scattered laughter and chatter to die down.

Destiny lowered her fork. His earlier words echoed in her mind: *"I have a few aces up my sleeve."*

"I can't begin to express just how much I appreciate this acknowledgement. I don't do this for accolades, and I don't do this for recognition. There are injustices that are eating away at our world, and I made a vow to myself years ago that I would help as best I could." He scanned the audience. "One cause that is near and dear to me is making sure we are keeping arts and music programs in our schools."

She grinned and covered her mouth with both hands.

"Lately, schools have treated these programs as if they are expendable. They'll do whatever they can to keep the football and basketball programs funded, because those events bring in money. Now…everyone knows that I love sports just as much as the next person. But music and art are being treated as less important than sports. I disagree with that stance." He lowered his eyes to the award in his hands. "Too often, we are putting value in *things*. This award is beautiful, but it's a *thing*. It shouldn't be a reason for donating our time to important causes. Money is also a thing. Once it's spent, it's gone. Money was never the main benefit of art. Art and music are creative expression for those who make it, and an escape for those who enjoy it. Art and music are a way for us to catalog major events or speak on politics, our society, culture, the *world*. The benefit of these programs is in preventing depression and gang violence, because instead of running around these streets, our children are learning to play the violin, write music, or sing their hearts out. It's encouraging celebrated art forms such as drawing, dance, sculpting, or whatever they set their little hearts on. These programs don't just benefit the children; we *all* benefit from these programs. The music you'll listen to on the way home tonight, the movie or show you're going to watch when you get home, the art hanging up in your homes *right now* are from artists. We are inspired by them every single day, and it is time they receive more respect. The kids attending school right now, and the children that will soon be attending school, are the next generation of artists. They are young and impressionable and need our support. We need to shift the way we think about these art programs. We need to prioritize them."

Applause erupted in the room. Instead of quieting it, he reveled in it this time. Most likely, he reveled in it because they weren't showering *him* with the attention, but his ideas and his cause. Many event guests stood while recording his speech on their cell phones.

This was his plan all along, Destiny realized. *If not at this event, he would've found another event to speak on this topic. No matter which event he'd done this at, he would have received a response just like this one. When everyone posts these videos to social media, his cause will pick up traction. This method of marketing might be even more effective than an interview would be. Network news reporters would still cover the story, without him having to give anyone an interview. If this was his plan all along, he isn't allowing me to interview him because he needs it. The interview would help me more than him.*

"I am spearheading a program that is intended to help save these programs," he announced.

The applause increased in intensity.

"I appreciate your support. I really do. Thank you. Several politicians are working with me on this program, and I can't wait to be able to tell you more about it. I've agreed to an interview with Howard University journalist Destiny Richards. That article will contain more details about the project." He held the award up in the air. "Thank you again for this and thank you for continuing to support these very important causes." As the applause reached deafening levels, he took a step back from the podium.

The event announcer appeared and excitedly ushered him off the stage.

Destiny awaited his return, not caring that her food was growing cold. Several people at other tables stopped him to commend him on his speech and to offer their support. Excitement coursed through her veins as he reclaimed his seat. "I can't believe you."

He grinned, setting his award on top of the table.

"When you said you had aces up your sleeve, I should have believed you," she said.

"You've barely touched your food," he noticed, gesturing towards her plate.

"Who could eat while you gave that brilliant speech?" Still, she picked up her fork and started moving her food around her plate.

He laughed, watching her.

"And you namedropped me. Why?"

"I want to make sure they're keeping an eye on your school paper," he responded. "There are journalists here, and they will trip over themselves to bring news back to their offices that out of all of the newspapers in D.C., I chose to interview with a college paper. It will drive them nuts. Get some tongues wagging. It'll also generate some buzz for you. Everyone will want to know who you are, since you were the journalist I chose to interview with."

"You're good," she said before eating a few bites of eggplant.

He finished his meal and wiped his mouth with his napkin. The award ceremony wrapped up, and the other couples seated at their table launched into a discussion about education.

"I can understand why the education system is being criticized," a tall, slender man said after gulping down his champagne. His hair was dark and looked suspiciously like a toupee. "But these days, kids have the internet. I don't even know if school is necessary. Kids these days have benefits we didn't have when I was in school. If they want to learn something, all they have to do is Google the topic. Kids these days can't find the different continents on a globe and does the education system deserve some of that blame? Sure, but I also put some of that blame onto the kids and their parents."

Destiny frowned and tilted her head to the side. "Respectfully, the education system was set up to educate our youth," she said, cutting into the conversation without asking. "People pay money, in taxes and in school fees, to make sure their children are getting the best that their school system has to offer. And the 'best' isn't getting their textbooks two months too late, cutting programs that are beneficial to the children, or slacking in the subjects that are being taught."

The man looked bewildered while André fought to hide a proud smile.

"And you dare to criticize parents who are working hard, often sacrificing time spent with their families, just to be able to save up to provide their children with a halfway decent college education. Meanwhile, the costs of college continue to increase, becoming more of a for-profit establishment each year. Parents work hard to pay for education for their children. A child shouldn't have to sit for 6-8 hours in classes and come home to parents teaching them the lessons that they should have been taught in school in the first place. That doesn't make any sense." Realizing that she was laying into a stranger who hadn't even formally invited her into his conversation, she stopped talking and lowered her gaze to her plate.

The man's wife interjected, "I agree with you, dear. I'm starting to think that the champagne is getting to Marty's head." The petite blonde woman scowled at her husband.

André slid an arm across Destiny's shoulders and pulled her close to him.

"I went a little overboard," she said sheepishly.

He shook his head. "I enjoyed every second of that. And you hit the nail right on the head." He kissed her on the temple and smoothed her hair back. "The event is winding down, so we'll be leaving soon. Will you come back to my hotel room with me? There is something I'd like to discuss with you."

Images flashed behind her eyes. The piano. Her hands mashing the ivory keys as he had his way with her from behind. The sound of moans and groans filled her head. Sensations, the feeling of his skin on her. The feeling of him inside of her. Her cheeks flushed deep red and she shifted in her seat, crossing her legs tightly together.

Intrigue filled his eyes. He dipped his head low so he could whisper in her ear, "Can I take that as a yes?"

8

Destiny didn't know what she expected the minute they stepped inside of André's hotel room. Maybe she expected a hot makeout session. A little bit of touching, groping, and kissing, maybe. What she *definitely* hadn't expected for him to do was flip the light switch on and make a beeline for a briefcase that was propped up against the suite's living room couch. *Does he want me to help him with the education program?* she wondered as she followed him to the couch.

"I want to talk about the contract with you," he said, sitting on the couch. Without any further explanation, he lifted the briefcase and set it on top of the coffee table.

Not knowing what to think or how to feel, she watched as he popped the briefcase open. *I guess I thought that maybe with the intelligence and support I showed him at the charity banquet, he might want to make an exception and be more than contracted "companions." Seems like that line of thinking was wrong.* She was silly to think that he'd forget about the damned contract and allow a real relationship to progress.

"Getting to know you has been one of the most thrilling experiences I've had," he went on, licking his fingertips and flipping through the paperwork in his briefcase.

"The feeling is mutual," she echoed, trying to keep the hurt she was feeling out of her voice.

He removed a small stack of paper, bound together with a mini binder clip. "Our interaction hasn't been...standard for me. This contract usually comes before the dates and the...intimacy. I don't want there to be any confusion or misunderstandings regarding where we stand. I think it's best for us to get this out of the way now." He looked up at her.

She took a deep breath and smoothed down the skirt of her shimmering golden dress as she sat on the couch beside him.

"A couple of times now, I have mentioned to you that I have very particular interests," he said slowly. "It was something I mentioned but never really specified. To be honest, I'm surprised you weren't more inquisitive about that."

"I figured you were into spanking women, rough sex, that kind of thing."

For some reason, that made him smile. "Those are elements that I enjoy, but my interests are a bit…broader than just a couple of sexual acts. I am a lifestyle Dominant, Destiny. Any woman that I become involved with, for the period of time that we interact, would be my submissive. Do you know what any of that means?"

"Dominant, so…you are the one controlling everything in the relationship?" *As if I didn't know he was controlling every aspect of our relationship already.*

"Not *everything*. As my submissive, you would trust me to make the vast majority of decisions. You would be trusting me to care for you, trusting me to train you to be my submissive. Essentially, you would live to serve me, to please me. In return, I would please you and reward you in just about any way you desired."

Her eyes widened. "I would *live* to serve you?"

"Do you have any questions about that?" he asked, searching her face.

"I…" *A lot of fucking questions, yes. But I don't even know where to begin.* "When you say I would live to serve you, you mean that my purpose in life would be fucking you."

"You would live to serve me and make me happy in whatever way I see fit," he elaborated, "whether that would be allowing me to take you to a play, allowing me to buy you gifts and shower you with presents, or fucking me within an inch of my life, yes."

At a loss for words, she remained silent beside him.

"I cannot explain to you in a quick twenty or thirty minutes what all I would expect from you," he told her. "This would be an ongoing dialogue between the two of us. The contract breaks down some of the basics: what I would expect from you and what you should expect from me, as your Dominant. It lists some of the sexual interests that I have and asks you to list your own. But this contract isn't the end all, be all. During your training, you would learn more about who I am as a Dominant and how I want you to service me."

"So…what you want is a sex slave that you can take on dates once in a while," she surmised, turning to look at him.

"That is a crass description of what I am looking for."

"But ultimately, that *is* what you're looking for?"

There was a long pause before he said anything. "The contract might be able to shed some light on what I am looking for," he said finally, holding the papers in his hands while looking at her. "I'm going to leave the room while you read the contract."

She frowned. "Why?"

He hesitated.

"You're afraid of me judging you?" she asked him.

"The content is…quite sensitive."

"I can't believe you've done this numerous times and you're still shy about it," she said, holding out her hand for the paperwork.

"I'm not, usually," he informed her, handing the papers over to her. "I will be in the bedroom. If you have any questions, just let me know. Otherwise, call for me when you're done." He stood and kissed the top of her head before leaving the living room.

What could possibly be in this contract that would make him fear my reaction? she wondered, flipping through the pages of the thick document. Sighing, she sat back on the couch.

THE CONTRACT
This agreement is a binding contract between André Damian Gaines (the Dominant) and Destiny Reneé Richards (the submissive).
The purpose of this contract is to:
1) Define the roles of both the Dominant and submissive, as agreed to by the signing of this document.
2) Ensure the safety and well-being of the submissive while under the Dominant's care
3) Ensure that both parties are discreet regarding this arrangement.
4) Allow both parties to explore their sensuality without the risk of judgement.
5) Outline the preferences and limits expressed by both parties.

How did he know my middle name is Reneé? I never told him that. Feeling anxiety beginning to creep in, she removed her heels from her feet and drew her knees up beneath her chin as she read:

REQUIREMENTS
1) Both parties agree that they are in healthy condition and free from disease or illness. Both parties agree to be tested for disease or illness. If at any time during this contract, either party is diagnosed with an illness, it is His/her responsibility to advise the other party immediately.
2) The Dominant reserves the right to remain non-exclusive and may take on other sexual partners throughout the duration of this agreement.

2a) The Dominant requires for the submissive to remain exclusive only to Him.

Destiny stopped reading and lifted her eyes from the document. He could have other women, but she had to remain faithful to him? *Unbelievable. He can't be serious.* She shook her head. *This explains why he didn't want to see my reaction. He knew he was crazy to even try this.*

ROLE: DOMINANT

1) The Dominant is responsible for the training, care, discipline, and well-being of the submissive. He will determine the time, place, and method of the submissive's training, with respect to the limits that the submissive has provided.

1a) *Training* in this contract is defined as the teaching of the skills the submissive will need in order to please the Dominant.

1b) Care and well-being in this contract is relating to the health and overall welfare of the submissive. The Dominant's first priority is the submissive's welfare at all times. He agrees to make decisions that will be to the benefit of the submissive's overall well-being. He agrees that He will not abuse His rights as a Dominant.

1c) *Discipline* in this contract is defined as the act of behavior correction. Disciplinary methods include but are not limited to: spanking, flogging, restraints, binding, sentencing to cage time, or any other form of punishment that the Dominant uses. It is the Dominant's responsibility to provide safe words for the submissive to use, so she can express when her limits are close to being reached.

2) The Dominant will make sure to answer any questions the submissive may have regarding this arrangement. If further questions arise after the signing of this contract, the Dominant agrees to answer those questions as well.

2a) The submissive will do her best to make sure her most pertinent questions are answered before the signing of this contract. It is understandable that questions may arise after the contract has been signed, but both parties are to keep in mind that this contract is a legally binding document.

3) Outside of work or school obligations, The Dominant reserves the right to make decisions for the submissive that directly relate to her well-being. This includes but is not limited dietary restrictions, the limiting of alcohol and the complete restriction of any drug use.

4) The Dominant will provide a safe, clean environment in which the submissive will serve Him.

5) The Dominant agrees to ensure that all equipment, toys or otherwise, are sterile, clean, and safe.

6) The Dominant agrees to respect the submissive's limits and/or concerns and address them as they arise.

7) The Dominant will care for the submissive in the event she falls ill or is otherwise incapacitated during the term of this agreement.

8) The Dominant accepts the submissive as His to control, own, train, discipline, and care for.

9) The Dominant agrees to carry Himself with self-respect and with a general respect for others. He also agrees to show respect to the submissive at all times, even when discipline has to be carried out.

10) The Dominant understands that if He does not fulfill His role as specified by the terms of this contract, the submissive reserves the right to terminate the contract.

ROLE: SUBMISSIVE

1) The submissive offers herself completely to the Dominant. The submissive agrees that she is the property of the Dominant. The submissive agrees that she is His to

own and control as He shall see fit, provided He is keeping her safety and overall well-being a priority.

2) The submissive will remain exclusive to the Dominant and will not take on any other sexual partners or romantic interests during the term of this agreement, which will be specified in the following section.

3) The submissive agrees that the Dominant has control over the men she is allowed to spend time with outside of work or school hours.

4) The submissive agrees to keep herself in healthy condition and agrees to refrain from smoking, excessive drinking, or any other harmful substances, such as drugs.

5) The submissive agrees to be available for the Dominant, within reason, outside of school and work hours. The submissive agrees to especially be free Friday-Sunday, unless work or school obligations exist.

6) The submissive shall not perform sexual acts on herself unless the Dominant permits it.

7) The submissive agrees to serve the Dominant in any way He sees fit, within the guidelines of the submissive's predetermined limits.

8) The submissive agrees to sexually please the Dominant in any way He sees fit. The submissive will not argue or hesitate when a sexual act is demanded of her. Either action will result in disciplinary action.

9) The submissive will not disrespect or insult the Dominant in any way and understands that if she does, she will be subject to disciplinary action.

10) The submissive will only look the Dominant directly in the eyes when she has been given permission to do so.

11) When in private quarters, the submissive will refer to the Dominant as "Sir," or "Daddy." She will refrain from using His first name, unless given express permission to do so.

12) The submissive will touch the Dominant only when she has permission from the Dominant to do so.

13) The submissive agrees to care for the Dominant in the event He becomes ill or otherwise incapacitated during the term of this agreement.

14) The submissive agrees to always carry herself with self-respect, and with general respect for others.

15) The submissive agrees to please the Dominant to the best of her ability at all times.

16) The submissive agrees to all of the terms outlined in this contract. If she has any concerns, questions, or requires for any part of this contract to be explained or revised, she will notify the Dominant before signing the contract. The submissive agrees that by signing this contract, she is agreeing to all the terms that exist in the contract at the time of her signing.

The contract went on and on. There were appendixes and a section for Destiny to fill out her chosen limits and safe words. There was a section that specified which sex acts each party liked. There was also a section for both parties to specify the acts they would not like to partake in.

Destiny ran a hand through her hair, overwhelmed with it all. She began to feel doubts that she could enter into an agreement like this. Could she allow André to date other women while she could only spend time with him? That would essentially be cutting off her own social life so she could be available for him *if* he chose to call. Knowing how assertive she was, could she really allow him to control most aspects of her life?

He'd already shown great care in how he handled her, but was that enough for her to trust that he would truly look out for her well-being? She noted that the agreement period specified by the contract was six months. *Six months where I cut off my social life, where I give myself only to him, and where I let him control who I hang out with and what I do.* There was no way she could make a decision on a contract this intense without taking more time to think about it. "André!" she called over her shoulder. A nagging reminder popped into her head. Once she signed her name on the dotted line, she'd no longer be able to call him André. She'd have to refer to him as "Sir" or "Daddy."

A moment later, the sound of his footsteps was audible. He entered the living room, rubbing lotion onto his wrists. He still had on his dress pants and dress shirt, but he'd taken off the suit jacket and tie. His dress shirt was completely unbuttoned, revealing his tattooed chest and abdomen.

That sight alone was almost enough to make her sign the contract. *Focus, girl.*

He approached her. "Did you read through the entire document?"

She nodded.

"What is your initial reaction?"

"I'm not sure if I can do this," she said bluntly.

He exhaled and sat beside her, smelling like cool water. "All right. Tell me what part of the contract makes you hesitate."

"I can't date anyone else, but you can?"

His eyes smiled, but his mouth didn't. "Yes. That is one of my stipulations."

"In what way is that fair?" she demanded to know. "I make myself available for you for the entire time that I am not at work or school. How is it fair that you aren't doing the same for me? And how is it fair that you can go out with another girl while sleeping with me?"

"I will make sure all of your needs are met and cared for," he stated, not breaking eye contact.

But if what I need is you, and you're off with another woman, then *what?* she wanted to ask him. "That doesn't completely answer my question," was all she said.

"I'm sorry if you feel that requirement is unfair," he said. "There are articles in that contract that are up for negotiation. That doesn't happen to be one of them."

"Why do you feel it's necessary to sleep with other women?"

"I feel it's necessary, because it helps to keep this arrangement in perspective. It would be important for..."

"For making sure you don't actually develop any real feelings for me?" she finished for him. "Is that why you feel the need to sleep with other women while we're in this twisted arrangement?"

A muscle in his jaw twitched.

"It's not that I don't understand why you should be allowed to see other women," she said, trying to ease the harshness in her tone. "It's more that I don't understand why *I* can't see other people."

"Because I don't want you to see other people," he said flatly.

Her brows drew together. "I don't want *you* to see other people," she returned. "There. How does *that* feel?"

He sighed and pinched the bridge of his nose. "I don't expect you to agree to these terms tonight," he explained. "I wanted to start the conversation and let you know about the lifestyle that I lead. The purpose of me showing you the contract is to give you an idea of what you would be signing up for by being involved with me. I expect for you to want some time to think it over, and that is completely fine with me. No pressure."

"So, you can't tell me why it's important for you to be able to see other people while I am only allowed to see you?"

"I can't give you the answer that you want, no," he told her. "I can only tell you that it's what I want. And you're right. It might not be the fairest request to make of you.

But if you agree to my terms, and you serve me, and please me, I will spoil you in ways that you couldn't even begin to imagine."

She stared down at the papers in her hand, her brows still furrowed.

He reached out and touched her hair. "Between the Jordan situation, the charity gala, and this contract, you've had a lot to deal with today. I propose that we get some rest tonight. Tomorrow I will take you back home, so you can have some time to think about whether or not you'd want to enter this agreement on my terms."

"All right," she allowed, setting the contract on the coffee table and standing. She held her hand out for him so she could help him up.

Visibly relieved that the discussion was over, at least for now, he took her hand and kissed it before standing. Then he led her to the bedroom, where he closed the door and turned off the lights. He guided her to the bed and stood behind her, trailing a hand down the length of her back. Mere moments passed before he unzipped her dress and lowered the fabric down her smooth shoulders.

She trembled at his touch and could feel tears gathering at the corners of her eyes. How was it possible that a man could be perfect in every other way except one? It was never a small imperfection. It was always an imperfection that teetered on the edge of being a dealbreaker. Her body quivered as he undressed her.

"Get in the bed," he ordered.

She did as she was told, without thinking. Lost in her own thoughts, she pulled the covers up to her chest and stared up at the ceiling.

He removed his clothes and joined her in the bed, immediately curling his arms around her and pulling her back against his chest.

She caressed the birthmark on his right forearm. "If I sign that contract, I wouldn't be able to touch you without permission," she commented.

"But you know that you would often have permission, right?" he asked her.

That response didn't satisfy her. None of his responses had. "I wouldn't be able to look you in the eyes without permission, either."

"Something else that you would often have permission to do," he said shortly before yawning.

"Then why even put it in the contract?" she demanded.

"The contract is standard. They aren't terms I came up with specifically for you."

"Maybe you should have drawn up a contract for me," she muttered.

He laughed in the dark.

"Your eyes are my favorite feature on you," she said, and she knew her voice sounded whiny.

He pressed a kiss to her bare shoulder. "And you would often have my permission to look into them," was his promise.

Still unsatisfied, she continued to trace the shape of his birthmark. Burning hot tears trailed down her cheek and dropped onto the pillow.

The next few days were a blur. Destiny functioned on autopilot and went through the motions of work and class. Wake, shower, eat, work, class, repeat. Wake, shower, eat, work, class, repeat. She found herself daydreaming in class. It was funny to her that out of everything mentioned in the contract, her brain was focused and locked in on the most mundane. Her brain was stuck on the fact that he would be allowed to have other women while she wasn't able to date other men. Meanwhile, she'd practically skipped right over the sections mentioning punishment by whipping, flogging, spanking, and cage time (whatever the hell *that* meant).

Her sexual experiences thus far had been traditional, to say the least. She wasn't a stranger to the doggy-style position and liked to vary positions to change things up. But whips? Chains? *Bondage*? Those concepts were new to her, nothing she'd tried before. She had never felt the urge to try those acts, and the only reason she was even giving them a second thought was because of the man who was requesting it of her.

She didn't realize that Carlos was staring at her with a look of pity until he made a clucking sound with his tongue. She hoisted a look in his direction.

"Are you going to continue staring into space like that, or are you going to help me with these croissants?" he asked with a hand on his hip.

"Are you giving me a choice?" she joked.

Carlos looked her up and down. "What's gotten into you, mija? You get rescued from the club by that gorgeous hunk of man, and you spend the night with him, and yet you look like a kid who's been told that Santa Claus doesn't exist."

I wish I could tell you, she thought. *I wish I could talk to you, or Candace, or Jasmine about this, but I can't tell anyone.* That was one of the worst parts about it. She had questions and wanted to know what they would do in her position. She took one look at Carlos, who looked to be having a fantasy about André right then and there, and she instantly knew what *he* would do. He would have signed the contract without even reading it, all *"Take me, I'm yours."*

Jasmine seemed liberal and confident enough to at least try it out. Candace was a bit more reserved in that regard. If André wasn't prepared to meet her parents and put a wedding band on her finger, she wasn't trying to even hear the word *sex* from him.

"Did he do something to hurt you?" Carlos asked, his expression changing from light-hearted to concerned.

She shook her head firmly. "No, nothing like that."

"I don't understand why everything involving him has to be so hush-hush," he grumbled as he started to stock the shelves with croissants.

"Because of who he is," she said with a deep sigh. "What if someone overheard us talking about him? I'd be mortified."

"Mortified? Pfft. I'm ready for my close-up, hunty," Carlos proclaimed with a wave of his hand.

Destiny laughed for possibly the first time in the past three days. She turned and assisted him with stocking the shelves. Surrounded by ball gowns and suits one evening and stocking bakery shelves the next. Was this her life, or had she stumbled into the pages of some bizarre adaptation of *Cinderella*?

"You can withhold the deets all you want, but just know that I know something major is going down between you two," he prattled on. "Both of your names are all over the news after he basically told the world that you're going to be interviewing him."

Yes, there was that. Jasmine had sent a flurry of texts once the videos of André's speech started circulating the internet. She wanted to know why she had to find out the news from social media. Candace hadn't been surprised, because she'd seen André in the flesh, the night of the charity banquet. It felt like overnight, Destiny Richards became a household name.

The door to the bakery dinged and a messenger wearing a purple and white hat and uniform entered, carrying a large, flat box.

Carlos frowned as he popped a piece of gum into his mouth. "What is this?"

Their manager, Samantha, appeared from the back and went to speak to the messenger. "The package is for you, Destiny."

Destiny's eyes widened. "I didn't order anything," she said, walking around the corner.

Her manager, whose dark hair was pulled back from her face in a ponytail, gestured to the return address on the package. "Does the company ADG sound familiar?"

ADG? Destiny peered at the return address. A spark of recognition lit her eyes. *André Damian Gaines.* "Umm... yes. Yes, I remember now." She hurriedly signed for the package and carried it to the front counter. She smoothed her hands over the cardboard box, staring down at it.

Carlos came to stand beside her. "Well? Aren't you going to open it?"

Can I open it? she wondered. *Or is a pair of fuzzy handcuffs going to fall out of the box?* Not that André struck her as the type to have fuzzy, pink handcuffs. He seemed like the type to carry the real thing, industry-grade stainless steel. No fluff, no gimmicks. With care, she opened one end of the box. She bent at the waist until her eye was level with the opening of the box. Peering inside, she breathed out a sigh of relief. A sleek, slim laptop was in the box, not a random assortment of sex toys.

"You forgot ordering a computer?" Carlos demanded to know, raising an eyebrow at her.

There was a sticky note stuck to the closed surface of the laptop. The note said, *"I respect your need to take some time to make a decision regarding my offer. I hope this helps with your research."* Her pulse raced as she slipped the note back into the box.

Carlos narrowed his eyes suspiciously. "You didn't order this, did you?"

"Carlos, shh," she hissed while placing the laptop back into the box.

He gasped and covered his mouth with his hands. "*He* sent that to you," he whispered. "ADG - *ADG*, André Damian Gaines. Of course!" He smacked his forehead with the palm of his hand.

"Carlos..." She threw him a warning glance.

He pinched his index finger and thumb together and drew them across his lips, indicating that his lips were sealed. "He bought you a computer? Why would he do that? Did you tell him you needed one?"

No, I didn't, she thought. "I have to put this in my locker. Cover for me?"

He nodded, but his eyes were filled with curiosity.

She carried the box into the back room and stored it in her locker. The text of the note advised that he respected her need for time before making a decision, but she could read between the lines. The laptop served to be a gentle, nudging reminder to make up her mind as quickly as possible.

Her cell phone vibrated in her pocket. No doubt it was André checking in to make sure she'd received her "gift." She sighed and, ignoring the buzzing phone, returned to work.

Destiny turned the shower knob. The cascade of water drops slowed to a steady stream before the drops ended altogether. She wrung her hair out with both hands. Then, she stepped out of the shower and grabbed the large, folded towel sitting on the corner of the sink. She dried herself off and wrapped the towel around her body, knotting the top of it above her bustline.

André was on her mind even as she left the bathroom and padded down the hall.

Candace, fully recuperated from her fainting spell, called to her from the living room couch. "Movie night?"

"Yeah, sure," Destiny called over her shoulder. She finished drying off in her bedroom and pulled her hair up into a ponytail.

The cardboard box, which by now she'd nicknamed *Pandora's box*, sat in the middle of her bed. She stared at it as she applied lotion to her arms, legs, and the rest of her body. *Just a few minutes of searching won't kill me,* she thought, sitting on the bed and opening the box. She slid the laptop and accessories out of the box, taking great care as she plugged the charging cable into the computer.

Truth be told, she owned a desktop computer. As a communications major and writer for *The Hilltop*, owning a computer was imperative. Between her own desktop and the computer she used in the *Hilltop* newsroom, she didn't have a pressing need for another computer. *Still, it's nice to have the ability to write or browse the internet from my bed instead of having to sit at my desk.*

She powered up the computer while it charged and went through the setup process while words and phrases from the contract occupied her mind. Then, she accessed the web browser. *Where do I even start?* she thought, tapping her finger on the matte silver mousepad built into the laptop. *I guess I'll start with the definition.*

The definition she found online:
"dom·i·nance ˈdämənəns/*noun*: power and influence over others."

She read the definition multiple times before changing her web search to "sexual dominance."

The first page that came up was a popular online encyclopedia site that mentioned and defined the BDSM lifestyle. What she realized, rather quickly, was that there *was* no searching this topic for a few minutes. This topic was a rabbit hole of information. One topic branched out to another and another.

There were so many pages about the topic, from well-known forums for those interested in the lifestyle to personal blogs written by couples that currently lived the lifestyle.

There were photographs of sexual play between Dominants and submissives. She saw photos of women bound with rope, women suspended from the ceiling, handcuffed, clamps attached to their nipples, women in cages (which reminded her that André's contract *had* mentioned a cage), and all sorts of other contraptions, positions, and disciplinary actions. There were examples of contracts, explanations of different relationship styles, and pages listing different BDSM-related conventions.

She read that some Dominants chose to take on more than one submissive under his care. They would often live together, in the same house. She blew air out between her lips. "Yeah, right," she muttered. "There is no way I would be down for that. Sorry, not even for you, André."

But isn't that what he's asking of you? a nagging voice in her head asked. *He wants to take on other lovers. Isn't it possible for things to lead up to him involving other women when interacting with you?* The thought alone made her shudder.

While women were beautiful, she had no intentions of sleeping with one. *But if you sign the contract, he controls you. He'd be able to tell you what to do. If he wants you to sleep with a woman, you'd be contractually obligated to sleep with another woman.* Another shudder. *Enough research for today.* She closed the laptop, drawing up her knees beneath her chin.

TEXT TO: Destiny Richards
MESSAGE: *Tomorrow? Dinner?*

TEXT FROM: Destiny Richards
MESSAGE: *I'm available tomorrow.*

TEXT TO: Destiny Richards
MESSAGE: *Bring your tape recorder.*

André leaned back in his chair. He was seated at a conference table listening to a Rush Limbaugh lookalike prattle on about how expensive an arts program like his would cost. It was the same drivel André had listened to for the past two weeks.

He presented the facts and numbers for the program to different politicians. Different suits, different faces, same old, washed up, money-grubbing mentality. All André needed was one person who had a brain and was capable of independent thought to believe in this project.

Funny how everyone was on board until the numbers were presented, he thought. Everyone had been ecstatic at the concept. "Save music and art programs? Help benefit underprivileged children? Of course! Wait, how much is it going to cost? Well, we may need to go back to the drawing board, here."

He tapped the end of his pen on top of the three-page meeting agenda. While he prided himself on being a man that held his composure, these meetings were an amazing test of his patience. More than a hundred hours of meetings over the past year, and to what end? They were still running around in the same circles, talking about the same topics, raising the same concerns, and getting absolutely nowhere.

The ringleader of the circus was a heavyset senator who went by the name of Harry Palmer. After breaking down a bunch of useless government fiscal data, he sat down and mopped his sweaty forehead with the handkerchief from his suit pocket.

Everyone at the table turned to face André.

"Oh, am I allowed to speak now?" he asked, setting down his pen. He rose from his chair and smoothed down his blue silk tie. He moved to stand near the canvas screen used to display projections, such as the bar graph being shown now. There was a definite lack of diversity and representation at the conference table. The one African-American politician seated was either afraid to voice his opinion and single himself out as the minority, or was too far removed from poverty to understand the true potential for trouble that young children faced when they didn't have supportive programs to dedicate their time to.

"I understand how dear to you this program is," Harry said, still dragging a handkerchief across his forehead.

"Do you?" André asked him with a tilt of his head. "Do you understand?"

The room was quiet.

"The truth is you don't understand. None of you do. If you understood how important this program is, you wouldn't mention that it is *dear* to me. You would say that the program is *necessary*. You would say that the program is worth the expense." André ran a hand over his head and extended a hand towards the projected bar graph. "I brought this program concept to you because I felt that if I had the government on my side, I would have the power to reach more schools. By reaching more schools, the program would stand to benefit a lot more children than if I executed the program on my own. But all of the time we have wasted in meeting after meeting, and the time we've spent on conference call after conference call...we've been at this now for more than a year. I took time out of my schedule to come here and get the program finalized. And essentially what is happening, is I'm being given the runaround. Now...while you were giving your brilliant speeches on how worthless these children's lives are to *you*, I had an epiphany."

The room was so quiet, you could hear a pin drop.

"It occurred to me that I don't need any of you to proceed with this program." He looked each of them in the face as he said these words. "I can get the program started on my own. I can get things going. I can oversee its campaign. I can enlist a few of my good friends in the entertainment industry. Once it gains popularity, none of you will have your names associated with it." He spoke calmly, but there was a hard, cold edge to his voice when he spoke. "If no one has anything else to say, I say we call an end to this meeting so we can get on with our day and actually do something productive."

There were a lot of low murmurs as he turned and exited the large conference room. He strode down the hall of the government office building, trying to keep his anger in check. He turned into the Men's bathroom and closed the door at his back. The bathroom had marble counters, sleek, glossy stall doors, and a beautifully tiled floor with a pattern that matched the marbled counters. He placed both hands on the countertop and closed his eyes while attempting to manage his emotions. The counter's surface was cold to the touch. The counters were made of real, genuine marble, none of that Formica shit. "This is what they would rather spend their money on," he said, opening his eyes and peering at his reflection. "They would rather make sure the decorations in their bathrooms are up to par than help greenlight a program that would potentially help hundreds of thousands of elementary, junior high, and high school kids across the country."

Anger welled up within him, a blinding anger that he could feel himself losing control of. He bellowed out and sent his fist flying into the nearest wall, cracking the expensive tile. The pain didn't even register to him. Once the pain did begin to crawl up his hand and forearm, it felt good. He was tempted to punch the wall again but didn't want to cause a scene. It was quite possible someone outside of the bathroom had heard the tile breaking.

Trying to get his anger under control, he proceeded to wash the blood from his knuckles. He closed his eyes, trying to steady his breathing. An image of Destiny popped into his head, and it had an immediate calming effect on him. He dried off his knuckles with a paper towel and discarded the paper towel in the nearest waste bin. After giving his reflection in the mirror one final look and adjusting the knot in his tie, he exited the bathroom and headed towards the elevator. Once in the elevator, he removed his cell phone from his pocket.

TEXT TO: Destiny Richards
MESSAGE: *I can't wait until tomorrow. I need to see you tonight. Now, if possible.*

He tapped the end of his cell phone on his chin as he awaited her response. The elevator doors slid open and he strode out of the elevator. His phone buzzed in his hand. He didn't hesitate in checking his phone screen.

TEXT FROM: Destiny Richards
MESSAGE: *I can ask if I can leave work early. What's wrong?*

If she had signed the contract, then asking her to leave work early would be considered a major no-no. It was selfish of him and a disregard for her welfare, since requesting for her to leave work early was putting her job in jeopardy. But his anger and frustration were eating away at him. He had to see her.

TEXT TO: Destiny Richards
MESSAGE: *Please ask. I'll explain when I see you.*

He accessed his call log and selected his driver's phone number, initiating a phone call. "The meeting is over. Pick me up out front." He disconnected the call and crossed the large lobby. His anger was already fading, making way for excitement at the thought of seeing Destiny again.

Destiny knocked on the hotel room door. André had offered to pick her up from work, but she'd insisted on driving over. She preferred to have her car here with her so he wouldn't have to drive her back home.

For the life of her, she couldn't imagine what was so pressing that it couldn't wait twenty-four hours. She frowned at her plain white polo and khakis in disdain. *I would have preferred to go home and change before coming over, but he kept texting me asking what time I'd be here.*

The door swung open and he filled the doorframe. His eyes looked so sad that she immediately felt concern for him. "What's wrong?" she managed to get out before he stepped forward and swept her up in his arms. The scent of alcohol was strong on his breath. Frightened for him, she pulled away from him. "Talk to me," she encouraged.

He pulled her into the hotel room suite and closed the door. When he finally released her, he retreated back to the couch. Once seated, he leaned forward to pick up the glass of Scotch he'd poured for himself earlier. "I should have known better," he said, swirling his drink and staring off into space. "Politicians. I trusted my program, my *baby*, to politicians." He took a long swig of Scotch and wiped his mouth with the back of his hand.

Some of her confusion cleared. Something had gone wrong with the execution of his program and that's why he was so distraught. "They're not going to move forward with it?"

"I gave them more than a year," he said between clenched teeth. "A year to get their shit together and get things moving. All they did was waste valuable hours talking about the same shit. Asking the same questions. All the while, they were getting paid. They probably knew from the beginning that they wouldn't move forward with it. The whole time, they've probably been milking it just to get paid for these meetings and show on paper that they care about what's going on in this country."

She touched his upper arm and caressed it through the fabric of his dress shirt. After a few moments of silence, she asked him, "Have you decided what you're going to do?"

"I don't know," he admitted. "All I could see was red. They angered me so much, I told them I was going to proceed with the program without them."

"You *should*," she urged, the gears in her mind already laying out how that would work.

He shook his head. "We are talking a *lot* of money here. Even with the money and resources I have, I don't have enough money to finance a program of that size - not on my own. It would take a lot to get it going, more than I'm capable of handling right now." Tears welled up in his eyes. "I don't think I can do it. Not without someone backing me."

But you own the biggest multimedia company in the country. How is it possible that you can't afford to put on the program, or would this program cost a lot more than I'm realizing? It was a bit jarring, seeing him cry. Up until now, he'd been a pillar of strength and dominance, a display of perfect poise. She grabbed his face in his hands. "You can do this, André. I know you can."

He continued to shake his head sadly, lowering his eyes. "It was a mistake to call you over here. I don't want you to see me like this."

"You say that as if feeling this strongly for a worthy cause is a bad thing," she said.

He continued to avoid her gaze.

She dropped her hands in her lap, chewing her bottom lip. Her mind was still in overdrive, laying out a blueprint. "It would be expensive to launch a nationwide program," she said slowly, thinking out loud. "But maybe you don't launch it nationally at first. Maybe you start with a few schools. Maybe you start with schools from Mississauga, and from Houston, since you were raised in those two cities. You start the program in those cities and campaign for it. When the program is considered a success, you'll get other people wanting to contribute resources to help."

Some of the sadness in his eyes cleared, replaced by contemplation. "You're right…the program doesn't have to hit all schools at once. That was the original plan, when I thought I had the government backing me. But I can scale it back a bit. Mississauga, Houston, maybe Atlanta. Start off small." He lifted his cell phone from the coffee table and sent a series of text messages. "I'm sorry, just give me a few minutes."

Relieved at his change in mood, she patiently sat back. "Sure."

Responses to his text messages started to come in. After setting the phone back down on the table, he leaned forward and kissed her forehead. "You are a beautiful, intelligent lifesaver."

Hours later, Destiny straddled André in the oversized hotel bed. They were both naked with a fine sheen of sweat gracing their skin. She lifted his injured hand and observed the scarring on his knuckles. "You must have punched the wall *really* hard."

"I was pissed the fuck off," he said. "I can't remember the last time I've felt that angry and helpless. I feel like... I feel like I'm the one that failed. You know? Like there was some better way I could have presented the idea to them. Explain the benefits of the program better, or in a different way. You know?"

She brought his knuckles up to her lips and kissed them. "Who needs further explanation than 'helping kids focus on art instead of gangs?'" she asked him.

His eyes widened. "I know, right?" A short chuckle erupted from his mouth. "I have friends who believe in crazy government conspiracies, all sorts of wild shit. I've always laughed that off, you know? But things like this...I can understand why those conspiracies exist. Situations like this make me feel like our youth is set up to fail. And when I think about it, *really* think about it, it's depressing. And sad. And..."

"Maddening?" she supplied for him.

"Infuriating," he added, lightly grazing her thigh with a finger. His expression turned serious. "I don't remember telling you to stop riding me."

Smiling, she leaned down and caught his bottom lip between her teeth. She sucked it before kissing him long and deep, moaning when she felt his arms circle around her. As instructed, she started to ride him again. This time, she took her time with him.

Beyond the partially open blinds, the sun spilled its very last rays across Washington, D.C.

André combed his fingers through her curly hair. "Have you made up your mind about whether you're going to sign the contract?"

Destiny's breath caught in her throat. She hadn't expected him to bring that up. "I'm...still thinking about it," she said, mentally kicking herself in the ass for not having a better answer than that.

"Is there a direction you're leaning towards?" he asked, kissing her shoulder and tightening his arms around her just slightly.

She stared at the blank wall facing her. "I'm...leaning towards..."

He pressed himself against her rear end.

She closed her eyes and moaned. "That's not fair," she muttered. "You're cheating."

He laughed in her ear. "You're leaning towards…?" he prompted, lowering the arm that was wrapped around her. He slid his hand down her stomach until it was nestled between her thighs.

"Yes," she moaned out.

He nipped at her shoulder with his teeth. "Good girl."

"*Leaning towards*," she emphasized.

He laughed again and buried his face in her neck. "Where is your tape recorder?"

She yawned. "My purse. The floor."

He pulled away from her and fumbled around the floor for her purse.

She giggled and turned her head, slanting a look over her shoulder. "What are you doing?"

"Interview me," he urged, handing her the recorder.

"*Now*?"

He nodded. "Now. I'm inspired."

The sheets bunched around her waist as she sat up. "I'm nowhere near ready for this right now, but…okay." She repositioned herself so that she was facing him. "I am conducting an interview with André Damian Gaines. The date is November 17th. The time is…" She checked the clock on the nightstand. "The time is 6:19pm. This interview will be recorded, if it is all right with you, Mr. Gaines." She tilted the recorder towards him so he could speak into it.

Amusement lit up his eyes. "I give my consent to record this interview," he said into the recorder, sounding like he was trying not to laugh.

"Word travels fast, and word has it that you've spent a lot of time in Washington, D.C. lately," she said into the recorder. "Can I ask why you've been spending so much time in D.C.?"

"Certainly." His voice turned a bit more serious as he said, "I have been in talks with some of our most respected politicians to spearhead a program that will launch new art and music programs in schools, and help improve the existing art and music programs in our schools." It had taken some effort for him not to choke on the word "respected."

"That sounds like an admirable project, Mr. Gaines. You recently attended a charity gala, where you were honored as Humanitarian of the Year. During that gala, you announced the initiative you are launching. Why did you feel it was important to announce the program at the benefit, when you've kept this project on the hush for the majority of your stay in D.C?"

His hand was on her thigh again. Lightly touching her thigh, he maintained eye contact with her. "While I was honored to be named Humanitarian of the Year, this program is important to me. There were a lot of important people present at the gala, and I felt like it was time for me to announce the project I've been working on. The only reason I kept everything quiet before is because I was still working on the launch. I wanted to make sure the program was fully backed before announcing it to the masses." His fingertips continued dancing across her thigh, making it hard for her to concentrate.

She cleared her throat. "Can you specify which grades this program would benefit?" Her voice went shaky towards the end of the question.

His fingers dipped inward, grazing her inner thighs. "This program would benefit elementary school students, junior high school students, and high school students," he responded, holding her gaze. "So...K-12."

She paused the recording. "What are you doing?" she demanded.

He grinned, boyish and devilish all at once. "I'm being interviewed."

"You know that's not what I mean."

"Turn the recorder back on," he instructed.

She stared at him for several minutes, trying to ignore the tiny shocks that his touch initiated. She took a deep, steadying breath and pressed the Record button again. "What inspired you to start this program?" she asked, having to draw an arm across her mouth to stifle any moans resulting from his feathery light touches.

"As most of the world knows by now, music is very important to me," he explained. "Music is...my life. I don't know where I would be without it, and I know a lot of people who feel the same way. We were all children once. We were children who sang along to the songs our parents played on the radio, or danced to music videos, or banged out a song using pots and pans or whatever our little hands could find." His own hand found what it was looking for and coaxed wetness out of her. "Without music, I could have easily fallen in with the wrong crowd. There are kids out there, who could be talented singers, or musicians, or painters. There are also people out there who *could have been* talented singers, or musicians, or painters. I want to help save those *could-have-beens*."

She switched off the recorder. "That was *nice*," she complimented.

"Thank you, but don't turn the recorder off again," he warned her.

She turned the recorder back on and stared at him, trying to read the look in his eyes. "You've reportedly been in D.C. for several weeks. Is there a date for when this program is scheduled to go into effect?" She turned the recorder in his direction while clenching her thighs around his arm.

"Actually, I'm wondering the same thing," he said, working his fingers inside of her. "The meetings I've been attending were supposed to set everything into motion, but the politicians who were working with me got scared. They felt the program would be too expensive. They've been dragging their feet."

All words escaped her mind. Spasms were making her body tremble. Fighting to catch her breath, she moved the recorder below her mouth. "Ahhh…"

He didn't stop. If anything, his fingers pushed deeper inside of her. "Were those the only questions you had for me?"

She shook her head, covering her mouth with her hand to keep from screaming.

"If you have more questions, ask me," he said calmly.

She tried to regulate her breathing before moving the recorder closer to her mouth. "I'm…I'm s-s-sorry to hear that," she stammered out, on the brink of ecstasy. "Umm... ah....so...what are your plans regarding the p-p-program?"

"I'm glad you asked," he said, his voice cheerful and buoyant. "Someone very dear to me gave me some of the best advice I've ever received. She said that I could start the program on my own. Start off small, in the towns that are nearest to my heart. With that being said, I will be launching these programs in Mississauga, Canada, Houston, Texas, and Atlanta, Georgia. These are all cities that helped raise me in one way or another. Each of these cities has helped me to become the man I am today. Since the schematics of the program have changed, I will need to get back to you with the exact date the program will be launching."

"It sounds like you are...very passionate...about the program," she said, her voice rising in pitch.

He leaned in close to her. "This program is my baby," he said, catching her bottom lip between his teeth and sucking on it.

She couldn't hold back any longer. Those words were the very undoing of her. She came with her thighs locked tightly around his hand.

"You realize that you're putting pastries you just baked into the freezer, right?"

Destiny scratched her head, trying to remember who she was, where she was, and what she was doing. *Your name is Destiny Richards, you're working at Eli's Bakery, and you almost fucked up royally just now,* she thought, wheeling around to face Carlos, who leaned against the food preparation table.

He sighed and pushed himself from against the table. "What is that man doing to you?" he asked, walking up to her so he could take the tray of pastries out of her hands

Everything. "Nothing," she said quickly. *André just has...an interesting way of conducting interviews.*

She planned on surprising him this weekend. Show up to his hotel, ready to sign the contract, wearing nothing but a trench coat. Or...something like that. She hadn't worked out the specifics yet. With his extensive sexual experience, he'd probably already had women show up to his door wearing nothing but a coat before. It was during her attempt at devising another plan that Carlos had caught her trying to deep freeze the pastries she'd just pulled out of the oven.

The kitchen door swung open. Samantha poked her head in. "Another delivery for you, Destiny," she said, sounding tired.

Destiny scratched her head and walked past Carlos.

Carlos was close at her heels as she pushed through the swinging kitchen door that led out to the front counter area. A messenger held the largest bouquet of roses she'd ever seen in her life.

Multiple colored roses peeked out from the silky looking material binding it. Not noticing that most of the customers were looking in her direction, she reached out to touch the bright-colored flowers.

"Not to rain on the parade, Destiny," Samantha said, tucking a pen behind her ear, "but we're going to have to start limiting these deliveries. They have the potential to disrupt business."

Destiny nodded, still dazzled by the colorful roses. "No more deliveries," she vowed, leaning forward to sniff a yellow rose petal.

The messenger held out a piece of paper and pen to her. "I just need you to sign for it, if you're Destiny Richards."

Destiny nodded and scribbled her name on the line marked "Recipient." She accepted the bouquet from him and buried her nose in the flower petals.

"I asked what he was doing to *you*, but maybe I should have been asking what *you're* doing to *him*," Carlos muttered, following her back to the counter.

She arched a look over her shoulder at him.

"Do you want me to take these to the back with me?" he asked her.

Still at a loss for words, she nodded.

He set the tray of pastries on their appropriate shelf and took the flowers from her.

Tonight, she thought giddily. *Tonight, I'm going to surprise him.*

After work, Destiny drove home. Her rose bouquet rested in the passenger seat. She'd put the seatbelt across it to keep it from falling forward whenever she brought the car to an unexpected stop. Once she got home, she showered. Massaged sweet smelling oil into her skin while eyeing her reflection in the mirror. She fluffed up her hair, wondering if she should flatiron it. André seemed to prefer it curly and natural. So tonight, she would keep it curly and natural. She did put some product in her hair to help tame it, though.

She pulled black panties up her legs and accompanied those panties with a matching black, lacy bra. She stepped into a slinky, black mesh dress and zipped it up the side, keeping her eyes on her reflection. Next came the application of light, subtle makeup, with eyeliner and dark red lipstick. She pinned her curls up and made sure a strand of hair wasn't out of place.

By the time she walked out of her bedroom with her purse slung over her shoulder, Candace was standing near the kitchen counter. Her eyes widened. "What are you trying to do?" she demanded. "Make him propose?"

As a matter of fact... Destiny laughed. "Don't wait up."

She felt jittery the entire ride to his hotel. *I am a complete bundle of nerves. Am I really going to sign a contract that would essentially make me his property? His to own and control? To dominate in every which way?* Why was she so willing to throw away her freedom?

Because after having met him, I can't go back to a life without him in it, she thought as she drove. The sky had darkened, and the streetlights were on. The streets were damp with rain.

Her nervousness spiked when his hotel came into view. She parked in the hotel garage and climbed out of her car. Once she was in the elevator, she had to resist the urge to send him a text letting him know she was here. What if he was sleeping, or busy? She glanced at the time on her cell phone. It was just after eight. Hopefully, he wouldn't be asleep this early.

The elevator reached the floor of his hotel room and the doors separated, allowing her to walk through. She stepped off of the elevator and immediately heard voices. She rounded the corner and saw André. A dark-skinned woman of average height and a shapely build walked behind him.

"You remember how this goes, right?" he asked, and his voice sounded different somehow. It sounded more monotone than usual. He reached into the pocket of his dress pants as they approached the door to his room.

The woman nodded. "Yes, Sir," was her enthusiastic response.

"That's right. Keep your eyes lowered."

Destiny retraced her steps back to the elevator and braced an arm against the wall to keep herself steady. She closed her eyes and clutched her chest. *It's not what it looks like,* she told herself. *She's just a friend of his.*

Why did she call him "Sir?" her nagging subconscious asked her.

She fought back the tears forming in her eyes. *Because...because she is his secretary or something.*

Why are they meeting in his hotel room on the weekend, this late at night, then?

Because...because he has a lot of work to do on the project now that he knows he's heading it on his own, she thought, wiping at her eyes and pressing her back against the wall. She put her face in her hands. *Get it together, Des. Don't make assumptions. You're going to walk right up to his room, and you're going to knock. They'll just be sitting on the couch, talking business.*

She took a deep, steadying breath and blinked her tears away. Gathering all of the willpower she possessed, she rounded the corner again. There was a sense of déjà vu as she approached his hotel room door. It wasn't that long ago now that she'd walked in on her ex-boyfriend, Jordan, kissing another girl. That had only been a few months ago. *Fate wouldn't be cruel enough to let something like that happen again,* she thought. *After the night that André and I had...he wouldn't be with another woman that soon.*

As luck would have it, the door to the suite was cracked open; it hadn't closed completely. She raised a hand and pressed her palm flat against the door, trying to control her shallow breathing. Briefly closing her eyes, she gave a push so that the door swung open.

There was the sound of giggling and a loud smacking sound.

No one was in the living room of the suite, as she had hoped. The sounds were coming from the bedroom.

The sounds should have been enough. The sounds should have been enough for her to turn around and leave and never come back. But they weren't. There was still a part of her that wanted to believe that the activities being carried out in the bedroom were innocent in nature. It was that part of her that drove her to pass the living room and walk down the hall of the hotel suite. Her hands were shaking. Her pulse rushed in her ears. She hesitated at the closed bedroom door. More smacking sounds. A moan.

She turned the doorknob and pushed the door open. And her heart broke in two.

9

André glanced up from the woman who was draped across his lap. His hand was raised in the air, preparing to smack at already reddened ass cheeks.

He was spanking her, Destiny realized. She turned and blindly stumbled down the hallway. She left the hotel suite and ran down the hall.

"Destiny!" he shouted from the hotel room door.

She knew that he was following her, running after her. That didn't stop her. She made it to the elevators and pounded on the Down button with her fist. She folded her arms across her chest and waited.

André rounded the corner. "Destiny. Wait. Stop."

She ignored him and pressed the Down button again.

"You told me you had to work through the entire weekend," he said.

The elevator doors opened. She went to step into the elevator, but he reached out and grabbed her upper arm. "Get your fucking hands off me!" she screamed at him.

"Destiny," he pleaded, sounding helpless. "You were *not* supposed to see that."

The elevator doors started to close, but she stopped them. "If you don't let me go, I'm going to scream," she warned him.

"I didn't know you were coming here," he explained.

"André." She really started crying then. "Please let me go."

He released her and stepped back.

She stepped into the elevator, pressed the button marked G, and kept her back to him.

He followed her into the elevator.

"What are you doing?" she demanded.

"I want to talk to you."

"I don't have anything to say to you," she stated.

"From the beginning, we said that this was a no-strings-attached arrangement," he reminded her. "That I would be allowed to date other women. The contract hasn't been signed, so even now - if you wanted - you could still date other men."

"I came here to tell you that I was going to sign the contract," she said, finally daring to look him in the eyes. "I was going to sign the contract and become your property. I was going to be something you owned. An object. While you would be allowed to…go off and have sex with whoever you wanted, I was going to sign a piece of paper saying that you would be the only man I'd be with. How could I be so stupid? So stupid, and desperate, and self-degrading?"

"You weren't being any of those things," he insisted. "We've formed a genuine connection and things are good between us. What you just saw…you weren't supposed to see that."

"But it still would have happened," she said sadly. "I can pretend all I want, but I don't want to share you. I don't want you going out with other women."

He lowered his gaze and stared at the floor.

"I want…I want you to *be* with me," she said, hating the sound of desperation in her voice. "I want us to be real."

The elevator doors opened once they reached the Garage level. André kept his gaze lowered. "You know I can't do that," he said in a soft voice.

"Why not?" she questioned. "What makes it so hard to stop seeing other women? What is it they're giving you that I can't?"

He shook his head, his lips pursed shut.

She sighed and wiped at her cheeks. "I know I'm young," she said. "I haven't achieved much in this life yet, but I could give you everything you could possibly ever want in a woman. Sexually, I don't have the most experience, but whatever I don't know, I could learn. I would be willing to learn, for you. I would support you, and be there for you, and love you."

"Destiny..." He settled his hands on her shoulders. "I'm just not that type of guy."

"Liar," she breathed out.

"Destiny." His voice turned firm.

"You're a liar!" she shouted at him. "You believe in love. You're just scared, and I don't know why. I don't understand you."

"You're right!" he shouted back. "You're absolutely right! You *don't* understand me. So how could you love me?"

She cowered in the corner of the elevator as its doors closed again.

"If you don't understand me, how could you possibly know that you could give me everything I wanted?" he went on. "You want me to believe in love, and then you say shit that makes no sense!"

With tears frozen in her eyes, she punched the Garage level button on the elevator control panel. The doors slid open and she walked out.

He growled in frustration. "Destiny!" he shouted, following after her.

When she reached her car, she whirled around to face him. "I don't want you to call me. I don't want you to text me. I don't want you to send things to my place of work." She laughed dryly. "And oh yeah. Roses? You sent me roses, knowing that you had a hot, steamy date with Mrs. Spanks in there? That's *sick*, André. You hear me? It's *sick*."

André stared at Destiny with a pained expression on his face. Long after she'd driven away, he remained standing, staring through a cloud of vehicle exhaust. Functioning completely on autopilot, he returned to his hotel suite. Instead of returning to the bedroom, where he knew the woman waited, he poured himself a stiff drink and sat on the living room couch.

The man who didn't even believe in love could feel his heart slowly start to break. He stared into space as he drank, trying to convince himself that Destiny's departure was for the best. In so many ways, she was innocent and naïve. Being involved with him would definitely tarnish some of that innocence, and it was one of the qualities he liked about her.

His guest tiptoed out of the bedroom and padded into the living room barefoot. "Are you coming back to bed?"

He swirled the strong liquor around in his glass and ignored her.

"Dré?"

"*Don't* call me that," he barked.

"I'm sorry...Sir," she said, bowing her head.

"Who told you that you could leave the bedroom?"

"I was worried."

"Worried what?" he prompted.

"I was worried, Sir," she said.

He downed the liquor in the glass and set the glass on the table. "You're released for the night. Please leave."

Her eyes widened. "Did I do something wrong, Sir?"

"Please leave," he repeated.

She returned to the bedroom, gathered what few items she'd brought with her, and left.

He continued to sit in the dark, staring into space. He tried to tell himself that he would be able to find someone else, someone who intrigued him as much as Destiny did. But he knew better.

Destiny told André not to text her or call her, but he did anyway. She didn't reply to his text messages or calls.

After days of receiving no response, he started to use the article as an excuse to communicate. He texted saying that she should still use the article, since it would do wonders for her career. Not even that message drew a response from her.

Her heart was crushed. It was difficult for her to focus on work or school. Fortunately for her, Thanksgiving break started soon.

She packed up the items she needed from her desk in the newsroom and slung her purse and backpack over her shoulder.

Jasmine, dressed in another one of her cute dress suits, stopped her in her tracks. "Are you okay?"

"I'm fine," Destiny assured, tucking straightened hair behind one ear.

Jasmine narrowed her eyes at her. "Whenever a woman says she's *fine*, she usually isn't *fine*."

"I just have a lot on my mind," Destiny said, avoiding eye contact.

"Anything to do with the fine, hot chunk of man who stopped in here for you a few weeks back?" Jasmine asked, smiling knowingly.

Destiny groaned inwardly and shook her head.

"You might as well tell me, Destiny. I already pretty much know."

"What do you know?" Destiny asked, curious as to her theory.

"I'm guessing he's the one who wanted you to be his girl on call," Jasmine said smartly, blowing on her nails. "He seems like the type. You tried to make it work because of who he is, or maybe because of how he makes you feel. From how down you've seemed lately, I'm guessing things didn't work out."

Destiny's brows shot up.

"I know my shit." Jasmine shrugged.

"Things didn't work out," Destiny echoed, shifting the weight of her backpack. "Huge understatement."

"What happened?" Jasmine perched on the edge of the desk.

Destiny sighed and lowered her backpack. "He didn't want a commitment. I did. I tried to be okay with what he wanted, but ultimately, I wasn't okay with it. I want more than he can give me."

"Ouch." Jasmine sucked air between her teeth.

Destiny didn't want to go into further detail than that. Even though he'd broken her heart, she didn't want to put his interests on blast. "Maybe it's for the best," Destiny said, trying to make her voice sound light.

The look in Jasmine's eyes was sympathetic. "If you believed that, you wouldn't be moping around here like this."

"I really need to get going."

"Destiny. Just know that everything that is meant to happen, will happen. Timing is everything. He might not want commitment now, but maybe he will later. Maybe now just wasn't the right time for you two to come together. There's nothing wrong with setting standards for what you want. Who knows? Maybe you'll be the one to show him that not *all* commitments are bad." Jasmine thought about it and added, "Just *most*."

Destiny laughed and nudged her in the arm. "I have to get going."

"Are you going home for Thanksgiving?" Jasmine asked.

Destiny shook her head. "No, but I will be going home for Christmas."

"Not going home for Thanksgiving?" Jasmine asked, wrinkling her nose. "Are you sure you don't want to come home with me?"

"I'll be fine. I have studying that I need to do, anyway."

Jasmine hugged her before she left. "If you change your mind, I'm just a text away."

When Destiny finally got home, Candace was waiting with her hands on her hips. Destiny frowned. "What?" she asked just as a powerful floral scent punched her in the face.

Candace stepped to the side. The living room was filled with roses. Roses of all colors were arranged beautifully around the room. "They're in your bedroom, too."

The scent of roses filled the place.

"Des...I could take the landline calls from Jordan. But André, too?"

Destiny's head whipped around. "I never gave him the landline number."

"Then he must be Inspector Gadget or Sherlock or some shit," Candace joked dryly. "Because he's been calling for you all day. If the education program and music industry thing doesn't work out, he should try out for the CIA."

Destiny shook her head in amazement. "Why doesn't he just let it go?"

"You put that good-good on him and now he's addicted," Candace guessed, walking over to the couch and sitting on it.

If he was addicted to it, he would have at least tried being in a relationship with me, Destiny thought as she joined Candace on the couch. "What are you watching?"

"A reality show about love and hip hop," Candace replied, popping a piece of popcorn into her mouth. "Hollywood or Atlanta or Miami, I can't tell which. They all seem the same at this point. Nothing but ratchetness. Just pure ratchetness."

The phone on the coffee table rang.

Candace stared at her. Destiny stared back. "What?" Candace asked, eating another piece of popcorn. "You're here now. I'm not answering that. I already know who it is."

Destiny sighed and leaned over to pick up the cordless phone. "Hello?"

"Destiny."

His voice was deep and low, his words curling into her ear and sending tingles of pleasure throughout her body. She closed her eyes, battling the sensations that his voice was causing. "Yes?"

"Can you please meet with me this weekend?"

"I'm busy."

He paused.

"Were you expecting me to jump up at your beck and call?" she asked him.

"I...don't know," he said finally.

"I don't want to see you," she told him. "And I don't want to talk to you. The phone calls, the text messages, the roses. It all has to stop, André."

"I can't stop," he blurted out. "I miss you."

She raised a hand to her temple and glanced at Candace before standing and heading to her bedroom. She entered the bedroom and closed the door behind her. "What do you want me to do?"

"I want you to meet with me," he answered. "I want to see if we can work this out."

"What is the point?" she asked him. "We want very different things. The issues we have aren't something that we can overcome by just having a talk. One of us would need to change their mind about what he or she wants. Have you changed your mind about what you want from me?"

"I can't stop thinking about you."

She sat down on her bed.

"I think about you all the time. When I wake up, before I go to bed, and most of the time in between."

"You know what I want," she told him firmly.

He sighed. "I can't give you that."

"Then this conversation is over, and we have nothing to meet about," she said, her words bouncing off of each other.

His voice dipped even lower. "I need to see you."

"Stop doing that."

"Stop doing what?"

"The voice thing."

"What?"

She groaned in frustration. "The thing you're doing with your voice, lowering it and making it all...deep and shit, stop it."

"I didn't do anything with my voice," he claimed. "At least, not purposely."

"I have to go, André."

"Wait."

With her nerves hanging on by a thread, she asked, "Did you have something else to say?"

"We still need to discuss the article."

"There's nothing to discuss. I'm not going to use it."

"Wait...you can't put that interview in the vault, Destiny."

She lapsed into silence.

"That article is imperative for what I'm trying to do with this program."

"What you want doesn't matter to me anymore."

"You know this is about more than just what I want. If you don't release that article..."

"You'll have to find a journalist who can conduct a *real* interview, instead of...whatever it was that *we* did," she finished for him, falling back on her bed and staring up at the ceiling. "It doesn't feel right for me to run that article. Someone else should interview you."

"You're lying down now," he said. "I can tell by the change in your voice."

She curled her body into the fetal position, hugging the pillow closest to her.

"I miss you so much, Destiny. That night, what you saw hurt you and I'm so sorry for that. I can make sure that something like that never happens again."

Tears started at the corners of her eyes. "I have to go," she said, and hurriedly disconnected the call. She cried into her pillow, annoyed that she had allowed him the opportunity to make her cry again. The phone rang. She touched the antenna of the cordless phone to her lip and cried even more.

The next morning, she threw each and every bundle of roses away. She mailed the laptop back to him. She didn't want anything that reminded her of him. The one thing she couldn't bring herself to throw away was the royal purple dress he'd bought her. It was entirely too beautiful. Instead of tossing it out, she hid it in the very back of her closet, out of sight.

Each day that followed was tough. She didn't have any classes, but she spent time catching up on the classes she'd taken to daydreaming in. She talked to her parents a lot over the next few days. Even though she didn't admit something was wrong, her mother was able to detect the sadness in her voice almost instantly. That was so...her mother. Quick to detect, quick to offer assistance. Sweet, loving, caring.

Candace and Jasmine offered their ears. She trusted them and at some point, wanted to give them a watered-down version of the situation. She just wasn't ready. She preferred to pretend that he'd never walked into her life, even though he continued to call. Less often, but still often enough to annoy her. He still continued to text her. Still reaching out. Asking her questions like how was she feeling? On a whim, she'd responded, "Heartbroken." To his credit, he'd replied, but she hadn't encouraged any further conversation.

School resumed and she immersed herself in classes. She still had the recorded "interview" with André, if you could call it that. Why keep it, when she couldn't even bring herself to listen to it? The last thing she needed was to be reminded of what he'd been doing to her during the recording.

Pathetic, how he could shatter her heart into a million pieces and yet the thought of him could still turn her on. Her body's reaction to just the thought of him was so strong. She wondered if that would ever change. She wondered a lot of things.

"What you need is a girl's night out," Carlos prescribed one night at work when the bakery was nearly empty.

It was raining outside, which was probably why the bakery was so empty. Raindrops dotted the windows and could be heard on the roof over their heads.

"What I *need* is a rubber room," she mumbled, resting her forehead against the cool counter.

"What you *really* need is to talk to someone about this," he told her. He held his hands up when she glared at him. "Look, it doesn't have to be me. But it needs to be *someone*. Holding in heavy shit just makes it worse. And it will make it harder for you to get over him. You need to vent. You need to let out all of that bad juju."

She raised her head off the counter and started pacing.

The bell over the front door rang. When Destiny saw who had entered, her complexion paled.

Tall, dressed in one of his trademark stylish suits, and completely rain-soaked, was André. He stood just inside of the door with sad eyes, as if he was afraid to approach the counter.

She stared at him without greeting him.

Carlos gave her a look that went unnoticed. "Welcome to Eli's," he greeted André, nudging Destiny in the arm. "Do you want me to take his order?"

"I'm not here to order." André slowly approached the counter.

Destiny backed away from the counter.

Carlos looked between the two of them, a frown forming on his face.

Without a word, Destiny turned and pushed through the kitchen door, wiping at her eyes. She walked over to the lockers, trying to blink the tears away.

The kitchen door swung open.

"Carlos, one of us needs to stay out front."

André strode into the back area.

She pressed her back against the locker behind her. "What are you doing back here?"

"I had to see you. You weren't replying to my messages or taking my calls."

She shook her head. "Coming here was *not* fair."

"I didn't know what else to do."

"Move on with your life, is what you're supposed to do," she said, turning her back to him. "That's what I'm *trying* to do. Since you don't believe in love, finding a replacement should be easy for you. Please go before you get me in trouble."

"Meet with me," he begged her.

"We've already talked about this."

"Please look at me."

"André, you need to leave."

"Destiny."

She whirled around. "What?"

His suit was completely soaking wet. He looked so distressed, so miserable. "I can't stop thinking about you. It's driving me crazy. That's not an exaggeration and it's not me trying to be cute. Living without you is literally driving me crazy. I can't...*not* have you in my life – not now that I've experienced life with you in it."

Those were pretty words, but the walls she'd built remained. "You know what I want, André."

"And you know what I want."

"We're at a stalemate, then, because I'm not settling for less than what I want." She tilted her chin up, trying to put on a strong front, even though she was sniffling and trying not to cry.

He took a step closer to her.

"Stop it," she warned, pointing at him.

He lowered his eyes and took another step forward.

She pressed herself flat against the locker, trying to keep as much distance between them as possible, as much as the small locker area would allow.

He closed the distance between them in two more steps and pressed himself against her. She could feel the wetness from his suit seeping into her clothes.

"André-" she started.

He grabbed her face in his hands and kissed her.

And she kissed him back, because it was *him*. Because other than his taboo interests and his need for dating multiple women, he was the kind of man she dreamed about. Because whenever she was near him, and even when she wasn't, every cell in her body cried out for him. It was crazy but now, even after all they'd been through, his kiss still made her soul sing. His touch still made her skin rejoice.

His hands were all over her and any minute, Carlos could come back here and find them, but she didn't care. That was the effect André had on her. She was no angel either, untucking his black dress shirt, desperate to feel his skin beneath her fingertips. She caressed his abdomen while he pressed her into the locker, wrapping her up in his arms and burying his face in her neck. His kisses were hot and hungry. If anyone witnessed the affection, they would swear that the couple had been apart for months, and not only weeks.

"André," she whispered against his lips.

"No."

She hadn't asked a question, but she knew what the *"No"* was in response to. When they were kissing and touching, they were in a bubble, a bubble unaffected by any other elements. Unaffected by rules, contracts, titles, jealousy, society, labels, and disappointments. He wanted to remain in that bubble. He wanted to keep his lips locked with hers and shut everything else out. While she wanted the same, at some point they would have to come up for air. "André," she whispered again.

He pulled back and looked at her with sad eyes.

"I'll meet you this weekend," she promised.

Hope flickered in his eyes.

"Only to discuss the article," she added.

The hope in his eyes dimmed but didn't completely die out. He nodded solemnly. "If I text you the day and time, will you respond?"

"Yes."

He touched her hair. "You straightened it again."

She brought a hand up to her hair self-consciously. "Wearing it curly reminded me too much of you."

"Destiny, I'm-"

"You need to get out of here," she said abruptly, cutting him off. "We don't want to be caught back here." She grabbed his hand and led him through the swinging door.

Carlos was leaning against the counter typing a text message into his phone. When Destiny and André came through the door, he lifted an eyebrow. When he saw that Destiny looked to be entering a wet t-shirt contest, the other eyebrow shot up. "O....kay," he said, pointedly staring down at her chest.

Destiny and André both looked down at her shirt.

André's face reddened. "I'm...sorry about that."

Carlos gawked at him in amazement.

"No worries, but you need to leave," she told him.

"Right." André pressed a kiss to her forehead. "This weekend?" he asked, backing up towards the front door of the bakery.

"This weekend," she agreed, waving him off.

He turned, opened the door, and walked out into the rain.

Carlos tapped his cell phone on the counter, staring at Destiny. "So...that Get Out of Jail Free card you've been using to avoid talking about this...no longer active. Spill."

Options were weighed quickly within a relatively short span of time. She regarded Carlos with an evaluating eye, ran through their short evolution of a friendship. If she was going to spill anything, it wasn't going to be in the front area of the bakery. Abruptly turning on her heel, she pushed through the door separating the front and back room of the bakery.

"Hey!" she heard Carlos calling after her, but she didn't stop until she was standing outside, behind the bakery.

Appearing confused, Carlos followed her out of the door. "Well?" he demanded, spreading his arms outward.

Destiny sighed and tilted her head back, staring up at the sky. The evening's rain had lightened into a drizzle. "Your assumptions were correct. André and I were seeing each other."

"No shit," Carlos said, withdrawing a pack of cigarettes from his pocket. "What I want to know is, what has both of you running around acting all crazy?"

Destiny sat on a low cement ledge and rested her elbows on top of her knees. She quietly observed the passing traffic before saying, "He is...a very intense man."

"Tell me something I *don't* know, girl," Carlos said, gesturing for her to get on with it.

"I'm trying," she said, covering her face with her hands. "This isn't easy for me to talk about. The whole situation is weird and complicated."

"All right, sweetie, take your time then." He checked the cigarette pack in his pocket. "I have six cigs left. I've got all the time in the world, honey."

She took a deep breath and lowered her hands into her lap. "He has very...specific interests. Sexually."

"*How* specific?" Carlos asked, tapping the end of his cigarette.

"Have you ever heard of Dominance and submission?" she asked him, genuinely curious.

His eyes widened and he sat down next to her. "No way."

"Way."

"Sex slave shit? *Him*?" Carlos laughed and took a long drag from his cigarette. "That tall, hunk of beauty who knows how to dress? Is into...what? Collars? 'Call me Sir'? Bondage? Spanking?"

"All of the above."

Carlos squealed. "Honey, when the juice is worth the *wait*. My Lord."

"Shh!" she hissed at him, slapping his arm.

"Oh my God, oh my God, oh my God, okay I'm sorry," he said, making an effort to bring down his excitement level.

"I can *trust* you, right?" she asked, suddenly worried. "I don't want this to get out. You have to promise me you won't talk to a soul about this."

He made a cross over his heart. "And hope to die, mija. Oh my *God*." He tugged on his curly black ponytail. "So...he's into that and, what? You aren't? That caused the tension you guys have going on right now?"

"There's more to it than that." She wanted a drag of his cigarette, even though she hated the smell of cigarette smoke. Anything to calm her nerves. "To be involved with him, I'd have to sign a contract. A contract saying what I can and can't do, and what he's supposed to do, as my Dominant. And...one of the things was that I couldn't date anyone else, while he could still date and sleep with other women."

Carlos twisted his mouth in disgust. "Some sexy points were definitely lost there," he remarked, nodding his head. "That would turn me off, too, yeah. I'm a possessive little bitch."

"*Right*?" she asked him, relieved that he understood. "I want him to myself. The thought of him being with another woman...I couldn't stand it. And I kept having these debates with myself, you know? Could I live with knowing he could be out with someone else?"

He shook his head. "Not me. I'm definitely not the one to put up with that."

"Well, I was going to try. I went to his hotel, prepared to sign the contract and give myself to him. But..." She fought back the imagery of the woman who'd been draped across his lap, eager to receive her punishment from him.

There was no telling what she'd done to warrant that punishment in the first place. "He was with another woman. Since I told him I had to work for the weekend, he decided to make other plans."

Carlos was still shaking his head. "It all makes sense, now. You've been dealing with all of this by yourself?"

"I do feel better, getting it out," she confessed. "But just when I thought I was beginning to get over him, he had to pop back up in my life. At my job. And mess up my head all over again."

"I can understand the confusion," Carlos said. "He's beautiful and perfect and you want to do whatever it takes to be with him, right? But it goes against everything you believe."

"Relationships are sacred to me," she said, nodding. "Between two people. He claims he doesn't believe in love, but I don't believe him. Or...if he doesn't, I think he wants to. I don't know."

"Hold up...Dré, *the* Dré, is claiming not to believe in love? As if we haven't heard a decade's worth of his music where he was singing and rapping about being heartbroken and breaking hearts and shit?"

"Something must have happened to change his mind," was all she could think of.

"Or something happened to scare the fuck out of him," Carlos suggested. "Some of that shit he was rapping about was so cringey, when it came to how women treated him."

"*And* when it came to how *he* treated women," she pointed out. "He wasn't a saint."

Carlos tipped his head in acknowledgement. "Well, by all means, show him the way, honey," he encouraged.

"He won't let me," she said, leaning forward and wrapping her arms around her knees. "He refuses to let me in."

Carlos sighed. "With something like this, there won't be an easy answer as to what you should do. Something like this, you just have to feel it out. Follow your heart.

Just don't be one of those girls who thinks you can change a man, because those plans almost *always* fail."

"I know."

"If you decide to go back to him, assume that he will stay the same for the entire time you're together. If that means he'd be seeing other women, then you'd have to be okay with that. If he *does* decide to let you in, that would just be a bonus – not the expectation."

"All of his other qualities are so perfect," she mumbled in disdain.

"Isn't that how it always goes?" Carlos queried, finishing off his cigarette and dropping it on the ground. "You find someone who is amazing, who completely rocks your world. Then there's always something major that rocks the boat. You can either stay in the boat and deal with it or jump the fuck out and swim as far away as you can."

She remained quiet.

"Oh *pobrecita,* come here." He gathered her in a bear hug. "Everything is going to work out. Somehow, some way. Trust me. I know these things."

"I'm usually an optimistic person, but I can't imagine any way for this to work out," she mumbled into his shoulder.

"Just because the way hasn't occurred to you doesn't mean that it doesn't exist," he said wisely.

She laughed and sighed as they pulled out of the embrace.

He lit up another cigarette. "I just need you to promise me one thing," he said, his tone turning serious.

"What?"

"If you do decide to go all *Secretary* on him and allow him to tie you up and a gag you up and shit, you'd better tell me. I need to know these things."

She laughed and shook her head.

André sent a car for Destiny on Saturday morning. He was stuck in the office all day and preferred to meet at the office, since his presence was required for the day. His office turned out to be in one of the tallest buildings in the city. He met her in the lobby. Seeing the expression on her face, he said, "Don't be too impressed. My company only takes up one floor of this building."

She shook her head in awe. She'd dressed in a cream-colored dress suit, but still managed to feel underdressed in a building that wasted no expense. The tiled floors gleamed as if they'd just been buffered and shined.

He placed a hand at her lower back and guided her to the elevators.

She clasped a small briefcase in her hands, gripping the handle for dear life. *Why did I agree to this?* For so long, she'd ignored his inquiries regarding the interview. After one steamy makeout session, she'd all but waved the white flag of surrender.

The elevator doors opened. She took a deep breath and stepped into the elevator. He followed suit and faced forward. The view of the nearly empty lobby was reduced to a sliver between the closing doors. Once the doors were closed, he turned and kissed her.

"André," she gasped, pushing at his chest.

He frowned down at her and lowered his gaze to where her hand was pressed firmly against his chest. "What's wrong?"

"This isn't why I'm here."

He stared down at her, looking confused.

She narrowed her eyes at him. "I'm here about the article."

"I know," he said, quickly recovering from a bruised ego. "I...I know. I just thought..."

She shook her head. "The night at the bakery...that was a lapse in judgement."

His brows rose. "Oh."

"I'm sorry," she said quickly. "I didn't mean to give off any other impression of what would happen today."

"No, my fault entirely," he said, reclaiming his position beside her. He straightened his tie. When the elevator doors opened, he was the first one off.

She followed him, feeling like she'd made a huge mistake in coming here.

He went to stand before two large glass doors flanked by floor-to-ceiling glass panels. The words "Gaines Enterprises" and a complex geometric logo was painted onto one of the glass doors. He withdrew a badge from his inside jacket pocket and used it to unlock the doors. "The office will be fairly empty today," he explained, leading the way past the reception area and down a long corridor. They passed offices, an open general office area, and more offices, until they reached the end of the line. He opened the door and entered a massive office.

Exquisitely decorated. Top of the line black and chrome furniture, tasteful matching floor lamps, well maintained potted plants, and one wall that served as a library, filled to the brim with hardcover books. The wall facing the entrance was made entirely out of glass. She went to stand in front of the glass windows. The office overlooked a small courtyard, complete with a pond and walking path. Local landmarks could be seen just beyond the courtyard. The view was breathtaking. An office like this had to make it easier to come to work every day.

"Do you like it?"

"It's beautiful," she breathed out.

He walked around his desk and seated himself.

She moved to sit in one of the chairs facing his desk. "You don't have a computer on your desk?" she asked, popping open her briefcase.

"It's *in* my desk," he said. "Hidden compartment."

"I'm impressed."

He smiled and leaned back in his chair. "Are you going to publish the article?"

"Yes."

He held his hands up in front of his chest and made a steeple out of his fingers.

"Most of the article is written, but it feels incomplete. I would like your feedback on what I have so far."

"All right."

She fished the draft copy of the article out of her briefcase and slid it across his desk.

"You want me to read it now?" he asked, shock registering on his face.

She nodded.

He collected the printed pages. "Most writers I know are self-conscious about having their work read in front of them."

"I know the article is good," she said, closing her briefcase. "Some of the aspects of the article are sensitive, so I want to make sure that the tone is right." She placed the slim, black briefcase on the floor and crossed one leg over the other while she waited.

He nodded and began to read. "Hmm," he murmured to himself. He tapped one of the lines on the first page. "Very nice."

She straightened her posture in her seat, trying to see which line he was tapping. Before she could get a good view of the line he was referencing, he flipped the sheet of paper and continued onto the next page. She settled back in her chair, chewing the inside of her cheek.

His short nails drummed on top of the desk for a moment before he scooted his chair back.

She craned her neck and watched as he opened the narrow middle drawer of the glass desk.

He removed a red pen and closed the drawer. Then he went to work on the document, circling certain words, underlining others, and adding notes in the margins. "I want to list the politicians by name," he announced.

Her brows shot up. "The politicians who wouldn't move forward with the project?"

He continued marking the article. "Yes."

"I don't know if you should do that."

He smiled. "That's advice coming from an aspiring journalist?"

She tilted her chin up. "You said to remain ethical. Yes, I want a good story, but not at the expense of your career or reputation."

"Good answer," he said, looking up at her. "I've had time to think about it. I won't drag their names through the mud, but I do think they should have to answer for their lack of follow-through. I want to list them by name."

"That's going to cause..."

"Mayhem," he finished for her.

"If that's what you want," she told him.

He slid the papers back over to her, keeping his fingers on them until she leaned forward to accept them. "You're right. The article is good. With a few edits, it won't just be good. It will be great."

She scanned over a few of his notes. "Your suggestions are valid," she said, glancing up at him.

He laughed. "You sound surprised."

She shook her head, speechless.

"I'm a businessman now, but I am first and foremost a writer."

"Evidently," she said, flipping through the pages and tapping her bottom lip with her index finger as she read. "I have a list of follow-up questions that I would like you to look at and get back to me on."

His eyes were boring holes through her while she rummaged through her briefcase for the questionnaire she'd typed out for him. She could feel the heat of his gaze. "You can't just ask me the questions now that we're both here?"

"I wouldn't want to monopolize your time."

"Not that long ago, all you wanted was to monopolize my time," he recalled, staring at her until she met his gaze.

"It's more efficient if you look over the questions and get back to me with your responses," she said, her voice tight as she slid the page across his desk.

He barely paid the document any mind, sweeping it aside with his eyes locked on hers. "I want to talk to you about us."

"There's nothing to talk about. We can't keep having the same conversation, André."

"You're right," he agreed, folding his hands together on top of his desk. "You're right. Wanting to keep you in my life is...selfish of me, knowing that we want different things. I've had time to think about it, and I know that now."

She lowered her gaze.

"Maybe you're right. Maybe I'm not the man you're meant to be with. Maybe you should run as far away from me as you can."

10

Destiny didn't have to be told twice. Run, she did. Burying herself in her schoolwork proved to be successful; there was definitely enough of it. Her time was split between school, work, and spending time with Jasmine, Candace, and Carlos.

Jasmine was elated to read Destiny's draft of the article. "An attractive man who cares about important causes?" She'd shaken her head and sucked her teeth. "Lethal combination."

Don't I know it, Destiny had thought at the time.

Destiny worked on the editing of the article, seated at her desk in the newsroom. Whenever she worked alone in the newsroom, she kept music playing. It relaxed her and helped her to focus. Her hair was piled on top of her head in a topknot and she wore a t-shirt, jeans, and sneakers. She hadn't even bothered with makeup. These days, she was just trying to make it to graduation day and makeup wasn't high on her priority list.

"You're like a well-tuned machine," came a deep voice from in front of her. The compliment came from Chad.

The last time they'd exchanged more than a polite greeting, she'd been...extremely drunk. She smiled shyly. "I want to make sure the article is perfect before I submit it."

"It's amazing that you were able to get the interview," he commended, going to sit in Jasmine's empty chair. "How did that happen?"

"He stopped into the bakery where I work," she replied, shrugging.

"And you asked him to do the interview and he said yes? Just like that?" Chad asked, his tone skeptical.

She shrugged and turned back to her monitor.

"I heard that he was the one who came and rescued you at the club that night," Chad went on.

"You heard that, did you?" She made a few quick edits to the article.

He laughed. "You're a stone wall, huh?"

"I mean...no offense, but it's none of your business," she said while typing.

"I'm just curious."

"I was just fortunate to get an interview, okay? If you want to insinuate that I only got it because I had some kind of...thing going on with him, that's fine by me. I don't care what conclusions you come to. Gossip is gossip. I'm not one to do it."

Chad held his hands up defensively. "Look, that's not why I was asking."

She rolled her eyes. "Then why were you?"

"Maybe I was just trying to see where your head was at," he said with a shrug. "Trying to see if you have been swept up by Dré Gaines. See if...you're still single enough for me to take you out to dinner."

Oh...I wasn't expecting that. She looked at him, *really* looked at him. Tall, deep brown skin, kind, dark brown eyes. The hint of a five o'clock shadow. Muscular, lean build. Dressed well. Currently wearing a nice polo shirt, jeans, and matching casual shoes. Attractive, intelligent, and he had been a dedicated athlete, an amazing team player in his sports heyday. She leaned back in her chair, studying him.

He mimicked the action, leaning back in his chair and returning the look of appraisal.

"When were you thinking of taking me out?" she asked him.

He glanced at the time on his cell phone. "How about now? Or whenever you're done with those edits?"

"I look...a hot mess right now."

"You look beautiful. You always do."

She tilted her head to the side. "There's no way I'd go out like this."

"We can stay in," he suggested.

She narrowed her eyes at him.

"Not like..." He wildly gestured with his hands, sitting up straighter in his chair. "Not like that. That's not what I meant. I wouldn't disrespect you like that."

She sighed and turned back to her monitor.

He dropped his hands in his lap and lowered his head. "If tonight's not a good night, then maybe another night."

She stole a glance at him out of the corner of her eye and smiled. "I'm almost done with editing," she told him. "Your place. Takeout. You pick the movie."

"Yeah, okay." He perked up in his chair. "That sounds perfect."

She nodded. "Okay. Hand me your cell, so I can put my number in it."

TEXT FROM: André Gaines
MESSAGE: *How is the article coming along? Do you know when it will go to print?*

"I ordered two different kinds of pizza," Chad called out when he returned from answering the door. "A veggie supreme and a regular supreme. I probably should've checked to see if you were vegetarian."

Destiny set her phone down on the end table next to Chad's couch. His one-bedroom apartment was tastefully decorated. Not too much decoration, not too little. Just a touch here and there. The crown achievement of the living room was its wide, dark wood entertainment center. She perched on the edge of the black leather couch, trying not to think about André's text message.

Chad stood in front of her, holding two pizza boxes. "Did you have a preference between the two?"

"Veggie sounds good," she said, snapping out of her thoughts.

He carried both boxes to the kitchen, where he prepared plates of pizza. He brought her back a plate and set a plate for himself on the coffee table. "Are you sure you okay?" he asked. "Are you tired? We can reschedule if you need to."

He's trying so hard to be accommodating, and all I can think about is a man who hasn't even tried to consider my feelings. She laughed uneasily and busied herself with grabbing a slice of pizza. "Are you kidding me? We're here and you already went through the trouble of getting the pizza. I'm fine, I'm just...hoping the article is well-received." After biting into the slice, she set it back on the plate.

"*Well-received?*" On his way back to the kitchen, he laughed. "Everyone thought he was in town for one of his music ventures. While blowing the lid off that theory in one of the most important speeches of our time, he namedrops *you.* It's well-known that he doesn't even interview anymore, and he announces that he'll interview with *you,* a non-established contributor of a college paper. Regardless of how the article is received, you're on the fast-track to becoming a nationwide sensation."

She shrugged her shoulders and wrapped her arms around herself. "I just...I don't know. Knowing that just makes me put more pressure on myself."

"You're a perfectionist," Chad commented from the kitchen as he poured liquid into a glass.

"Maybe a little," she said, feeling like she was being psychoanalyzed. "One minute, I think the article is perfect the way it is and ready to print and the next minute, I can think of a dozen ways to improve it and make it better."

"That comes with the territory of writing," he told her. "It's the same for me. I'll write an entire article and submit it, then remember an amazing play that I forgot to mention. When it comes to art, there are always ways to change it up and make it different. That is why it's tough to feel like a project is truly perfect."

"If only knowing that helped get rid of my anxiety."

"Just...relax. Have faith in yourself and your talent." He returned with two glasses of amber liquid. "Apple juice," he explained. "It's all I have, other than water and protein shakes. I should probably go grocery shopping more often."

She laughed. "Apple juice is fine." When she accepted the glass from him, their fingers brushed against each other for the briefest of moments. The touch didn't send electric shocks throughout her body, the way André's had. She settled back on the couch and nursed her drink. "So, what are we watching?"

"I wanted to leave that up to you," Chad said, seating himself.

"You're giving me free reign?" she asked. "Reality show? Chick flick? I can pick anything?"

He laughed as he picked up the remote control from the arm of the couch. "Anything. Just...don't be cruel. All I ask."

She flexed her fingers, grinning devilishly. "Oh, you're a brave man."

"What did I just get myself into?"

It was nice to be on the receiving end of that question, for once.

André peered out the window of the jet plane, lost in his own thoughts. He wondered what Destiny was doing this very minute, wondered if they'd ever meet up again. It wouldn't be any time soon. He was on his way back to Mississauga to visit family and friends. He straightened the cuffs of his suit jacket.

He remembered a time when his private jets were filled with laughter and good vibes. When he was an entertainer, his crew would travel with him. Lifelong friends who all now led their own lives. Married with children, homes filled with light, laughter, and contentment.

The group of people he had around him when he was a music artist were proof that unconditional love existed. If he had chosen to stay in the business of making music, they would have supported that decision. When he made the decision to fall back and sign other artists instead of *being* a music artist, they didn't question it. The empire he'd built back then had served to line their pockets, but on more than one occasion, they'd each proved to him that they were not riding for him because of the money. He had heard horror stories about other artists wanting out, but their friends and family pressuring them to stay in the business for the sake of keeping their wallets fat. That was never an issue with the crew he had around him. When he wanted out, they supported his decision to bow out.

The timing couldn't have been any better, either. As soon as he ducked out of the hunger games quest that was being an entertainer in the music industry, two of his boys entered into what would become serious relationships resulting in marriage. Nearly all of them had left the party life behind, and they'd grown the hell up. They still checked in on him, made sure he was good, reminded him that they were around if he ever needed their help. In turn, he still checked in on them, made sure they were good, and showed up to their events whenever he was in town.

As a result of all of them moving on with their lives, though, private jet flights were now unnervingly quiet. No one was cracking jokes at the back of the jet anymore, no one pulling pranks, no one starting ten-minute rapping sessions, no one getting it on in the room at the back of the jet. The life that he led these days was quite lonely. *Well, whose fault is that?* a nagging voice sounded at the back of his head.

"Did you need me to refill your drink?"

He glanced up at the stewardess, then dropped his gaze to the empty shot glass on the table in front of him. He gave a slight shake of his head.

"Is there anything else I can help you with?" she asked, not budging from her spot in the aisle.

She was tall, slender, blonde. No hips, no curves, but pretty in the face. Her shape, or lack thereof, in no way appealed to him. Her eagerness to maintain her status in the mile-high club also did nothing to add to her appeal. All it did was cause him to wonder how many other rich men she'd made the proposition to.

"I'm good," he said. "Thank you."

She attempted to mask her disappointment, gave a curt nod, and walked away.

To fill the silence and help pass the time, he played music. The benefit of flying private was that he never had to wear headphones; his music played directly from the device. Being at the forefront of a multimedia company, he had to stay in the know of emerging talent. That meant he was always listening to new music, whether from submitted demos or artists he'd stumbled across on music streaming sites.

The jet touched its wheels to the ground close to its projected landing time. He gathered his carryon luggage and exited the jet once the pilot announced he was able. At once, he was reminded why he hated airports. Airport environments were loud, chaotic, and disorienting. Fans either approached or called out to him, and he responded with quick waves. He walked briskly through the airport and glanced at the designer watch on his wrist.

Loud screams followed him throughout the airport and bright lights flashed as fans and reporters snapped photos of him.

He brought a hand up to shield against the blinding, flashing lights that went off in his face.

"Dré Gaines! Dré Gaines! You've singlehandedly caused mayhem in D.C. with your remarks in *The Hilltop* about the politicians that failed to back your arts education program. The politicians are responding to that criticism. Do you have anything to say?"

"Why did you name the politicians who wouldn't help with the project?" another journalist asked.

"I have a lot to say, actually," André said, slowing his steps and coming to a full stop. "Which camera should I look into?"

"Mine!"

"Ours!"

A crowd started to gather around them. André smiled and chose one camera to look into.

"You're not getting tired of having these movie dates?" Chad asked, flipping through television channels.

Destiny shook her head. She sat on his couch with her feet tucked beneath her rear end, eating ice cream out of the carton. "We can go out next time," she told him.

"You said that the *last* time I asked you about it." As he flipped channels, there was the briefest glimpse of a familiar face.

"Hold it," Destiny said, lifting her hand. "Flip back."

Chad angled a glance at her. "Okay." He hit the Last button on the remote.

André's face filled the television screen. Behind him, people were hurriedly walking in both directions, and an illuminated sign displaying flight numbers and times was just over his head. He looked to be standing in an airport.

"We wanted to know why you decided to name the politicians in *The Hilltop* article," a journalist who was off-screen questioned, thrusting a microphone in André's face.

"The answer to that is simple," André responded. "There were individuals who vowed to do all they could to get the program off the ground. Those individuals failed to keep their word. I felt that they should be held accountable for that."

"Why did you conduct an interview with a university publication instead of one such as the *Post*?" the same journalist asked.

"There are not many journalists who I trust to remain ethical in their writing," André said, and his eyes were focused off-camera, most likely at the journalist who was asking the questions. "I agreed to do the interview with Destiny Richards of *The Hilltop* for several reasons. I have a high respect for Howard University. I always have. I also have a high respect for Ms. Richards as a journalist. After meeting with her, I felt that she would write the article from an ethical, unbiased perspective."

"What was your reaction once you read the article?" a different journalist asked.

"I thought the article was written very well," André said, and at this point he turned his eyes to the camera.

Destiny's heart skipped several beats.

"I want to thank Destiny for agreeing to interview me. The interview went...very well." He smiled and held up his hands. "Thank you. That is all I have time for today. I will report back when the program is a thriving success."

Ice creamed dripped from her spoon onto her lap as she stared at the television screen. The coldness of the dessert didn't even register to her, she was so lost in the image of André's face on the screen.

"Destiny," Chad said softly.

She blinked over at him. "Yes?"

He gestured to the spoon in her hand.

She lowered her gaze to the spoon and cursed under her breath. Drops of melted ice cream were beginning to make a colorful pattern on her jeans. She set the spoon in the carton and placed the carton on the table so she could work at rubbing the ice cream out of her jeans. "Better my jeans than your couch," she joked, still working at getting the ice cream stains out.

"What he said just then...that the interview went very well," Chad said, rubbing his temple. "Are you sure that nothing happened between you and him?"

She shrugged her shoulders without looking up.

"Destiny."

"What?"

"You can be honest with me."

She looked up at him. "I thought the only reason you asked that night is because you wanted to know if I was single."

"That *was* the reason," he said. "But now I'm asking because I want to know."

She ran a hand through her hair. "Something happened between me and him, but now it's over," she said simply. "Are you happy? Does knowing that help you?"

"Why couldn't you just tell me that?"

"I didn't think it was any of your business," she said honestly. "And I don't make a habit of talking about past relationships or past...whatever that was."

"What happened? Why didn't it work out?"

"You don't need to know all of that, Chad," she said. "But yes. Something happened. Since it's over now, it's a non-factor."

"So, you two are completely done?" he asked her. "He doesn't text you or call you anymore?"

She glanced at her phone, which she'd set on the coffee table. "We don't communicate through texts or calls, or any other form of media." Words chosen very carefully.

Chad nodded.

"Can we watch a movie now?"

"Yeah, sure," he said, and changed the channel.

André's face faded from the screen, but not from her mind.

Mississauga was good for André's soul. There was an energy the area had that nourished the very essence of his being. His mother worried that he wasn't eating enough and cooked large meals. His friends continued to pour in, and they would reminisce about the old days.

Word traveled quickly in this part of the world. Within a few hours of him having touched ground in Canada, the women he used to spend time with started to text him. The televised interview had a hand in that, since he'd been filmed in the Toronto Pearson International airport.

After much deliberation, he'd responded to a few of the text messages that he received. He wasn't quick to reject their advances. During his stay here, he would appreciate the company of at least one of them. Anything that would help him get his mind off of Destiny.

He'd texted Destiny several times, wanting to know whether or not she'd seen the interview. As expected, she hadn't responded.

Her name was being juggled around in the press. Soon, they'd start stalking her, too. Stick cameras in her face, ask her how she'd scored the interview with *the* André Gaines. They would ask her if she was involved with him. They would ask her a lot of things. He sipped his hot cocoa, wondering how she'd respond.

Standing near the living room window of his mother's house, he gazed outside. He felt very much like a fish in a fishbowl. Snow blanketed the yard but had already been plowed from the sidewalk and streets. Specks of snow shone beneath the sunlight. He wore a coal gray, long-sleeved cashmere sweater that his mother had purchased for him and dark jeans.

"Are you going to stand there all day?"

André turned and grinned at the sight of Oscar Al-Katim, former manager and friend of more than a decade.

"I was thinking about it," André joked dryly. He walked across the room and embraced his friend. "It has been a long time."

"Indeed," Oscar said, peeling the black trench coat from his shoulders and draping it across the back of the couch near the entrance to the room. "Talk to me. You couldn't get anywhere with the politicians, so you're going to tackle this beast of a program launching on your own?"

"As you know from my text, I had...what you may call a strong reaction after the final meeting. I was so angry that I lost control."

"Meaning you went off," Oscar interpreted. He sat on the long, cream-colored couch in the center of the room. After shaving his head completely, he'd grown his hair back out. The dark curls stopped just above his shoulders. There were no traces of judgment in his bright green eyes.

André remained standing and returned to his spot near the window. "Meaning I went off," he admitted.

"Did anyone witness that?"

André shook his head. "It was in the bathroom, after the meeting."

"Thank goodness for that," Oscar muttered, breathing a sigh of relief. "Okay, so...on the phone, you said that you wanted to start small, just a few cities."

"Someone pointed out that once the program is shown to be a success, other powerful people would jump on board. The psychology makes sense."

"So, this random person you keep referencing," Oscar said, narrowing his eyes, "would it be anyone I know?"

André took another sip from his cup.

"A woman, I'm guessing," Oscar said, continuing to study his friend.

"You'd be correct."

Oscar nodded silently and draped an arm across the back of the couch. "So..."

"She was the student who interviewed me."

"And you...what? Like her?"

André didn't know how to respond, so he remained quiet.

Oscar gave a slight shake of his head.

"You don't have to worry about my image anymore," André reminded him. "I'm no longer an entertainer you manage."

"That doesn't mean that I can just stop caring about how you come off to the press and the public," Oscar told him. "Certain things are still going to concern me, if they have the potential to threaten the empire you've built."

André tapped his fingertips on the ceramic mug. "I like her," he admitted finally. "But it didn't work out."

"How much does she know?" Oscar asked pointedly.

André pressed his lips tightly together.

"You can trust her to be discreet?" Oscar pressed.

"Yes."

"After you basically threw those politicians under the bus, they're going to come after you," Oscar warned him. "If you have dirt out there, dirt that hasn't been *managed*, it will come back to bite you."

André squinted his eyes as he stared out of the window, watching a kid across the street attempt to build a snowman. "I can trust her," he said firmly, echoing his previous sentiment. "We don't have to worry about her."

"Is she the one who advised for you to namedrop the politicians?"

"No. That was all me."

"All right. When it comes to getting the program going, what do you need from me?"

"I need you to reach out to schools for me," André said. "Start with the schools I went to. I also want to cover schools in Atlanta and Houston."

Oscar pulled his cell phone out of his pocket and started typing in a notepad app. "You're covering the cities that raised you first," he said as he typed. "Then planning to expand from there?"

"Yes."

"Good idea. Okay."

André nodded and took another sip from his mug. "She had several of those."

Oscar paused typing and gave him a long look.

"What?"

"You *really* like her," Oscar observed. He made it a statement and not a question.

"We're not going to do this," André said, downing the last of his hot cocoa and exiting the room.

Oscar jumped off the couch and followed him down a short hall, to the kitchen.

"Did you want anything else to eat?" André's mother asked, standing near the kitchen stove. When she realized that her son wasn't alone, her whole face brightened up. "Oscar!"

"Mama Mandy," Oscar greeted, hugging her. As he pulled back from the embrace, he hooked a thumb over his shoulder. "You should ask your son about the girl he fell in love with, in D.C."

André's facial expression turned stony.

"Girl? Love?" André's mother, a short Irish-Canadian woman with shoulder-length blonde hair, excitedly clapped her hands.

"Oscar is pulling your leg because he's cruel like that," André said in an apologetic tone. He shook his head at Oscar. "If I had something to throw at you that wouldn't cause you permanent damage..."

Oscar chuckled.

"What is this about a girl?" his mother demanded to know.

"I met someone. It didn't work out." André's eyes were still shooting daggers at Oscar. "I'm sorry he got your hopes up like that."

Oscar leaned a hip against the counter. "No, man. I saw the look in your eye. She got to you."

His mother grinned and swatted Oscar on the arm. "You're in the way."

"You can't fool me, man," Oscar teased, moving away from the counter. "I've known you for far too long and I know you *far* too well."

"You already know my viewpoints on love," André said, leaning over the counter and inspecting the leftover food arranged in chinaware that varied in size and shape.

"You claim not to believe in it," Oscar said.

"Claim?" André repeated with one lifted eyebrow.

"I think you believe in it, but just don't want to be hurt," Oscar said with a shrug. "We all think that."

"We're not going to have this conversation." André stretched an arm across his mother's shoulders. "Dinner was amazing, as usual." He kissed the top of her head.

She started wrapping up the leftovers. "If there was a girl you loved, *really* loved, you would tell me, right?"

He glared across the room at Oscar. "Of course, Mom."

She looked up at him and waited for him to meet her gaze. "You would *tell* me, right?" she asked again. Her tone had that edge that his had sometimes, the *I'm not playing around* tone he knew all too well.

His brows furrowed, but he looked her in the eyes as he repeated, "Of course, Mom."

She searched his eyes for an answer beyond the one he'd verbally spoken. Satisfied with whatever she found in the depths of his eyes, she nodded. "Good." She cupped her hands around her mouth. "Who's ready for dessert?"

Dating Chad was safe. Chad was sweet, attentive, and had a great sense of humor. She enjoyed spending time with him. Whenever she was around him, though, she found herself *trying* to have feelings for him. He was the ideal guy to fall in love with. He was intelligent, funny, physically attractive, and she could tell he truly cared for her. Even with all of those qualities, he didn't excite her. It was perplexing. She felt like she *should* love him.

Months into their relationship, she watched him when he didn't know she was looking. She'd watch him and think, *Can I picture spending the rest of my life with him? Can I see myself marrying him?* The truth was, she could imagine marrying him and having children with him and having a nice, peaceful life with him. She imagined having dinner at the same time every night, putting the kids to bed at the same time every night, maybe being intimate a few times a week. There was nothing wrong with that scenario, was there?

Sure, he didn't cause butterflies to flutter in her stomach. The thought of going on dates with him didn't fill her with a nervous excitement. The thought of him touching her didn't cause her knees to grow weak, but was all of that needed for a long-lasting, healthy relationship? Another factor in all of this was the fact that they hadn't gone all the way yet. Maybe that was a part of why the excitement wasn't there? *Although, I didn't have to go all the way with André before I felt butterflies. All he had to do was touch my face or put his hand on my lower back for me to feel all tingly. The butterflies and that tingly feeling aren't a requirement for a happy relationship, though, right?*

After months of asking, she still hadn't come up with an answer. There were other distractions in her life to keep her from dwelling on that age-old question. Paparazzi had taken to following her everywhere she went. They were probably hoping to catch a glimpse of André.

From the short interview he'd given in the airport he'd touched down in, it was evident that he was in Canada. The press still trailed her everywhere she went, though. They still demanded to know what her connection was to André. It was overwhelming.

She refused to talk to them, but Chad encouraged her to. "They're not going to leave you alone until you answer at least *some* of their questions," he pointed out. "You know better than anyone else how they work, since we're technically in the same field."

"The paparazzi are not real journalists, and I don't have anything to say to them," she maintained.

They attended their school's basketball game on a cold, mid-February night. She dressed for the cold weather in a long, baby pink sweater, jeans, knee-high boots, her black pea coat, and a stylish black beanie hat. Chad opted for a beige turtleneck sweater, jeans, dark boots, and a long, black trench. Friends of theirs stopped them to remark on how cute they looked together.

They watched the game intently, commenting on the skillset of certain players. Several times, Destiny stood up and shouted in frustration.

Chad laughed at her, amused by her passion for the game.

"Don't judge me," she told him, lightly punching him in the arm.

He slid an arm across her shoulders.

After the game, they exited the stadium with their arms linked together. A tall, dark-haired man wearing wire-rimmed glasses approached them. "Destiny?"

Chad's pace slowed, but Destiny kept walking, forcing him to keep up with her. "Yes?" she asked the stranger, who was also forced to keep up the pace with them.

"Can I talk to you for a minute?"

"Do I know you?" she asked him.

He withdrew his cell phone from his pocket and held it up to her. "Destiny, what is your affiliation with André Gaines?"

She rolled her eyes. "Oh my God," she muttered, halting her steps and burying her face in Chad's chest.

"She doesn't want to talk to you, all right?" Chad raised a hand to shield his face from the reporter's cell phone camera.

"Who are you?" the dark-haired man asked. "Are you the boyfriend?"

"I am," Chad said proudly.

"Don't *talk* to him, Chad," she mumbled into his chest.

Chad obediently zipped his lips shut.

"We just want to know how you were able to get an interview with André Gaines. The first interview he decides to give in a long while goes to a college paper. It's a bit odd." The journalist shrugged. "Help me out."

Feeling a surge of confidence, she turned to face the man. "You want me to help you out?"

He nodded eagerly.

"Are you recording?"

The journalist checked. "Yes."

"I met André Gaines in the bakery, where I work," she said, focusing her attention on the lens of the cell phone camera. "There is no glamorous story behind it. He was a customer. I took his order. In casual conversation, I mentioned that I was a writer for *The Hilltop*. He was nice enough to let me interview him. The impression I got from him is that he is dedicated to helping people. I'm evidence of that, because he didn't have to give me such a big opportunity – but he did anyway."

The journalist frowned. "That's it?"

"That's it," she confirmed. "That's what you have all been hounding me for. Absolutely nothing."

"No romance, no tryst?"

She rolled her eyes and started walking again. Chad walked alongside her.

"Can you confirm that you had no relationship with André Damian Gaines?" the journalist yelled after her.

"I can confirm that I did not have a relationship with André Damian Gaines!" she yelled back at him. "There is only one man who I am in a relationship with, and his name is Chad!"

Chad pulled her closer to him as they walked. "At least now they'll leave you alone," he told her.

She shuddered, even though his embrace was warm. "We'll see," she muttered.

"Can you confirm that you had no relationship with André Damian Gaines?"

"I can confirm that I did not have a relationship with André Damian Gaines! There is only one man who I am in a relationship with, and his name is Chad!"

André paused the entertainment news footage so that the close-up shot of Destiny's face was frozen on his television screen. He tapped the remote control against his bottom lip while he stared at her face. Sighing and leaning forward, he set the remote control on the table. He poured himself another stiff drink. Looked over the top of his glass at that beautiful face, that beautiful mouth. A mouth that formed the words claiming another man as hers. He swirled the glass of liquor around in his hand while staring at the screen.

After the stunt Oscar had pulled, it had taken another half an hour or so to convince his mother that he wasn't in love with anyone. She hoped and prayed so hard that he would find love. There was nothing more that she wanted for him, and it was sweet of her. He simply did not believe in it.

But...

If I don't believe in it...then why does the sight of Destiny with that man piss me off? he wondered. He tried to tell himself that the sight of her with another man pissed him off because if things had gone according to plan, she would be his. She would be his to own and control, and instead of being his, she was someone else's. He tried to tell himself that it wasn't a matter of *love*; it was a matter of possession. He didn't possess her, and he wanted to. That's what he told himself, anyway.

If she was just going to be your property, isn't she something that can be replaced? his subconscious nagged at him. *Couldn't you find another girl who would be just as good of a submissive, if not better?*

He took a swig of the strong liquor and continued to swirl it in his glass, lost in his own thoughts. Lost in his own justifications of his feelings. Making up excuses as to why he felt so strongly about her being on the arm of another. His fingers tightened on the glass. He picked up the remote control and rewound the news coverage to the beginning.

"Destiny, what is your affiliation with André Gaines?"

She groaned. "Oh my God."

"She doesn't want to talk to you, all right?"

"Who are you? Are you the boyfriend?"

"I *am*."

André paused the footage again, this time on the young gentleman's face. This must be the Chad she referenced at the end of the interview. The glass in André's hand shattered, and cold liquid splashed on his hand. He barely felt the glass break, barely felt the liquid cascading over his hand. He was filled with that much anger and jealousy.

11

"Can you believe it's all over?" Jasmine screamed. She adjusted her graduation cap, so the tassel wasn't hanging in her face. "It feels like just last year, we were clueless freshmen!"

Those words rang true. Just four years ago, Destiny's future had seemed far off. Now that she was graduating, the future was *here*. The future was now. It turns out, the future was a lot less intimidating when it was years off and much more so when it was staring you in the face. Ever since she'd entered her teens, she'd started charting out the path her life would take. She'd made a blueprint for the rest of her life, but now, everything seemed so uncertain.

Chad stood proudly at her side with his arm around her waist. He was all smiles, laughing and bumping knuckles with his friends whenever they passed by. "I have to go find my seat," he said, giving her a squeeze.

She nodded. "All right."

"You two are *so* adorable," Jasmine gushed, watching Chad jog towards the area he'd be sitting in.

"Have you seen Candace?" Destiny asked, turning her head and surveying the crowd of students gathered on the field of Greene Stadium.

Jasmine shook her head. "Nope, not yet. But she *has* been all about her new man lately, so..."

"She's moving out today," Destiny said. "When she announced that she was moving out is when all of this became real for me. Even now, it's making me pause. Like...she won't be my roommate anymore, after today."

"Chances are, you'll never have to have a roommate again," Jasmine commented. "Have you decided which offer you're going to go with? The rumor mills are telling me that you've received offers from *The Post* and *New York Times,* just to name a few? How are you not bragging about that to *everyone*?"

Writing for *The Washington Post* was Destiny's dream, something she'd wanted for years. "*The Post* did give me an offer, but I haven't given them my decision yet. I know how crazy that sounds, so I haven't told anyone about it yet." Destiny nervously fidgeted with her graduation cap.

Jasmine's mouth slanted. "You got an offer from *The Post* and you're not jumping on it? What is *wrong* with you, girl?"

"I don't know if I want to stick around D.C.," Destiny stated.

Jasmine frowned at her.

"I know."

"What about Chad? Where is he going?"

"He has a contract offer with ESPN," Destiny replied.

"Oh, right," Jasmine said, snapping her fingers. "Does he know where he'll be working?"

"New York."

"Hmm. So, are you leaning towards accepting the offer from the *New York Times*?"

"You'd think so, right? He is putting the pressure on me to accept the *Times* offer, but…I'm not sure that is what I want."

A voice over the loudspeaker came on. "We need all graduates to find their seats. The ceremony is about to begin."

The two girls exchanged excited looks and embraced each other. Jasmine tilted her head back and squealed. Once the embrace ended, they split up and went in search of their seats.

Destiny placed her cap on her head and checked her hair to make sure that her curls weren't disturbed. After scanning the lawn for her parents, she found her seat and sat down. No matter how hard she tried, she just couldn't calm her nerves. This was it. College was done and after today, she would officially be a college graduate.

She surveyed the other students. If they were nervous, they did an amazing job of hiding it. Everyone else was all smiles and energy. After minutes of searching the area behind where the graduates were seated, she was just barely able to locate her parents and wave to them, when a voice rang out through the speakers spread throughout the field.

Two rows of professors were seated on the stage behind the podium. One stood from his seat and approached the podium. After a short introduction, he spoke words of encouragement to the graduating class. A few more robed professors followed suit before the final professor introduced the dean.

"I would like to welcome the Class of 2021!" the pretty, dark-skinned dean greeted. "There has been talk about who would give the commencement address for this year's graduation ceremony. Several candidates were considered, but there was one that stood above the rest. This man is known in the entertainment industry as a triple threat and is currently making major headway as the front man for an organization responsible for saving educational art programs across the country. I would like to welcome none other than André Gaines, whom we have always had a good relationship with. Please put your hands together and welcome him."

Destiny's palms started to sweat. *This isn't happening,* she thought in disbelief.

The applause was thunderous. André stepped onto the stage and walked across the wide platform in measured, long strides. Dressed in a classic black suit with a black dress shirt, top button undone. No tie. He grinned and greeted the dean warmly, first shaking her hand and then embracing her. He spoke into her ear and laughed before moving to stand before the podium.

Destiny gripped the edge of her seat as he gazed out over the audience.

"I am honored for that warm welcome, thank you," he said, adjusting the height of the microphone. As he angled the microphone, he glanced out across the audience of college students and looked beyond them to the families seated behind the graduating class. "She isn't lying when she tells you that I have a very longstanding relationship with this university. In my early years as a rapper, I performed college tours. This was one of the first colleges that I performed at. I was grateful for that opportunity." He paused for a moment before continuing. "The irony is not lost on me, the fact that I am standing here before college graduates when I barely graduated high school. But I have lived. I have lived through experiences that I believe will help you in your own lives. With that being said, I would like to share with you my general outlook on life and success."

The chatter in the crowd of students died down.

André didn't have cue cards in front of him and from what Destiny could gather, there was no teleprompter supplying him with words. Instead of relying on script, he seemed to have chosen to wing it. "On the road to success, you will encounter what I will refer to as obstacles. These obstacles will manifest in a variety of different ways. People. Critics. Situations, financial or otherwise. Your own self-doubt. Time constraints. Challenges. Lack of opportunity. The list goes on and on. In this life, no matter which industry you choose to embark on, you have to have faith in yourself. Faith in your craft. Having that faith is not always easy. *Much* easier said than done. When you are greeted with others who are doubting you or your vision, it is quite easy to begin doubting yourself." As he was speaking, he did a great job of giving different sections of the audience a few moments of attention. That may have been something he'd learned to do as an entertainer. "I didn't know whether or not I was going to have the guts to share this story with you, but I will. As many of you know, I have spearheaded a program to help save music and arts programs in schools."

Applause erupted again. Destiny glanced around at her fellow students, pleased at their encouragement.

"Thank you," André said into the microphone. His eyes combed over the crowd. "Most of you know by now what the program is about and how long it took for me to get the program going. What you probably *don't* know is the toll that it took on me. I had to fight against my own self-doubt. I became very fed up with the stonewalling and the delays. I came close to having a mental breakdown, I'll be honest with you."

Destiny leaned forward in her seat and rested her elbows on her knees.

"I'll also let you all know one of the reasons why this program is so close to my heart. Growing up as a youngster, I went through some pretty tough times. My mom, who loved me with all of her heart, was a single mother. Just trying her best to make it, for her sake and for mine. I can honestly say that she tried to give me the best life that she could. She tried to hide all of the stress that came along with that, but I saw it. I saw it and I felt helpless. Like...I wanted to help her. I was willing to get a paper route, whatever I needed to do to help her. I didn't know just how little that helped at the time. But...seeing her go through all of that stress, it killed me. Not having my dad in the house, only being able to visit him so often, that weighed on me, too.

"Even though my mom is one of the most approachable mothers I could have been blessed with, there were times when I felt like I couldn't go to her with the things that I was dealing with. She had her own problems and worries, and I didn't want to add more stress to her life. Everyone goes through periods like that, times when you keep the things that you're dealing with inside. Maybe you feel no one else would relate to what you're going through, or maybe you feel that admitting your own problems and frustrations will only burden those who are close to you. I went through a lot of phases like that. When I couldn't talk to anyone, music was there for me." His voice started to shake with emotion. "Music *saved* me. I don't know how else to put it. It saved me from turning to alternatives that would not have been beneficial to me as a young man. It saved me from being swallowed up in my own angst, my own depression. It gave me something to hold onto. It gave me something to believe in."

"We love you, Dré!" one of the students shouted.

He laughed into the mic and hung his head.

The audience started cheering and chanting his name.

He wiped his brow. "Can I get some water, actually? My throat is getting dry. I think I'm talking too much. It sounds like I'm rambling. Am I rambling, or am I making sense?"

The students continued cheering him on while the dean hunted down a bottled water for him.

"Thank you, I appreciate it." He unscrewed the cap of the bottle presented to him and took a long sip. Then, he wiped his mouth and set the bottle on top of the podium. "I don't want to delve too deeply into all of that. I think you get the gist. Music became an important part of my life, even before the acting. That is probably my father's influence. Listening to music, singing to it, dancing to it, it was all an outlet for me."

A few students in the front row started shouting out lyrics to one of the first songs he ever released, and soon nearly every student rapped along to the words.

Destiny joined in, clapping her hands and making limited dance moves in her seat. Even some of the parents in the back were singing and dancing.

André's mouth stretched into a wide grin at the sight of everyone singing and dancing. "All right, all right. Thank you for that moment. That was one of my early hits. Long before I dropped that song, music was my life. Singing in my room by myself. singing with my dad. Going to his shows, watching him play. Singing with his band. Those were the moments that I looked forward to. For you, music might not be your free therapy. Your free therapy of choice might be drawing, painting, dancing, sculpting, writing, filming, or something else. Each of us has that one thing that helps us through tough times. For that reason, I wanted to make sure that the program continued to move forward, with or without help. But...I didn't know what to do. I'm a little out of my depth, here, because I've never launched a nonprofit organization before. What am I supposed to do, being just one man without the strength of the government helping me to jumpstart this thing? Right?" He searched the audience and his eyes found Destiny.

She shrank down in her seat.

He smiled warmly, a smile that reached his eyes.

She could feel her cheeks grow hot as he stared at her. Her feelings for him came rushing back, washing over her like a tidal wave. After half a year of not having seen him, there were still those memories of how it had felt to be touched by him, kissed by him.

"I was faced with a lot of obstacles," he said into the microphone, not taking his eyes off of her. "But I was fortunate enough to have an angel on my side. This angel suggested that I start the program on my own. Start it small. Make sure it's a success so other people jumped on board. And, needless to say, her idea worked. It worked like magic.

"I say all of that to say this: you will have ideas. You will have goals. There may be obstacles that stand in the way of those goals. If you truly believe in your idea, or your goal, it is up to you to defeat those obstacles. You may not have an angel over your shoulder the way I did." He hunted Destiny out in the crowd again.

His gaze was so intense that a few students in the row in front of her turned around in their seats to look at her.

"During those times, I ask for you to remember what I am telling you today. Remember me telling you that if no one else believes in you, I do. Not to sound cliché, but I believe that each of you is capable of succeeding at your goals. You just have to be willing to work hard for it. Put in the hours. Put in the effort. Put in the research. Success isn't obtained easily. It takes hard work. It takes trials and tribulations. It takes time. It takes networking. Sometimes it takes failing before you get there. Failure is only a temporary setback. Keep your head up. Keep striving. Keep the faith in yourself and in your craft. And you'll get there." There was a deafening smatter of applause and he held his hands up with his palms facing outward, a signal for them to quiet down. "Before I leave here today, I want to thank one of your own, Destiny Richards. She is the student who interviewed me for *The Hilltop*. She believed in me at a time when I didn't believe in myself. If anyone deserves applause here today, it's her. And it's all of you. You already have a major accomplishment to be proud of. You've survived four years of college, and now you are onto the next amazing chapter of your lives. A round of applause for yourselves. Congratulations to the class of 2021!"

Everyone stood from their seats, clapping loudly. Destiny slowly rose from her seat, clapping her hands. When she was finished clapping, she wrapped her arms around herself.

André turned and shook the hands of the robed professors seated behind the podium. Then, he walked around the podium and beamed at the audience. His eyes locked with Destiny's again, as the dean approached him.

One of the professors walked up to the podium and announced that they would now begin calling the names of the graduates. Watching each student accepting their college diploma only cemented that this was the end of an era. It all felt so *final*.

As Destiny walked across the stage to accept her own diploma, she could feel André's eyes on her. She turned just to confirm that she was right, and there he was, flashing a bright, encouraging smile at her.

More inspiring words, a loud cheer, and then the tossing of graduation caps followed. Everyone blindly turned to the person beside them and hugged them, regardless of how long or short of a time they'd known the person. It had taken long nights of studying, long shifts for those who'd had to work jobs to help support themselves, and countless long days locked up in lecture halls, but they'd all done it; they'd all graduated onto the next chapter of life.

André was now off the stage and wandering along the side aisle, briefly speaking to the new graduates gathering around him.

Eager to put distance between herself and him, Destiny sought out her parents. Her mother, who looked like an older, shorter version of herself, was quick to hug her. "I cannot express to you how *proud* I am right now," Mrs. Richards said into her daughter's ear.

"You definitely should be," a deep voice sounded behind them.

Destiny straightened and whirled around. Her heart started to pound in her chest. "André."

"Hello."

Shock morphed Mr. Richards's face. "You're the head of Gaines Enterprises," he told André, as if André had to be reminded of who he was. "The one our daughter interviewed."

"The reason she's getting hounded by all of those reporters," Mrs. Richards added, pursing her lips tightly.

"Guilty on both charges," André said, stepping forward and giving both parents a firm handshake.

"He's also the reason why I have so many offers from different publications across the country," Destiny told her parents. "You should be thanking him."

Her mother's facial expression softened. "I guess you're right about that." She turned around. "I thought we were going to get to meet Chad."

Destiny's eyes widened and her cheeks reddened. "He's...he's around here somewhere," she stammered. "You will meet him soon enough."

André stretched his neck, searching the crowd. "I wanted to meet him too," he said, turning his attention to Destiny.

Destiny glared at him. "That isn't necessary."

"It's very necessary," he argued with a polite smile on his face. "I'd like to shake the hand of the man who has been...taking care of you."

She glared at him.

He returned the look, but a slow smile curved his lips.

Mrs. Richards looked between the two of them and after a moment, touched her tall, light-skinned husband on the shoulder. "Your father and I are going to give you two a moment," she told her daughter.

"We are?" Mr. Richards asked, his face puckered in confusion.

"We are," Mrs. Richards confirmed, steering her nosy husband away.

Destiny clasped her hands together in front of her. "Out of all of the colleges you could give the commencement addresses for, you decided to come here."

"I've had a long history with Howard University," André reminded her, sliding his hands into the pockets of his suit pants. "Since *The Hilltop* helped garner attention for my program, I felt it was only right to give the address here."

"And what is this about you wanting to meet Chad?" she asked him, frowning.

"Walk with me."

She took a deep breath. "I really don't have the time for this, André."

"Please?" He offered her his arm.

With a sigh, she accepted his arm and walked beside him. "Don't think I'm going to let you off the hook. I want to know why you want to meet Chad. What could you *possibly* have to say to him?"

"I just want to meet the guy that swept you away."

She walked alongside him in silence, trying to convince herself that the nervousness she felt was not because he was near her.

He led her quite far away from where the other students and families convened on Greene Field. They came upon a large maple tree and it was at this point that she removed her arm from his. She went over to the tree and touched its trunk.

"I missed you."

"That's nice," she said, keeping her back to him.

He moved closer to her. She could hear the faint sound of bending grass, and she could feel the distance between them closing. She held her breath and a moment later, felt his arms on her shoulders. "Destiny. I *really* missed you."

"I have a boyfriend, André," she hissed in a voice barely above a whisper. "What do you expect me to say?"

"Do you love him?"

"What kind of question is that, especially coming from someone who doesn't believe in love?" She whirled around to face him and instantly regretted it. He was so close to her. Close enough for her to smell his cologne, close enough to feel the body heat radiating from him.

Still he moved forward, forcing her backwards until her back was pressed flat against the tree trunk. He braced his arms on either side of her. "Tell me that you don't miss me, and I'll leave you alone."

The bark from the tree was poking her in the back, but that tree was the only thing keeping her upright. Being this close to him was beginning to turn her knees into jelly. She didn't respond to him, but she didn't have to. Her traitorous eyes were probably giving her away.

He drew his face closer to hers.

"Don't," she whispered, trembling. "Please don't do this to me."

The briefest doubt flickered in his eyes, and he pulled back.

Tears filled her eyes and she wiped away at them. "I need to get back to my parents. I need to get back to Chad."

"Destiny!"

She wiped her eyes again and smoothed her hair down.

André backed away and turned his back to her.

Chad rounded the tree and stopped short when he saw André. He turned his head and saw Destiny standing near the tree. His strides were quick as he made his way to her. "Hey," he greeted breathlessly, draping an arm across her shoulders. "What's going on?"

"We were just having a conversation," André replied.

"All the way out here, huh?" Chad squinted his eyes and looked out across the field towards where the other students congregated with their families. "Must be some conversation."

"We were discussing whether or not you both would consider joining me for dinner," André said.

Destiny shot daggers at him with her eyes. "I was telling him that isn't necessary. But thank you, André, for the offer. My parents are in town. They want to meet Chad. We wouldn't have time-"

"We could make time," Chad interjected smoothly, tightening his arm around her. "We'd love to accept your offer."

"Chad," Destiny said, looking up at him.

He gave a nonchalant shrug, as if none of this was bothering him. "What? Is there a reason why we shouldn't have dinner with him?"

André withdrew his cell phone from his pocket and checked the notifications on his screen. "You'll probably want to spend tonight with her parents, since they are in town, but maybe tomorrow night? Say, seven o'clock?"

"Perfect," Chad said with a smile plastered on his face. The smile didn't quite reach his eyes, so she couldn't figure out his angle in all of this.

Why would he want us to go to dinner with André, knowing that there was something between us? she wondered.

André nodded and walked away.

Chad watched until the other man was far out of earshot. With his eyes still on the man's back, he asked Destiny, "Are you going to tell me what that was really about?"

"It's not important, Chad," she said, moving away from him.

"To hell with that!" Chad shouted, all composure lost.

His tone of voice rocked her and reminded her of the rage Jordan had displayed the night he'd come face-to-face with André. "Excuse me?"

"I know something is going on between you and him, Destiny. I'm not a fucking idiot." He plucked at the buttons of his graduation gown so he could slide it off his shoulders. He draped the garment across his arm. "Let's go."

"We're not going anywhere until you calm the hell down," she told him through clenched teeth. "Nothing happened."

"But he tried, didn't he?" Chad asked, the vein in his neck protruding.

She stared at him without answering.

He turned on his heel and started off in the direction André had gone.

Flashbacks from the night Jordan had attacked André came rushing at her. Alarmed, she ran after Chad and grabbed him by the elbow. "Chad, stop it!"

"Do you think I'm going to just stand here while he disrespects me like that?" Chad demanded. "I don't give a fuck *who* he is."

"He and I haven't seen each other in a long time, and we haven't talked since the last time he was in D.C.," she explained. "I don't think he knew that I had a boyfriend. Once I told him, he understood. So, please stop this."

Chad's chest heaved, but he stopped walking. He ran a hand over his face. "And his invite to dinner?"

"Probably his way of apologizing for his behavior," she said. *More like a cover-up for why he brought me all the way out here in the first place,* she thought.

Chad nodded and thumbed his nose. "You're a nice person who wants to see the best in people, and I love you for it. But I'm a guy. The way he was looking at you…he didn't invite us out to dinner to apologize. He is trying to get you back, trying to make moves on you. I don't *like* him, Des. More importantly, I don't *trust* him. Neither should you."

"We can cancel the dinner plans. We *should* cancel the dinner plans."

Chad shook his head. "No. We're going."

She scratched her head in confusion. "But why would we, if you think he's trying to get me back?"

"Because you're going to get dressed up," Chad said, setting his hands on her shoulders. "And you're going to look beautiful, as always. We're going to show him just how *together* we are."

"You're not serious."

"I'm as serious as a heart attack."

She rolled her eyes. "You're going to show me off, like I'm some trophy? You want to show off that I chose you instead of him? Trust me, he is already aware of this fact."

Seeing her agitation, took some of the wind out of his sails. His puffed-out chest deflated a bit and some of the anger in his expression faded. "Okay, okay…maybe I kind of lost it there. I'm sorry."

"Maybe? Kind of?" she repeated. "My parents are wandering over there somewhere, excited to meet you and you're obsessing over someone from my past. You're giving him more attention that I am."

"Just tell me one thing."

Don't ask me what you're going to ask me, she thought desperately as she lifted her eyes to meet his. "Yes?"

"Do you still have feelings for him?"

Her gaze drifted towards where their fellow students were talking and laughing it up, making plans to go to dinner or meet up later that week. She wished she could be any one of them, to escape having to answer this question.

"It's a simple question, Destiny," he told her.

Her gaze anchored to the ground. "Actually, it's not that simple," she said. As much as she hated to admit it, she *did* still have feelings for André. They were feelings she'd fought against for a long time. Seeing him today had brought those feelings surging to the surface. How was it possible for her to turn off feelings for someone who had awakened a part of herself that she hadn't even known was there? After meeting him, her life was forever changed. As much as she wanted to, she couldn't dismiss that.

"If the question isn't simple, then your answer is yes," he countered. "Which would explain why you won't take the *New York Times* offer, knowing New York is where I'm headed."

"Chad..."

He held up a hand. "No. No need to explain. I hear you loud and clear."

"*Chad.*"

"What?" he asked, his tone harsh. The expression on his face was hard, cold. He was putting up a brave front, but his eyes told the truth he was unable or unwilling to speak. His brown eyes were pleading with her. His eyes were pleading for her to give him a reason to stick around, pleading for her to choose him. Despite the anger he'd just shown, she *wanted* to choose him in that moment.

I want to say something that would make you stay. I want to ease your worries about André. She wanted to be the girl for him, because he was *safe*. André was anything *but* safe. She never knew what to expect with André. Having any sort of feelings for André was dangerous. But Chad...Chad was stable. Chad knew what he wanted, and he went after it. And once he had it, he nurtured it. He did everything he was supposed to do. "You are...an amazing man," she said slowly.

His face fell. Even though she was giving him a compliment, he looked crushed. He was smart enough to read between the lines, to know the subtext of what she was telling him. "You can stop there," he said, his voice choked up with emotion.

"No, I *can't* stop there," she insisted. "You're an amazing man and I have love for you."

"You *have* love for me."

"I have love for you, and I respect you. I *want* to be the girl that you end up with, but...deep down, I don't feel like I am."

"You couldn't figure that out months ago?" he asked her, sounding more hurt than angry. "What have we been doing all this time, if you don't feel the same way I do?"

"I'm sorry," she apologized, feeling miserable.

"I don't know what I expected. I'm going off to New York. You don't even know which job you're taking yet." He sighed and ran a hand over his head. "Maybe...I don't know, maybe the timing is just bad."

Her eyes welled up.

"Come here," he said, bringing her in for a hug.

She hugged him. She clung to him for dear life, because she didn't know what awaited her after she let him go.

Destiny stared at her reflection in the apartment bathroom mirror. She gripped the edge of the sink and lowered her head, closing her eyes while the events from the previous evening played in her mind.

"I thought we were going to meet Chad," her mother had said, her voice tinged with disappointment.

"Chad and I had a talk, and we decided to cool things off for a while," Destiny had told her parents.

"But...you told us he was a great boy," her mother had said, sounding confused.

Destiny lifted her head and surveyed her appearance. She looked like a wreck. Mascara-tinted tears coursing down her cheeks. Liquid eyeliner ruined. Nose running. She took the heel of her hand and wiped at her tears.

"Chad is a great person," Destiny had explained to her parents. *"But our careers are about to take off and now just isn't the time."*

"But...if you find a great boy, you hold onto him until it's the right time," her mother had responded. *"There's no telling if you'll find another one."*

"You shot yourself in the foot," her father had agreed.

"You should call him up right now and work things out," her mother had suggested.

More tears welled up in Destiny's eyes. *What am I doing with my life?* she wondered. *I had everything planned. I knew exactly where my life as going, and now I don't know anything. Everything is falling apart, and I don't know how to stop it.*

"If it is meant to be, it will be," she'd told her parents. The restaurant was crowded last night. She'd distracted herself by watching patrons at the other tables. Anything to help her avoid making eye contact with her parents.

Because what was I going to tell them? she wondered now. *Your daughter broke up with a nice guy, a sweet guy, a loving guy, so she could...what? Try to make it work with a man who would rather keep his options open while he dates me?* More tears fell. This time, she didn't wipe them. She looked at herself, *really* looked at herself. Who was she? What exactly did she think she was doing? Had she made a terrible mistake in leaving Chad?

She hadn't felt that she was in love with him, and shouldn't she know? He had felt like a backup plan the entire time she'd dated him. While she felt horrible for thinking of him that way, it was the truth of the matter. During their entire relationship, he'd made her a priority. He'd loved her, and he had shown it. She'd never caught him in a lie. She never saw or heard of him flirting with other girls. He'd definitely had offers. She'd heard about those from fellow students. But he'd politely turned them down. He had respected her enough to be honest with her.

"And what do I do?" she asked her reflection as more tears continued to stream down her face. "I *leave* him. I leave a guy that most women would hope for."

It was a conversation she'd had with her friends a few years ago. If you met a nice guy, a guy that treated you well, did you stay with him and marry him because he was nice and treated you well? Or were girls supposed to wait for that magical kind of love, the kind you hear about in fairytales?

Each option had its drawbacks. Stay with the nice guy that treats you well that you aren't in love with, and it's possible you were settling. Sentencing yourself to never knowing what true love felt like. But if you chose the other option and waited for the magical, fairytale kind of love, it was quite possible that you would never find it. It was quite possible that you would waste your life away and wind up alone because you were looking for a myth.

People were often marrying out of convenience, or to do right by children that were conceived out of wedlock. For some couples, it worked. Some couples who wed out of convenience grew to love each other over time. It was all a matter of what kind of love you wanted: a stable partnership that seemed more like a marriage between best friends, or wild, passionate love that was the stuff of romance novels. Some of Destiny's friends had claimed that the romance novel type of love didn't exist, just as André had, but she had a hard time believing that. She felt it existed, it was just rare.

She peered into the hallway of the apartment. The place felt so empty now. Candace had already cleared her stuff out with the promise of checking in on Destiny within the next few days. Everyone was moving on while she didn't even know which staff writer job she wanted to take.

While sniffling, Destiny removed the makeup she had applied. She washed and rinsed her face, dried off with a fluffy pink towel. She clasped her shaking hands together and waited for the shaking to stop. Then, she withdrew small capped tubes from her makeup bag and reapplied her makeup. As she was reapplying makeup, her phone vibrated on the bathroom sink.

Ignoring the phone, she applied lip gloss to her lips and smacked them. Gave her hair a light toss. She stepped back from the mirror and smoothed down the skirt of the sleeveless ivory dress. She looked...acceptable. Her eyes were red from crying, but hopefully that would clear up. She blinked them now, to help along the process.

The image of Chad's hurt face flashed in her mind. She lowered her eyes and stared at the floor, willing away any other tears that dared to fill her eyes. She didn't want to have to apply makeup a third time.

A knock sounded on the apartment door. Blinking back tears, she hurriedly packed her makeup back into its bag. After turning off the bathroom light, she walked down the short hall. A million different thoughts and memories ran through her head, memories of how it felt to have André touch her. Memories of how it had felt to walk in on him with another woman. The happy times with Chad. The look on Chad's face when he realized that she was trying to break up with him in a way that spared his feelings.

She grabbed the strap of a shimmery blue purse, slung carelessly over the back of the couch. Then she went to answer the door. "Hello, André." Points for her. Her voice didn't sound as shaky as she'd expected it to sound.

He smiled and looked beyond her, into the apartment. "Where's Chad?"

"He won't be joining us tonight," she informed him.

His smile widened and he offered her his arm.

She stared down at his arm. Still worrying, still wondering, still blinking back stubborn tears. Pushing the memories out of her mind, she attempted to focus on the present. The man standing before her looked stylish and suave in his black designer suit and striped dress shirt. The look in his eyes was intense, but he displayed patience. After taking another deep breath, she accepted his arm.

In the limousine, André wiped tears from her cheeks. "Do you want to talk about it?" he asked.

She shook her head quietly and stared out the window.

"If you do, I'm here."

She nodded.

The ride was quiet. The limousine pulled up in front of one of the most highly regarded restaurants in D.C., located on the Potomac River. He helped her out of the car and escorted her into the establishment. They were shown to a premium table where André pulled out her chair for her, always the gentleman.

A man was playing the piano in the corner of the room. Well-dressed people ate, drank, and conversed.

"Have you ever been here before?" André asked her.

Wordlessly, she shook her head.

"Their food is top-notch."

A tall, dark-haired waiter arrived with their menus and described that evening's specials.

"Could we have a few minutes?" André asked him.

The lanky young man nodded. "I will check back on you both in a few minutes."

André watched him leave and turned his attention to Destiny. "I tried to give you some privacy, but seeing you in pain like this is killing me. Talk to me."

"Chad and I broke up," she blurted out. "Right after you left."

"I'm sorry to hear that."

"Are you?" she asked him, meeting his gaze.

He was quiet for a long time. "No," he said finally, after seeming to weigh how he should respond. "I'm not."

She shook her head and looked away from him.

"I'm not sorry that you two broke up," he amended, "but I *am* sorry that you're hurting."

"He was an amazing guy," she told him. "He loved me. He was sweet to me. He did everything he was supposed to do. He did everything *right*."

"Then why did you break up with him?" André asked softly.

"Because I didn't love him."

"You realized that the day of graduation?".

She blinked back tears. "I knew for quite a while."

"Why did you stay with him so long, if you knew that he wasn't the man for you?"

"Because I wanted him to be the one," she said frankly.

He nodded. After a moment, he gestured to her menu. "You need to look over your menu. Decide on what you want."

She sniffled and dabbed at her eyes with the napkin before picking up the menu. She could barely see past the veil of tears in her eyes, but she settled on grilled salmon with a side of vegetables. She wasn't particularly hungry.

When the waiter returned, André relayed her order and put in an order for pan seared scallops on a bed of linguine and a side salad.

"Is that all you're ordering?"

"Did you expect for me to order the entire menu?" he asked, passing the waiter their menus.

She shrugged.

"I spent a lot of time in my hometown," he explained. "While I was there, I spent most of my free time with my mom. My mom cooks. She *really* cooks. She's the type of mom that makes sure you're fed. Turn down a plate, and she'll force it on you. You can imagine how much I ate while I was there. I'm trying to make up for that now."

"I've been there," she said.

He smiled. "There's a method to my madness, trust me."

She clasped her hands together on top of the table and glanced around the restaurant again.

He watched her. "Is it safe to tell you that I've missed you?"

"That's sweet of you to say."

"You didn't miss me at all?"

Her mouth set into a grim line.

"It's okay," he said. "You don't have to return the sentiment. So...Chad. You wanted him to be the one for you, why? Because he was nice and sweet and loved you the way he was supposed to?"

She nodded. "Yes, exactly."

"When he called you to set up a date, did you feel excited?"

Was he a mind reader? "No," she answered honestly.

"When you made love to him, did he even come close to making you feel the way I do?" He lifted his hand and touched a fingertip to the rim of his water glass.

"None of your business," she snapped at him.

"That would be a *no*," he supplied for her.

"That would be a *none of your business*," she clarified.

He sat back in his seat.

"You know what?" she asked, changing her mind. "Fine. Let's put all of the cards on the table. Yes. You turn me on more than he does. Yes, I prefer making love to you than him. *But*." She held up an index finger. "He was able to give me something that you couldn't. Exclusivity. He was mine and I was his."

"You were settling," André told her, the expression on his face stony.

"And if I choose you, I'm *still* settling," she hissed, trying to keep her voice down, "because you can't give me everything I want."

He rubbed his chin and nodded. "Maybe I can't," he admitted. "But I do have a proposition for you."

"*Another* one?" she remarked, rolling her eyes.

"Come work for me."

"As what, exactly?"

"Public relations representative."

This offer was unexpected. She didn't know how to feel or react. "Based out of...where?"

"Your time would be split between Mississauga and Los Angeles," he replied.

"I don't know anyone in either of those places. I'd only know you."

"Is that a reason to hold back your career?" he asked, his eyebrows raised.

"No," she said slowly, mulling over the proposition. He was offering her an amazing opportunity. He was revered in the fields of music, film, publishing, business, and philanthropy. *But...it's him,* she thought. *You'd be around him all the time. Can you handle that?* A question occurred to her. "Would you require for me to work exclusively for you, or would I have the option to be a contributing writer for other publications?"

"Very smart question to ask."

"I didn't know whether or not your exclusivity hangups extended to your business relationships," she quipped.

He chuckled in surprise. "Usually, employment offers that I give are conditional, based upon exclusivity," he said, his dark eyes sparkling. "But if you would be willing to show me the articles you write for those publications and as long as those articles don't present a conflict for Gaines Enterprises, I don't see a reason why we wouldn't be able to come to an agreement."

"Hmm."

"I don't expect an answer tonight," he told her quickly. "You'll probably need time to think about it."

"No, I don't," she said. "I would need to look at the specifics. What my responsibilities would be and what my salary would be. If everything lines up the way it should, then yes. I accept."

A pleased smile stretched across André's face. "I have the paperwork back in my hotel room."

"Of course, you do," she muttered under her breath.

The waiter soon showed up with their meals. They ate in silence, listening to the music and casual chatter around them.

"Will you come back to my room with me tonight?" he queried, spearing a scallop with his fork.

"I don't think that's a good idea," she said. "Maybe I can meet you at your office tomorrow."

He grinned, holding his fork near his mouth. "If you want me to behave, I'm capable of behaving. I *do* have self-control."

But do I? she wondered.

"We'll keep it short," he promised.

"Fine," she relented.

"You don't have to be so guarded with me," he said before sliding the fork into his mouth.

"Yes, I do," she argued. "Because if I'm not, then..."

He arched an eyebrow at her while chewing.

"Then I let you back in, and things get messy," she finished.

"Why did you come to dinner with me, if Chad wasn't coming with you?" he asked. "You could have called and cancelled."

"That would have been rude," she stated, sectioning off a piece of salmon and popping it into her mouth.

He smiled. "I thought we were putting all of our cards on the table."

She tilted her head to the side, frowning at him. "All right, because...I wanted to see you."

"And?"

She looked upward. "And...okay. Cards on the table. I missed the feel of you on me and in me. I missed waking up to your adorable, sleeping face in the morning. I missed the way you smelled, the sound of your voice. I even missed your bossiness."

He grinned and lowered his eyes to his plate.

"And I hate myself for missing those things," she added quickly. "Because I shouldn't feel that way after walking in on you with someone else."

"We weren't exclusive," he reminded her.

"I know that," she said, glaring at him. "But it still hurt me. It still made me feel...expendable. Replaceable. I shouldn't feel that way, not with someone I..."

His eyes were intense as he waited for her to continue.

She stared at him, her eyes welling up.

"Someone you...?" he prompted.

Her heart hammered in her chest. Emotions contorted her face as she fought to force them into the nether regions of her mind. The tears were coming, she could feel them. She took a deep, steadying breath. "I need...I need to go to the Ladies' room," she said as calmly as she could manage, pushing her chair back and standing.

"You're not going to finish your statement before you go?" he asked quietly. "Cards on the table, remember?"

What is the point in finishing that sentence, knowing that you won't even believe me? She shook her head slowly. "I'm keeping that card up my sleeve," she replied. Then, she went to find the bathroom. Weaving in between tables, trying to ignore the happy couples dining together. Those couples had the luxury of worrying about normal things. Was the babysitter taking good care of their children? Making surprise birthday plans, family vacation plans. Those were the types of conversations she'd be having with Chad ten years from now, if she'd stayed with him.

Tears clouded her vision, but she still managed to find the short hall where the bathrooms were located. She pushed open the door to the Ladies' bathroom. The bathroom had a sitting area consisting of two loveseats and an armchair near the entrance. Beyond that, the bathroom sinks were off to the right and the lilac painted stalls were off to the left. She made a beeline for the nearest bathroom sink and gripped the edge of it. Her tears dropped and fell into the sink, one by one.

Chad's words from the day of graduation echoed in her mind. *"I know something is going on between you and him, Destiny. I'm not a fucking idiot."*

She lifted a hand to her temple and closed her eyes, trying to shut out the memory.

"Do you still have feelings for him?"

"I do," she confessed to her reflection. "God do I feel stupid for it, but I do." Even her reflection regarded her with judgment.

"I don't know what I expected. I'm going off to New York. You don't even know which job you're taking yet. Maybe...I don't know, maybe the timing is just bad." Even though he had been hurting, he had been sweet enough to leave the door of his heart cracked open a bit to give hope that they might reunite at a later time. That was the kind of man she'd just kicked to the curb.

The job offer she was accepting was the opportunity of a lifetime. She should be excited about it, but instead, she couldn't feel more miserable. Holding onto the sink was the only thing keeping her on her feet. She'd had a good man, and she had let him go. "I broke his heart, and I deserve for my heart to be broken." Those words, once spoken, held a certain weight.

She sniffled, wiped at her nose. Washed her hands, dried them. All the while, looking at the girl in the mirror. The young woman who was still struggling to find herself, find her place in the world. The young woman who felt so much guilt over breaking a good man's heart, who was beginning to doubt her own choices. She closed her eyes and lowered her head.

The bathroom door swung open. She heard soft footsteps on the tile. Not quite the sound that high heeled shoes made. Soft, solid footsteps. Coming to a stop just behind her. She felt a pair of hands grab her by the waist. Those hands pulled her against a firm, warm body. She held onto the sink and tilted her head back, opening her eyes.

André stood behind her. She could see his reflection in the mirror. He was looking back at her while sliding his hands up and down her waist.

How was it possible for one man to be so beautiful? And how was it possible that they looked so perfect together, had such amazing conversation, and such great chemistry and yet were doomed to be reduced to a casual fling?

He lowered his head and kissed her shoulder, dropping his hands to the skirt of her dress. Slowly, he raised her dress until it bunched around her waist.

Her eyes met his in the mirror. She turned around to face him, intent on telling him that they shouldn't do this here. Her intention was to tell him that at any minute, someone could walk through the door and see what they were doing. But the look in his eyes was pure unbridled lust. She lifted a hand to his face and felt that his skin, as always, was smooth to the touch.

His hands settled on her waist again, but this time so he could lift her up onto the sink. He parted her legs and moved to stand between them.

Her eyes widened in surprise. "André-" she started.

He leaned forward and kissed her. Lightning quick, no hesitation. Cutting off her protests, not giving her a chance to stop a good thing.

Andre's kisses were demanding. He hadn't tasted her sweet lips in so long. He had to make up for lost time. He stood between her thighs, feeling the heat radiating from the apex of her thighs. The lust he felt for her was indescribable, but strong enough for him give up anything just so he could feel her again. He had wanted to maintain his composure throughout the evening. He'd wanted to be on his best behavior, but whenever he was around her, he was so tempted to be on his worst.

She was the sweetest, cutest, most tempting little thing. She'd gone toe-to-toe with him this evening and had expected for that to turn him off, most likely. If only she knew how sexy she was when she challenged him.

One hand was tangled in her hair while the other delved between her thighs. Panties to the side. She sucked on his bottom lip, a move that was quickly becoming his weakness. He groaned against her mouth and felt her hands tugging at his dress shirt, untucking it from his dress pants. Unbuttoning his dress pants, unzipping. He felt her hand sliding in and wrapping around the length of him. It was almost enough for him to lose it right then and there.

During her absence from his life, he had tried his hand at other women. When he and one woman were done, he moved on to the next. That was how it went. And he had tried. He'd invited women to his place in Mississauga. Test drives before introducing the contract to them. They hadn't engaged him. Not one. Not one woman out of the several he'd invited had even remotely aroused him. They'd been beautiful, some had even been successful in their own right. One of them had even been sexy beyond belief. A part of him felt like he *should* have been turned on by her, but he wasn't. She was sexy, she was beautiful, but she was missing something. They *all* were missing something.

They weren't Destiny, he realized now as he ravaged her mouth with his tongue. Once that thought entered his mind, he pulled back suddenly, staring into Destiny's eyes. *Don't go down that road,* he told himself. *That line of thinking is dangerous.*

Those shapely strong thighs were wrapped around his waist. Her eyes anchored to his lips. One of her hands was in his dress pants, working him. Stroking. Caressing. Rubbing her thumb over the tip, and he briefly wondered where she'd learned that move from. Her free hand moved to cover the hand he had frozen between her thighs. She pushed at his hand. "Who told you to stop?" she asked.

Using his own words against him. He leaned forward and caught her bottom lip between his teeth. Using her move against her. Her little moans were bringing him to the edge, so he withdrew his hand from her thighs. Gently removed her hand from the inside of his pants. Enjoying the look of surprise on her face, he roughly pulled her against him as he entered her. She bit into his shoulder to quiet her own moans.

"André," she cried out. She leaned back and met his thrusts. Lips pouty and eyebrows drawn together to form an expression of pure ecstasy.

He was so addicted to her. She was crack and he was the fiend. He couldn't get enough. Even when he had her, even when he was inside of her, he wanted more of her. He tasted her, and he wanted to taste more of her. He filled her up, and he wanted to fill her up even more. He buried his face into her neck and groaned as he climaxed. A burst of warmth exploded inside of her.

She rode the wave with him, clinging to him and kissing the spot behind his ear. Her thighs tightened around him.

He stayed that way for several moments. He didn't want to move, didn't want to budge. He should. They were in a public place. Anyone could come walking in and see them. But it felt so good to rest his head on her shoulder. It felt good to have her arms around him, and his arms around her. He lifted his head and stared down at her. Even now, she didn't lower her legs from his waist; her legs remained tight around him, as if she was just as reluctant to let him go. He smiled and kissed her forehead.

The door to the bathroom door swung open and two middle-aged blonde women entered, chatting nonstop. They stopped short when they saw André and Destiny, Destiny posted on top of the sink and André locked between her thighs. He arched a look over his shoulder at the blonde women.

One of the blondes lifted her eyebrows in interest, while the other looked appalled.

Destiny shifted and André stepped back so she could lower down to the floor and stand. He helped her down, fully aware that the women were gawking at them. With a confident smile, he tucked himself back into his pants, buttoned them, and zipped them up. "Good evening, ladies," he greeted them as he adjusted his dress shirt, deciding to leave it untucked.

"Good evening," the interested blonde returned, her gaze pointedly lowered at his midsection.

André helped Destiny straighten her ivory dress and affectionately brushed her hair back from her face. Then, he took his time in washing and drying his hands. Destiny followed his lead. When they were finished, he offered her his arm. On their way out of the door, André told the two blondes, "Enjoy the rest of your night."

André and Destiny barely made it out of the bathroom before they heard one of the blondes saying, "I'll have what *she's* having."

Destiny buried her face into Andre's arm, nearly collapsing in laughter.

"I tried to get over you. I surrounded myself with other women. I invited them over. The usual. It did nothing for me."

Destiny's fingertips traced around his birthmark. The bedroom of the hotel suite was dark, but her eyesight had adjusted to the darkness. Her head rested on his bare chest. He had one arm propped behind his head as he stared up at the ceiling.

"I haven't experienced that in a long time, and only one other time. Moving on is generally not a problem for me."

"I wonder what that means," she returned.

"It means you're special," he told her without pause. "It means that I have to have you."

She searched his eyes and released a long, deep sigh. *"I broke his heart, and I deserve for my heart to be broken,"* she'd said to herself earlier in the restaurant bathroom. "I'll sign the contract," she whispered, her voice choked up with emotion.

He frowned down at her. "What did you say?"

She cleared her throat. "I tried to get over you, too, and it didn't work. You can't give me everything I want, but maybe I don't deserve everything I want. Especially after I broke someone's heart in the process of trying to get over you. Maybe this arrangement is what I deserve."

He sat up abruptly, forcing her to move aside. He planted his feet on the floor, turning his back to her. She could hear his knuckles cracking.

She rose on her knees and stared at his back. "Did I say something wrong?"

"You make being with me sound like a punishment," he said, his voice gravelly.

"Wouldn't punishment be involved?" she asked, remembering the phrasing of the contract.

"Punishment is warranted only if you misbehave. The entire setup isn't about punishment. It's not even about sex."

She wanted to reach out and touch him but suppressed the urge. "Then what *is* it about?" she demanded. "Tell me, because I don't understand."

He leaned forward. How she wished she could see the expression on his face right now. "It's about...a bond. Trust. A mutual understanding of each other. A mutual sense of adventure and exploration. Being honest and open with each other. Being able to tell each other anything. Carnal desires, yes, but it's about letting go. Completely letting go of all of your inhibitions and trusting that you won't be judged for it."

"Okay."

"I want that with you," he said, "but I don't want you to feel like you're *settling* for me."

"I honestly don't know how to prevent that, when I'm having to share you," she told him, tucking strands of hair behind her ear. "I'm too tired to even think about all of that right now. All I know is that I'm here with you, right now, and it feels like this is where I'm supposed to be."

"I leave back out for Canada next week," he informed her, shifting on the bed so that he could see her. "Will you come with me?"

She nodded.

"And you'll sign the contract?"

She hesitated only briefly before nodding again.

They met in the middle of the bed and wrapped their arms around each other. He gently kissed her lips and held her against him.

This particular flight to Canada was one of the most enjoyable he'd ever experienced. This was Destiny's first time flying private, and her excitement was infectious.

She remarked on nearly every feature that was available in the jet for the first half an hour. Only once he queued up a movie, did she quiet her exclamations and settle in next to him.

It felt good to have her beside him, felt good to wrap his arm around her while they enjoyed a movie together. For the first time in a long time, the flight didn't stir up feelings of loneliness and emptiness.

He hadn't forgotten the fact that she'd referred to their arrangement as a punishment she was enforcing on herself for the treatment of Chad. Hearing those words had crushed him a little and he now found himself searching for signs that she still felt that way. It was tough to read her these days. Sometimes she seemed genuinely happy to be with him. Then there were times when she seemed worlds away from him. Distant. In those moments, was she remembering Chad? Did she regret leaving him? Did she feel like she'd made some sort of mistake in returning to André? *Only time will tell,* he thought, pulling her a little closer to him as the movie reached its climax.

The flight landed smoothly in Toronto. A sleek, black luxury SUV awaited them. The driver of the vehicle hopped out to help transfer the luggage from the jet to the trunk of the car.

André greeted his driver, a tall dark-skinned man with dreadlocks pulled back into a ponytail. After their brief catch-up, he gestured to the pretty woman standing beside him. "KC, I'd like to introduce you to Destiny. She is going to be staying with me for a while."

Destiny stepped forward and shook hands with KC.

KC offered her a warm smile and tilted his head forward. "Welcome." He played off the introduction smoothly, as if this was his first time being made aware of Destiny's existence. In truth, he had already received a lengthy text message from André advising that a female guest would be living with him and working alongside him.

Whenever there was a drastic change to André's living or working situation, he alerted his team. Certain chess pieces needed to be moved in order to make this particular living situation work. At some point, Destiny would require a company car, feminine items, and her own work area in his condo. All of that would require a little bit of help from his team and assistant. As a courtesy, he'd sent out a heads-up text to his entire team the day following Destiny's acceptance of his job offer.

"I need to call my parents to let them know I've made it safely," she announced to him as he helped her into the car.

"By all means," he allowed, appreciating the fact that she'd checked with him first.

She called her parents. From what he could decipher from her end of the conversation, they didn't hesitate to voice their concern over her being so far away. He could just barely make out a woman's voice expressing love and affection on the other end of the line. Destiny voiced the same sentiments and ended the phone call.

Once he was comfortably seated beside her, André spoke low into her ear. "The flight was long. I figured we would just relax today. I want you to stay with me tonight, but after tonight, you will have a choice. You can either stay with me throughout your stay here, or I can have a condo prepared for you."

Her mouth dropped open.

His lips curled into a smile. "When I tell you that I will spoil you in ways that you could never imagine, know that I'm not a man who makes a habit of exaggerating."

She laid her head on his shoulder, lapsing into silence for the rest of the drive.

Upon their entrance into his condo, he hung behind Destiny and watched her explore. Commissioned artwork graced the walls. Cherrywood floors ran throughout the space. Floor-to-ceiling windows had blinds hung from mechanical rods that could be controlled with a remote.

The place also boasted a huge kitchen, large, decadent bathrooms, and bedrooms the size of living rooms. Even though the condo complex had its own gym that residents could use, he'd had a full-sized gym built inside of his condo unit.

"People kept coming up to me, asking for autographs while I was trying to work out in the gym on the main floor," he explained as she walked around the home gym. "I've also never liked the idea of working out on machines that hundreds of other sweaty people have used. I use public gyms when necessary...for example, when I'm traveling and staying in hotels. But when I'm home, I much prefer having my own gym equipment to use."

"I've never seen a condo this gigantic," she breathed out in awe.

"This space was originally two separate condo units," he explained. "My future home has been in the works for a couple of years now, but getting zoning and permits squared away for it has been a complete nightmare. At first, I stayed in hotels, thinking that within a year I would be able to move into my new house. When that started to drag out, I had to make a decision: I could get a temporary house or buy a condo that I could rent out or allow friends to stay in. A condo made the most sense at the time. I loved the community here, but their condo units were way too small to accommodate my needs. It took a lot of convincing before the property management company allowed me to remove the unnecessary second kitchen and knock out the wall separating the two condos. In the end, money did the talking for me."

During the tour, he casually gestured to the different rooms as if his condo were run-of-the-mill. There was one door, however, that he paused in front of. "I can show you this room later."

She laughed. "Just show me now. We're standing right in front of it."

Still, he hesitated. *Don't show her this room yet. She needs more time. She needs to learn more about the things that I like, more about the lifestyle.*

Rolling her eyes, she reached out and turned the doorknob. After pushing the door open, she froze in place.

Without realizing it, he sucked in his breath and held it.

She turned and looked at him, her facial expression disbelieving.

His face remained a blank slate, but his thoughts were all over the place. *Please don't judge me for what you find in this room. Please don't run from this condo building screaming, because you think I'm some kind of weirdo. Please don't change your mind about staying with me just because my interests in this lifestyle run a bit deeper than you may have been expecting.*

She turned back to the room and stepped inside, pressing the light switch as she entered. Recessed lighting bathed the room in a warm glow. The room was filled with racks and shelving, and wood contraptions with wrist straps. The shelves contained paddles, chains, and some tool that looked like it consisted of leather tassels. A long cage stood in the corner. There was no telling what she may have thought that cage was for.

She covered her mouth with her hands as she walked further into the room. Toys as far as the eye could see. Shackles mounted to the walls. Rows of silky material in a multitude of different colors. Several times she cast glances at him. He remained in the doorway, watching her. Silently gauging her reaction.

"What are your thoughts?" he asked her.

Her response didn't come immediately. She seemed to take a few moments to gather what her thoughts even were. "When you said you had 'particular interests,' that didn't translate to you having a room dedicated solely to kink. I thought this room was going to be a home office or something like that."

He burst out laughing and walked further into the room. Touching some of the items brought a wistful smile to his face. "I do have a home office. It's in an upstairs loft. We haven't gotten to it yet. I'm still working out where your home office would be, if you decided to stay here with me."

He could feel her eyes on him as she asked, "You're really into all of this?"

"Yes."

She exhaled and nodded. "Okay."

He looked amused. "Okay?"

"There are definitely things that you'll have to teach me," she clarified. "This is all new to me. I've seen kinky movies, but I've never used any of the things in this room. I'm willing to learn about them, though."

Relief washed over him.

"Where's the contract?" she asked him. "I'm ready to sign."

He studied her while his fingers caressed the handle of a wooden paddle. "The contract is in my briefcase. I was thinking that you might want to learn about some of this first, before-"

"I'm ready." She held out her hand.

Pause for a minute and think about why she would be ready to sign the contract after seeing a room full of things she'd never tried before. Just take a minute and think about that. His subconscious nagged at him, but he didn't want to pause to think about anything. The woman he was currently enamored with had seen a fairly sizable part of his identity and hadn't run away with her arms flailing. Even though he probably should have, he didn't want to question the gift he'd been given. He lowered his gaze to her extended hand. Lifted his eyes back up to her face. Lowered his gaze again as he accepted her offered hand. He led her out of the room, turned off the lights, and closed the door.

"Upon signing this contract, you will need my permission to do anything unrelating to your health, education or career." André stood behind a beautifully carved wooden desk in his home office. "I want to make sure you understand that once you sign your name on this line, you will belong to me."

She sat before his desk, still dressed in the black tank top and jeans she'd worn on the flight. She'd pulled her hair back into a ponytail before they went over the finer details contract, which had been a long, drawn out ordeal. There were safe words that needed choosing, sexual acts that needed clarifying, preferences to be made and filled in.

"You don't have to sign this today," he reminded her. "We've both been through a lot and it has taken a lot for us to make it to this point. There's nothing wrong with taking a day to relax."

She teetered the pen between her fingers, leaning over the desk. "I want to sign it," she said stubbornly.

He smiled. "All right."

She took a deep breath and steadied the pen in her hand. Gave the details of the contract one more cursory, brief read-through. She didn't have the energy to read the entire contract again. It was dense with information regarding the rules and roles, this, that, and the other. She flipped to the last page and pressed the tip of the pen to the dotted line. Her heart thumped in her chest. Before she could really think about how she was essentially signing her life over to someone else for a six-month period, she hurriedly signed her name on the dotted line and dropped the pen on the desk. Then she leaned back in the chair, making sure to keep her eyes lowered.

The contract slid out of her view and a moment later, she heard the telltale scratching of pen on paper. His eyes bore holes into her while he replaced the cap on the pen. "You may look at me."

She lifted her eyes.

He laughed. "Let's not start with this today. There is still much for you to learn. Today, we can just relax. We'll start fresh tomorrow." He walked around the desk. "Come with me." He held his hand out.

She grabbed his hand and stood up from the chair. He led her down the winding staircase and into the kitchen, where he gestured for her to sit on a stool. He walked around the island counter and started to gather food items and utensils. "You cook?"

"Are you kidding? Of course, I cook."

"I guess I assumed you had a personal chef."

"I did for a long time, but I've always loved to cook. When your tastes are as specific as mine, it helps to know how to cook. I can be very..."

"Picky?" she supplied, resting her elbows on the counter.

"I was going to say *selective*," he said as he rolled up the sleeves of his dress shirt. "Better connotation."

She grinned, appreciating that he even knew what the word "connotation" meant.

"Do you cook?" he asked while peeling leaves off a head of lettuce. "I mean, I know you work in a bakery, but do you *really* cook?"

"Yes."

"Oh, so you throw down a little bit?" he asked, a small smile teasing his lips.

"I do," she told him confidently. "Chicken - baked, fried, grilled, however you want it. Soul food. Pasta. Mexican, Asian and a little bit of Thai. I can do a little something in the kitchen."

"I like that," he said softly, rubbing his hands together.

"Is there anything I can help with?" she asked after watching him for several moments. "I feel like dead weight, just sitting here."

He shook his head. "I want you to relax today. Today, you're my guest."

"But I want to help," she said, her mouth forming into a pout.

He rubbed his chin. "Okay. Umm..." He surveyed the vegetables he'd gathered. "All right. Come here."

She hopped off the stool and rounded the counter so she could stand beside him.

"How are you at dicing tomatoes?"

"Dicing tomatoes is easy."

He carried the package of tomatoes to the sink so he could thoroughly rinse them. As an afterthought, he did the same with the lettuce leaves he'd plucked. He set the tomatoes in front of her and provided her with a sharp dicing knife. "Be careful with this," he cautioned. "It's very sharp. You wouldn't even feel the cut if it happened – I know that from experience."

She went to dicing, standing with one foot raised and resting on the calf of the other leg.

He watched her work for a minute. "There's a better way to do that," he informed her.

She gave him a look.

He raised his hands, palms outward, in a defensive gesture. "Or you can keep doing it like that," he said, grinning.

She snuck peeks at him out of the corner of her eye as he moved onto rinsing off a handful of carrots. "What is the better way?" she finally asked him.

After wiping his hands off on a towel, he went to stand behind her. His hands settled on top of her shoulders and slid down her arms until they covered her hands. He repositioned the knife in her hand and made a series of cuts into the top of the tomato. Then, he turned the tomato and made another row of cuts, crisscrossing the first row. "A lot faster," he said into her ear as he turned the tomato on its side and made a similar series of cuts. "A lot more efficient than the other way, and not as messy."

She nodded, half-listening to what he was saying and half-trying to prevent herself from collapsing at the sound of his voice that close to her ear. "Thank you."

He resumed his position beside her and started slicing the carrots. Then, he turned on the stove. He moved around the kitchen fluidly.

As if I needed another quality to love about him, she thought. *Articulate, intelligent, attractive, sexy, talented, caring, and on top of all of that, he knows how to cook.* "You're like Kryptonite," she blurted out as she diced the last tomato.

His brows furrowed. "What?"

She hadn't realized she'd spoken the words out loud. *Ugh. I really need to learn how to keep thoughts to myself.*

"What was that?" he asked, returning to her side.

"Just ignore me," she said, wiping her hands on the towel that he'd tossed on the countertop.

"I want to know what you said." The expression on his face was pleasant, but the tone of his voice was serious.

"I said...you're Kryptonite."

"Meaning what exactly?"

"Meaning it's as if you were built to be a weakness for women everywhere."

He laughed and wrapped his arms around her. "I'm your weakness? Is that what you're telling me?"

"I said 'all women,'" she said, savoring the feeling of his arms around her.

"'All women,' *including* you, correct?"

"Technically, yes."

He laughed again and kissed the top of her head. "Good. I'll take that." He held onto her for a few minutes, then released her and continued cooking.

They moved around the kitchen, and around each other. There was a lot of flirtation and a lot of affection. He would suddenly stop what he was doing and wrap her up in a bear hug. She didn't take those moments for granted. For, in those moments, she felt like she'd made the right decision in choosing him. In those moments, she was grateful for him, grateful that she'd been open-minded enough to sign the contract. Granted, signing that contract had been a subconscious way for her to punish herself for hurting Chad. But it was possible that something good could come from this, something organic. Something real. Something beautiful.

12

Destiny rolled over in bed and came face to face with a gorgeous sleeping man. Thick eyelashes, the hint of a five o' clock shadow, full lips. Her heart fluttered at the sight of him, a reflex that she was going to have to learn how to control.

His eyes slowly opened, and he shifted in bed.

She lowered her eyes immediately, remembering that the contract stated she couldn't look him in the eyes without permission.

A slow smile curved his lips. He pressed a kiss to her forehead. "You may look at me," he told her, propping himself up on one elbow.

Wordlessly, she peered up at him.

He laughed. "And you may talk to me."

"I'm sorry, this is all just...very..."

"New to you," he finished, remembering her words from yesterday.

She nodded, pulling the sheets up to her chest. The previous evening had been a dream. They'd cooked together, eaten together while talking about his company and the educational program that he'd started. Then they'd cuddled on the couch while watching the most recent *John Wick* movie. After the movie was over, the kissing and touching had started, and that soon led to a variety of other intimate acts. They'd started in the living room, with her on his lap, and wound up in the bedroom with her bent over the bed. It had been the perfect night. Their interaction had been perfectly normal, and now... now that she was locked into a contract with him, the scope of their relationship had changed. "Normal" was no longer a word that could be applied. She was in foreign territory. A lot of interaction that people took for granted, such as eye contact or ways to greet someone, were interactions that were now being controlled by a piece of paper she'd signed her name on.

He lifted his hand and touched the curve of her breast, only stopping once his hand met the top of the sheet she'd pulled up to her chest. "What are you thinking right now?" His voice was groggy with sleep.

"I'm thinking that I don't know how to do this," she admitted with a nervous laugh.

He dragged his eyes down the length of her. "Today will mostly be training for you. Your training will last a while. Don't worry about getting everything right at first. You're still in the learning phases."

"Can we go back to being how we were last night?" she asked, her voice sounding hopeful. "Just...normal?"

He hesitated before answering. "The longer we are... *normal*, as you put it, the more difficult it will be for you to learn the lifestyle and my preferences. These things are easier to learn when you start applying them right away. You lowered your eyes and waited for me to give you permission earlier. You're already doing a great job."

But it's weird having to do that, she thought. *It's strange to need your permission just to look at you. How come you can't see that?*

An unreadable expression crossed his face and for the briefest moment, she feared that he was a mindreader. He brushed her hair back and said, "Before we do anything, I think we should have a conversation about this lifestyle. My experiences in the lifestyle, how I first encountered it, and what it means to me." He turned his head and glanced at the clock on his nightstand. "First, we need to shower. Then I'll make us breakfast."

"Okay."

He smiled again. "The appropriate response is, 'Yes, Sir,'" he corrected.

She covered her mouth. "I'm sorry."

He raised his eyebrows.

She furrowed her eyebrows. "I'm sorry...Sir?"

He laughed and kissed the tip of her nose. "Up. Shower."

She rose into a sitting position, clutching the sheets to her chest.

"You don't need to be modest around me," he told her.

She stared back at him and didn't budge.

"Meaning that you can drop the sheet," he elaborated.

She looked down at the sheet and slowly released it. It fell around her waist.

He admired her body for a moment before saying, "If this wasn't your first day, that hesitation would have earned you a punishment."

Great. I'm failing already, and this is just day one.

He sighed and placed an index finger beneath her chin, tilting her chin up. "You're new to this. I understand that, which is why I didn't punish you this time. I'm going to try my best to ease you into this. There is a lot for you to learn, and it would be impossible for me to cover every single scenario or potential situation in a training session. This means that your learning will be ongoing, even once your training has ended. Whenever you display an action that would garner a punishment or reward, I will let you know. Understood?"

"Yes, Sir," she said softly. The words felt weird to say, almost like she was talking an entirely different language.

"Good. Now, up. Shower."

She stood up from the bed but didn't move. She clasped her hands together in front of her. "Are you coming with me?"

"Coming with you..."

"Are you coming with me, Sir?" she asked. "Do I really have to say it after every sentence?"

He shook his head as he stood up from the bed, naked with skin that looked - and *was* - smooth to the touch. He had a lean muscular build, and his perfect grooming didn't end at his five o' clock shadow. "You don't have to say it after every sentence, but I want you to while you're training. The more you use it, the more quickly it will become a habit."

She nodded in understanding.

"And yes, I'm joining you." He held his hand out to her.

She accepted his hand and trailed behind him as he led the way to the most high-tech bathroom she'd ever seen in her life. The shower had a television embedded into the beautifully tiled wall with a control panel below it. The control panel gave the user options of different mist scents to spray into the stall. There were also multi-colored LED lights installed into the ceiling.

She didn't have much time to appreciate the different features that the shower had, because the minute they were in the stall with the water pouring down on them, he pulled her against him. Then his mouth was on hers and he was lifting her up and holding her against the shower wall. Just as eager to feel him as he was to feel her, she wrapped her legs around him. They proceeded to get dirty before they got clean.

"So...the lifestyle." Shirtless, barefoot, and wearing white linen pajama pants, André set a pan on top of the glass stovetop and turned on the burner. "I'll start off with how I came into the lifestyle."

Destiny sat on a stool at the island counter. Ever since she'd met the man, he'd been a mystery to her. He didn't believe in love, and she couldn't fathom why – especially when so many of his songs were centered around the topic. Now that she was about to discover more of his background, maybe some of her questions would finally get answered.

"The women I've been involved with have developed theories about why this lifestyle appeals to me. I've heard it all. Some women assume I was abused as a child or had some dark, crazy past. That couldn't be any further from the truth." He walked over to the refrigerator and pulled one of its doors open. He withdrew a carton of eggs and set it on the counter beside the fridge. "Because I'm a public figure, I can save you a lot of the backstory. You probably know most of it already. My parents split up when I was young. I spent my time between here and Houston. I'm not going to lie and say my life was easy. But I was loved, and I knew I was loved. I love my family now, and I loved them then." He continued to pull ingredients from the stainless steel refrigerator: butter, cheese, tomatoes, mushrooms, spinach, and green onions.

She watched him in fascination.

"A psychologist would probably dig up some reason as to how my interest in BDSM is tied to my childhood, but in my opinion, it's not. At all. Despite having dominant traits for my entire adult life, I actually stumbled upon the lifestyle by chance." He arched a glance at her over his shoulder. Their eyes met and he smiled before turning his attention back to the vegetables he'd set on the counter. "There was an exotic dancer that I dated back when I was an entertainer. Beautiful girl. Society has a stigma against exotic dancers, but she was extremely intelligent. We had good chemistry. She starred in one of my music videos. We joked between takes, and one thing led to another. We became involved. Our first lovemaking sessions were, as you'd call it, *normal*. 'Vanilla' is generally the term used to describe what you call 'normal' sex, or a 'normal lifestyle'. Using the term 'normal' loosely, of course.

"My first few times with her were vanilla. Enjoyable, though. Vanilla is what I was used to at that time; it was pretty much all I knew. But she slowly started to introduce kink into our relationship. At first, I just thought she was adventurous or experimental. I thought we were trying new things together. She later explained to me that it was a tactic she used to introduce men into what she called 'the lifestyle.'" He glanced at Destiny while removing an egg from the carton. "If we go into the meaning of BDSM, the meaning of 'the lifestyle,' it can get *very* convoluted *very* quickly. The lifestyle means different things to different people. There are so many different aspects to it. Some people just have kinky sex. A little bit of spanking here, a little bit of flogging there. Toys. A little bit of blindfolding, a little bit of bossing each other around. Others just like to feel pain or inflict pain on others. That would be the sadomasochism aspect. Then there are those who immerse themselves into an actual lifestyle, meaning that even the periods of time throughout the day when they're not having sex, they are still fulfilling their role as a Dominant or submissive." He cracked the egg against the edge of the counter and spilled its contents into a clear bowl. "Even for those who choose to live a lifestyle, there are many different ways for them to do that. It all depends on the couple. The lifestyle is ultimately what each couple makes it, and that is one of the things I love about it. In no way is it cookie-cutter or a basic mold. Couples choose how they fit the lifestyle into their own relationship."

"Am I allowed to ask questions during this, Sir?" she asked him.

He smiled at her. "Very good, and yes."

"Is there a reason why you feel the need to live the lifestyle instead of just having kinky sex once in a while?" she asked him.

"That's an excellent question," he said, proceeding to crack another egg. "To answer that, I would need to finish my story. The exotic dancer that I dated, she slowly introduced me to the lifestyle. She was into everything. The toys, the kink…she even took me to these sex clubs where we would be intimate in front of other people."

Destiny's eyes widened. The first thought that occurred to her was, *You don't expect me to do that, do you?*

He cast a glance at her and smiled as if he knew what she was thinking. "Again, I'm going to ease you into this. Don't worry about that. It will only overwhelm you."

You think?

"One interesting thing about the way she operated, was that she chose to alternate between being Dominant and submissive," he went on, beating the eggs he'd cracked with a whisk.

Destiny frowned. "She...dominated you?"

"Hard to believe, isn't it?"

"Very."

He laughed. "This was back when I was new to all of this. I have to admit, I liked being dominated back then. At that time, I was at the height of my career. Women were throwing themselves at me, willing to do anything just to spend a night with me. It was rare that I got to experience the chase with women back then – they were too busy chasing me. In those situations, I was always the one in control. It felt good to have a woman tell me what to do, for a change. It felt good to have her act or feel superior to me. It felt good to have to work for what I wanted. I don't know if you're going to understand that."

"I get it," she said.

"I liked it at first, but she kept switching back and forth, between being Domme and submissive. It was confusing. I like consistency. She would switch up without notice and it threw me off. Over time, she and I didn't work out and I was on to the next girl. But now that the dancer had introduced this entire way of living to me, I couldn't just drop it because I was moving onto someone else. I was already fascinated with it by that point." He spoke as he continued to cook. "While dating this new girl, I started researching BDSM. Movies, videos, tutorials, books, and websites. I joined online groups anonymously, to meet other people who lived the lifestyle. Nothing kinky. Just conversations with like-minded individuals. Sometimes the groups held meetings at coffee shops and lounges. I had to wear disguises in order to attend these meets, but they were worth it. I learned so much and met lifelong friends that I still talk to.

"Through time, relationships, and experimentation, I felt like I discovered myself. I realized that I wasn't submissive, not by nature. Submission is something that I liked earlier on due to my career, my status in the industry. If I hadn't been an entertainer...if I had been just a normal guy working an entry-level office job, my nature would be to dominate." The ingredients in the pan sizzled. "Once I realized that, things came a lot easier to me. Knowing who I was and what I wanted made it easier to search for women who had similar interests."

"So, you prefer the lifestyle to just kinkiness because you prefer consistency?" she asked.

"In so many words, yes," he responded. "For me, there is a thrill in the very nature of BDSM. It's not all about the sex for me. Some of it is, of course, but I also like the teasing. All of the interaction in between. There is a great deal of trust exchanged between a couple involved in the lifestyle. Trust hasn't been a running theme throughout my life. At the level I am at, finding someone who I can trust - *really* trust, with my deepest and darkest secrets, is difficult. If someone asked me to use one word to describe what the BDSM lifestyle is about, the word I would choose is *trust*. That is the element that appeals to me the most. In a lifestyle like this, you are trusting that you can be open and honest about what you like and the things you want to try, without being judged by your partner."

"You say that, but then you become involved with so many women," she pointed out. "How do you know you can trust them not to run to the media with stories about their experiences with you?"

"They're contractually obligated to remain discreet," he reminded her.

"What if they didn't care?" Destiny pressed. "Sure, you could sue her, or whatever you would do. But the truth would be out there, and people would know."

He shrugged his shoulders. "I honestly don't know how I would handle that. Occasionally, I ask myself the same questions you're asking me now. I wonder whether it would matter if everyone *did* know. People have become desensitized and aren't as prudish as they've been in the past. Would they care if they found out that I have a room filled with whips and chains and shit? I don't know." He used a spatula to flip a perfect omelette onto a clear glass plate and proceeded to make another.

Another question occurred to her. "If you prefer consistency, why are the contracts only for six months? Wouldn't you just want to stay with the same woman?"

"I would not object to being with the same woman over a long period of time," he said slowly. "But the contract length is for six months, because I want to make sure that both parties have a chance to re-evaluate whether or not the setup works for them. After six months, you very well could say, 'You know what…this isn't for me.' Or maybe you would like some aspects of the relationship but would want to change other aspects and have that noted in the next contract."

"So…you would not object to being with the same woman for a long period of time, as long as you could date other women during that time frame?"

He finished making the second omelette. "Yes."

His proclivity to dating other women was a known fact and yet her heart still broke a little whenever he confirmed that it was necessary for him. Her mouth slanted in disapproval, a facial expression she only felt comfortable wearing when his back was to her, as it was now.

"Do you still have reservations about me seeing other women?"

To tell the truth, or to not tell the truth, she thought, wringing her hands.

"You have to be honest with me," he said, throwing her a warning glance as he turned to open the door to the fridge again. "This arrangement will never work if you feel the need to lie to me."

"Yes, I have reservations about it," she said. "I always will."

He smiled. "It's the strangest thing," he remarked. "Seeing other women is completely necessary for me, but for some reason whenever you are possessive of me like that, I don't know...I kind of like it."

Breakfast consisted of the omelettes he'd prepared, a small bowl of fruit, and a glass of filtered water.

They seated themselves at his dining room table, a long black modern furniture piece with a glossy surface. The table was placed beside a wall of tall windows. André sat at the head of the table. He indicated that she was to sit at his side instead of the other end.

He set his cell phone next to his plate. "I'm surprised you don't have more questions," he told her as he watched her pick up her fork.

"I have a ton of them," she contradicted. "I just...don't even know where to start with them."

"Just ask whatever you want to ask."

She sighed and took a few moments to collect her thoughts. "You explained that this kind of lifestyle can mean different things to different people," she said slowly. "And I read the contract and you've given a vague idea of what you expect. But...on a day-to-day, how does something like this work? I don't know how to act around you."

Using his knife and fork, he sectioned off a piece of omelette. "I don't want to change who you are," he stated. "I'm attracted to your personality. A submissive doesn't need to change who she is. I've seen submissives lose complete sight of who they are, because they were trying so hard to be the perfect submissive. Perfection doesn't exist for submissives *or* Dominants. In training you, I may make a mistake or there may be times when I am unclear when giving you an instruction. No one is perfect, and there is beauty in imperfection. I don't want you to bend over backwards trying to conform to what you think I want. Continue being yourself while being mindful of the rules that are in place. What you learn in your training will only enhance what is already there, not create an entirely different personality."

"But I'm not supposed to question the decisions you make, or the orders you give me," she said. "Questioning things is a part of my nature. That's one of the reasons why I chose journalism as my field."

He forked a piece of the omelette into his mouth and chewed on it thoughtfully. "I want to make sure you understand that the calling me 'Sir,' the making eye contact and touching with permission only, and the rule against questioning my authority are not put in place for selfish or egocentric purposes. There are Dominants out there who take advantage of rules like this, certainly. But true Dominants don't enforce rules like these because of a superiority complex."

"I can't imagine what else it would be about," she said honestly.

He smiled and lifted his glass of water. "I appreciate your honesty. Your honesty is what will help you to learn." He took a sip of water and dabbed at his mouth with a cloth napkin. "Those rules are about respect. The Dominant is the authority figure in the relationship."

"Can I speak freely, Sir?" she asked him.

He chuckled. "Yes. You've done well by asking first."

"You don't think that the 'Sir,' and all of that has at least a *little* to do with ego stroking?"

He thought about it. "To a certain extent, maybe," he admitted. "It would be a small extent - at least as far as I'm concerned, anyway. I don't need titles to boost my ego. You're here with me. I'm smart enough to know that means more than you calling me 'Sir' or any other title."

She shook her head. "I feel like I'm never going to understand any of this."

"It's a lot of information to take in," he said. "I mean, think about it. It's an entire lifestyle. Learning an entire lifestyle takes time. You aren't expected to understand everything in a twenty-four-hour period."

"Can you clue me into some of the basics of what you would expect from me?"

He nodded. "Every day won't be the same, of course, but typically, we will wake up. If you behaved the night before, we would wake up together in bed. If you have disappointed me in some way, you may not be permitted to sleep with me. Either way, we would wake up. Work out. Shower. Get dressed. Eat breakfast. If it's a weekday, we would go to work. By the way, at work you would not call me 'Sir,' just to be clear. At work, you can call me Mr. Gaines or André. Understood?"

So many rules. How am I going to remember them all? "Yes, Sir."

He reached over and covered her hand with his, visibly pleased that she'd addressed him correctly. Then, he removed his hand from hers and continued, "After work, we would come back home. Whatever we do from that point will ultimately be up to us." He paused and took time to eat some of the food on his plate. "I'll give you a few specifics on what I expect, just to give you an idea. When we are at home, and I am seated, you are to kneel beside me. This is with the exception of meals or if I say otherwise. Whether we are here or elsewhere, you don't ever walk ahead of me, unless I say otherwise. I lead, you follow. General rule of thumb. Whenever we go to an event, you are to stay at my side. Always, unless you are otherwise instructed. Outside of work, you will ask my permission to do everything. And I mean everything. Recreational activities, answering your phone, pleasing yourself. Everything.

"Any signs of disrespect will result in punishment. I will be lenient with you at first since you are still learning. That leniency does dissolve over time. Acts of disrespect include questioning me or a decision I have made, talking back, or hesitating before obeying. Do you have any questions?" He took another sip of water.

"If...if I choose to live here with you," she began, her voice timid, "would you bring other women here?"

He set the glass back on the table without breaking eye contact with her. "Most of the time, I would not bring other women here, out of respect for you."

"*Most* of the time?" she repeated.

"There may be times when I deem that it is necessary to bring other women here," he told her. He must have seen the frustration in her eyes because he continued explaining. "Entering into this arrangement, we already have one obstacle to overcome. I don't believe in love and you do. If I see that you are developing feelings for me, feelings that are stronger than they should be, I may feel the need to bring another woman here to discourage those feelings. To remind you where we stand."

Confrontational words leapt to mind, and she had to clamp her lips shut before she spoke those words out loud.

An amused glint sparkled in his eye.

She stared at him wordlessly.

"Understood?" he asked her.

She didn't respond.

He lifted an eyebrow. "*Understood?*" he repeated, this time his voice taking on a harder edge.

She blinked and fought for control of her emotions. "Understood, Sir," she said quietly.

He wiped his mouth with his napkin and evaluated the clothes she'd put on: a black tank top and matching shorts. "Today, we're going to go shopping. As my submissive, you are a reflection of me. I want to make sure that when it comes to your wardrobe, your skin care products, your hair care products, everything - you have the best of the best." He picked up his cell phone to check the time, since he hadn't bothered to put a watch on. "We will leave out in approximately an hour. When you get dressed, be sure to wear a skirt or a dress. You will not often be permitted to wear jeans. Do you have any other questions?"

"A ton of them," she returned.

"When we come back from shopping, I'll address more of your questions," he promised.

They finished the rest of their breakfast in silence.

The streets of Mississauga were left behind for this shopping trip. André drove Destiny into the Toronto city limits for that day's excursion. As he drove, she peered out of the passenger window. She saw all walks of life strolling the streets or playing in parks around the city.

Seated on the northwestern shore of Lake Ontario, Toronto was a beautiful city. It had stunning architecture and a richness of culture. Many of the streets boasted French names. She commented on this, which prompted him to give an overview of the historical ties between Canada and France.

The mall was a beautiful structure capped off by a glass dome. The sun's rays streamed through the glass and created bright patterns on the gleaming mall floors.

Walking through a mall with André was an experience unlike any other. Some shoppers walked past him as if they were used to seeing him around the city, whereas other fans squealed and approached him. Even though he'd been out of the rap game for a while now, many of his fans still clung to the hope that he would eventually drop another album. They said as much and rapped his lyrics to him. It was adorable.

He was very gracious to his fans and took the time to talk to each of them for a few minutes. When they asked him to take photos with them, he politely obliged.

Destiny hadn't had many boyfriends in her life, but the few she'd had dreaded accompanying her to the mall. Even her male friends talked about the long, endless waiting times they'd endured while their girlfriends tried on clothes. André, however, did not seem to have that same outlook on shopping. He was extremely interactive, choosing which stores for them to visit and reviewing the selections of clothes on the racks.

"We're only going to purchase some of your wardrobe from this mall," he'd explained while evaluating different pieces of clothing. "We're going to grab the rest from designer shops. You deserve better than clothes that come off the rack." He draped several dresses across his arm.

One of the store clerks, a pretty brown-skinned girl with her hair pulled back in a ponytail, approached them. "Did you need help finding any-" She cut her question short and her eyes widened with recognition. "You're Dré."

Destiny remembered that her father had said something similar when meeting André for the first time. She wondered how many times a day he heard that statement.

He smiled, continuing to search through the dresses on the rack. "I am, yes."

"Oh my God." She covered her mouth with both hands. She blinked a few times, then dropped her hands and called over her shoulder, "Brianne! It's Dré! Dré is here! In our store!"

He angled a look down at Destiny, who was trying hard not to laugh.

"My name is Shayna," the clerk went on. "I have all of your CD's. I don't just stream your albums. I also buy the physical copies. Oh my God, you're really here. You're really standing in front of me right now. Brianne, hurry up! Bring my cell phone!"

"You shouldn't leave the cash register unattended," he warned her, looking concerned.

"My manager is cool," Shayna said with a flip of her wrist.

André's eyebrows shot up. "Well...I mean, all right, as long as your manager is cool." He gave Destiny another pointed look.

"Please, just one picture," Shayna begged him.

"A quick picture," he granted. He lifted the dresses draped over his arm and laid them across the top of the rack. Then, he unbuttoned the cuffs of his white dress shirt and rolled the sleeves up his forearms. "Where do you want to do this?"

Shayna glanced around the store. "Umm...right here is fine. No one will be looking at the background if you're in the picture."

Brianne, a short, petite blonde, approached them and handed Shayna her cell phone.

Destiny took a few steps back to give them room to take the picture.

Shayna leaned in close and held the cell phone up, using the front-facing camera. André flashed one of his most charming smiles. When she was finished taking the picture, she reviewed the photo. "Ugh, I look so ugly in this. Can we take one more?"

"Sure," he allowed.

Shayna handed the camera to Destiny. "Can you take the picture for me this time? I think it will look better if someone else takes it."

Destiny started to step forward, but André covered Shayna's hand with his. "She's not here to take your photograph, Shayna. You can have your friend take the picture."

Shayna blinked in surprise. "Oh...okay." She handed her cell phone to Brianne.

Brianne took the picture and returned the cell phone to her friend. Shayna reviewed the photo and smiled in relief. "This one is a lot better, thank you." She looked up at André. "I didn't mean anything by asking your...lady friend to take the picture. She was just closer at the time."

"It's fine," he told her. "We have to get going, though. It has been a pleasure to meet you, Shayna. You too, Brianne." He left the two friends to shriek in private while he led Destiny back to the rack they'd been standing at before the interruption.

Together, they hunted down the dressing rooms. He instructed her to try on different outfits for him. "Don't just try them on and then take them off," he added. "I want you to step out so I can see how the clothes look on you." There were some pieces he didn't like, and he was blunt when expressing his opinion.

The last dress she was given to try on was by far her favorite. She'd loved most of them, but the last one was a modest silk dress with a fitted skirt that ended at the knee. The sleeves were capped. She smoothed the material flat against her stomach, studying her reflection in the mirror mounted to the wall of the dressing room.

There was a light knock on the dressing room door.

She walked over to the dressing room door and turned the knob. Cracking it open, she asked, "Yes?"

André stood on the other side of the door, peering in at her through the crack.

She opened the door wider.

His eyes scanned down the length of her. His eyes drank in every curve of her frame. His responses to the previous ensembles she'd tried on had been swift. "Yes, I love it," or, "This one goes back on the rack. I'm not a fan." This time, he didn't respond at all. Instead, he glanced over his shoulder.

Destiny stood on her tiptoes, trying to see what he was looking at.

When he turned back, he stepped forward and into her personal space.

Forced to take a step back, she searched his eyes. Trying to read what he was thinking, she took another step back. "Sir?"

He stepped forward again and she took another step back. He turned, his movements slow and calculated. Closed the dressing room door behind them.

Her heart pounded in her chest. *What is he...?*

When he turned to face her again, he took another step forward.

The space was cramped and could barely fit them both. Her back was pressed against the dressing room wall. She couldn't take another step backward and he knew that.

His eyes locked with hers as he tenderly touched her upper arm. He silently trailed his fingertips down her arm. "Turn around," he ordered.

But two of your fans are working somewhere out there. They probably followed us and could be out there right now. Her eyes darted around him, landing on the dressing room door.

"You're hesitating," he told her. "That would normally result in punishment."

Swallowing the lump that had formed in her throat, she slowly turned around. She felt his hand at the nape of her neck. That hand brushed her hair aside and grabbed a hold of the zipper on the dress. Very slowly, he dragged the zipper down. Her body shuddered in anticipation as he moved the zipper down the length of her spine. A moment later, she felt his lips on the back of her neck and his hands moving the dress sleeves down her arms. Her knees went wobbly. Once the dress was a puddle around her feet and her bra was removed, she lifted her hands and pressed her palms flat against the wall. She arched her back, stared up at the ceiling, and surrendered herself to him.

His kisses continued down her back. Those kisses dipped so low that he was gradually kneeling to the floor. He didn't stop until his lips came into contact with the top of her lacy, white panties. "I love the way white lace looks on brown skin," he commented shortly before dragging the lacy garment down her legs. He kissed and bit the curve of her rear end, then pulled back. "Turn around," he ordered gruffly.

This time, she didn't hesitate.

Heat burned in his dark eyes as they scanned across every inch of her exposed skin. "Do you think you can stay quiet?" he asked her.

"I...don't know," she told him honestly.

"You don't know..."

"I don't know, Sir," she said, correcting herself.

He smiled and blinked up at her a few times before moving his head forward and licking the skin beneath her belly button.

She clamped a hand over her mouth to keep any sound from escaping.

While caressing the sides of her thighs, his lips moved lower. He grabbed the waistband of her panties between his teeth. Slid one of his hands between her thighs and parted them. Moved his lips to her inner thigh. Continued kissing, biting. Slowly, but surely, he was working his way up her thigh.

The closer his mouth moved to her center, the more her thighs began to tremble. She feared that she was going to fall over and *really* embarrass herself. She raised her hands to her hair and buried her fingers in her tresses, overwhelmed by the sensation his lips were causing.

He pulled back, used his hand to tease her. Open her up. Then he put his lips together and blew air across her skin. The lightest puff, a small gentle action that pulled a dramatic physical response from her body.

A small moan escaped her lips.

He rose to his full height and started to unbutton his dress pants. "Move closer to the bench."

She went to stand beside the bench that was attached to the dressing room wall.

Once his pants were removed, he joined her and sat down. He admired her body for a moment and said softly, "Come here."

She moved to stand in front of him.

"Sit on me."

She straddled him.

"Good girl." He grabbed her by the waist while staring up at her. "Ride me."

That was an instruction she was more than happy to follow. Setting her hands on his shoulders for balance, she lowered onto his lap. A small moan did escape her lips as she felt him filling her up, and another when he circled an arm around her waist and drove even deeper inside of her. A loud knock sounded on the door. She gasped and grew tense.

"Are you okay in there?" Shayna, the store clerk asked.

"Did I tell you to stop?" André whispered harshly, his voice rough with desire.

The "No, Sir," she knew he was expecting was on the tip of her tongue, but she couldn't bring herself to say it - not with someone else standing on the other side of that door. *Is he serious?*

"I didn't tell you to stop. Keep riding."

She started moving again.

"Tell her that you're fine and don't need any help," he whispered.

"I'm fine," Destiny called out to the store clerk, making an effort to keep her voice level. "I don't need any help. Thank you for checking."

"Okay, just checking," Shayna said.

Destiny glanced towards the door again and could still see Shayna's silhouette through the slats in the door. *If I can make out her shape, there's no telling what all she can see.*

"Look at me and don't take your eyes off of me until we're done," André commanded.

She followed the command.

Shayna knocked softly again. "I'm sorry to keep bothering you, but...do you know where Dré went? He was out here, but now he's gone. Your shopping bags are out here."

André leaned forward and caught one of Destiny's nipples between his teeth.

She tilted her head back and gasped. He started to suck, softly, and her gasp turned into a moan.

"Are you...*sure* you're okay?" Shayna asked. Then there was the sound of whispering.

Destiny didn't care. All she cared about in that moment was André and what he was doing to her. She continued to ride him. She wrapped her arms around his neck, half-expecting him to reprimand her for it. He didn't. He kissed every part of her body that he could access from this position, groaned against her mouth, guided her hips with his hands, bit into her shoulder, and filled her completely.

Many hushed moans and breathless sighs later, she surveyed her reflection in the mirror and straightened her knee-length, floral print dress. Behind her, he hoisted his pants up over his hips. His head was bent down as he zipped his fly. In that moment, she had to pause and ask herself if this was really her life. If she, a recent college graduate, was truly having a tryst with one of the most well-respected men in the music industry. Had she really, for the *second* time, hooked up with him in a public place? It sounded more like a fantasy than real life.

I thought he wanted to be discreet, she thought. *But those sounds we made were far from discreet.*

"How are you feeling?" he asked, raising his head and looking at her.

"I'm good," she assured him, giving her hair another pat. "I just can't believe that this happened."

The smile he gave her was boyish. Dangerously handsome. So damned attractive. He had a face that was so adorable, she couldn't imagine ever being mad at him for long.

Then, she remembered how it had felt to walk in on him with another woman draped across his lap. Maybe her earlier sentiment was a slight exaggeration. Depending on the situation, she could stay mad at him. It just wouldn't be easy.

"I think we're ready," he announced before cupping her face in his hands and kissing the top of her forehead.

They exited the dressing room hand in hand. Destiny had expected to see Shayna and Brianne standing right next to the door, but the girls were helping customers at the register. Destiny closed her eyes and breathed a sigh of relief.

Destiny and André gathered the shopping bags they'd accumulated and headed towards the cashier's counter. Brianne handled her current customer. Her eyes widened when she saw André and Destiny. Her cheeks flushed red. "Did you...find everything okay?"

André grinned and withdrew his wallet from his pants pocket. "I found everything just fine," he confirmed.

Brianne laughed nervously and started ringing up the clothing items. Shayna, standing behind Brianne, gawked at André openly, without shame.

Destiny kept her gaze lowered. The girls knew what had happened in the dressing room, and how couldn't they?

"Thank you for helping me so much today, I appreciate it," André told both of them.

"No problem," Brianne said quickly.

"Of course, anytime," Shayna said simultaneously.

He handed Brianne one of his credit cards and waited patiently for them to bag the items. He turned, lowered his head and whispered into Destiny's ear. "That last dress you tried on, by the way...looks *amazing* on you. Seeing it on you will make me want to rip it off."

The expressions on the two store clerks' faces were beyond priceless. Their eyes were wide with disbelief.

André accepted the bags from a speechless Brianne and thanked her again. He reclaimed Destiny's hand and led her towards the store's entrance.

Destiny glanced over her shoulder at the two clerks as André led her out of the store. Shayna said something to Brianne. She couldn't quite make it out, but she thought she heard the word "lucky."

"Can I ask you a question without you getting offended, Sir?" Destiny asked him while he drove.

"Questions that come with disclaimers are never good."

"The question isn't *that* bad. I'm just curious about something." She tugged on a curly strand of her hair while staring through the windshield of his luxury car.

"You can ask me," he decided.

"The sex in public thing...is that going to be our thing?"

He laughed until he saw her expression. "Wait, you're serious?"

"Yeah."

"*Yes*," he said emphatically. "Say '*Yes*,' not 'yeah.'"

"Yes, Sir, I am serious."

He stroked his chin with one hand while steering with the other. "If you're serious, then I should apologize to you. I am putting too much emphasis on the sexual nature of our arrangement. I try not to, I do. But..." He glanced at her and shook his head. "Resisting you is...difficult for me."

She couldn't help but feel flattered and relieved that her inability to resist him was at least mutual.

"The times we had, in public, were those the first times you've been intimate like that in public?"

She laughed outright. "Yes."

"What do you think about it?"

"I mean...I don't know how to feel about it. I can't even believe I did that."

The smile still hadn't left his face. "How did it make you feel, though?"

"It was sexy," she said. "*Very* sexy. But I was worried that those girls were going to come barging in the dressing room or demand that we leave. I was freaking out on the inside."

"But there was a point in time when you didn't care if they *did* barge in," he guessed, pressing his foot on the accelerator pedal when the traffic light turned green. "I saw it. I saw it and it turned me on."

The butterflies in her stomach were going crazy. The sun had long since set, but you couldn't tell from how many people were outside laughing, loving, and enjoying life. "I felt...like a sex goddess," she said after several moments.

He continued to drive with one hand. His other hand slid across the console and squeezed her thigh. "You were," he confirmed.

When Destiny and André returned to his condo, he led her into what he referred to as the playroom. The name was fitting, considering there were a myriad of toys stored there. He explained what each device, toy, and prop was. Some were for fun and play, while others were used to carry out punishments. Some items could be used for both pleasure *and* behavior correction.

There was so much information to remember, she felt like disappointing him was inevitable. There were certain ways to greet him, specifics on how she should sit during relaxation time, and his permission required for routine things that had become habitual for her. All of that was expected of her and they hadn't even begun training yet.

"How did women respond to you when you explained your interests to them?" she asked curiously. "I'm trying to imagine their reactions to you showing them some of this stuff."

"Some women looked at me like I was crazy," he admitted, laughing. "Others ran the other way and never looked back. A lot of them at least gave it a chance. After giving it a chance, about half of them decided that this kind of life was not for them, which I had to respect. This way of living is not for everyone."

"Dating had to be daunting for you," she remarked. "Never knowing who would give it a shot and who would call it quits then and there."

He shrugged. "To be honest, that was my dating life even *before* I introduced BDSM into it. Some women were okay with my celebrity lifestyle, whereas others walked away because they couldn't stand the craziness of it all. From the outside looking in, dating a celebrity can seem appealing, but my partners tend to go through a lot of grief. The media digs up their identities and sometimes stalks them. Women can be overt when flirting with me, even when I have a woman on my arm. Whenever I am interested in a woman, I am automatically asking a lot of her. I am asking for her to be a phenomenal woman. I am asking for her to put up with my crazy life. I am asking her to submit herself to me completely and totally. That is a lot to ask of a person."

"And you still ask it."

A hint of a smile teased his lips as he affirmed, "I still ask it, yes."

"Have you ever come across a woman who made you consider giving up the whole BDSM thing?"

"Yes," he replied, "but it never got past the point of me considering. At this point, the lifestyle is ingrained in me. I cannot separate myself from it; it is a part of me now. Incorporating the lifestyle into my relationship is just as important as the woman I choose to be my partner."

She reached out and touched one of the silk blindfolds on the nearest shelf. "That's deep."

"If you remain involved with me after our contract period, you shouldn't do so in the hopes that I will ever renounce the lifestyle in order to be with you," he said, and his tone was very serious.

"The lifestyle is here to stay, got it," she acknowledged, trying to ignore the disappointment dropping into the pit of her stomach.

He approached her and brushed the back of his hand against the side of her face. "Some aspects of the life that I lead are overwhelming, especially at first. There is still so much for you to learn and experience. While it may be difficult for you to imagine now, I suspect that some of my preferences will resonate with you. It is quite possible that over time, you will grow to love it as much as I do."

Pfft. As dismissive as she wanted to be about all of this, she couldn't help but admit she was curious. If he wasn't even willing to consider having a relationship outside of BDSM, there had to be some redeeming qualities about it.

After they left the playroom, they relaxed in the living room for a bit. She asked his permission to respond to text messages while he set up a hookah machine near the couch.

TEXT FROM: Carlos Villegas
MESSAGE: *I can sense the multiple orgasms all the way from here, bitch. Where are you? Why aren't you responding to texts? Has anyone told you that you are a horrible friend? You don't give me deets or juice. You're leaving me to my own imagination - which is running completely wild, let me tell you. Text me back.* ☺

TEXT FROM: Jasmine Brown
MESSAGE: *This is your weekly reminder that if things don't work out with you and Mr. Right Now, I will gladly take your place.* ☺ *Just kidding, of course. I think.*

TEXT FROM: Candace Patterson
MESSAGE: *Girl, I think this guy might be the one. You know me. I have never said that before. I need help, though, because I'm thinking of taking that next step with him. You know - THE step. I need tips, pointers, wisdom, tricks, I need it all. When would be a good time to call you? I don't know what kind of schedule you're on these days.*

TEXT FROM: Mama Bear
MESSAGE: *Your father is driving me crazy, asking about you. How are things there? Has work started? Is it too soon to be asking that?*

A cloud of hookah smoke billowed around André and spread throughout the room. She sniffed the air. There was a sweet scent to the smoke. The multicolored light from the lamp near the couch gave the smoke a magenta hue.

She typed in responses to her friends and parents with her feet tucked underneath her. It felt weird, kneeling on the floor with André seated on the couch behind her. His movements were subtle, but at times she could tell he was peering over her shoulder at her phone. Perfectly round smoke rings floated past her while she typed.

When he finished smoking, he announced that dinner that evening would be shrimp with sautéed vegetables.

"Do you always eat this healthy?"

"I alternate between periods of bulking and cutting," he explained. "During bulking periods, I eat carbs and other crazy shit. Those are periods when I am trying to put on a massive amount of weight. After I put the weight on, then I start cutting. That is when I work out and eat healthy to build muscle, shed fat and gain definition. Now happens to be a cutting period for me."

"I was just curious," she said. *Mainly because most guys I know call salad and veggies rabbit food.* "I always made a vow to myself that I would start eating healthier, but that's easier said than done in college."

"In college, you were probably always on the run, or in need of a meal that was quick," he guessed. "With my career, I faced some of those same challenges. I just had to make it a priority."

"Can I ask you something?" she asked while he sautéed vegetables in a large pan.

"May," he corrected, stirring the vegetables in the pan. "I let that slide a couple of times, but you're a writer. You should know better."

Burying the urge to scowl at him, she rephrased, "*May* I ask you something?"

"May you ask me something..."

She sighed deeply.

He glanced at her over his shoulder while continuing to stir.

"May I ask you something, *Sir?*" she asked him.

"Yes, you may."

"Would you ever consider rapping or singing again? Or is that something you're completely against?"

He stopped stirring and turned to face her. "I thought you were going to ask something related to your training. What inspired that question?"

"I was remembering the first night we were... together," she said, avoiding his gaze, "and I remembered how you sounded when you were singing. Your voice...it seems like a shame that you aren't still sharing it with the world. It seems like the fans we ran into at the mall agree. I'm sure everyone who was at my graduation agrees. All over social media, your fans are hoping you'll drop an album at some point."

She had expected him to soak up the compliment. To her surprise, his expression grew somber. "This isn't a subject that I really like to talk about."

"Oh. I'm sorry."

His eyes were *so* sad.

His sadness tugged at her heartstrings. "Permission to speak freely, Sir?" she asked him.

He lifted his eyes and stared at her. "You may..." He hesitated and looked down again. "Yes, you may speak freely," he said finally. There was a look in his eyes that begged her not to make him regret the decision.

No pressure, Destiny, he just might hate you after what you have to say, she thought. "I want..." She nervously chewed on her bottom lip. "I just want to make sure that you know you can talk to me about anything. Even things you don't talk about with anyone else. I mean, didn't you say that this lifestyle is about trust and not being judged?"

"You are correct."

"I wouldn't judge you," she vowed. "I'm here for you. I'm on your side. I just...I just wanted you to know that." She bowed her head and stared down at the floral print pattern on the skirt of her dress.

She felt the heat of his gaze on her long after the words she spoke. Then he slowly walked around the counter and came to stand in front of her. He just stood there, with his arms still crossed over his chest. It was a posture that one of Destiny's psychology courses claimed was defensive. "I'm not sure if I deserve you."

When she dared to look at him, his dark eyes were filled with emotion. Gratitude.

"Thank you, Destiny. You're completely right. Since you are my submissive, I should trust you enough to talk to you about anything. I am the one that is failing you here. Talking about entertaining...is hard for me."

"Because you miss it?" she asked him, her voice barely above a whisper. She didn't know when permission to speak freely expired.

The muscle in his jaw twitched. He looked away from her and took a deep breath. "Yes, because I miss it," he replied. "A day doesn't go by that I don't miss it."

"Why wouldn't you just go back to it?" she pressed.

He ran a hand over the top of his head. "Because... because it's not easy to do that after having stepped away from all of it," he told her. "I told myself that I wouldn't be a middle-aged entertainer still rapping about money and women and cars. Other artists are out now. My job now is to support them. I can't just abandon my current position and go back to being an entertainer."

Her brows furrowed. "Didn't you support your artists while you were entertaining though? You collaborated with them, toured with them, and posted about them on social media."

"I did, yes."

"Then why-"

"I don't want to talk about this, Destiny."

Her next questions died in her throat, but her frustration continued to fester. "At some point, you're going to have to talk about this."

"You've spoken freely," he stated. "Now, that time has passed."

She felt and probably *looked* hurt for the briefest moment before she fixed her face into a blank expression.

He returned to the stove and continued preparing their dinner.

"I still think you should go back to entertaining," she said stubbornly.

"Destiny, I'm warning you."

"You can punish me if you want," she told him. "But you should still be making music. You can't deny that. You *know* it. That's why you don't want to talk about it. You're just...scared. It's okay to be scared. Just because you're this...Dominant guy, doesn't mean that you aren't allowed to feel scared sometimes. You haven't been an entertainer for a while and you probably don't know if people would accept you if you tried to do it again. It's okay to feel that way, but don't let it keep you from rapping and singing when your voice and words are beyond amazing, André. The fans that we saw in the mall and everyone who rapped your song at my graduation… those are all positive indicators that you *would* be accepted if you tried entertaining again."

His arm froze in mid-air at the mention of his name, but he didn't speak.

She closed her eyes and cursed under her breath. "I mean, Sir," she said in a small voice. *I've really stepped into it now. He's pissed off at me. He hates me and is already regretting having signed into a contract with me.*

He finished making dinner, arranged the vegetables and shrimp on a plate for her, and led her to the dining room table. All of this, he did without speaking one word. Then, he returned to the kitchen and made a plate for himself.

Instead of eating right away, she watched him. He made his plate and carried the plate with him as he returned to her. "When you're done with your dinner, you are to stay seated at this table for the remainder of the evening. I will come to collect the plate from you and after that, I will return once you are allowed to leave this table. Is that understood?"

Tears started to well up in her eyes, but she nodded.

"Is. That. Understood?" he repeated, his voice seething with anger.

"Yes, Sir, I understand," she said, fighting to keep the tears from falling.

He turned away from her and carried his plate upstairs, to his home office, where he ate alone.

She lowered her eyes to her plate, trying to keep her composure. And failing.

After she finished eating, she continued to sit at the table, as instructed. During her punishment, she had time to think about her actions. She tried to put herself in his shoes so she could try to understand why he'd gotten so angry with her.

He'd been subtle in expressing his anger, but she'd seen the flash in his eyes. *And now he's withdrawing from me,* she thought. *Or at least, that's what it feels like. He isn't even willing to sit down to dinner with me, all because I tried to help him see just how important music is to him.*

She heard sounds upstairs, the clinking of silverware. Then she heard his footsteps on the staircase. He appeared a moment later, holding a dinner plate that he'd cleared. He walked over to the table, gathered her dishes, and carried them to the kitchen.

Her heart clenched as he walked away from her. She desperately wanted to say something. For some reason, she felt like apologizing would only make matters worse. The last thing she wanted to do was intensify his anger.

He passed by her again but didn't stop by the table. Instead, he sauntered into the living room and sat on the couch. He picked up the remote control from the coffee table and turned the television on. After some time, sweet hookah smoke wafted over to the table.

For the first hour or so, listening to the television served as entertainment for her, something to keep her from being bored beyond belief. But after that point, even the sounds of television couldn't save her from boredom. She leaned her head on her hand, and soon she was blinking slowly. Tiredly.

It was at this point, when she was teetering between consciousness and unconsciousness, that he finally spoke. "Do you understand why you're being punished?"

She straightened her posture and rubbed her eyes. "No, I do not, Sir," she said.

He was seated on the couch with one foot resting on the knee of his other leg, arms spread across the back of the couch. "Why do you think you're being punished?"

"Because I hurt your feelings or your ego by telling you the truth," she said flatly. Then, almost as an afterthought, she added, "Sir."

"You are incorrect."

She stared down at the table.

"You are being punished because you failed to obey a simple command," he explained. "I instructed you to stop speaking and you showed a blatant disregard for that instruction. Even in the early stages of training, that is not something that I can tolerate. You knew better than to do that. You said that I could go ahead and punish you, you wouldn't care, and that is not an attitude I can encourage over the course of this training. When I express to you that I prefer not to talk about something, it is your duty as my submissive to respect my wishes instead of pushing those boundaries. I give instructions. You follow them. Those are our roles in this arrangement."

His words stung.

"Do you now understand why I punished you?" he asked her.

"Yes, Sir," she said.

"I want you to come to me," he said.

With her head bowed, she stood from the table and took a step towards him.

"I don't want you to walk to me."

She halted her steps, frowning in confusion.

He lifted his hand and pointed an index finger down at the floor. "I want you to crawl to me."

She almost laughed out loud. *Is he serious?*

"Any hesitation will result in punishment," he advised, the expression on his face quite serious.

She lowered onto her hands and knees, trying to ignore how awkward and silly this felt. *Is this an extension of the first punishment he gave me? What is the point of having me crawl to him?*

He remained silent on the couch, patiently waiting for her to come to him.

When she pictured herself crawling, the image that formed in her mind looked comical. Far from sexy. Still, she crawled out of the dining room and into the living room. She didn't stop until she reached his feet.

He pointed to the side of his right knee. "Kneel. Here. Facing the television."

She positioned herself in a kneeling position, resting back on her haunches with her hands folded on top of her thighs.

"Good girl. I have something for you. I'm going to get it. I'll be right back." He stood from the couch and left the room.

She continued to focus her eyes on the television, but she couldn't have named the show that was on. Her mind was elsewhere, wondering why he'd wanted to see her crawl towards him, why he'd gotten so angry with her to begin with. That led to her wondering what she'd truly gotten herself into, and whether or not she would be able to handle it.

When he returned, he held what looked like a black leather strap in his hands. He reclaimed his seat on the couch and reached out to touch her shoulder.

She flinched away from his touch, thinking that he was going to hit her with the strap. Maybe her punishment wasn't over after all.

"I'm not going to hurt you, Destiny." There was a hint of concern in his voice.

She turned her head, not quite brave enough to look him in the eyes.

He smoothed her hair over one shoulder and gently touched the back of her neck. "I had to punish you because you disobeyed a direct order," he explained, his voice still soft, "but that doesn't mean that I disagree with you. You have given me something to think about. When I give you an order, though, I expect you to obey it."

The apologetic tone in his voice gave her the courage to look at him.

"I had time to think while I was eating alone upstairs," he said. "And you may be right. About everything." He lowered his gaze and stared at the leather strap in his hands. "This isn't a belt. It isn't something that is used for hitting. This is a leather collar. By wearing this collar, you are agreeing to submit to me completely. This piece of leather serves as a reminder that you belong to me."

She looked down at the leather in his hands.

"No one else has worn this," he said, stroking the leather with his fingertips. "I bought this collar for you. This is the first time I am offering to collar a submissive before she has passed training. I'm not offering this to you because of your opinions regarding my music career. I am offering this to you because of what you said before the opinion you gave. When you told me that I can talk to you about anything, that you're on my side, I appreciated that more than I can say. There is no doubt in my mind that I want you as my submissive. Even though you've signed the contract, I am still giving you one last chance to back out. Whether or not you accept this collar is your choice."

According to the contract, he was supposed to be her Dominant, in charge of her well-being. There were times when his words or actions gave her the feeling that he *was* a man who could very well care for her. But there were also times when she glimpsed small cracks in that strong, brave, strong-willed persona. Those glimpses revealed a man who was broken. Not a man that needed fixing, per se, but a man that needed to be cared for as much as he needed to be the provider of care. Should she get out now, while the getting was good? Or should she stand by his side and be that person who cares for him? Wasn't caring for each other what real relationships were about? After some deliberation, she said, "I accept."

"Kneel in front of me," he ordered.

She followed the instruction without pause.

He smoothed her hair again. "Hold your hair for me."

She swept her hair to one side and held onto it.

He reached his arms around her and secured the collar around her neck. Checked its tightness to make sure she wasn't uncomfortable. Then he lowered his head and pressed a kiss to her shoulder, his lips caressing her skin through the fabric of her short-sleeved dress. "Thank you for reminding me that I could trust in you," he whispered. "Once you complete training, there is another collar that I will give to you, one that looks...prettier than this one."

"I'm sorry for not respecting your feelings earlier," she told him. "I wanted to apologize to you while sitting at the table, but I thought I would make you angrier if I did. I know I disobeyed you. I was just trying to encourage you and inspire you. That's all."

His hands stilled. Then he kneeled on the floor with her and wrapped his arms around her.

Her heart swelled to the point that it felt like it would explode. All of this was quite perplexing. Only moments before, she'd been sentenced to a Time Out of sorts, as if she were a preschooler. *I feel like I should be running away from him instead of towards him,* she thought. And yet whenever he showed true affection, it felt there was another dimension to his actions.

Her heart filled with emotion, happiness, and she hated to admit it, but love. Love was also there.

13

The following morning, Destiny awoke to the sound of loud running water. She lifted her head off the pillow and quickly surveyed the bedroom. André was nowhere in sight, not in bed beside her. Nowhere in the room. She sat up and rubbed her eyes.

The previous night, he'd worked late in his home office while she slept. By the time he'd joined her in bed, she was taking a tour of slumberland. She faintly remembered the sensation of him wrapping her arms around her, but that could have been a figment of her imagination.

She brought a hand up to her hair and extended one curl. *I'm in dire need of a trip to a salon, stat.*

André strode into the room, bare-chested and wearing nothing but ocean blue pajama pants. He held a towel in his hands and used it to mop a sheen of sweat from his face. "Good morning," he greeted.

"Good morning, Sir," she returned, her voice still raspy with sleep.

He ran the towel across his chest while moving across the room.

The sight of his tattooed torso definitely had an effect on her. She had to turn her attention elsewhere just to be capable of coherent thought. "Did you just finish working out?" she asked, the loud running water nearly drowning out her voice.

"Yes," he responded. After wiping the sweat from both of his arms, he dropped the towel into a silver cylindrical clothes hamper. "Tomorrow, I want you to start working out with me. I almost woke you up today, but you were sleeping so peacefully. I couldn't bring myself to wake you. Now that you *are* awake, I'd like for you to come with me."

She pushed the sheets and covers aside and stood up. Last night, she'd worn one of his dress shirts to bed. Now, she nervously tugged on one of the cuffs as she followed him into the master bathroom.

Standing near a beautifully tiled bathtub, he bent at the waist and lowered the faucet handle to cut off the running water. The tub was rectangular in shape, and deeper than any tub she'd ever seen. Billows of steam rose up from the clouds of bubbles resting on top of the bathwater.

She was hypnotized by the flexing of his back muscles as he dipped two of his fingers into the water so he could test its temperature. The tattoos on his back rippled with every movement he made.

He straightened and angled a look at her. "What?"

She blinked and lifted her eyes. "Um...you have a nice back." *You have a nice back? Could I possibly be any more awkward?*

He laughed and beckoned her over. "Come here."

She walked over to him.

He affectionately touched her hair, a smile curving his lips. "We need to make a salon appointment for you."

"Is that your way of saying my hair looks like a hot mess?" she queried, lightly touching her hair. Despite having the very same thought just minutes ago, she now felt self-conscious.

He shook his head. "No. It's my way of saying we need to make a salon appointment for you. I think a salon visit once a week is reasonable." He lowered his hand from her hair to the collar of the dress shirt she was wearing. "This shirt looks better on you than it does on me."

Her face brightened at the flattery.

His eyes held hers captive. With his smoldering gaze threatening to burn right through her, he slipped the top button of the shirt through its hole. Then he proceeded to unbutton the rest of the shirt, perching on the edge of the tub once he got to the lower buttons. When the lapels of the plain white dress shirt fell open, he drank in the sight of her body with hungry eyes. Those dark eyes locked with hers as he leaned forward and pressed a kiss to her stomach. He pulled back and smoothed his hand down the flat curve of her belly. "Shirt off," he commanded softly.

She slid the sleeves of the dress shirt down her arms and allowed the garment to fall to the floor.

His finger moved from her collarbone to her pelvis. "You have the most amazing skin."

Her cheeks grew hot. Other areas grew hotter.

His gaze was passionate, intense. "In the tub. Now."

While she settled in the tub, he knelt to the floor and picked up the dress shirt. She stole quick glances at him as he folded the dress shirt and set it on top of the sink counter. He eyed his own reflection for a moment before removing his pajama pants. Those pants joined the folded dress shirt on top of the sink counter, and then he moved out of sight. When he returned to the tub, he came bearing towels. "Scoot forward."

She planted her hands on the bathtub floor and slid forward.

He stepped into the tub and lowered himself behind her, causing small splashes of water to lap up at her back. He set two folded washcloths on the edge of the tub. Then, he lifted the wrist of her right hand and pulled off the black hair tie tightly circled around it. "I know it's convenient to wear these around your wrist and it's proving to be very convenient now," he told her, "but from now on, don't wear these on your wrist. It's bad for your circulation."

"Yes, Sir," she responded.

He gathered her curly hair in his hands and wound it into a bun at the top of her head. Some tendrils escaped the bun, but he left them and even playfully pulled on one. With her hair secured and out of the way, he reached over and grabbed one of the folded washcloths.

She was aware of movements he was making behind her, but she couldn't see everything he was doing. There was the sound of a cap popping open, and then he was dipping the washcloth in the bathwater to dampen it.

"I want you to tell me something about yourself that I don't already know," he said as he squeezed body wash onto the washcloth.

"Hmm. Well...I've written ever since I was little. Ever since I *could* write, I did."

"Really? What did you write? Not articles all the way back then, so...what? Stories?"

After the question was asked, she felt the warm cloth being pressed to the back of her neck. Her back arched and she found herself leaning into his hand as he worked the washcloth up and down her back. "I did write articles, actually. Whenever something dramatic happened in our family, I would write an article about it. Then I'd sell the article to them."

"You charged them to read about their own drama?" he asked, laughing. "Savage."

She laughed along with him. "A quarter a pop. They bought them, too. Goes to show how much people love drama."

"Or maybe they loved you and wanted to support your writing," he suggested, continuing to wash her back.

"Maybe," she said, tilting her head back. "I miss them *so* much. One of the toughest parts about being in college was being far away from them. I can't wait to see them."

"We can fly out to see them next week."

Her head whipped around quickly enough to give her something akin to whiplash. "*We*?" she repeated.

He dipped the washcloth into the water again. "You don't want me to come with you?" he asked wryly.

"I didn't say that. I just..." She faltered, unable to find the words to express how she felt about him visiting her family. "I guess I just...didn't expect you to *want* to come with me. We aren't in a real relationship or anything."

"Our relationship may not be traditional, but it's just as real as any other," he said, squeezing more body wash onto the towel. "I would be interested in having a better understanding of where you come from, *who* you come from. I met your parents very briefly at your graduation ceremony. They seemed very nice and supportive of you. I would like the chance to sit down with them. Understand how you came out to be this...amazing, unique creature."

"I'm flattered, but..."

"But...?"

"I wouldn't know how to act around you, with my family there," Destiny worded carefully. "The thought of you being in the same room with them...kind of frightens me, to be honest."

He laughed outright. "Frightens you?" he repeated.

"I don't know, I just get this image in my head of you putting me over your knee and spanking me right in front of my parents," she mumbled.

He continued laughing while washing her arms. "I'm not a complete degenerate," he said. "I wouldn't do something like that in front of your family. Most aspects of that lifestyle are for us to experience in private. Any public play we decide to participate in wouldn't be in the presence of your mom and dad."

"We would be a normal couple for that time period?" she asked.

"I'm not a fan of the word *normal*," he reminded her. "But we would give the impression that we are a vanilla couple, yes."

She lifted her eyebrows. "Oh."

He smiled knowingly. "I had a feeling you'd like that. Stand up and turn around to face me."

Holding onto the railing attached to the wall, she stood and turned around.

"Tell me something else about yourself that I don't know," he requested as he proceeded to wash her legs.

She focused on the ceiling and exhaled. "Hmmm...I had my first kiss when I was twelve, and my first boyfriend at sixteen," she confessed. "When it comes to intimacy and all of that...I started pretty late."

"I could tell," he said.

She frowned. "What is *that* supposed to mean?"

He raised his eyes and stared at her.

"I mean, was I...bad?"

He gave a slight shake of his head. "No. But there's something very pure and very innocent about you. It's a part of what makes you so irresistible. When I think about it, it's kind of crazy. Throughout most of my adult life, I've had an interest in experienced women. In many ways, you are the complete opposite of my usual type."

"In what ways?" she asked quietly.

"Your innocence and inexperience, as I've mentioned."

"I'm not a virgin," she muttered defensively.

"No, but you are a lot less experienced than I'm used to," he responded. "Also, a lot younger than I am used to. I tend to date older women, or women my own age."

Does that mean he finds me inferior to those women? she couldn't help but wonder.

He continued to wash her. "It's not good or bad." When she didn't respond right away, he added softly, "And I think you already know how much I enjoy what you do to me and your reactions to what I do to you. I don't think I need to remind you of that."

Her cheeks flushed and she finally met his gaze.

He finished washing her, then told her to stand in the shower and wait for him. He drained the tub and joined her in the shower. "Baths are a great way to relax and decompress," he told her, "but for as long as I can remember, I've never been a fan of the thought of sitting in dirty bathwater. After taking a bath, I always shower. If you ever take baths without me, you are to do the same."

"I always shower after bathing, for the same reason."

"Good girl." After twisting the shower knob, he pressed the screen on the control panel. Soft, melodic music started to play. He turned and pressed a fresh washcloth into her hands as plump water droplets fell from the showerhead above them. "Wash me."

There was something undeniably appealing about a man's chest, shoulders, and abdomen and that was doubly the case for instances when those body parts were covered in steady streams of water. His muscles rippled beneath the water pouring down his skin.

"You're hesitating," he said, but his voice was light. Teasing.

"I'm sorry," she was quick to say, fumbling for the bottle of body wash that sat on the shower ledge. After dampening the washcloth, she wiped his brow and drew the cloth down to his jawbone. Aware that his eyes were on her, she applied a dab of translucent bodywash to the washcloth. It was tough focusing on the task at hand when he was fucking her with those dark, beautiful eyes. She ran the washcloth down his neck, shoulder, one arm and across his chest, slowly circling each pectoral muscle. Her hand fell away from him as she took a minute to admire how gorgeous he was.

"Done already?"

She shook her head, wrung out the washcloth, and dampened it with water again.

His eyes lowered from her oversaturated hair, to her face, to her body.

She followed his gaze, saw beads of water rolling down the crest of both breasts. Was she as beautiful to him as he was to her? *I wish I knew what was going through his mind right now.* Instead of trying to guess, she continued washing him. With water cascading all around her, she knelt to the shower floor and moved the washcloth along the angles of his pelvis.

"Seeing you kneel in front of me like this is enough to make me want to pick you up, slam you against the wall, and fuck the shit out of you," he said bluntly. "Since I feel like I am putting too much emphasis on sex, though, I'm trying to resist that urge." As if to prove his point, he remained immobile as she washed him. Only one part of him seemed stubborn and moved on its own.

When she was finished washing him, she looked up at him.

"You can stand," he allowed.

She stood up, wringing the washcloth out with both hands.

Staring at her intently, he took a step forward. He braced his hands on the shower stall wall on either side of her, lowering his eyes to her lips. "Open."

Giving him a confused look, she opened her mouth.

He slid his index finger between her open lips. "Suck."

She flicked her tongue along the length of his finger, raised her hands to cover his hand, and started to gently suck his finger.

He groaned and pushed her against the wall. His face contorted as he struggled to keep his own libido in check. "How am I supposed to resist you when you look so damned delicious all the time?" he demanded. "As your Dominant, I'm supposed to be in control at all times, but how can I be in control when the sight of you, even fully clothed, turns me on so damned much? When one single touch from you drives me crazy?"

Caught off-guard by his outburst, she blinked at him.

He withdrew his finger and kissed her. It was a gentle kiss that grew to be deeper, more demanding. Then he was pressing her into the shower stall wall with water pouring over them. It didn't take long for his hands to roam over her body, and then it was impossible for either of them to stop. Together, they both teetered on the edge of losing control.

Following their steamy shower, André announced that he was going to make crêpes for breakfast. He gestured for her to sit at the counter and proceeded to describe his daily routine in greater detail. "On a normal weekday, I get up, work out, shower, and make a healthy breakfast," he advised, whisking eggs and flour into a mixing bowl. "After eating breakfast, I dress and head to work. During the week, my days are generally filled with meetings and conference calls. Within the next few days, I will give you a tour of the office so you have an idea of where you will be working. What I do after work depends on whether there are any important business functions that require my presence. There are concerts, parties, and interviews that I am expected to show up for. If my company is hosting a charity event, I prefer to be there. On nights when I have nothing scheduled, I may meet up with a friend. On nights I spend at home, sometimes I read, catch up on a show that I'm behind on, or check in with friends and family. Sometimes I'm required to take work home with me. It all depends on what is going on."

"Will your schedule remain pretty much the same with me here?" she asked.

He paused before answering. "That would depend on whether or not you choose to live with me throughout the contract period. If you live with me, most evenings will be dedicated to your training. Occasionally, I will test you on the knowledge you have retained. If you decide to live on your own, you'd have the option of only training on the weekends."

"How long does training typically last?"

"That can depend on the submissive. A submissive who has been trained previously and is well-versed in the lifestyle may only need to learn my personal preferences. Someone like you who has to learn the key elements of the lifestyle, the tools of the trade, the safety aspects involved, *and* my personal preferences would require significantly more time to train. The bulk of your training could wind up taking a full month. That isn't counting the ongoing learning that will be required of you throughout the rest of our time together."

Out of our six months together, a full month will be dedicated to training? she wondered in disbelief.

"My advice is to take your training a day at a time and retain what you can. Whenever in doubt, ask me. Do you have any questions before we begin training for the day?"

"What do you have against pants?"

"What do I have against pants?" His face puckered in confusion.

"You said that I should always wear skirts or dresses."

"Skirts and dresses are feminine, demure. I prefer them. I also prefer the access that they give me." As he spoke, he added other ingredients to the mixing bowl: a dash of sugar, whole milk, water, and a few drops of vanilla extract. Then, he resumed whisking while she struggled to figure out how it was possible for her to find even that action hot. "During your training and when we are out in public, you are required to wear either a skirt or a dress. You will be permitted to wear yoga pants or shorts when we are working out. You will also be permitted to wear lingerie or sexy eveningwear for me. Those are the only exceptions, barring any special circumstances."

No more leggings, no more ripped jeans or cute shorts. How many times was he going to break her heart, really?

"You're pouting. I take it that you don't care for that rule."

Unaware that she'd been pouting, she attempted to fix her face. "I'm going to miss wearing shorts and jeans."

"When you are out and about, you are a representation of me," he explained. "People will see you on my arm and they will be curious about you. Everything about you will be evaluated, from your clothes to your hair, to your makeup, to your posture, to the way you speak, and the way you carry yourself. You are to be mindful of that and ensure that you are sitting or standing straight, without slouching. You should speak clearly and with confidence. Continually introduce new words into your vocabulary, something you should strive to do anyway, since you are a journalist. I will pay for your hair and nail salon visits. I am also willing to pay for your wardrobe, and any other expenses incurred from the requests I am making of you. Your face is naturally beautiful, so any makeup you wear should be minimal. Whenever you walk into any room, walk with the confidence that comes with knowing you are mine."

His words sent a shiver crawling up her spine. "When we are at public events, how am I supposed to act?"

"Vanilla," he responded. "Our visit to your family will be good practice for how you should interact with me when we are in public. I'm not looking to raise eyebrows at corporate functions or public events."

"When we go to visit my family, and when we are at business functions, I no longer need to ask permission before answering text messages or phone calls?"

"During business events, your phone will be in my possession," he answered, setting the whisk in the sink. He carried the mixing bowl to the refrigerator and placed it inside. "You will have the ability to check your phone after the event."

She took a deep breath.

"People have their faces in their phones all the time these days," he said with a dismissive wave of his hand. "While we are at a business function, our attention should be on that function, not on messages from Carlos."

"I understand, Sir."

"Because you will be on my arm at these events, our relationship won't be a secret for long. In the office, you will still refer to me as André or Mr. Gaines. We must remain professional in the office at all times."

"I understand, Sir."

"I booked our Phoenix flight for next Tuesday. I'll text you the flight details so you can let your family know our arrival time. Before we make that trip, I want to give you a tour of the office and have you fill out the necessary paperwork to begin employment with Gaines Enterprises.

Our office in Los Angeles will process your employment paperwork."

This is really my life now. For the next six months, I will belong to this man, and work for this man, and spend nearly every minute of the day aiming to please this man. Something told her that all the information he had given her was only the tip of the iceberg. This was only a peek into what her life would be like for the next six months and not the full picture.

"You will have a lot of questions as you advance in your training, and I fully encourage you to ask whatever questions come to mind. No question is too stupid if it will help you to become a better submissive for me. Do you understand?"

"Yes, Sir."

"I have a question for you. Do you consider yourself a submissive by nature?"

"I'm not sure I know what that means," was her timid reply.

"Thank you for being honest. Is it in your nature to try to please others?"

"Yes," she answered.

"Do you feel you have a nurturing personality?"

"Yes, Sir."

"When you disappoint someone, do you feel a sense of failure?"

"Don't we all?"

"Not all," he said. "Answer the question, please."

"Yes, Sir."

"Are you very critical of yourself?"

"To a fault, Sir."

"Thank you for answering my questions." He flipped up the sink faucet and promptly washed off the whisk he'd used. "The crêpe batter will take about a half an hour to chill. While we wait, I'd like to take you into the playroom and test your retention of the items you learned about yesterday."

Trying her best not to succumb to nervousness, she followed him down the hall and into the playroom.

The quiz was relatively short, and she managed to surprise herself with how many items she'd remembered.

Throughout most of the session, he'd worn a pleased smile on his face. "Some of these items won't be fully understood until they are experienced," he said, standing beside a large wooden structure at the back of the room. "I can explain to you the benefits of sensory deprivation, but until you've felt those benefits for yourself, you will not understand how enjoyable it can be. It is the same with some of the other items in here."

"Some of the things in here look very intimidating," she said cautiously. *"Scary"* was the first word to come to mind, but she didn't want to offend him.

The way he touched some of the items as he walked around the room, it seemed that some of them were an extension of him. "Everything new seems crazy and intimidating, until it becomes a part of your daily life. Then you find yourself waking up and looking forward to it. Some more time passes, and you feel *off* if you go a day without it."

"I can't imagine feeling that way about this stuff," she said, tugging on the shackles mounted into the walls.

"Give it time. Remember that once upon a time, I was like you. I didn't know that this world existed. Someone had to introduce me to it. All of this seemed crazy at first, so I questioned everything. I questioned why she would be interested in doing these things and my own sanity for being curious about it. I questioned whether I was weird for liking some of this shit. Becoming involved in this life has taught me a great deal about who I am. It helped to realize why I prefer some of the sexual acts I prefer in the bedroom, such as rough sex or edging."

"Edging?" she echoed.

"All in due time," he promised with a wink.

She moved around the room. Most of the wall space was padded, the only exception being a small area of wall where the shackles were mounted. "What is up with the padding on the walls? Did you have that done just in case one of your girls goes crazy?"

"Soundproofing," he responded, giving the nearest wall a pat. "Different levels of pain and pleasure are felt in this room, and I do not want that to cause any disruptions for my neighbors."

She had to respect the fact that even though he was into all of this, he still cared enough about others to pay for soundproofing. That couldn't have been cheap.

He answered a few more of her questions and then they broke to eat. They returned to the kitchen and he removed the mixing bowl from the fridge. All she could do was watch him in fascination as he proceeded to cook crêpes. One minute, they were talking about rough sex, and the next he was standing at a stove making her breakfast.

Did he find himself having to explain everything he had explained to her, to all the submissives who signed contracts with him? The life that he led generated a lot of dialogue. There were so many questions she'd asked him, and there were many more questions burning beneath the surface. *It can't be easy, having to explain all of this each time,* she thought, feeling a twinge of sympathy for him. *I'd get tired of repeating myself whenever I meet someone new.*

But isn't that a part of the dating process? Whenever you start dating someone, you tell them about yourself. If it doesn't work out, you're having to do the same thing with the next person. It's not much different from that.

He was quiet while he cooked, and she appreciated the silence. It was a chance for her to reflect upon what they'd discussed. She felt like she was beginning to peel back the layers that made up the man she was trying desperately not to fall for. The silence was briefly interrupted when he asked what kind of filling she wanted in her crêpe, and again when he expressed surprise at her choosing cheese and mushrooms.

The crêpe he made was delicious, and discussion was kept light. The sweet crêpe he'd made for himself was filled with fruit and topped with a hazelnut spread.

After breakfast, it was back to training. He told her that he would prepare most meals, while she would be responsible for the cleaning. "I do have a housekeeper come in weekly, and she goes over the place with a fine-tooth comb. The cleaning you would be responsible for is just daily upkeep. Dishes, laundry, things of that nature."

"Will I ever get the chance to cook for you?"

Warmth lit up his eyes, and he looked like he might be holding back a smile. "Thank you for wanting to cook for me. If you did make anything for me, I'd want it to be scallops. Pan seared. My tastes are pretty particular, as I've said before, but I can show you the way I prepare my dishes."

When she thought to check her phone, she had missed calls and text messages from Carlos, Jasmine, Candace, and her parents. It was always a bit jarring to see their names in her notifications list. There was an entire side to herself that she couldn't share with them.

As instructed, she asked for André's permission before answering phone calls or text messages. He wanted to see the text messages before she responded to them, which amused her. Why was he so possessive to the point of wanting to make sure that other men weren't texting her? It seemed silly, when they both knew that he would be seeing other women.

Awaiting his permission before answering a text or phone call, in and of itself, was not as easy as it would seem. When her phone rang, it was habitual for her to grab it and answer it. Fulfilling this request required a complete rewiring of her brain impulses.

Against her better judgment, she asked, "If this lifestyle is about trust for you, then why do I have to show you my phone before responding to calls and messages?" She'd asked the innocent question while they were relaxing in the living room, him seated on the couch with his work laptop and her kneeling on the floor at his feet.

His eyes widened at the question. "Asking permission before making a call or sending a text is a sign of respect."

"But isn't it a hassle for you? If you're in the middle of something and I interrupt you to ask if I can call Carlos back, isn't that a bother? You could just trust that I would never call or text someone that I shouldn't be speaking to."

"We are still building trust in this stage."

"I guess I get that."

"Tell me something about yourself that I don't know."

This again. "If I hadn't chosen journalism, I probably would've become a teacher."

"Really?"

"I have a lot of teachers in my family," she told him. "My grandmother was one. My mother went to school for it, but then she met my dad and got pregnant with me. One of my aunts taught elementary school and she was always decorating her classroom in the cutest ways. The kids seemed to love her. I had great teachers growing up, too. I've always had the utmost respect for them, you know?"

"My mother would be happy to hear that," he said, his voice soft.

Now it was her turn to be caught off-guard. He rarely mentioned his mother in their conversations. "Oh?" She wanted to hear more about his mother.

"She taught for a long time," he elaborated. "You could say that she is the reason I started writing. She really *was* and still *is* an amazing teacher."

"I didn't know she was a teacher. Even though I haven't met her, I already respect her."

Affection filled his gaze. "Teaching can be a thankless job at times."

"It feels like all careers have those days or phases."

"You're wise beyond your years," he remarked.

"Am I..." *Don't ask what you're thinking of asking.*

"Are you...?"

"You're going to be meeting my parents next week," she prefaced, her hands fidgeting with one of the coasters on the coffee table. "Am I ever going to meet your mom?"

"Probably," he replied, his tone casual.

"Cool." *That's it, Destiny. Just be nonchalant. Nice and easy, like meeting his mom isn't a big deal, or anything.*

"Once we're finished with dinner, there are a couple of books I'm going to assign you to read," he announced. "When I'm working, you can read these books, or clean, or conduct your own research on BDSM. I would like for you to write down any questions that pop into your head."

"Yes, Sir."

He flashed her a smile. "Good girl."

With all of the learning going on, Destiny started to feel like she was back in college. She was given material to study and was quizzed on that material. It was no wonder his mother was a teacher; some of her skills must have rubbed off on him. To André's credit, he tried to provide breaks from the monotony by showing her around his city. He showed her the lot where his home was being built. A larger-than-life skeleton of a structure stood before a beautiful, meadowy backdrop.

"Zoning has been a bit of a nightmare," was his only comment about the house. There was longing in his eyes as he'd spoken the words. It seemed like he noticed the curious expression on her face, because he attempted to change the subject. "Today is as good of a day as any for us to visit the office."

As they pulled up to the Gaines Enterprises building, Destiny pressed her hands against the car window. Her mouth dropped open in amazement.

"Unlike the office in D.C., this entire building *is* ours," André explained, seated beside her. He hadn't felt like braving the Monday morning traffic, so he'd had his driver chauffer them around for the day. "Feel free to be impressed." He unbuckled his seatbelt and leaned forward to give his driver instructions regarding when to return.

The surface of the building looked to be all glass and steel, beautifully crafted. Sunlight bounced off the glass panes. The building had a jagged, layered design.

The driver stepped out of the car and opened the door for them. Destiny accepted his offered hand and angled her head back, trying to get a full view of the building's height. Thirty stories. At *least*. When she turned her head to survey the other buildings, she realized that this building was a part of the Toronto skyline.

"Do you like it?" André asked as he stepped out of the car to join her.

"This building is so beautiful."

"Thank you. We pay a lot for it, so it had better be." He smiled and placed a guiding hand at her back. As he escorted her into the lobby, multiple sharply-dressed business executives greeted him. Just as with fans who had approached him, he was polite and courteous, but kept conversation brief.

The lobby had a classic-meets-modern elegant look to it, glossy tiled marble floors with chrome accents. He led her to a row of elevators and pressed the Up button.

"This building..." She shook her head, at a loss for words.

"This building is where your office will be located," he finished for her as the elevator doors slid open.

"Office? I get my own office?"

He laughed and gestured for her to enter the elevator.

She stepped into the elevator, suddenly feeling like her black, knee-length dress and simple black pumps were too understated for this office building.

"Your job will be very important," he informed her, following her into the elevator and pressing the button for the thirty-fifth floor. "So, yes. You will have your own office."

A horde of other people joined them on the elevator, men dressed in tailored suits and women wearing chic dress suits. Each of them carried a briefcase. There were more cordial greetings to André, who they referred to as "Mr. Gaines."

Destiny and André pressed their backs against the back wall of the elevator. They exchanged a look briefly before shifting their gazes forward.

The elevator stopped at the fourth floor and a few of the business executives got off the elevator.

André's hand lightly brushed against hers.

She looked up at him, but he was staring straight ahead, his face expressionless. She gently bumped his hand with hers, turning her focus to the front of the elevator. Out of the corner of her eye, she saw the briefest hint of a smile on his lips.

The elevator stopped on the tenth floor, and more employees stepped off the elevator.

André coughed into his left hand while grabbing her hand with his right.

Destiny's pulse raced. She was having a difficult time catching her breath. Excitement sent small electric shocks that started at her fingertips and moved up her arm and throughout her entire body.

The eighteenth floor. Two more people stepped off the elevator.

André slid closer to her and his entire arm was pressed against hers. His fingertips grazed her thigh.

She closed her eyes and parted her lips.

One of the men in front of them turned around. "André, there was a report that I needed to show you."

"I look forward to it," André responded, his fingers still caressing Destiny's thigh.

"There are some discrepancies that I want to go over," the man, a tall redhead, said while pushing thick-rimmed glasses up his nose.

"I'd be more than happy to sit with you," André said. His fingers raised slightly, teasing Destiny's hip, eliciting a small gasp from her. He arched an eyebrow at her.

The redhead man turned his gaze on Destiny. "Are you okay?"

"She's fine," André assured him.

She lowered her eyes to the elevator floor.

The man's brows furrowed, but he nodded and turned around to face the elevator doors just as they slid open to reveal the twenty-third floor. "Well, this is my stop," he announced. "We'll have that meeting soon, then?"

"Call Bridgette, have her set up a date and time," André said.

"Thank you, André."

"Anytime, Steve," André returned.

Only three other people remained on the elevator. Two of them got off on the twenty-seventh floor.

André nudged Destiny's breast with his arm.

The elevator stopped at the twenty-ninth floor and the final employee got off. The minute the doors opened, André's arm snaked around Destiny's waist. The minute the employee stepped off the elevator, he pulled Destiny closer to him. When the elevator doors started to close, he turned, pushed her against the wall, grabbed her face, and ravaged her mouth with his.

Passion threatened to overtake them. Whenever they touched, it was easy to get lost in the sensation of being joined. Somehow, when the elevator doors slid open, they were the picture-perfect display of propriety. The only hint that anything inappropriate had happened was André's hand, deftly straightening the tie at his neck. He strode off the elevator and checked over his shoulder to make sure Destiny followed.

The carpeting on the thirty-fifth floor was colorful and gorgeously patterned. Triangular sconce lights lined the hall walls, their lighting muted by the daylight pouring in the tall, narrow windows posted at each end of the hall. Straight ahead of them were large glass doors with "Gaines Enterprises" etched into the glass panes.

He opened one of the doors and led her into a formal lobby, complete with a receptionist's desk, sitting area and vertically-mounted television showing current events and company accomplishments.

The receptionist seated to the right greeted him in a cheerful, lilting voice. She was a petite blonde whose glance at André was more than brief and more than polite. He didn't seem to notice. The blonde turned her gaze to Destiny and the look of wanton lust morphed into one of curiosity.

Destiny trailed behind him as he led the way down a long walkway. General office sections stretched out to the right and left of the walkway, and these sections were buzzing with chatter, the sounds of typing, and activity. There were hushed whispers. She could only imagine what the whispering was about. *"It's Mr. Gaines! Shh! Look busy!"*

Some of the chatter died down. Several women were checking their reflections in their compact mirrors before turning to face André. She became fascinated with the effect that he had on women. He was oblivious to it all. Instead of paying the employees around him any mind, he told her which department they were passing at any given time. To the few people he *did* talk to, he introduced Destiny as their new public relations associate.

The aisle opened into another lobby with a secretary's desk placed at the right. Another television was mounted to the wall of this lobby, displaying the same events and company accomplishments. A pretty brunette wearing a headset looked up from her computer monitor as they entered. "Mr. Gaines," she greeted, removing her headset.

"Hello, Bridgette." He turned to Destiny. "Destiny, Bridgette is my executive assistant. Bridgette, Destiny is one of our new PR associates. I'm giving her a tour."

Bridgette blinked with a smile frozen on her face. "And you're going to show her your office?"

André smirked. "Is there something wrong with that?"

Bridgette shook her head, causing her dark brown waves to bounce. "Not at all," she was quick to say. She turned her attention to Destiny. "It's a pleasure to meet you, Destiny."

"It's nice to meet you too," Destiny said politely.

"Hold my calls, and anyone who comes in waits in the sitting area," André told Bridgette.

The assistant nodded, but the curious look hadn't left her eyes. "Certainly, Mr. Gaines."

André gestured for Destiny to follow and ushered her past the reception area towards another set of frosted glass doors. He pulled them open and led the way inside of an expansive office. A wall of windows faced them. Tall, potted plants marked each corner of the room. A sleek glass desk sat near the wall of windows, a huge behemoth of a desk with two plush black chairs in front of it. A bar counter with cabinets lined the wall on the right, along with a couch and entertainment center. A closet and private bathroom took up the left side of the office.

"Wow," she breathed as she walked over to the wall of windows. His office had a spectacular view of the city and Lake Ontario.

"Once in a while, hard work pays off," he said, moving to stand beside her.

Destiny shook her head. "Your life...your *entire* life, is unreal."

He smiled.

"You're more like a character in a movie," she went on. "Real people just don't live like this."

"Some do," he said quietly. "A small percentage do. I am in that group, and now, so are you."

They stood side by side in silence for several minutes, enjoying the view and each other's presence. Without warning, he turned and walked to his desk, where he took a seat.

"I take it you like the office," he said, wearing a smile that gave the indication he already knew the answer to the question.

"It's an amazing office," she remarked.

"I'll show you your office before we leave," he told her. "We will also drop by HR so you can fill out the necessary paperwork. I just want to take a minute and relax."

She moved away from the windows and sat in one of the chairs facing his desk. "I'm kind of surprised," she admitted. "I expected this floor to only have executives. It looked like you had entry-level staff out there."

He leaned back in his chair, tapping his fingers on the right armrest. "A lot of executives are full of themselves, or shit, or both," he said flatly. "In previous buildings, I've had my office on the same floor as the executives. I hated it. Most of them lacked personality - or hid their personality in favor of kissing ass to those above them. There was a lot of phoniness, and I cannot stand that for extended periods of time. That is why I bowed out of the industry and stopped doing interviews."

Her eyebrows shot up.

He smiled. "I vowed to myself that when we moved to our permanent office location, my office would be on the same floor as the front line. They are the true foundation of this company, an amazing team of people. Bright, dedicated, and pleasant to be around. I love those people out there."

"You barely acknowledged them," she pointed out.

"The women were primping for me," he explained with a shrug of his shoulders. "I don't want to encourage that kind of behavior. Whenever they start fussing with their hair like that the minute I walk in, they are ignored."

"So, you *do* know how women react to you."

"Good at reading people," he reminded her, tapping his temple. "And naturally observant."

"Just when I think you can't impress me more, you do."

"I'll go for the home run, then," he said, grinning. "The first receptionist you met, Samantha, has a crush on me. She probably hated you on sight. There are co-workers who will sit and eat lunch with her, but they all talk about her behind her back. She's too self-involved to notice that she has no real friends. Bridgette, whom you met just now, *used* to have a crush on me. Somewhere along the line, she formed the thought in her mind that I was gay - probably because I never made a pass at her. She liked to tell me stories about men who randomly hit on her. She thought stories like that would arouse my interest or make me jealous. Wrong on both counts. But that preconceived notion she had about my sexual preference, is the *only* reason why she'd be bold enough to question why I would show you my office. Right about now, she's wondering, *Could I have been wrong? Maybe he's not gay. Maybe he just didn't like me.* At which point, she would be correct. Being a woman yourself, you're credible enough to gauge my potential for accuracy. How did I do?"

She stared at him like he'd sprouted another head. "Where did you *come* from?" she asked him.

Instead of answering that hypothetical question, he showed her where her office would be located. Public relations, media, and marketing were all located on the thirty-fourth floor. The thirty-fourth floor was a lot quieter than the thirty-fifth. He introduced her to a few members of management. Then he showed her the office designated for her. It was approximately a third the size of his office and still a much larger space than she was expecting upon accepting his job offer.

The tour of the thirty-fourth floor was kept very brief. As he walked her back to the elevators, he withdrew his cell phone from his suit pants pocket and dialed his driver. "We'll be ready in about half an hour."

As soon as he ended the call, Destiny asked him, "How did you become so good at reading people?"

He chuckled as he pressed the Down button on the elevator. "You're still on that?"

"I don't think I've ever seen a man give such an on-point analysis of a female's psyche."

"Then you've never heard my songs."

"I mean someone other than you," she amended.

"I just pay attention to people," he said with a shrug. "When someone is talking, a lot of people are only half-paying attention, waiting for their own turn to speak. Me, I'm listening. Not only am I listening, but I'm watching. Picking up on quirks, gestures, subtle tics in their facial expressions. Most communication is made through body language. Once I learned that, I prioritized studying body language."

The elevator dinged and the doors opened. He gestured for her to step inside and then he followed.

"I wasn't what you would call popular in school," he explained as he pressed the button for the first floor. "If I had been, I would not be the person I am today. I would be some mediocre individual who was too busy hanging out with friends to write and rhyme and practice my craft. I'd be one of those people who waits for his chance to speak instead of listening to the person who is already speaking."

"I've never met anyone like you before," she said.

"I expect you never will again," he responded with a cocky grin.

The Human Resources and security offices were on the ground floor of the building. André led Destiny into the HR office and had her complete an official application, after explaining that it would allow the company to run the necessary background checks. "Your employment offer paperwork is being drawn up, and you'll be able to review it before your first day." To the shock of the HR staff, he sat beside her while she filled out the application and walked her out of the office once her application was submitted.

Since it was near noon, André had his driver take them to a small bistro in the heart of Toronto. The lunch crowd in the restaurant was in full effect, but he seemed not to care. "It gets a little crowded in here from time to time, but the food is totally worth it," he said as he moved between tables. He spotted a booth in the far back corner and led her to it.

As she was sliding into the booth, the phone in her purse started to ring.

He watched as she opened her purse flap and withdrew the phone from the bag.

Her heart started pounding in her chest when she saw the name flashing on her phone screen.

"Let me see it," André commanded. When he saw the name on her phone, a frown immediately morphed his features. "Chad?" he asked as the phone continued to ring in his hand.

"I don't know why he'd be calling me."

He pressed the on-screen Ignore button and handed the phone back to her. Then, he took his seat across from her. "I'm going to buy you a new phone," he said. "New phone, new number. You can give the new number to the people who need it. Your family, your friends. People like Chad and Jordan can stay in the dark."

"Yes, Sir," she said.

The frown on his face disappeared just as a waiter approached and presented them with menus. "Give us a few minutes," André requested.

The short, brown-haired waiter nodded. "Sure, I'll give you guys some time. It's always great to see you here, man."

André opened the menu and perused the lunch selections.

"This is...not really the right place to ask, but I have a question," she said.

He looked at her over the top of the menu. "Ask it."

"The...playroom that you have. We haven't used any of the things in there yet."

Amusement lit up his eyes. "Did you want to?"

Her cheeks burned. "Not necessarily. I mean...I'm not complaining. I guess I was just wondering why."

An unreadable look entered his eyes. "That day I took you shopping and we...did what we did. After that, we had a conversation in the car. You asked if public sex would be our 'thing.' At the time, you didn't mean much by it, but it showed me how much emphasis I was putting on sex. Yes, I have the playroom. There have already been a few occasions where I've...gotten a bit reckless in public places with you, but I want much more than just sex with you."

At his mention of sex, she cast a glance around the restaurant to see if anyone was within earshot of their conversation. When she turned back, André's eyes were on her. "I appreciate that."

"I could have taken you into the playroom the first night you signed the contract, and I was tempted to," he said. "I could have rushed you into it. There are several reasons why I didn't. For one, I care about you."

Hope filled her eyes and she struggled to keep her own emotions in check.

He licked his lips and leaned forward, covering both of her hands with his. "Not to confuse caring with love, I have grown to care for you," he clarified. "And as such, I want to ease you into this lifestyle. You're new to it. There are elements to this lifestyle that could be misunderstood or traumatizing if a couple is reckless with an arrangement like this. That is why I'm trying to take my time with you, explain things about myself and the things that I like to do, so you can understand it a little before participating in it. If I'd told you on the first night that I met you that I wanted to see you naked in a cage, what would you have thought of me?"

The absurd question caused a laugh to come bubbling out of her. "I would have thought you were a psycho," she answered.

He laughed and settled back in his seat. "Now that you have a better knowledge of who I am and how I feel about you, what would you think of me if I said that I wanted to see you naked in a cage?"

"That you are a psycho," she said, laughing.

He laughed along with her. "I expected you to say that. A part of me is surprised you didn't go running around screaming after seeing some of the items I have in the playroom."

The waiter started to head over to their table again.

André gave a slight shake of his head, indicating that more time was needed. "You need to look at your menu, decide what you want to order."

Whenever she was in a restaurant with him, the last thing on her mind was food. There were so many things that she wanted to know. She could barely focus long enough to read the words printed on the menu, much less decide what she wanted to eat.

After they each put their respective orders in, he asked her, "Is there anything else you're curious to know?"

"I'm just curious about all of it," she said.

"Anything in particular?"

"Just a few things," she said sheepishly. "Nothing I can really mention here."

"I want you to tell me," he said firmly.

She tucked strands of her hair behind her ear and took a deep breath. "I'm curious about...the spanking," she answered finally, speaking the words in as low of a voice she could manage without whispering.

"Is that all?"

"And the cage. I don't understand the cage."

He grinned. "The cage is for punishment purposes." He reconsidered his own words and then added, "Usually."

She looked confused.

He laughed and shook his head. "Tonight, I'll give you a crash course to satisfy your...curiosity."

14

The living room was dark, lit with an assortment of candles. The flickering flames cast eerie shadows across André's face. He was seated on the couch with both feet planted firmly on the floor and his legs parted. Shirtless, with the scattered tattoos on his chest, abs, and arms visible. His hands rested on his thighs. He'd ordered for Destiny to undress in the bedroom and return to him after retrieving her collar. "Putting on your collar should be the first thing you do after walking through this door - unless we are otherwise preoccupied."

He patiently waited for her while Massive Attack's "Unfinished Sympathy" played from the speakers of his high-end entertainment system.

She emerged from the hall with her head bowed and her eyes lowered. Shadows played over her beautiful brown skin and the light from the candles caused the entire left side of her body to glow. Her curls hung down her back and over the tops of her breasts as she moved across the room.

His eyes roamed over her body, then remained locked for several moments on the black, D-ring leather collar circled around her neck. He loved the way the accessory looked on her, loved having a reminder that she belonged to him. Anticipation welled up in him at the sight of her. He watched her slow approach and felt his throat tighten. "Look at me," he urged softly, just barely loud enough to be heard over the music.

She lifted her eyes. Her gaze met with his as she walked towards him.

He very deliberately dragged his eyes down the length of her, appreciating every dip and every curve of her frame. "Lie across my lap," he commanded, lifting his eyes back up to her face once he was done perusing.

She lowered onto the couch in a kneeling position and bent over his lap.

He adjusted her positioning so that her rear end was dead center in the middle of his lap. After rubbing her rear end affectionately, he said, "Just to issue a disclaimer, this is not a punishment. You were curious about spanking, and I'm just giving a demonstration of what my spankings would feel like. Understood?"

"Yes, Sir," she said, propping herself up on her elbows.

"Good girl," he said, giving one of her butt cheeks a squeeze. He raised his hand into the air.

She tensed, preparing for the blow.

He smacked her ass. Hard.

She gasped and looked at him over her shoulder, her expression reflecting shock and indignation. Tears sprang to her eyes at the unexpected sting of pain.

He looked her in the eyes as he lifted his hand into the air again. He repeated the act, smacking her ass so hard that it bounced back against his hand.

She turned and faced forward, digging her nails into the couch cushion and ducking her head down.

After that second slap, his hand smoothed over her rear end, caressing the pain away. "Spankings are usually a punishment," he explained. "I've had submissives who would disappoint me on purpose so they could get a spanking from me. Back then, I was a lot more...*gentle* with punishment. I learned to be a bit firmer. The firmer I was, the less a submissive was inclined to manipulate me into giving her a spanking. I spank at varying degrees of intensity, and those varying degrees will depend on what you've done to disappoint me. What I am giving you now is only mid-level."

She turned her head to the side and rested it on the couch cushion.

He continued caressing her rear end, admiring the view of her draped across his lap. "For the record, if you ever want a spanking from me, a playful one, all you have to do is ask me."

"I understand."

He raised his hand, held it in the air for a moment, and then smacked her again.

She moaned out loud.

Submissives often experienced conflicting emotions when receiving a punishment such as spanking. On one hand, they experienced the urge to protest. Pain was being inflicted upon them and as such, their defense mode sometimes kicked in. On the opposite end of the spectrum, however, were those tingling sensations that the pain left in its wake. Shortly after the pain, there was pleasure. He could see this conflict in Destiny's face. Her lips were parted. Ecstasy filled her eyes as she clenched the cream-colored Italian leather couch cushion.

He continued to spank her and watched her face as he did it. After about the tenth spank, she no longer reacted to the pain...only the pleasure that came after. She didn't even realize it, but minute by minute, she started to arch her back, raising her rear end higher and higher. Anticipating the smack. Wanting it.

He smiled and gave her rear end a final pat and gentle caress. "I think you get the idea," he said.

"Are we done already?" she asked, her voice sounding like she'd just woken up from a good dream.

"Already?" He made a show of checking the watch on his wrist. "We've been at it for quite a while. Up."

She rose into a kneeling position and remained that way, awaiting further instruction.

He stood from the couch and stroked her cheek with the back of his hand. "I have something to show you. I'm going to be right back." He exited the living room and walked down the hall. When he returned, he had his fingers hooked through the sturdy metal wires of the large, long cage from the playroom. He set the cage down beside the end table near the couch.

The minute she saw it, her back went ramrod straight and her eyes widened slightly. A wary look entered her eyes and she became watchful of his every move.

Feeling her eyes on him, he opened the door to the cage and gestured towards her. "Get in," he ordered.

She stared at him blankly.

"You're hesitating," he chided her lightly.

She stepped off the couch and hesitatingly walked up to him. Taking a deep breath, she lowered down to her hands and knees and crawled into the cage.

He knelt to the floor and closed the door to the cage. He engaged the combination lock that hung loosely on the latch and tugged on the lock to make sure it was secure. "This is where you will sleep tonight," he advised her.

She opened her mouth and looked like she was going to protest.

He arched an eyebrow at her. "Did you have something to say?"

She thought better of it and swallowed her words, shaking her head in response.

"Good. Good girl. Again…this is not a punishment. This is just a demonstration of what cage time is like. There's some work that I have to get done before the night is over. I'll check on you before heading to bed." He reached through the opening in the cage and caressed her hair. Then, he turned and left her.

Whenever Destiny shifted in her sleep, her elbow hit something metal and solid. The metal was hard enough that it woke her up a few times. She jerked her head up and squinted, checking her surroundings. Where the hell was she? The living room. *In the cage,* she realized with a start. She sat up, as much as she could in a four-foot-tall cage, and rubbed her eyes. The condo was quiet. *I have to hand it to him...this is definitely a punishment.*

No cell phone access, no television access. There was nothing at her disposal that would provide entertainment. She hummed to pass the time, tried to imagine what her first day of work would be like. Then, her mind played back special moments between her and André. At some point, even that lost its entertainment value. She couldn't think of anything else to do, and she was still having trouble falling asleep. So, she waited.

Sunlight pushed at the blinds hanging over the living room windows, but the light wasn't allowed in. The living room remained relatively dark.

Approximately an hour after she cracked her eyes open, she heard a toilet flushing. She perked up and grabbed the wires of the cage, peering towards the hall. While she was waiting for him to enter the room, she had to wonder why someone would willingly sleep in a cage like a dog or some other animal. There was a pillow cushion lining the bottom of it, but it was still very much a cage and felt very much like a prison. Even considering that someone would have to do something to earn this punishment, it seemed inhumane.

André padded down the hall wearing a pair of crisp, white linen pajama pants and nothing else. He came to a stop at the hall entrance, drying off his hands with a small towel. "Good morning," he greeted, bypassing the living room and entering the kitchen. She saw light flood the kitchen. Some of that light overflowed into the living room.

"Good morning, Sir," she returned, eager to get the hell out of the cage. *I'll never express curiosity about a punishment again,* she vowed to herself. The sound of a running faucet reached her ears.

A moment later, he reappeared with a glass of water. He set the glass of water on a coffee table coaster and knelt to the floor. Quietly, he twisted the combination to the lock and removed the lock. He opened the door to the cage and assisted her out.

She was surprised that she wasn't sore and said as much.

"I wouldn't allow you to sleep in there if it was going to hurt you," he explained as he closed the cage door. "I'm supposed to care for your well-being."

"At the restaurant, you hinted that the cage could be used for...good things, and not just bad. I can't imagine how." She rubbed her elbow, frowning down at the cage.

He gently grabbed her arm and inspected it. Small impression marks from the cage's wires were pressed into her skin. He sucked his teeth and gently rubbed his hand over the marks, smoothing them out. "Maybe I should check to see if there is a more comfortable cage."

The words sounded absurd. "More comfortable cage?" she repeated.

He laughed along with her. "It sounds crazy, I know. But if I ever want to see you naked in a cage, or fuck you through the cage bars, then I'd feel better knowing that you were comfortable."

She didn't even have time to fully process what he'd said.

The doorbell rang, a pleasant tinkling sound.

"I'm not expecting anyone. Umm..." His eyes scanned over her, taking in her nudity and the collar that was still buckled around her neck. He chastely kissed her on the cheek. "Wait for me in the bedroom." He backed away from her and jogged to the door.

She scurried out of the living room and into the bedroom. Upon searching for the nearest piece of clothing she could throw on, she wound up grabbing one of André's dress shirts from the closet. She buttoned it as quickly as she could, missing several buttons. Then, she tiptoed over to the bedroom door and poked her head through the crack. Two male voices were audible.

"I don't mean to be unprofessional or anything, but I'm a *huge* fan. My friends are not going to believe I got to meet you today. Hopefully, I'm not interrupting you or anything."

"No problem at all. I just wasn't expecting the delivery for another few days. You can come in."

She saw André lead a uniformed man of average height into the living room. She pushed the door open a little further, praying that the hinges didn't squeak. They didn't. Leave it to André to make sure the hinges on all of his doors were properly maintained. She eased herself through the crack in the door and pressed her back flat against the wall, feeling like a character in a James Bond film. When leaning away from the wall a bit, she was able to catch a glimpse of the uniformed man, who was facing her general direction.

"I need you to sign here, here, and here," the uniformed man said, adjusting the cap on top of his head.

She crept down the hall and stopped about a foot from the hall entrance. The deliveryman was staring down at a digital device he was using to capture André's signature. A large package had been set in front of the coffee table. *I wonder what's in there,* she thought, her eyes shifting from the box to André. His back was to her as he signed the digital document.

"Is that it?" André asked.

"Unless you had any questions," the uniformed man said, taking a minute to glance around the condo. At this point, he saw Destiny.

Her eyes widened and she pressed herself back against the wall.

"No questions," André said. "I appreciate your service. Thank you for carrying the package in."

Destiny leaned away from the wall again, slowly.

"That's what I'm here for," the uniformed deliveryman said, still checking out André's condo. "This is some sick place you have here."

"Thank you."

The deliveryman's eyes landed on the cage sitting near the couch. He instantly got excited. "You have a dog?" he asked, walking over to the cage.

André scratched his head. "Umm..."

"Can I see it?" the deliveryman asked. "I'm a huge dog person. Where is he?"

Destiny released a small giggle without meaning to. She clamped her hands over her mouth.

"This is a *big ass* cage!" he exclaimed. "What the hell is it, a Doberman? Your dog must be big as hell!"

"I don't...have a dog," André said.

The deliveryman gasped. "Oh." He frowned down at the cage. "Then..."

"Yet."

"Huh?" the deliveryman asked, looking up at André.

"I don't have a dog *yet*," André improvised. "I ordered the cage first."

The deliveryman nodded. "That makes sense. Usually when someone has a dog, you can smell it. And I don't smell dog in here."

André gave him a strange look. "That's a relief. Let me walk you out." He walked the uniformed man out of the condo and Destiny heard his sigh of relief right before he appeared at the entrance to the hallway. When he looked down at her, she was sitting on the hallway floor, trying in vain to cover up her laughter. He shook his head. "That guy was a nut job," he muttered.

Destiny uncovered her mouth. "Says the guy who has a cage in his living room but no dog," she said through her laughter.

He laughed with her and bent down to help her up. "Funny," he said. "You're a funny girl."

She tried her best to quiet her laughter. "I'm sorry, I had to say it."

Tears had formed at the corners of her eyes from laughing, and he wiped them. "You know that technically

I could punish you for not waiting in the bedroom for me like I asked, right?"

That sentence served to quiet her laughter completely.

He smiled. "You slept in a cage last night when a punishment wasn't even warranted, so no. I'm not going to punish you. I'm just letting you know that I could."

"*Technically*," she said, using the same word he had.

His smile stretched wider. "Yes. Technically." He draped an arm across her shoulders and steered her in the direction of the bedroom.

"So, what breed of dog were you thinking of getting?" she asked him, collapsing into a fit of laughter all over again.

André pulled his luxury car rental into the driveway of a two-story brick colonial house, put the car in the Park, and turned off the car. He glanced over at Destiny, who was peering wistfully out of the passenger side window. "Are you ready to go in?" he asked her.

"Not really."

"Everything is going to be fine."

"My mom is a sweetheart," she told him. "She's the sweetest person you'll ever meet. She's going to love you. But my dad...he has a very quirky sense of humor. It can take time to warm up to it. He's very silly. Unless you piss him off, and then he's a beast."

"Everything is going to be fine," he repeated. "Going by that description, he kind of sounds like my own dad."

She racked her brain for the information she felt that he needed to know. "My parents are spiritual. Not religious, per se, but they are all about love and happiness and peace and treating people the way they'd want to be treated."

André nodded slowly.

He thinks I'm being extra and he's indulging me, she thought, trying to steady the trembling hands clasped in her lap. "This is my family," she said emphatically. "My family is important to me. I just...I want this to go well."

"You're worried that it won't?" he questioned.

She shook her head. "I don't know what to expect."

"You don't have anything to worry about. Here, I'm just André. We're dating. That's it. That's all they need to know."

She flipped the visor down, checked her appearance, and flipped the mirror back up.

"I didn't expect you to be this worried," he said.

"Last night, I spent the night in a cage," she reminded him. "It's hard to feel normal after something like that. I know you hate the word 'normal,' but I don't know what other word to use. I feel like a freak. I feel like...if I walk in there, they'll smell it on me. That I'm different, that I've been..." She looked at him, at a loss for words.

He arched an eyebrow at her. "That you've been what?"

"That I've been some superfreak who's been having sex in public and sleeping in cages and getting spankings even though I'm a grown ass woman," she finished in a fast, long string of words that ran into each other.

He laughed.

She frowned. "I'm glad you find it funny."

He shook his head and tried in vain to stop laughing. "I'm sorry. I'm sorry." He closed his eyes and willed the laughter away. "The feeling you've described, I've felt it before. Back when I first got into all of this. That feeling goes away."

"Knowing that it goes away *eventually* doesn't help me right now," she muttered.

"I'm going to grab the door for you. We can't sit in the car for forever, and I'm starving." He pocketed the key fob and opened the driver side door.

Once he opened the door for her, she stood out of the car and smoothed out the skirt of the white lace dress he'd bought.

He reached past her and closed the passenger door. Then, he gently pushed her against the car and kissed her.

She placed her hands on his chest, intending to push him away. Her pushes were futile and eventually ceased altogether. Within seconds, she was kissing him back.

When he pulled back, he had a dopey smile on his face.

"You don't know my parents," she told him chidingly. "They could have been looking out the window this entire time."

"Then they definitely just got a show," he said in a low voice, offering her his arm.

She accepted his arm and rolled her eyes.

They walked along a stone walkway flanked by green, perfectly manicured grass. "Your family's house is beautiful," he commented.

"My dad worked blue collar jobs for most of his life," she explained as they walked up the two short steps leading to the porch. "But he was very frugal, saved up his money. He was a dependable worker. Over the years, he slowly started moving up through the ranks."

"Admirable," André remarked.

She beamed up at him, glowing with pride for her father.

André leaned down and kissed the top of her head.

She reached out and rang the doorbell. There was a lot of commotion and yelling behind the closed front door before the door was yanked open. A woman who looked like an older version of Destiny grinned at both of them. Destiny detached herself from André and threw her arms around her mother.

Her mother ushered them into the house and closed the door behind them.

"Where's Dad?" Destiny asked, looking towards the living room entrance and then down the hall leading to the kitchen.

"In his chair like always," her mother answered. "He's talking to your Uncle Kevin."

"Uncle Kevin?" Destiny echoed. "Does that mean Nyla is here?"

Her mother nodded and smiled, her eyes crinkling at the corners.

Destiny excitedly looked up at André. "Nyla is the cutest little thing you'll ever see in your life," she told him. Then she remembered she hadn't even given the formal introduction. She gestured towards André. "This is André, Mom. You met him at graduation."

"I certainly did," her mother said, hesitating only a moment before giving André a hug. "I've heard a lot about you."

Destiny's eyes widened slightly as she exchanged glances with André. She laughed uneasily. "Let's go say hi to Dad."

André grabbed Destiny's hand and they followed her mother into the family room. He leaned close so that his lips were right next to Destiny's ear. "I hope you only told her the good things," he said before playfully nipping at her earlobe.

"...And then he said, 'What stapler?'"

The dining room table erupted in laughter at Mrs. Richards's story. The dining area was a large room with a cathedral ceiling, beautiful cherrywood oak cabinet, and long cherrywood table. Destiny and André were seated at one side. Destiny's uncle, Kevin and his wife sat on the opposite side. Destiny's parents sat at opposite ends of the table. Through the archway leading to the kitchen, Kevin's children were visible. They were seated at the kitchen table, temporarily dubbed "the kid's table."

Nyla was the youngest, an adorable toddler, wearing a pink and purple jumper with her hair pulled up into a curly ponytail. Nyla had two older brothers, Evan who was eight and Marcus who was twelve.

"Destiny mentioned having aunts who were teachers," André stated.

"They don't live in town anymore," Mrs. Richards informed him. "I'm sure they would have flown in, if they had more notice."

"This trip was very last-minute," Destiny chimed in. "I told André that I missed being around you guys so much and he just...made the trip happen."

"So...André, is it?" Kevin's wife Tasha queried.

"Yes," André confirmed, looking up from his plate.

"How long have you and Destiny been dating?"

Destiny forced a mouthful of mashed potatoes down her throat and wiped her mouth with a napkin.

"I've had an interest in dating her since before she interviewed me for the article late last year," he replied, maintaining eye contact with Tasha. A playful spark lit up his eyes. "But she wouldn't give me the time of day, so we started dating shortly after she graduated."

"You two make an *interesting* couple," Tasha said. She had beautiful, dark brown skin, dark almond-shaped eyes, and full lips she'd applied crimson lipstick to. Her attire was chic: a black, loose-fitting top that complimented her petite build, tailored khaki slacks, and stylish black heels. Ever since Destiny could remember, she'd thought her aunt Tasha to be beautiful, if not a bit...outspoken.

"What makes us interesting?" he asked, tilting his head to the side.

"Destiny's a bit young," Tasha said. "She's fresh out of college. You're this...well-established businessman. How many years are there between you? Ten?"

André blinked and set down his fork.

Kevin, medium brown-skinned with a faded haircut, cleared his throat and tugged at the collar of his plaid button-down shirt. "Babe."

"What?" Tasha asked innocently, waving her fork in the air. "It's just a question, and I'm sure we were all thinking it."

André smiled charmingly. "Not that it matters, but yes. There are about ten years between us."

"I can't imagine what you would have in common," Tasha said.

"That's enough, Tasha," Destiny's mother chided. "He is our guest and you're being rude."

Tasha shrugged and returned her attention to her plate.

Destiny looked up at André, hoping that he would just let the subject drop. But by the look in his eyes, she could tell that he wouldn't. His intense stare was on Tasha. The expression on his face was calm, but by now she could tell when a storm was brewing beneath the calm facade.

"You can't tell what we would have in common?" His voice was tight. "Maybe similar tastes in literature and films? The common bond of both of us being writers? To be honest, that is more than enough to provide us with a strong bond. We also have stimulating conversation. She is knowledgeable in world events, most likely attributed to her interest in journalism. She is intelligent, funny. She is more woman than a lot of self-proclaimed women these days and has challenged me in ways that other women your age haven't accomplished. Age doesn't necessarily indicate a certain level of maturity. You should know that by now."

Tasha stared at him with an unreadable expression.

An uncomfortable silence fell over the table, until Destiny's father whooped with laughter.

André's smile widened and he flashed two perfect rows of teeth. "Now mind you, I didn't give this explanation because I felt a need to defend the relationship that I have with your niece. My hope is that this explanation helps to open your very closed mind. There are many ways that people can relate to each other, many things that can cause two people to connect. Too often, focus is put on elements that don't matter. I love being around her. I take care of her. I treat her well. Be sure of that. And to answer the question you have no doubt asked yourself, no I do not make a habit of targeting younger women. I typically date women that are older. But Destiny... is special." He cast a glance at Destiny's mother. "I'm sorry that you had to hear all of this."

Destiny's mother shook her head. "No apologies are necessary. I think you are a very well-spoken young man. I'm honored to have you seated at this table, and I am pleased to hear that you view our daughter so highly."

"Tasha, on the other hand, should be sitting at the kiddie table," Destiny's father muttered under his breath.

Destiny turned her face into the sleeve of André's suit jacket to stifle her laughter.

After dinner, the family settled in the living room. The children sat on the floor, playing a board game while the adults sat on the couches and armchairs. Mr. Richards spoke passionately to André about a business idea he had, a non-profit for unemployed people with blue collar work experience.

Destiny sat beside André, only half-listening to his conversation with her father. She was relieved that they'd all gotten past the Tasha Inquisition. Even Tasha had to respect André's response to her nosiness. As a result of that discussion, Destiny's parents also had an entirely new level of respect for him.

Realizing that his conversation with her father wasn't going to end any time soon, she kissed his cheek and slid down to the floor. She crawled over to her cousins, and the sensation of crawling triggered vivid memories.

Even though her father was talking to him, André had his eyes on her. Desire flickered in the depths of his dark eyes. One corner of his mouth lifted into a half-smile. He knew what she was thinking about. That smile and that fiery look in his eyes were his way of communicating that he was thinking about the exact same thing.

André watched Destiny playing with her cousins. This entire evening had been quite the experience. Both of her parents were as loving and endearing as could be. He couldn't say the same for Tasha, Destiny's aunt. *What is her deal and why is she so hostile? Her questions were bizarre and highly inappropriate.* Maybe she'd lost an ex to a younger woman? Whatever the case, she seemed to take his relationship with Destiny as some sort of personal affront. Thankfully, she'd backed off after his response. The rest of the evening was quite pleasant.

After dinner, he had an interesting and enlightening conversation with Mr. Richards. Destiny had been right; Mr. Richards definitely had a quirky sense of humor, but André liked it. The man was very likeable, and he had a great head for business. In some ways, he reminded him of his own father.

Once Destiny left his side, he had a hard time focusing on her father's words. Seeing her crawl across the floor was enough to rile him up. She caught his gaze and held it, smiling seductively before joining her cousins. He enjoyed watching her play with them...laughing, chasing, and tickling them. He could clearly see the love that her cousins had for her.

"My goodness, Destiny, do you remember this?" Mrs. Richards called out to her daughter, standing near a tall, wide bookcase that took up the majority of the far wall of the living room. A heavy, hardcover book was in her hands.

Destiny finished tickling Nyla and glanced up. Her eyes widened. "Mom...Mom, no."

Her mother laughed. "What? Don't you think André would want to see these?"

Destiny stood up and raised her hands, palms facing outward. "Mom, if you value your life..."

Mr. Richards laughed heartily.

Kevin and his wife wore mirroring expressions of confusion. "Angela, what is that?"

"A ton of baby pictures and kid pictures of Destiny," Mrs. Richards responded, wiping a hand over the top of the photo album.

André lifted an eyebrow. "I'd like to see them."

Destiny turned her head. "You...don't need to see that."

Ignoring her, Mrs. Richards walked over to André and handed him the photo album. She gave her daughter a pat on the back. "The pictures are adorable, everyone thinks so."

André laughed at Destiny's discomfort as he flipped the photo album open. The first picture was a small photo of baby Destiny, taken at the hospital the day she was born. A hospital wrist band was visible on her tiny wrist. There were several newborn photos, and then a series of photos that had been taken in a photography studio. Baby Destiny, with her hair pulled up into a curly ponytail like Nyla's, seated on a platform. She had adorable chipmunk cheeks, sparkly eyes, and a nearly toothless smile that could melt anyone's heart. He lifted his eyes and looked at Destiny.

She covered her face with her hands and turned her back to him.

He flipped the page. Baby Destiny in her crib, sleeping. Baby Destiny trying in vain to open a Christmas present with impossibly tiny hands. Quietly, he flipped to the next page. Baby Destiny wearing a chiffon lilac-colored dress, possibly for Easter.

Destiny went back to playing with her younger cousins.

He continued flipping the photo album pages without speaking, tuning out the sounds of Kevin's and Tasha's chatter. Tuning out the sound of Mr. and Mrs. Richards's flirtation as Mrs. Richards sat on her husband's lap and hugged him. As André flipped the pages, the child in the pictures gradually started aging. Toddler pictures in the park, her first day of pre-school, the falling out of her first tooth. Birthday parties, holidays, Halloween costumes. Her childhood was immortalized in photograph form.

There was even a picture of one of the first articles she'd written in colorful marker. The article was about her uncle Kevin cheating on his girlfriend Tasha, which made André chuckle before he continued flipping throughout the rest of the album. He lifted his eyes over the top of the album and peered at Destiny.

As if she could feel his eyes on her, she turned and looked back at him. She held Nyla in her arms. Without breaking eye contact with André, she pressed a kiss to one of Nyla's chubby cheeks.

There was something in that moment, a feeling that he couldn't name. He didn't know if it was the photo album, or the sight of Destiny holding the adorable little girl in her arms, but it felt like his heart was swelling in his chest.

Later that evening, André lie in bed with Destiny's head resting on his chest. He'd expected that they would have to sleep in separate rooms, but since Kevin, his wife, and his kids were also spending the night, bedrooms were in short supply. Mrs. Richards had advised that André and Destiny could share Destiny's old room.

Mr. Richards, who'd been funny and chill the entire evening, had turned serious all of a sudden. "But I expect for you not to disrespect me in my own house."

More than understood, Mr. Richards, André thought now, brushing Destiny's hair back from her forehead.

"I thought you were sleeping," she murmured sleepily.

"No, just thinking."

"About?"

"How adorable you looked playing with your cousins and how cute your baby pictures were." When he closed his eyes, he could still see those photos.

"Can we pretend like you never saw those pictures, actually?" she asked him. "That was so embarrassing."

He grinned in the dark. "You have absolutely nothing to be embarrassed about. You were a beautiful child."

"Speaking of kids..." She hesitated, looking for the right words. "What is your viewpoint on them?"

"Children are amazing little people," he said, knowing that his response didn't fully answer the question she was trying to ask.

She hesitated again. "Yeah, I know, but...I mean, are you planning on having any? Ever?"

He brought an arm up and rested it beneath his head. "I love children, but they don't really fit into my lifestyle," he told her.

"Oh."

"You?"

"I want to have them one day," she said softly.

He stared up at the ceiling. Watching her tonight with her younger cousins, he could imagine her as a parent. "You'd make a great mother," he told her.

"Thank you."

He decided to change the subject. "Your family is..."

"Crazy?" she finished for him.

He laughed quietly. "I was going to say amazing."

She lifted her head off his chest. "Even after Tasha's questions?"

He shrugged one shoulder. "Her questions were out of line, but her wacky questions don't affect my opinions on your family. Your parents are very kind, warm. Loving. Hilarious."

She laughed. "My dad."

"Both of them."

"They're amazing people. I'm fortunate to have them."

"You are," he agreed. And he didn't speak the words aloud, but he now understood how it was possible for her to grow up in this day and age still believing in love. Her parents were still together and were extremely flirtatious with each other. Seeing the way her parents were together was enough to make anyone believe in love...

Destiny fell asleep on his chest. He continued to stare up at the ceiling, plagued by his own thoughts and fears.

15

Destiny woke up early, tossed on a t-shirt and a pair of shorts, pulled her hair into a topknot, and went into the kitchen to cook everyone breakfast. It felt good to cook. She felt spoiled whenever André prepared meals for her, because he was a very skilled chef. Truth be told, she missed cooking.

She stood at the stove, balancing her weight on one leg with the other raised and bent at the knee. She held a pan over the stover burner, tilting it at an angle and watching the square chunk of butter melt into a sizzling golden liquid. She hummed to herself and danced as she cooked.

"Won't you make the adorable little housewife?"

Destiny recognized the voice.

Tasha sauntered into the kitchen wearing a blue robe and purple hair bonnet. She sat at the round kitchen table and crossed one leg over the over, dangling a slippered foot.

"Good morning to you, too, Tasha," Destiny greeted.

"Aren't you chipper?" Tasha quipped, resting an elbow on the table.

Destiny shrugged while scrambling eggs. "I have every reason to be. I'm spending time with the people that I love most in this world."

"Including your man André?"

Destiny hesitated in responding.

Tasha arched an eyebrow.

"It's...a bit soon for declarations of love," Destiny answered finally, trying to keep the nervousness out of her voice.

"Fair enough," Tasha allowed. "While we're being honest, I still don't understand how anything between the two of you could work. He has been around the block more than once. Gossip rags talk about his exploits. So here he is, this very *experienced* businessman who has lived a crazy life as a hip-hop star. Sure, you both may be writers at heart or whatever dream he was trying to sell me, but you are still a baby, Destiny. You just got out of college, so what would you know about the world? But if it works for you, hey."

"He already explained to you why we connect. If you still don't understand, then maybe it's not for you *to* understand," Destiny said as she poured the scrambled eggs onto a platter, next to the pancakes she'd made. "I'm curious to know why you are putting so much time and energy into analyzing my relationship, when you have your own. Moving forward, you can keep your opinions on my relationship to yourself. I'm here to enjoy some time with my family while I can."

Tasha crossed her arms over her chest. "Aren't we Miss Thing this morning?"

Destiny turned, and the expression on her face said she wasn't joking.

Tasha rolled her eyes and waved a hand in the air dismissively. "All right, fine. I'll leave you two alone."

"He's a great guy," Destiny added, setting the pan in the sink and washing her hands. "He's not some predator, the way you make him out to be."

"I appreciate that, baby girl." André walked into the kitchen, shirtless with only a pair of gray sweatpants on.

Tasha gave her hairnet a pat and clutched the lapels of her robe as her eyes scanned over every inch of André that was visible to her. "Oh my," she muttered.

He grinned. "I appreciate that, too," he told Tasha.

Tasha's eyes widened and she averted her gaze, realizing that she'd been staring. Sputtering under her breath, she shifted in her chair.

He crossed the room and kissed the top of Destiny's head. "I don't like waking up without you."

"I wanted to make breakfast for everyone," she told him.

The sounds of footsteps could be heard over their heads.

"And it sounds like everyone else woke up right along with you," she said, surveying the food she'd loaded onto the dishes she had lined up on the island counter.

He leaned over to inspect the food she'd made. "You made all of this without any help?"

She nodded proudly.

"I would have helped you," he told her, his brows furrowing.

"You *always* cook. I wanted to feed you for a change."

André wrapped his arms around her waist and pressed a kiss to her temple.

"He cooks too?" Tasha asked, almost to herself. "What *doesn't* he do?"

Destiny couldn't help but smile as she looped her arms around his neck. "I haven't figured that out yet."

André stared down at her.

She stared back. At first glance, the look in his eyes said that he wanted to kiss her. After looking deeper, she realized that his eyes said that he wanted to do a hell of a lot more than kiss her, but he was trying to be respectful to an aunt that hadn't shown either of them much respect thus far.

Destiny trailed an index finger down his chest. "You're going to want to put a shirt on," she warned him.

"I was going to, but when you weren't there..." He stopped himself and said, "I just...wanted to make sure everything was okay."

"Putting on a shirt takes about thirty seconds," Tasha grumbled.

André hoisted an annoyed look in her direction.

Tasha held her hands up in a defensive gesture. "I'm just saying."

There were more sounds of footsteps.

Destiny pushed at his chest. "Shirt on. Now."

He looked amused. "Are you getting bossy with *me*?"

She met his taunting gaze head-on and told him, "I guess I am. Don't make me bend you over my knee."

His eyebrows shot up in surprise. He took a step closer to her, just slightly, but the movement was enough to make her stumble backwards.

She reached out behind her and caught hold of the kitchen counter. With a defiant look in her eyes, she tilted her chin up. "If you want, we can take this outside."

"I was thinking more along the lines of taking this out on you when we get home," he said, lowering his voice.

She blinked, worry briefly flashing in her eyes.

He gave a slight shake of his head and leaned in close to her. "I'm kidding." He straightened his posture. "I'm going to follow your advice and put on that shirt."

Destiny cleared her throat and looked at her aunt, who was still staring off in the direction André had gone off in.

By the time he returned, her parents and little cousins were in the kitchen, creating pure chaos.

"You made eggs, pancakes, waffles, grits, and sausage, but no bacon?" Mr. Richards demanded with his hands on his hips.

Mrs. Richards hugged Destiny. "That's his way of thanking you for preparing this meal for us," she said before throwing her husband a scolding look. "You aren't supposed to eat bacon. Remember what the doctor said."

He shrugged and muttered under his breath.

Nyla sat at the kitchen table with her brothers, tugging on her curly ponytail while her brothers argued about video games.

André entered the kitchen while adjusting a black t-shirt featuring a popular rapper's album cover.

"Look who's up and at 'em," Mr. Richards greeted with a grin.

"Good morning, Mr. Richards," André returned. His eyes shifted to Destiny, who stood at the kitchen counter preparing plates for her cousins. He went over to help her. "What do you need me to do?"

"Can you take these plates to them?" she asked, lifting one plate higher than the other. "This one is for Nyla, since she eats so little."

He accepted the plates from her and delivered them to the kitchen table.

Nyla, dressed in a pink t-shirt, jeans, and sneakers, looked up at André. "Are you my cousin, too?" she asked him.

"Uh..." He looked back at Destiny.

"He's a friend of mine, Nyla," Destiny called over her shoulder.

"Oh," Nyla said, picking up her plastic fork. She tried to gather eggs onto her fork, but the fluffy yellow bits kept falling off the utensil.

André watched her a few times. "Do you want me to help you?" he asked softly.

She shook her head. "I know how."

He watched her make a few more attempts.

She sighed in frustration. "Okay, show me."

Laughing, he knelt beside her. He guided her hand and successfully speared some of the eggs with the fork.

Destiny eyed them, leaning a hip on the island counter while wiping her hands off with a kitchen towel. She tilted her head to the side. *Just when I think he can't get any more adorable, he finds a way,* she thought.

He smiled at something Nyla said, and repeated the tutorial on how to get her eggs to cooperate with her fork.

He doesn't want to have children, but he's so good with them. She didn't know what she expected, especially with his viewpoints on love and relationships. *I guess, despite Carlos's advice and despite my own vow, I still hoped he would eventually change his mind about what he wants.*

Breakfast was a relatively short affair. Conversation was light and good-natured, but minimal. Everyone was eager to get on with the rest of the day. Nyla attached herself to André and developed a kiddie crush of sorts. She requested for him to pick her up several times throughout the day. Each time Destiny caught a glimpse of him holding the little girl, she caught herself wishing that the relationship she had with him was different. She wished that they were just two people who could fall in love, get married, and raise a family together.

Just last through today, Destiny, she told herself while the family settled in the living room to watch a movie together. *Tomorrow morning you're back to Mississauga, where you won't have to see how irresistible he is when he interacts with children.*

Nyla sat on André's lap swinging her legs back and forth. Destiny sat beside them, focusing on the television, or trying to. Whatever she did, she was trying not to notice just how cute it was to see Nyla sitting on André's lap and talking to him like he was a trusted longtime friend. Or how cute it was when he smiled at Nyla, a full thousand-watt smile.

Destiny's father fumbled around with the remote to the television. "Never figured out how to use this damned thing," he muttered. "You have regular TV and then all of these little side apps and programs. Why can't everything just all be on the same thing?"

Mrs. Richards waited near the light switch, waiting for her cue to turn the lights down. "Destiny, will you please help your father figure out the remote? At this rate, we'll be here all night waiting for him to get it together."

"Of course, Mom," Destiny said, and moved from her spot on the couch. She approached her father and held her hand out for the remote. Once the movie started playing, she reclaimed her seat next to André and Nyla.

Mrs. Richards turned off the lights and sat in the armchair beside her husband's.

Completely uninterested in the movie, Marcus and Evan sat in the corner playing handheld video games.

"Can I kiss your cheek?" Nyla asked André as the film production studio trailer rolled across the television screen.

André's brows drew together. "Um, sure."

Destiny's eyes met his in the dark as the little girl's lips came into contact with his cheek. He held Destiny's gaze for a moment, long after Nyla twisted around in his lap. Destiny broke eye contact first, following Nyla's lead and returning her focus to the flat-screen television mounted on the wall.

About halfway through the movie, André reached out and took Destiny's hand. He gave her hand a reassuring squeeze. A gesture to signify that he knew what she was thinking, but they would be okay. She appreciated the gesture; she truly did. But she knew that what she wanted for her future drastically contradicted what he wanted for his, and that left her feeling *far* from reassured.

The return to Canada was bittersweet. Destiny was excited to embark upon her career in public relations. She was also excited to have alone time with André. As soon as the wheels of the plane tucked into the aircraft, the feelings of missing her family set in. The time she'd had with them had seemed so short. She would also miss the normalcy between her and André. This trip had revealed another side of him that she hadn't seen before.

On the flight back to Toronto, he was quiet, lost in his own thoughts. He would stare at her for long periods of time, as if she were a mystery he was trying to solve. She wished she could read his mind, the way he seemed to be able to read hers.

The minute they stepped in the door, she headed to the bedroom. She located her collar on the nightstand next to the bed, brushed her hair to the side and strapped it around her neck.

André came to stand in the doorway and leaned against the doorframe. "I'm proud of you for remembering that," he said softly.

She clasped her hands together in front of her and kept her head bowed.

"I have to get caught up with work today. I won't have much time to share with you. You are free to relax. Watch a movie, read, whatever you want...just relax and enjoy yourself. Since I'll be so busy, you should spend the night in the guest room. Tomorrow morning, I want you to work out with me. After breakfast and a shower, we will head to the office. Understood?"

She nodded. "Yes, Sir."

He pushed himself from against the doorframe, turned, and disappeared down the hall.

The first thing she did was run herself a bath. While the bath water ran, she scoured through the bookshelf in his bedroom. The collection of his books ranged from non-fiction studies of human psychology to thriller novels to erotic fiction with a BDSM twist. She plucked one of the erotic fiction books from the shelf and returned to the bathroom.

She read and bathed to her heart's content. After the bath, she showered to rinse off. Wearing one of his black, unbelievably soft robes, she exited the bedroom and went to the kitchen. Sounds of his typing carried down into the kitchen. She hummed while making a sandwich and then carried the plate into the living room, where she settled in to watch a movie.

It was nice to have a day to herself, but her mind ran a mile a minute. André had been quiet on the flight back home. The silence hadn't felt like the comfortable silence they often had. *Maybe spending time with my family took a lot out of him,* she reasoned. The thought was so valid that she *might* have believed it, if it wasn't for the fact that he was now secluding himself upstairs. It felt like he was distancing himself from her. *You're just overanalyzing, girl. We flew to Arizona on a weekday that he would have normally been in the office. Maybe he really needs to catch up on work.*

The typing sounds stopped abruptly, and Destiny felt a burst of hope. Maybe he was going to take a break from work, come down and talk to her for a few minutes. Her heart stopped beating as she waited.

Her waiting was in vain. The typing resumed moments later. She lowered her eyes and tried to ignore the feeling of disappointment that settled in the pit of her stomach.

André tapped the end of his pen on top of his desk while leaning back in thought. As much as he attempted to direct his focus to his work, all attempts failed. He would successfully work for a few minutes and then his thoughts would jumble into an incoherent mess. All he could think about was Destiny. How beautiful she was, how amazing her family was, how naturally maternal she was with her little cousins. Thoughts of how amazing her family was led to troubling thoughts, thoughts he hadn't had in *years*. Thoughts involving whether he *could* possibly have his own family at some point.

With a frustrated sigh, he set the pen down and leaned forward. He rested his elbows on the desk and put his face in his hands. Those were thoughts that he didn't want to have. He had come to terms with the fact that most likely, he was fated not to have kids of his own. Children didn't fit into the lifestyle that he'd chosen for himself. He couldn't imagine putting his future son and daughter to sleep and then taking their mother into his playroom. The corners of his mouth turned downward. *My playrooms are always soundproofed, but still. It would be weird to live that kind of life with kids around. Chances are, they'd stumble upon something or see something that they shouldn't.*

He stood up from his desk and pushed his chair back. *Stop it, André. Stop it. No kids. No wife, no kids. No family.* He pinched the bridge of his nose as he paced the length of his home office. This was no good. He was beginning to lose sight of who he was. He was beginning to lose sight of the path he'd laid out for himself.

He closed his eyes and tried to push out the visuals of Destiny playing with her cousins. The image of her stuck in his mind, stubborn. Resilient. *If I can't get rid of these images on my own, I'll have to force them out,* he thought, walking over to the railing and looking down.

Destiny was seated on the couch, watching a movie. She wore his robe, which was ridiculously oversized on her. Her hair was piled up into a topknot and she had her legs tucked underneath her. As if she sensed that he was watching her, she tilted her head back and looked at him.

His pulse quickened the moment her eyes met his. He shook his head sadly. *If I can't get rid of these images on my own, I'll have to force them out,* he thought again. *And there's only one way to do that.* He turned away from the railing, returned to his desk, and picked up his cell phone. He held the gadget in his hand for several moments before powering on the screen and dialing in a number he hadn't used in a long time.

Destiny was curled up on the couch, teetering on the edge of unconsciousness when the doorbell rang.

André appeared at the upstairs railing. "Can you answer that for me?" he asked. Those were the first words he'd spoken to her in hours.

"Sure," she said, sitting up and rubbing her eyes. In disdain, she checked her hair with one of her hands and determined that it probably looked like a mess. Would another deliveryman be on the other side of the door? It was late in the evening, but maybe someone with André's wealth could afford to have deliveries made to his home no matter what hour it was.

A brown-skinned woman stood on the other side of the door. Half of her hair was sectioned into a high ponytail. She wore a short, colorful dress that showed off shapely thighs and a curvaceous figure. The pink lipstick she wore was several shades too light for her complexion.

Destiny didn't have time to cover her surprise. "How may I help you?" she asked.

The woman's eyes anchored on the collar circled around Destiny's neck. "I'm Reese," she greeted. "I'm here to see Dré."

The corners of Destiny's mouth turned downward.

Reese shifted her weight from one heeled foot to the other. "Can I come in?"

"Yes. Yes, I'm sorry." Destiny stepped back, allowing the woman to enter.

Reese's cell phone rang. "*Mierda*," she muttered under her breath, pulling the phone out of a sleek, glossy black Chanel purse. She lifted the phone to her ear. "Hello?"

Destiny folded her arms over her chest. She heard André's footsteps on the staircase and eagerly awaited his arrival so he could explain why this woman was standing in his condo.

He approached them. "Reese."

Reese ended her phone call with lightning speed and went to embrace André. "Baby."

Baby? Destiny's hands balled into fists. She stuffed them into the pockets of André's robe.

Reese stood on her tiptoes and whispered into André's ear.

Destiny struggled to keep her anger under control.

André rubbed both of Reese's upper arms and moved away from her. He went to stand in front of Destiny. "I need you to go into the guest bedroom," he told her. "Stay there until tomorrow morning."

While you two are doing what? Destiny wondered, feeling her emotions bubbling to the surface. "Why is she here?"

"Not that I owe you an explanation, but she is here because I invited her," André explained.

"And what are you two going to do?" she pressed on.

He wordlessly stared at her.

"You're not going to answer me?"

Reese was giving Destiny a strange look. "Maybe I should come back another time, Dré," she said, adjusting her purse strap.

André looked at her over his shoulder. "No. You stay." He turned back to Destiny. "*You.* In the guest room. Now."

Destiny didn't budge. She looked past him, at Reese, whose beauty and sexiness couldn't be denied. This was a woman who was going to fuck the man Destiny was falling in love with.

"You're hesitating," he said in a low voice.

"Why does she get to call you by your first name?" Destiny demanded.

"And you're questioning me," he reminded her.

"Then punish me," she taunted him. "We have an audience this time. Maybe that will turn you on."

He stared at her for a long time. "You and I are going to talk about this tomorrow. You can stay here if you want." He grabbed Reese by the hand and tugged her towards the master bedroom.

Destiny was tempted to follow him, throw a complete fit, and force him to send Reese home. Force him to reschedule whatever little tryst he was trying to throw in her face. But she only had a small amount of dignity left, and she wanted to hold onto it. Not knowing what to do, she stood with her back pressed against the door to the condo.

She could hear Reese's giggles all the way from where she stood. The melodious sound broke her heart. Tears filled Destiny's eyes. She slid down to the floor, drew her knees up to her chest, and cried.

Reese was an attractive woman. Shaped just the way André liked, naturally seductive. Fun to be around. She loved to please him. It *excited* her to please him. Once upon a time, he thought that she could be the one.

They had an intricate history and had known each other for the better part of a decade. At first, neither of them took the other seriously. But before they knew it, they'd stumbled into something serious. That was until he caught her texting the paparazzi their whereabouts so they could capture her and André on vacation together. That act of betrayal demonstrated to André that she was definitely *not* the one, but from time to time he still enjoyed spending time with her.

This time, he hadn't called her over because he missed her company. He'd called her over because he needed a distraction. Destiny was starting to dominate his thoughts in a way that was not good for him. She was beginning to make him question the very lifestyle that had been good to him for the past several years. Even worse than that, she was beginning to change him, and that frightened him. He didn't see a need to change. He didn't *want* to change.

Reese kneeled between his legs. She was going to town on him, but he couldn't get into it. He was sitting on the edge of the bed with a gorgeous woman tending to his every whim, and all he could think about was Destiny and how he was breaking her heart right now.

Once Reese realized she wasn't getting the reaction out of him that she usually did, she sat back on her haunches. "Is something wrong?"

He shifted his gaze to her. "Did I tell you to stop?"

"No, but-"

"Then keep going," he ordered.

She did as she was told.

In his experience, the women he came across usually did. Destiny was the only exception, the only one who thought to speak her mind whenever she deemed it necessary. She was the only one who challenged him whenever she thought he was wrong. *Which is why she's the only one you have true, genuine feelings for,* his conscience reasoned. "Stop it," he whispered.

Reese stopped immediately and sat back.

He closed his eyes. "Not...you. Not you."

"Then who?" she asked.

He sighed.

"What is going on with you? You're starting to freak me out."

He shook his head.

"Is it about the girl out there?"

"This was a mistake," he said softly.

Reese stood up.

"Where do you think you're going?"

"This is a mistake," she spat at him. "I'm leaving."

"No." He grabbed her hand. "You're not. Get in the bed."

She gave him the side eye.

He maintained eye contact as he repeated, "Get in the bed. Now."

She muttered under her breath in Spanish, a bunch of colorful words to describe how he was acting.

"Don't think for a minute that I don't understand what you're calling me," he told her.

She quieted immediately.

"Seems to me like you're begging for a spanking," he said. "On all fours. Now."

Reese brightened into a smile and eagerly obliged.

16

The condo was quiet. André rose up on his elbows and shifted a glance down at the sleeping female figure beside him. At first glance, he thought it was Destiny. Same spill of dark hair, similar complexion. Hair falling across her face. It didn't take long for the events from the previous night to come rushing at him. He placed the flat of one hand to his forehead. He'd been a complete and utter dick to Destiny last night.

Granted, he'd had his reasons.

He glanced at Reese, who was murmuring in her sleep in Spanish. It was a habit she'd had the entire time he'd known her.

He stood up from the bed, pulled on a pair of pajama pants, and left his bedroom. Taking a deep breath, he pushed open the door to the guest room. A frown etched into his face. The bed was perfectly made and perfectly empty. A lump formed in his throat. He closed the door, counted to three, and opened the door again. His eyes hadn't been playing tricks on him. The bed was empty. His hand trembled on the doorknob as he closed the door.

He continued down the hall. The living room couch was also empty. He turned his head towards the entrance door to his condo. Destiny sat with her back against the door, her head resting between her knees and her arms covering her eyes.

Relief filled every inch of his body as he walked over to her. He knelt down to the floor, kissed the top of her head and gathered her up into his arms. A million different thoughts ran through his mind as he stood up and carried her into the guest bedroom. He kicked the door closed with a bare foot and crossed the room, stopping only when he reached the bed. Holding onto her with one arm, he drew back the covers.

She curled against his chest.

Emotion welled up in him. He'd invited Reese over to help get rid of the feelings that were developing for Destiny. That tactic hadn't worked. He was starting to believe that nothing would. That thought frightened him, but he shoved that fear to the back of his mind. The fear of losing her was a lot more frightening than the fear of the feelings he had for her.

He was hesitant to lay her down; he liked the feel of her curled up against his chest. Realizing that he was getting entirely too sentimental, he laid her on the bed. He wiped at the dried tear tracks marking her cheeks.

Her eyes fluttered open.

He wanted to greet her, but he didn't know what to say. A strange feeling was taking a hold of him. What was it? Shame? Guilt?

She closed her eyes and rolled to her other side.

"Destiny."

"Don't talk to me," she croaked in a sleepy sounding voice.

He walked around the bed so he could see her face, then sat on the edge of the bed. "Destiny."

She opened her eyes. When she did, her beautiful brown eyes were filled with tears. "You're a monster," she whispered vehemently.

The words surprised him, and he didn't know why he was surprised. He'd known that she would be angry with him after what he'd done. Anyone would be under the same circumstances. "That is a disrespectful thing to say," he said quietly, trying to regain his composure and control of the situation.

"What you did was disrespectful to *me*," she threw back at him.

"You were aware that I would be free to sleep with other women."

"You came with me to spend time with my *family*," she hissed at him. "You didn't even wait a week after we got back here before inviting her. We just came back from seeing my family. My *family*, André."

His expression turned hard.

"Don't tell me to call you Sir," she said, pointing at him. "Not after you bring that...that...*girl* in here. Not after you let her call you by your first name. She's different. She's not one of your little sex slaves. You're...different with her."

"I've known her for a long time," he explained in a quiet voice. "Since before the lifestyle."

Destiny sat up slowly. "Oh? So, you...have normal sex with her? She's allowed to be normal with you because she knew you first?"

"We will talk about this another time." He stood up from the bed.

"No, we'll talk about this now," she argued.

"We'll talk about this after she leaves," he said, his voice firm and leaving no room for argument.

"You're a fucking *monster*," she repeated. "A monster of the *worst* kind." She laid back down and hugged the nearest pillow.

He could feel his heart fracturing as he left the room. His life up to now had been so perfectly planned out. He'd maintained a unique sense of control over everything that happened in his life, and now he could feel everything falling apart all around him. He leaned his back against the door. Tears started to form in his eyes, but he willed them away.

His bedroom door opened to reveal Reese, who was completely naked. Pouting prettily, she leaned her head against the doorframe. "I guess this is my cue to leave?" she asked him.

Without saying a word, he nodded.

She turned and proceeded to gather her clothes. That was the beauty of the understanding he had with Reese.

Feelings weren't involved. No offense was taken when he told her to leave. She simply got dressed and went to kiss him goodbye. No harm, no foul.

He turned his head to the side so that her kiss landed on his cheek.

She pulled back with a confused look on her face.

"Thank you for coming on such short notice," he said.

She laughed. "You're welcome, Mr. Dré Gaines," she returned, mocking the formality in his voice.

"Goodbye, Reese."

She reached out and touched his arm. "I wish the best for you, Dré. I always have. I barely spent a night with you and even I can see that you have feelings for that girl in there. If that's true, she has succeeded where the rest of us conquests haven't. She's gotten through to this...right here." Her hand moved to his chest, indicating his heart.

He closed his hand around hers and smiled. "I think...I think I fucked it up."

"She has feelings for you too," Reese told him. "She was ready to claw my eyes out last night. Mine *and* yours. Understand that she was only that angry because she cares so much. I'm the same way."

He nodded knowingly. "I remember."

She laughed. "You know how I am, yes. Talk it out. Apologize, apologize, apologize. Then buy her Chanel. It works for me."

He nodded again.

"You know that, too," she said, beaming at him. "I hope it works out, honey." She raised on tiptoe, kissed him on the cheek again, and then she was gone.

He remained standing with his back against the door to the guestroom another moment before turning, opening the door, and entering.

"Oh, so you have time for me now?"

André closed the door behind him. "I know that you're angry with me. I owe you an explanation for my behavior last night."

Destiny sat in bed with the sheets bunched around her waist. Still wearing his robe. Strands of hair had escaped her topknot, but she still looked beautiful. Always did.

He took a deep breath and approached the bed. "My timing...was bad."

"You think?"

"I can understand why you're angry with me," he said slowly, sitting near her feet. "But I'm going to have to ask for you to keep the sarcasm to a minimum. I have an extremely low tolerance for disrespect."

She folded her arms across her chest.

"You and I had a conversation about whether or not I would invite women here," he started.

"And you said that you would invite women over if you felt I was starting to fall in love with you," she said. "I remember. Is that why you invited her? You feel like I'm falling for you?"

He didn't respond.

"Because I'm not falling for you," she said quickly. "We had a great time at my family's house. We bonded. We had a good time, but I'm not...falling in *love* with you or anything."

He gave her a doubtful look but remained quiet.

She threw her hands up in the air. "Okay, fine. Maybe I did start falling a little bit. You were holding my cousin and being all cute with her, and...it was hard to keep my feelings in check after seeing that. But it's not like I went overboard or declared my love for you, though. I kept it cool, didn't I?"

"Destiny."

"I just don't understand why you'd invite her before talking to me about it," she told him. "Can't you talk to me if you think I'm getting out of line with my emotions, or whatever?"

It took a few minutes for him to compose his own thoughts. "While your feelings for me were beginning to become a concern, I didn't invite Reese over because I felt you were falling in love with me," he said, staring down at his hands.

She scratched at her temple. "I don't understand. Why, then?"

Releasing a deep sigh, he shifted his focus to the wall. It was safe to look at the wall. The sight of the wall didn't make him feel weak, didn't turn his insides to jelly. "I didn't invite her over because of anything you did."

Her eyebrows drew together.

"I invited her over because of me," he admitted finally, meeting her imploring gaze. "I invited her over because I'm falling for you."

She stared at him in shock, her lips parted. That damned hope springing into her eyes. "Well...you act like that's a bad thing."

"Because it *is*," he said, standing up.

"Falling in love isn't a bad thing," she argued. "It's a beautiful thing, a wonderful thing."

"I don't believe in love. I told you that."

She tucked her hair behind both ears. "But you do. I mean...if you're falling for me, you do."

"But I *can't*."

Her hands clutched at the bedsheet. "So...the problem isn't that you *can't* fall in love with me. The problem is that you don't *want* to fall in love with me."

"You're making this about you, and it's not about you," he said emphatically.

"But it is!" she disagreed.

"*No*." He tried to sort through his emotions. "This isn't about you. It's...about me. How I feel for you is becoming a problem. It's distracting. It's...changing who I am. How I operate. And I can't allow it to." He risked a glance at her and wished he hadn't.

The hope in her eyes flickered and died, replaced by a look of sadness and rejection. "So, even if I do what I'm supposed to do, and keep my feelings in check, you can punish me by bringing other women here?"

"Destiny," he pleaded, his voice sounding strained.

She jumped out of bed. "No. I need you to answer this question for me."

"Yes," he said, meeting her gaze head-on. "*Yes*. Okay? If either one of us starts feeling too strongly about the other, then yes. I will need to bring other women here to try to...put things into perspective."

"And having me answer the door without warning me who was going to be on the other side?" she asked him quietly. "Is that how you put things into perspective?"

The muscle in his jaw twitched.

"You don't even understand how cruel that was, do you?" she asked him. "Are you so far removed from human emotion that you don't understand how mean it is to have me, the girl who *lives* with you, the girl who cares for you, answer the door for the woman that you're going to sleep with *while* I'm under the same roof? You wanted me to sleep in the guest bedroom, where I would have *heard* everything. You felt that all of that was necessary? To what...to put things into perspective, as you call it?"

"I went too far," he confessed, fighting to keep his voice level. "I realize that, and I apologize for that."

"I almost left you," she said, tears rolling down her cheeks. "I came *so* close. I walked in on my ex cheating on me, and I was done with him. Completely done. My feelings for him were shut off. I walked away and I never looked back. You pretty much do the same thing to me, right under my nose, and I'm still here. Why am I still here?"

"Because we established pretty early on that this was a possibility," he answered. "I never lied to you or betrayed you."

"It's not fair. It's not fair to me." She bit her bottom lip and stared up at him. "I don't think I can do this."

He closed his eyes. *And now it's time to* really *make her hate you,* he thought. "It doesn't matter what you think," he said. "You're under contract. I own you. You belong to me, as outlined by the contract."

She narrowed her eyes at him.

"If you should attempt to breach your contract, I will not hesitate to take legal action against you," he added.

Anger and indignation flared up in her eyes. "You... you *wouldn't*."

"Today, I'll give you a pass for your behavior," he went on. "I can understand why you're angry with me. Starting tomorrow, your training resumes. That means your words and your actions will be punishable."

"You would take legal action against me if I decided to leave?" she whispered with tears frozen in her eyes.

He maintained eye contact as he replied, "Yes."

She backed away from him. "I'm not good enough to fall in love with, but you want to keep me here?"

"I want you here with me," he said, keeping his facial expression blank, emotionless. "I refuse to let you go."

She covered her mouth with her hands and gave him a look that caused more cracks to embed themselves in his heart. Because she was looking at him like she really believed he *was* a monster.

Destiny felt like a prisoner in her own home. What was perplexing is that while she was horrified that André would even think to take legal action against her for leaving, there was *still* that small part of her that was relieved he wouldn't let her go. That small part of her didn't want to let go of him either.

That tiny part of herself made her question her own sanity. After last night's events, she shouldn't want to be with him. Anyone seeing the situation from the outside would judge her for staying. She imagined Candace or Jasmine in the same situation. Candace would somehow flip the script on André and have *him* carrying out *her* orders, whereas Jasmine would probably enjoy the setup - legal threats and all. Jasmine was a different breed, often amused by rough sexual elements that would scare off most sane individuals.

How Destiny wished she could speak to her friends right now. Candace would tell her to kick the bedroom door down and run for her life. Jasmine and Carlos would tell her to fuck André wherever he stood and make sure to capture it on video. Those two possessed a savagery that she did not. Her heart was completely shattered in two, and the man who had shattered it was holding a contract she'd signed over her head.

Why am I obediently staying in this room instead of kicking the door down and running for my life? she wondered as she stared out of the guest bedroom window. The answer to that was obvious. Even after everything that had happened, her feelings for him were still strong enough to keep her here. *What I feel for him - is it love or some bizarre form of co-dependency?*

He'd been quick to remind her about the contract, but there had been one major catalyst that caused her to sign that document. *I believed that I deserved some form of punishment for hurting Chad, but do I really deserve treatment like this?*

Did she deserve having to open the door for the women that he brought to the condo? Did she deserve having to clean up their mess once the women left?

As André had pointed out, there had been no lies, no deceit…only a lack of warning. The problem was, she interpreted that lack of warning as a lack of respect for her.

I had suspicions that he was broken, and he has pretty much confirmed those suspicions. So, now what? I stay here and continue to tolerate his self-indulgence?

A soft knock sounded on the door. "Lunch is on the dining room table," he announced through the closed door.

"Thank you, Sir," she returned automatically, without thinking. Immediately, she covered her face and blinked back tears. *I'm not ready to see him or talk to him. I don't even know what to say to him right now.*

She reluctantly looked down in disdain at the robe she was *still* wearing. Sliding the robe off her shoulders, she walked over to the long mirror in the corner of the room. The hem of the robe dragged behind her on the floor. She touched the black leather collar at her neck. It wasn't quite a piece of jewelry. It was like a brand. A visual, tangible reminder that she was a possession.

While studying the shape of her body in the mirror, she found herself comparing her curves to Reese's. That hadn't been her intention, but it seemed that most women were genetically inclined to compare themselves to each other. Destiny's curves weren't nearly as exaggerated as Reese's, but her body had a nice shape.

She left the guest bedroom and entered his bedroom. He wasn't a fan of jeans; he'd implied as much. She didn't feel like putting on one of her new dresses, not without showering. She settled for a t-shirt and shorts, not really caring what he thought about it.

With her nerves rattling, she dragged a brush through her curls to help herself look at least halfway presentable.

She expected for him to eat lunch in his home office, but instead he sat at the head of the dining room table. *Definition of awkward,* she thought. *This moment. This moment right here.*

"I made chicken Caesar salad," he told her just as his cell phone buzzed.

"Thank you, Sir," she said, eyeing the plate he'd set out for her. He'd set the plate at his left. Not only was he going to eat at the same table as her, but he wanted her to sit close to him. She took a deep breath and sat down.

He gave a pointed look at her choice in clothes.

"I haven't showered yet today, so I didn't want to put on one of my dresses," she said. "I would have taken a shower, but I didn't want to keep you waiting."

"You can shower after lunch," he told her.

She lifted her fork.

His phone buzzed again. This time, he checked it. He ran his fingers over the glossy screen on the gadget and cleared his throat. "Just so you have warning, Reese is coming back tonight."

When he spoke those words, Destiny forgot herself. She forgot her role in their relationship. She forgot about the contract she'd signed. In that moment, she was just a woman. "Excuse me?"

"Reese is coming back here, and she is spending the night," he repeated.

She pushed her chair backwards and stood up.

"Sit down, Destiny," he commanded softly.

She glared down at him.

"I said, sit down," he ordered, his voice harder than it had been the first time.

She gripped her fork in her hand so hard that it started to hurt. There were so many words on the tip of her tongue, *none* of them nice. It took a maximum amount of effort, but she was just barely able to hold her tongue. She slowly started to sit back down in her chair.

"Tell me what you're thinking."

She didn't respond.

"Destiny."

"Permission to speak freely, *Sir*?" she asked.

"Granted," he allowed.

She squinted at him, trying to see past the nonchalant expression plastered on his face. More than anything, she wanted to see beyond the dominant persona and bravado to the man who was underneath. "I'm wondering how you came to be so broken."

He drew back in his seat.

"You come from a broken home," she stated. "That is common knowledge, since you rapped and sang about it. I understand how much of an impact that can have on someone. I have friends and family whose parents split up or divorced. I understand that it's traumatizing. I do. But none of them are so afraid of falling in love that they are willing to risk the only true love they've ever experienced. None of them have become as jaded as you seem to be."

"Destiny," he said, his tone grave with warning.

"You gave me the permission to speak freely, did you not?" she asked, pounding her fist on the table and standing again. "Do you know what I see when I look at you?"

He stared back at her, and there were cracks visible in the mask of composure that he was putting on.

"Come on, André," she taunted, leaning close to him. "Don't you want to know?"

He stared up at her without speaking.

"I see a frightened, scared little boy when I look at you," she told him, her voice dripping with pity. "I see a little boy who is so fucking scared, he's willing to make me believe he is a monster. He'd rather me believe he's a monster than believe that he knows that love exists."

"Shut your mouth," he said quietly, finally breaking eye contact.

"Has my free speech expired so soon?"

"Destiny, I'm warning you." He closed his eyes.

"I hear your warning, but what I *don't* hear is a denial of anything I've said," she yelled at him. "And do you know why? Because you know I'm right. I guess you're not the only one who is halfway decent at reading people."

He shoved his chair back so hard that it flew across the room and toppled on its side. When he stood up, he braced his hands on the table and drew his face close to hers. His face flushed red with anger. "If you don't shut your mouth as I've instructed, I'm going to shut it for you."

Her heart pounded wildly in her chest. She knew what he meant, and she knew where this was heading, but she didn't let up. "And how are you going to do that?"

He reached up, curled a hand around the back of her neck, and drew her face closer to his until their lips met.

It was another kiss where she could tell he wanted to stay in their bubble and shut the rest of the world out. There was a desperation in the way he kissed her, like he was pleading for her to stay. She kissed him with the same desperation, only her kiss was pleading for him to accept the love he felt for her.

The kiss lasted for so long, and still it ended way too soon. They stared at each other wordlessly. He glanced over his shoulder at the chair he'd nearly destroyed and closed his eyes.

The air was tense with both of their emotions cranked up to the highest of levels. Her gaze anchored to the floor while she tried to make sense of her own feelings. She tried to cling onto the anger she felt towards him, because she knew that he deserved it. That anger was already slipping away because it was *him*. How could she stay angry with him, when she felt she needed him as much as she needed her next breath? "Would it really be that bad for you to just love me?"

"Reese coming over isn't about you," he said, echoing his earlier sentiment. "It's about me. Me regaining control over what I'm feeling. I'm sorry that my involvement with her causes you pain, but I need this."

She sighed and walked away from him.

He followed her into the living room. "You are correct about my parents splitting up having something to do with why I can't open myself up to...to the idea that..."

She turned and looked at him.

He stopped walking. "Don't pity me."

He said those exact same words the night he came to find me in the newsroom, she remembered. "You can't even speak the words."

He blinked rapidly.

And just like that, she could see through his polished exterior. It was as if a curtain had been drawn. She wanted to assure him that he could trust her with his secrets, his heart. He didn't have to be afraid of falling in love with her, because she loved him and would never do anything to hurt him. *I slept in a cage, for God's sake,* she thought. *How can't he know that I would do anything for him?*

"My parents' relationship has influenced my views on love," he said finally, in a voice just above a whisper. Vulnerability dwelled in the depths of his sad eyes. "I've also had experiences as an adult, relationships where I put everything into them and was taken advantage of. I vowed to myself that I wouldn't ever go through that again."

"So did I, when Jordan cheated on me," she told him. "I know what that feels like. I wouldn't *ever* do that to you."

He looked away from her and closed his eyes, as if the act would shut out sound.

She stood before him, looking hurt. "You don't believe me?"

"It's not that I don't believe you," he said, his eyes still closed. "It's not that I don't believe that *you* believe you're telling the truth. The relationships I see...someone always winds up getting hurt. As much as I *wish* I could, I can't take the risk of putting myself through that again. It broke me the last time I went through it."

Her frustration was coming to its boiling point. "I can promise you," she said, walking over to him. She laid her hand on his arm. "I can swear on anything you want me to swear on."

He backed away from her the minute she touched him. "Destiny. It's not that simple."

Near the point of screaming, she raised both hands to her temples. "Oh my God, what is *wrong* with you?" she cried out.

"I don't know!" he bellowed at her, his voice booming throughout the condo. The windows vibrated against their panes and the glasses on the dining room table trembled. He strode over to the couch and sat on it. "Okay?! I don't know. Please stop asking me that. Please stop referring to me as broken. *Please*...just stop."

"Okay." She followed him to the couch, wanting to reach out and touch him or hug him. From how tense his body appeared to be, she could tell that he didn't want to be touched right now. Instead, she knelt to the floor. "I don't want to keep repeating myself, so I'm just going to make this known. By now you have to know that I love you. Okay? There, I've said it and it's out of the way. Before, I wouldn't have told you because I knew that if I did, you would invite another woman over. But you're doing that anyway, so..." Her sentence trailed off and she lapsed into silence.

His eyes were still full of sadness.

"I love you and I want you to know that. I would never hurt you. *Ever*. I respect you. I admire you. I appreciate having you in my life, despite you bringing Reese here. Despite you bringing her here again." She paused and tried to sort her thoughts out. "Basically, what I'm trying to tell you is that loving me wouldn't be a risk, because I would never ever hurt you. I love you too much. I'd hurt myself first."

The glimmer of tears shone before he lowered his gaze.

She sighed. "I feel like...I feel like you *want* to love me."

There were words that he wanted to say, but he seemed to be weighing the risk of saying them. Finally, he lifted his eyes and looked at her. "I do."

Despite the recent events that had just transpired, she felt hope surging within her. Tucking wayward strands of curly hair behind her ear, she started to ask, "So then why...why can't we just..."

"Because I don't know how," he insisted in anguish. "Because I'm too scared to relearn how."

She tried not to let the disappointment show on her face. "I'd be willing to work with you, though. We can at least try."

André ducked his head down. He wanted to believe her so badly. He would gladly trade all his money and all his empire for her if there was a one hundred percent certainty that she would never hurt him. The problem was, there were no one hundred percent certainties in relationships. You were dealing with someone entirely separate from yourself, and that created factors and elements that were beyond your control. As much as you loved someone, and as much as you felt like that person was your soulmate, that person's feelings could change over time or maybe were never reciprocated at all.

The look in Destiny's eyes was enough to pull at his heart. He wanted to be the man that could stand up, pledge his life to her, marry her, give her beautiful children, and make her the happiest woman in the world. While he wanted to be the man that could give her those things...

I don't feel like I am the man that could *give her those things. If she doesn't hurt me, there's a chance that I would wind up hurting her.* He'd shut himself off to love for so long, he didn't know how to begin to express it again. In his stumbling, he was likely to break her heart.

Tears filled his eyes as he said, "I want to. I want to try. But...I can't."

Hope had lit up her eyes when he said that he wanted to try and died when he said that he couldn't. "Well...I don't want Reese to come over tonight," she stated, her facial expression stony.

"She *is* coming tonight. I need her to."

"Then I don't want to be here."

"I told you that if you try leaving, I will take legal action."

"Then take legal action."

Those words caught him off-guard, and he racked his brain for a rebuttal. "I'm not bluffing, Destiny."

The expression on her face said that she didn't care whether he was bluffing, and that facial expression alone was enough to scare him. "Neither am I. Take legal action. I don't care. I'm going to pack my bags. Have one of your drivers take me to the airport." She stomped away from him.

Frowning, he jumped up to follow her. *You can't let her leave. Hurry up and think of something.* He trailed behind her as she exited the living room and paused once he reached the master bedroom. "My lawyers are sharks. They would eat you alive."

"Hello, newsflash to André, I don't own anything!" she shouted as she walked around the bed. "All you can take away from me is my college debt. You're welcome to help yourself to that."

He ran a hand over his head. Control was slipping away from him so quickly, that he couldn't get a hold of it. She was holding all the control now; she was the one leading this discussion, the one holding all of the cards. It had been years since he'd felt such a loss of control in a relationship. "You can't leave," was all he could think to say. He hated the sound of desperation in his own voice, hated how weak those words had sounded.

"This isn't *Phantom of the Opera*," she said flippantly, opening his closet door and hunting down her luggage. "This isn't *Beauty and the Beast*. You can't keep me here."

Fear seized his heart. He could feel his chest growing tight as he watched her. "Destiny, please stop."

She hefted her luggage out of the closet and lifted one of the cases on top of the bed. "No, André, *you* stop." Her movements were jerky as she unzipped the suitcase.

He had a knack for knowing which words would pull his preferred reaction from someone. Many of his past lovers had accused him of manipulating them. But in this moment, he was at a complete loss for which words would get Destiny to stay - other than the obvious words she wanted him to say. He moved around the bed and silently stood beside her while she flipped the suitcase open.

She turned and made as if to move, but he was blocking her. "Excuse me."

"I'm not moving."

"Really? Like I can't just walk around you?" She stepped to the side.

So did he.

She glared at him. "This is juvenile, André."

"Please don't leave."

"Please don't invite Reese over," she countered.

He blinked at her without responding.

She stepped to the side again.

Again, he blocked her path, but he knew that it would take more than that to keep her from leaving. "Okay," he said finally.

"Okay, what?" she prompted.

"Okay, I'll text her and cancel," he said.

She folded her arms across her chest. "For me to stay, you can't keep seeing other women."

"Your contract stated-" he began.

She shook her head. "I don't care."

His gaze shifted to the suitcase on the bed. That suitcase would be packed tight with her clothes within the next few minutes if he didn't give her the answer she wanted. His options were limited: give her what she wanted or remain stubborn and lose her. "I don't...I can't..."

She took a step closer to him. "I have a question for you."

His jaw tensed. "All right."

"When you slept with Reese last night...how did she make you feel?"

Don't answer that.

Destiny searched his eyes and looked to have found her answer. "And this morning? When you woke up to her? How did you feel then?"

If only you knew…

"I can answer both questions for you." She lowered her gaze to his right forearm and touched his birthmark. "Both times, you wished she was me. You wished she was me, because I can do more for you than any other woman can. On some level, you know this. That's why you couldn't get over me the last time I walked away from you, and why you're trying to do everything in your power to keep me from walking away from you right now. Can't you see that?"

"I won't deny that," he worded carefully.

"Then you also have to admit that there is no point in bringing Reese, or any other woman here ever again," she reasoned.

"I can give you my word that I will cancel tonight with Reese, Destiny, but I cannot promise to be monogamous."

"Then move out of my way," she demanded.

"No." He took a deep, shaky breath. "Earlier, you said you would work with me, right?"

She went still. "Yes, I did say that."

"Look…I'm willing to cancel with Reese tonight. For you. But asking me to go from the way I was, to being the perfect boyfriend overnight isn't realistic."

She avoided eye contact with him. He'd made a valid point, and even as angry as she was, she couldn't deny it.

"All I'm asking is for you to accept me as I am," he said, touching her cheek. "You might think I'm broken or flawed or whatever it is you want to call me. But this is how I was when you decided to come here with me. It is no secret that I care about you a lot. You can tell that just by the way I treat you, and everything I'm willing to do for you. You missed your family. Despite the effect that had on my schedule, I made it happen. Professionally, I have always supported you and encouraged you. While I wish I could tell you everything you want to hear right now, I can't. I'm not the guy who would lie to you or mislead you just to keep you here."

She wrapped her arms around herself. "How could you want me to stay so badly, but not even be willing to just... *try* to be with me? I just asked you to *try*. I haven't given you a reason to distrust me." After a brief pause, she shook her head. "You are right about one thing, though. I signed the contract with the understanding that you'd be allowed to sleep with other women. You were very clear about those terms. That contract, however, does not state that I have to be under the same roof when you do it."

He frowned.

"So, that condo you offered me on my first day here? I'm going to need that condo - in my name. I'm also going to need a car." She sidestepped him and made her way to the dresser so she could pull some of her clothes out. "I'll fulfill the rest of my contract, because I'm a woman of my word and because I don't need a legal case being brought against me. But once the contract period is over, I'm out."

He watched her as she packed her clothes into the large suitcase. "I understand," he said quietly. He left the room so she could pack in peace.

For the remainder of the day, Destiny avoided André. Despite her desire to be understanding, she couldn't stand the sight of him. His views on love were warped due to seeing a lot of disastrous, destructive relationships. That much was understandable. But when she was in the throes of anger and frustration, she couldn't help but wonder if all of those excuses were just a clever way to keep her compliant while he ran around with other women.

The thought was dismissed nearly as soon as it popped into her head. She'd seen the look in his eyes and the tears.

But let's be real here, Destiny, he's an actor, she thought. *Or, at least, he used to be. All of that could have been an act.*

She summoned an image of his face when he thought she was leaving. That's all it took for her to come to the final determination that it hadn't been an act. In many women, there was that urge to nurture. Nurture and fix. A guy is proven to be a "bad boy?" *Let me nurture him and fix him*, was most women's instinct. It often led to a heartbreak that Destiny was trying to avoid.

I feel crazy for even thinking this, but is it selfish for me to want to walk away from him so I can protect myself? Wasn't love about accepting someone as they were, and sticking with them through the tough times? People were always told they shouldn't have to change who they are for someone who claims to love them.

This situation was so aggravating. There was no easy answer. She could live life with him and learn to deal with him sleeping with other women, learn to be satisfied with whatever little slice of his life that he offered her. Or she could live life without him. In both cases, she felt doomed to be miserable.

If she walked away from him, she could meet a nice, stable guy like Chad. No matter how great the man was, André would always be there, at the back of her mind and in her heart. At any given time, she'd still wonder where he was, who he was with, or what he was doing. Those thoughts would lead to her wondering whether he still thought about her.

He'd had such a huge impact on her life, that she would always compare the men in her life to him. God forbid André happened to cross paths with her and make a pass at her. Most likely it would be a pass that she accepted, regardless of what other man she was dating. Why?

"Because I love him," she said out loud, tears filling her eyes. "Because I love him. And God, I don't *want* to. I want to hate him. Hating him would be so much easier. But it's impossible to hate him when I love him so much."

On the other side of the bedroom door, André had both arms braced against the doorframe. At the sound of her words, his own eyes filled with tears. Smiling through his tears, he hung his head. "I love you too," he whispered. "I just...I can't tell you that yet. Just...be patient with me. Give me time and I promise I'll show you how much you mean to me." Words that he could whisper now, because she wasn't standing right in front of him making demands and ultimatums. Words that he could whisper now, because he knew that she couldn't hear them.

This time, as he stood there on the other side of that door, listening to her pleading and crying out for him, he did let the tears fall.

17

André was a man of his word. He showed her the condo he would set her up in. The unit was in the same building as his, a cute one-bedroom number with an amazing view of the complex swimming pool. Several cars were at his disposal and he told her that she could have her pick. She chose a pearl white Range Rover Velar, and he gave her the keys without hesitation. He even offered to have the title transferred to her name.

He would have given her just about anything she asked for, anything other than commitment. She was standoffish with him, keeping him at arm's length. As long as she was still around, he was okay with that. All he needed was time.

She reminded him that she was only contractually obligated to be available to him Friday through Sunday.

He confirmed that and reminded her that he had final say and approval over who she could spend recreational time with. He gave her a list of names of approved friends that she could communicate with via phone calls and text. Carlos, Jasmine, and Candace were all included in that list. All members of her family were approved without question.

She agreed.

He glanced around the condo he was giving to her. It was a unit that he'd rented out over the years, one that he used to live in. "Someone from my staff will go grocery shopping for you," he announced as he walked throughout the unit. Since the condo was empty, his voice bounced on the walls around them, causing a slight echo effect. "A maid comes in once a week, just like my place."

She followed him, uncharacteristically quiet.

He poked his head into the barren bedroom. "I'll have furniture delivered within the next few days."

"Do I get to pick it out?"

He turned and gave her the side eye. "You're milking this."

"I'm not!" she exclaimed. "I'm just...picky when it comes to furniture."

He shook his head and smiled. "You can pick out the furniture."

"This is more space than I imagined."

"I lived here before moving to the unit I'm in now," he explained. "I didn't think I needed more space than a one-bedroom condo. I was wrong."

"Hard to have a playroom with only a one-bedroom unit," she remarked.

"Exactly," he agreed, grateful that her disposition was positive enough for her to joke. "At the time, I also needed a studio. Over time, that studio became my playroom."

She avoided his gaze.

He reached out and touched the D-shaped ring on her collar. "I want you to wear this, even when you're here."

"Yes, Sir," she said, still avoiding his gaze.

He cleared his throat and raised his eyes. "So, you need groceries, furniture. The Range should be checked out for any possible issues. I haven't driven it in over a month."

"I need a television," she added.

He slanted a look at her.

"Just *one*," she said.

"...And a television," he amended.

She walked away from him, moving down the hall and into the space that would be the designated dining room. Coming to stand in front of the dining room windows, she murmured, "It's so beautiful."

"And now it belongs to you," he said from behind her.

"It's hard to believe I own it. None of this feels real."

"I'll complete the work of getting the condo and car title transferred to your name," he said, eyeing his watch.

"There will be documentation that you need to sign. Working and owning property in Canada will require for you to file tax returns in Canada. There are accountants I can get you in touch with, to brush you up on that."

"Since I don't have to worry about a house or car, the only debt I have to worry about is my school loan," she said, more to herself than him.

"I'm going to take care of that when you start work next week," he advised.

Her head whipped around. "You don't have to do that," she said. "When I said what I said, we were in the middle of an argument. I don't really expect you to take care of my student debt."

"I know I don't *have* to," he said, closing the distance between them. "I *want* to. Even though you signed a contract, I know that being with me isn't easy."

Her hands balled into fists that she kept at her sides. "It won't change how I feel," she warned him. "I'll still want to leave once the contract period is over. You can't bribe me to stay."

"My intention isn't to bribe you," he said, touching her upper arm. "My intention is to show you that I appreciate you. That sometimes gets lost in translation."

"Easy for that to happen with other women walking around," she muttered.

He let his hand fall to his side. "That free day I gave you ended yesterday," he reminded her.

She closed her mouth and lowered her eyes.

He sighed. "I want us to move past that."

"Okay," she said.

"Okay?"

She nodded. "Yes. I can move past that."

His eyebrows drew together. "That was...easier than I expected."

She shrugged her shoulders. "I'm going to take a page from your playbook and remove my emotions from this situation," she said. "You want me to do your bidding and follow orders? I can do that. I'll be just like your maid, someone else under your employ. This is your show. I'm just another bit player playing a role. Right?"

He frowned down at her.

"I mean, right, Sir?" she corrected, holding out the skirt of her dress on both sides and attempting to curtsy.

Instead of responding, he said, "Since we have to wait for your furniture to be delivered, you'll spend the next few nights with me. Follow me."

She followed him out of the condo and waited for him to lock up. Then, she followed him to the elevator, where he pushed the button for his floor. Once the elevator doors slid open, she followed him down the long, familiar hall to his own condo. He unlocked the door, entered, and told her to close the door behind her.

After dropping both sets of condo keys on the narrow table near the entryway, he headed to the playroom and stopped just in front of the door. "Mockery and disrespect aren't something that I can tolerate, Destiny." He reached out, grabbed the doorknob, and opened the door.

The lights were left dim.

Time moved slowly as André sauntered around the room, evaluating the various toys and tools on the shelves.

If his intent was to intimidate her, then this method was working. Anticipation built up within her as she waited in the center of the room. She didn't know what to expect. There was a thrill in that, but there was also an underlying, foreboding sense of fear.

Each moment that passed without a word only served to increase her fear. When he came to stand in front of her, he held several items in his hands. He looked her in the eyes with a stoic expression on his face. "Come."

She didn't want to move from her spot in the middle of the room. In the middle of the room, she felt safe. But she knew that if she didn't move within seconds of his issued command, she would be scolded. Reluctantly, she stepped forward and followed him.

He stopped right in front of a tall, wooden contraption. *Contraption* was the only word Destiny could think of to describe it. It looked like something from the medieval times and was the one item he'd never explained in their previous visits to this room. He set down the items he was holding near the base of the large behemoth of a construct. Then he set a hand on her shoulder and moved to stand behind her. He brushed the back of his hand against the nape of her neck before grabbing the zipper on her dress and dragging it down. Slowly, he parted the two sides of her dress. His breath left a hot, steamy trail down the length of her exposed back. Next, he slid the garment off her shoulders and down her arms. They both watched the dress fall to the floor. With her bra and panties left on, he extended his hand to her.

Now was when the worry and survival instincts started to kick in. "I'm sorry I mocked you," she apologized.

"Apologies come easy. Corrective action is a better training tool than the acceptance of a verbal apology." The briefest hint of a smile touched his lips as he spoke the words. "Come."

"I won't mock you again," she promised. "I know I crossed the line."

"Don't make me repeat myself, Destiny," he said.

Maybe I wouldn't be so hesitant to follow your orders if this weird platform-thing didn't look like a torture device that was used back in the 1400's, she fretted, swallowing the lump that had formed in her throat. Once she accepted his offered hand, he guided her up a step and onto the contraption.

"Face me."

She turned around and try as she might, she couldn't keep the worry and fear off her face. Thick wooden beams were on either side of her as she faced him.

He bent at the waist to retrieve one of the items he'd set down earlier, an item that looked similar to some of the others. It was a circular cuff with a chain hanging from it. He bowed his head and walked to the side of the wooden contraption.

She angled her head, trying to keep an eye on him to see what he was up to.

"Look straight ahead, please," he instructed.

Rolling her eyes heavenward, she turned her head. She stared straight ahead as he stepped up on the platform of the strange wooden structure. He reached out and grabbed her right hand, then opened the cuff and circled it around her wrist. Next came connecting the chain of the cuff to its proper post on the wood beam. She tugged her wrist to test the strength of the cuff. It held.

"The mocking *did* bother me," he stated as he wrapped a cuff around her left wrist. "But that's not what bothered me most."

Over the past twenty-four hours, she'd definitely made a show of testing his patience with sarcastic responses. As much as she would have loved to pretend it was because she'd become a savage overnight, the sarcasm was more of a defense tactic. It helped her to take him less seriously, helped her to keep her feelings in check.

"What bothered me most was you saying that you would take emotions out of this - that entire portion of the conversation. You said you would be like another one of my employees." He secured the cuff on her left wrist to the wooden beam and tested it before moving to the pile of items he'd left on the floor. "I don't want you to be some lifeless robot, Destiny."

"I won't be," she told him earnestly.

"I didn't give you permission to speak," he cautioned, proceeding to cuff both of her ankles.

A sense of helplessness overwhelmed her. "I know I'm not allowed to speak, but it's not fair for us to have these conversations when you're doing this."

"Doing what?" he asked her.

"Cuffing me to a device they used to decapitate kings and queens back in the medieval times," she told him.

He laughed as he finished connecting the cuff of her left ankle to the post. "The device you're referring to is called a guillotine. That's not what this is."

"It's still not fair. If you want to talk to me about what I said, it should be done..."

He looked up and arched a brow at her. "Let me guess. *Normally?*"

She searched her brain for a synonym that wouldn't irk him as much. "Or *vanilla* as you would say."

Laughing, he stood up. "I'm not in a mood to talk," he said, giving her a pointed look.

She tugged at both wrists.

"You've been extremely vocal lately," he said, picking up something that looked like a large, black bicycle handlebar tassel. "I've allowed you to speak freely, a lot more freely than I've allowed submissives to in the past - a lot more freely than most Dominants would ever allow. I think I may have been too lenient with you."

Her eyes zeroed in on the item in his hands. The item looked harmless, but the look in his eyes did not.

"You say that you want to take feelings out of this. You want to be like an employee to me. I'm going to show you what that would be like." As he spoke, he lightly slapped the black tassels against one hand. "I want to make sure you understand that my feelings for you are what caused me to be so lenient with you. My feelings are why you haven't experienced a real punishment dealt by me.

"But if you want feelings out of it, we can do that. You can dive into this lifestyle headfirst and see what it's like when someone is cold, and unfeeling, and doesn't give a shit about you."

His words made her cringe.

"This here," he said, indicating the item in his hand, "is called a flogger. I'm a huge fan of the flogger, because it is a multi-purpose instrument." He continued slapping the black leather tassels against the palm of his free hand. "This item can be used to cause sensations of pleasure or pain. It all depends in how you use it."

She watched as he stepped back onto the platform.

"I can lightly touch you with it, like this..." He lightly touched the tassels to her belly and moved it back and forth.

Her stomach convulsed as the leather tassels moved across her skin.

"If you've done something that warrants punishment...I can do this." He flicked the tassels of the flogger at her stomach with a lightning quick jerk of his wrist.

She gasped out loud. The smack was hard enough to send a dozen tiny little stinging pricks of pain across her stomach.

"That was tame, compared to what I could do," he told her. "If I didn't care about you, I could do a lot worse."

"I understand," she told him.

"You understand...?"

"I understand, Sir."

"Tell me what it is that you understand."

That I should maybe keep my sarcasm to a minimum from now on. "You're using this room and these...*things* to show me how much you've sheltered me, and how you've tried to ease me into this. You're trying to show me that you care about me."

He lowered his head and stared down at the flogger. "With other women, I needed these things. I needed them to get excited, or to have something to look forward to. With you, I don't need them. Don't get me wrong, I still like them. There are some items I'd very much like to use on you, in time. But...when it comes to you, *you're* what I look forward to."

She could feel tears gathering in her eyes.

"I can't become the perfect man overnight," he told her sadly, looking back up at her. "If I could, for you, I would.

But I can't. There are...things that I have to work through. Issues that I have. All I wanted was time. Time to try to get my shit together. I was willing to let you live in that condo, away from me. I was willing to live without you for most of the week, willing to give you space if you needed it. But when you said those things about taking emotions out of it and being like an employee to me...that got under my skin."

"I was mad at you," she said, her cheeks wet with tears. "You knew what bringing that girl here would do to me and you threw it in my face. Just as I was starting to move past that, you invited her back."

"That entire situation was handled poorly," he said. "I didn't know what to do and acted out of desperation. I'm sorry for how that made you feel."

Her mouth dropped open in shock. "Thank you...Sir."

With deft movements, he lifted an arm and started to uncuff her right wrist.

"But..."

A single eyebrow arched. "What is it?"

"I'm interested in finding out more about how floggers could be used for pleasure," she confessed.

An expression of pleasant surprise settled across his features as he stepped down from the platform.

At first, Destiny thought he was leaving the room, another form of punishment. But he lingered in the room, moving slowly between rows of shelving units, scoping each shelf's contents. He stopped near the end of the row, picked up an item, and draped it across the palm of his hand. A cerulean, silk blindfold - long and wide.

"Touch and sensation are very fun to experiment with," he explained as he returned to her with the shimmering fabric. "To a certain extent, I can control how intensely you feel sensation." With those words spoken, he stepped back onto the platform and moved behind her.

It was hard *not* to feel vulnerable and helpless when you were cuffed, spread-eagle and wearing very little clothing. His fingertips danced down her spine and she shivered in response.

"Sensory play. When one or more of your senses are cut off, you feel the others more strongly. Your brain, and your nerves, can focus all of their energy on those senses that are still active." His fingers walked back up her spine, eliciting another shiver. Chuckling, he lifted the blindfold over her head and in front of her eyes. "There are also medical benefits to sensory deprivation beyond sexual enjoyment. It can help aid in improving sleep quality and the body's ability to relax. The way we will use sensory deprivation today will cause you more excitement than relaxation, since you are so new to this."

She tugged at her wrist cuffs as he secured the silk garment in front of her eyes and knotted it behind her head. Lights out. She could see nothing but black.

"Is that too tight?" he asked, adjusting it on her head slightly.

"No, Sir," she responded.

"Good girl," he commended, and moved. Only...she could no longer tell *where* he was moving. She could hear the slight rustle of his dress shirt, the click of his shoes on the wooden platform. A moment later, the sounds of clicking stopped.

Not knowing where he was in the room was causing her a bit of anxiety. She strained to hear any sounds at all. A fingertip grazed along her collarbone, causing her to gasp. That fingertip moved down her chest and traced a pattern around her navel. Her skin tingled in the areas he touched. Her skin tingled in the areas he *didn't* touch. She found herself arching her body towards him, craving the feel of his hand.

He chuckled again and withdrew his hand. Even that chuckle sounded richer when it was all she could focus on.

She whimpered the moment his hand left her skin. The feeling of his hand was soon replaced with the feeling of about twenty long, hard tassels. The feeling was familiar. *That must be the flogger,* she realized. The fringe tassels from the flogger shook against her belly, then the feeling was gone. There was a light smacking sensation. The sensation triggered a series of small shocks throughout her body.

"Did that hurt?"

She shook her head. "No, Sir," she said breathlessly.

"How did it feel?" he asked, his voice low.

"It felt..." She writhed, slightly pulling at her restraints as a shudder rocked her body. "It felt good."

He smacked her again with it, a bit harder.

She moaned out loud.

He dragged the tassels across her skin again, soothing the spot he'd just struck.

"Mmmm." She bit her bottom lip.

The flogger lashed out, pulling another moan out of her. The wooden boards of the platform creaked as he stepped down. She heard his footsteps, close at first and then much further away. Heard the door to the room swing open and shut. Confusion set in, but she waited until she heard the door to the room swing open again. There was the sound of his returning footsteps, and then there was another sound...a light, clinking sound. There was also a scent there. Something sweet, fruity. The sweet scent teased her nostrils.

"It's so interesting to me," he said, his voice sounding close. "Women have always been easy to tease. I could tease them for hours and think nothing of it. But with you...I don't know. It feels like when I'm teasing you, I'm teasing myself. The longer I wait before touching you, before kissing you, before entering you..."

His words caused tremors to run along the length of her body.

"The longer I wait, the more torturous it is for me. It's like edge play, which I also like and will teach you about."

She felt something cold touch the spot between her breasts and gasped in shock. The cold sensation moved over the curve of each breast, and lowered to one nipple, which was still covered by a lacy white bra. Ice. The clinking sound she'd heard earlier were ice cubes. She twisted her torso to the side, shying away from the cold.

She heard him step onto the platform and could feel his closeness. "Don't turn away from me," he ordered softly.

She untwisted her body but cringed before he touched the ice to her skin again. The ice left a wet trail down her stomach. He tucked the ice cube in the waistband of her panties and left it there. Then she felt his hands sliding up the length of her arms, felt his fingers intertwine with hers. She arched her body towards him again and felt his mouth come crashing down on hers. Memories from the past forty-eight hours faded. The anger she'd felt towards him was forgotten. The only thoughts that ran through her mind in that moment were how good his lips felt and how much she wanted to see him.

He broke the kiss off abruptly, and she felt him rest his forehead on her shoulder. Then he moved away from her.

"I want to see you," she told him.

"Is that what you want?" he asked her, sounding further away now.

A moment later, she felt something touch her bottom lip. A million different visuals sprang to mind as the object was pushed against her mouth, trying to pry her lips open. She opened her mouth. The object was plump.

"Bite down," he instructed.

She sank her teeth into the object. Strawberry juice exploded into her mouth and coated her throat while the ice cube tucked into her panties continued melting.

He removed his hand and left the strawberry in her mouth. Then she could feel the blindfold around her eyes loosening. The silk fabric fell away from her eyes. He stood in front of her, and she would have sworn that he'd somehow gotten more beautiful in the brief time she was blindfolded. He lowered his head and wrapped his lips around the end of strawberry protruding from her mouth. He pulled the strawberry out of her mouth and bit down into it. Translucent liquid moistened his lips and ran down his chin as he chewed. He chewed slowly as he stared at her.

She wasn't one to be eager. But with André standing in front of her, gorgeous, sexy, and with a presence that was larger than life, her entire body cried out for him.

The look in his eyes said that he knew the effect he was having on her. Instead of fulfilling her wishes, he took a step back and started to unbutton the cuffs of his dress shirt. His hands moved up to the shirt collar. Turning his back to her, he slid his dress shirt down his shoulders. With the dress shirt removed, he next raised his undershirt over his head.

She got a great view of the artwork tattooed on his broad, muscular back and on the back of his upper arm. There were faces of the people who were most important to him. A detailed flying bird resembling a raven. Roman numerals, a few quotes from his own songs. His muscles flexed as the shirt fell to the floor and she felt her entire body grow hot. He angled a look at her over his shoulder. "You're blushing," he observed.

"Well that solves the mystery," she joked. "Black girls *can* blush."

He grinned and lowered his eyes.

She followed his gaze. He was looking at a bucket of ice. *But...I thought we were done with the ice,* she thought, watching him closely.

He bent at the waist and plucked a piece of ice from the bucket. He put it into his mouth and clenched it between his teeth. Then he looked up at her and stepped back up onto the platform. Ducking his head down, he grazed her shoulder with the piece of ice.

Her breath caught in her throat as he moved the piece of ice down to her collarbone, between her breasts, where he paused and lifted his gaze. She stared down at him with her lips parted.

He dragged the rapidly melting piece of ice over the slope of her chest and to the tip of one bra-covered breast. Her nipple hardened beneath the cold wetness of the ice. He sucked what was left of the ice into his mouth, along with the tip of her breast.

She could feel the wetness and heat from his tongue through the lacy fabric of her bra. That, mingled with the intermittent coolness of the ice drove her crazy.

He pulled back and hopped down from the platform. When he returned, he had another piece of ice between his lips. This time, he started beneath her breast and moved downward. He lowered down to his knees. His hands sloped down the curve of her waist and stopped when they met the waistband of her panties. His fingertips were warm to the touch as he slid her panties down her legs.

She shuddered uncontrollably. The sensation of the ice traveling towards her center, along with the image of his face *right there* was too much to handle.

He teased wetness out of her with his fingers before touching the piece of ice to her most sensitive area.

She tossed her head back and moaned loudly, thankful that he had the foresight to soundproof this room.

He slid his hands down to her outer thighs and used the piece of ice on her until it was completely gone. Once it was gone, he *still* didn't stop. He used his lips and his tongue to send waves of pleasure crashing throughout her body.

Spasms caused her to unknowingly tug at her restraints. "André," she cried out, already close to the brink of climax.

He stopped and looked up at her. "What did you call me?" he asked, his eyes darkening.

"I meant Sir," she said, her voice shaky. "I'm sorry. I meant Sir. Please don't stop." *If you stop, I'm going to lose my mind. I'm going to go completely crazy and...*

He stared up at her with dark, luminous eyes, cutting off all her thoughts. Those eyes...her weakness. He moved his face forward again and flicked his tongue against her. Then he turned his head and nipped at her inner thigh with his teeth. He slowly stood up and deftly removed the cuff that was circled around her right wrist, then did the same for her left. He did the same for both of her ankles. Then he went to stand in front of her. Raw desire flickered in his eyes as he lifted her and slung her over his shoulder.

He left her dress, her panties, and his dress shirt on the floor as he carried her out of the playroom and into his bedroom. Once in the bedroom, he laid her in the middle of the bed.

She watched as he unbuckled his belt. Her right hand rested on her thigh, but at the sight of him undressing, that right hand shifted and moved between her thighs.

"You're not allowed to do that without my permission," he reminded her as he unbuttoned his pants.

She withdrew her hand and set it beside her on the bed.

His grin was wolfish. "You have my permission."

That was all it took for her to dip her hand between her thighs again. She parted her thighs so she could get a better view of him as he dragged his pants and boxer briefs down his legs. Naked André was a sight to behold. Truly too much beauty in one man.

He watched her touching herself with hungry eyes. Then he lowered both hands onto the bed. He raised one knee onto the bed and slowly moved forward. His eyes stayed on her hand for several minutes, then moved up to her face. "Do you know how sexy you are?" he growled.

I was going to ask you the same thing, she thought.

He nipped at her inner thigh with his teeth again as he watched her push her index and middle fingers in and out of herself. The groan he released sounded wild and carnal, beastly. He loomed over her, positioned in between her shapely brown thighs. Stared down at her like he wanted to eat her alive. Reached down between those thick thighs and covered her hand with his. He pressed on her hand, pushing her own fingers deeper insider of her. Then he kissed her.

She moaned against his mouth.

He lifted his head and nudged her hand, indicating for her to remove her fingers from herself. He brought her hand up between them and inserted her index and middle fingers into her mouth. "Suck," he ordered.

She sucked on her fingers, tasting herself. Her juices were sweet and succulent. With her eyes closed, she let out another moan.

He reached down between their bodies again, this time to guide himself inside of her.

The sensation of the length of him pushing its way inside her made her cry out. Her voice was muffled by the fingers she still had in her mouth.

He dragged her hips downward as he pushed in and out of her, then pulled her hand out of her mouth. He ducked his head down and kissed her. He sucked on her lips and raised his head suddenly. "I can taste you. You taste so fucking good, Destiny." He buried his head in the crook of her shoulder. "Why do you taste so fucking *good*?"

She could have exploded right then and there. Those words, spoken by *this* man. She could have climaxed at that very moment. But he wasn't there yet, and she wanted to climax with him.

He lowered her bra so that both breasts were exposed and teased them with his mouth as he made love to her.

She almost called out his name again, but this time she caught herself. "Sir," she called out. It felt awkward, but she was willing to call him whatever he wanted to be called, as long as he kept fucking her.

He groaned and sped up the pace.

"Oh my God," she cried out.

His eyes were drunk with lust, and the sounds coming out of him were music to her ears. Alternating between fast and slow pacing, he ran his thumb over her bottom lip and pushed her hair out of her face. He started to speed up again.

Does he know how good he is in bed? He has to, right, with how many women he's been with? They probably tell him how good he is. Guys in college liked to brag about their skills in bed, but this man is a certified lover, boy. She raised her head off the bed and kissed him.

Both of their worlds exploded simultaneously during that kiss. He groaned against her lips as their climaxing caused both of their bodies to quake. He wrapped his arms around her and pulled her against him. His strokes slowed and stopped altogether, but he didn't pull himself out of her. He stayed in her warmth, in her wetness, and continued holding her. "Once the contract period is over, you're not allowed to leave me," he told her. "You're not allowed to *ever* leave me. Understood?"

She stared back up at him, her brows furrowing.

"Any hesitation will result in punishment," he said, his voice cracking. The dominant words clashed with the vulnerability in his voice. He'd made the words sound like an order, but in actuality he was begging her not to leave him.

Her heart expanded with love for him. "Understood, Sir," she returned.

Relief flooded his eyes, along with a flash of another emotion that she didn't dare try to name. Before she could question whether she'd really seen it, he lowered his head and kissed her again.

18

The following morning, Destiny felt André remove his arm from her, felt him shifting in bed. She lifted her head and blinked sleepy eyes at him.

"Morning workout," he explained, his voice groggy.

She *loved* how he sounded first thing in the morning. *Hell, I love everything about the man. Well...almost everything.*

"Come work out with me," he encouraged, standing and looking around for his boxer briefs.

It was too early. She barely felt capable of *thought*, much less jogging around on a stationary machine without falling and busting her face. Her first urge was to protest, but then she remembered whose offer she was about to decline. His words had sounded like a casual suggestion, but this was André. She couldn't tell if she really had a choice. With everything they'd been through recently, she decided not to risk disappointing him.

She tried focusing her eyes so she could see through the darkness shrouding the room. A glance at the window told her that the sun hadn't even risen yet. "Um...sure," she responded finally. "I'd love to, Sir."

He laughed. "That wasn't an order. You can stay in bed a little longer, if you want."

She ruffled her hair with one hand. "I'm awake now. I can work out with you."

"Good." He sourced a fresh pair of boxer briefs and pulled them up his thick, muscular legs.

She wondered how he was so chipper this early when he'd woken her throughout the night, nudging her, poking her, kissing her, and biting on her shoulder to let her know that he was turned on again. Not that she had complained in the least. Well - she hadn't *then*. She kind of wanted to complain now that he was up at the butt crack of dawn and in need of a workout buddy.

He flipped on the nightstand lamp and they moved around the room, collecting articles of clothing - him from the closet and her from the dresser drawers. She started to reach for her collar, but he called out for her to leave it. "Don't wear it while working out. It's real leather. Sweat isn't good for it."

That wasn't how you felt last night, she thought, several mental images coming to mind. But she turned away from the nightstand and gathered her hair into a ponytail.

The home gym was located beneath his home office. It wasn't huge; there was only so much space in the condo. But it had most of the essentials: an elliptical machine, bicycle machine, free weights, a few weight machines, a couple of weighted fitness balls, a punching bag, and a large workout machine with chin up bars and weighted cables. A television was mounted in the corner of the room. For all intents and purposes, it felt like a hotel gym.

"You can pick a machine," he urged.

Easier said than done, when he was looking as good as he did. He'd thrown on a pair of gray sweatpants from one of his own clothing lines. No shirt. Just sweatpants and boxer briefs. Muscles and tattoos. Skin that tasted just as delicious as it looked. At the sound of his voice, she tried to look alert, like she hadn't just been checking him out.

"I will...take the elliptical machine," she said, already moving towards it.

Stretching an arm across his chest, he headed over to the weight rack and bent at the waist to flip open a compartment. An assortment of gloves filled the storage area. He pulled a glove onto one hand while she turned her focus to figuring out how the elliptical machine worked.

After a few moments of watching her struggle, he coached her through the different selections. He backed out of the selections she'd chosen and had her go through the menu options again, to make sure she got the hang of it. He strapped the second glove around his left wrist as he watched her pressing the different selections on the screen. "You got it," he said as the machine started up. He gave her ass an encouraging smack.

Startled, she reached back and rubbed her butt cheek.

He backed away from her with a devilish grin on his face.

She was no stranger to working out, but she'd definitely slacked a bit towards those last several months leading up to graduation. In high school, she'd played volleyball and soccer. Throughout most of her college years, she ran on the track at night, usually after leaving the newsroom. That was before Chad, before André. Pushing those thoughts out of her mind, she increased the speed and resistance settings on the machine. Even though she tried not to, she found her gaze wandering over to André.

Having returned to the free weights, he bent down and wrapped his hands around the bar of a long dumbbell with a seventy-five-pound disc on each end. He lifted the bar and performed several curls. From the relaxed expression on his face, those curls were light work to him. His arm muscles rippled and flexed as he curled the bar upward towards his chest and downward with his arms extended. He kept his elbows tightly tucked in at his sides.

How are my legs even moving at this point, and how is it possible that I haven't fallen off this machine? They had to have been moving on their own, because all she could concentrate on was how amazing he looked. Her eyes lowered from the focused expression on his face to his bulging biceps and flexing triceps. Sweat started to bead on her forehead and she couldn't tell whether it was from her own workout or the sight of André.

His eyes slid over to her as he pulled the bar up to his chest. His eyes scanned down the length of her body, to the brown legs pouring out of her tight, white shorts and back up to the red tank top that was beginning to stick to her skin with sweat. He grunted as he pulled the dumbbell upward one last time before adding more weight to the bar.

Again, she increased both the incline and speed on the machine. She increased the speed until she was practically sprinting. Her curly ponytail flopped around behind her and she pumped her arms as she ran.

He set the dumbbell down and turned away from her.

That was how the rest of their workout progressed. They worked out quietly while sneaking lustful glances at each other. He moved from the dumbbells to one of the weight machines. She moved from the elliptical machine to a workout mat, where she proceeded to do a set of one hundred crunches.

He appeared out of nowhere and helped her to stand after she finished her last crunch. His arms glistened and sweat droplets ran down his forehead. He moved forward, forcing her backward until her back hit a wall. The look in his eyes was intense as one of his hands slid beneath her tank top.

She boldly slid her hand down the front of his pants and wrapped her fingers around the length of him.

He groaned and closed his eyes. "I didn't give you the permission to do that," he ground out between clenched teeth.

Her hand froze.

He cupped one of her breasts in his hand and stroked the nipple. "But you have my permission."

She stood on her tiptoes and caught his bottom lip between her teeth before sucking on it.

The workout they had completed paled in comparison to the workout that soon followed.

After their workout(s), André and Destiny showered together. He washed her, and she washed him. Both made a conscious effort not to initiate another lovemaking session. Flirtatious looks and a few short kisses were still exchanged, but they didn't take their interaction beyond that.

After showering, they got dressed on opposite sides of the bed.

"You'll have the condo to yourself today," he told her. "*Both* of them, actually. Francesca, my cleaning lady, will be in to clean up the place. So, you don't have to worry about the cleaning. Ugh, shit."

She finished zipping up her peach-colored dress and looked over at him. "What is it?"

"I can't get this knot to work," he muttered, frowning at his reflection in the bedroom mirror.

She walked around the bed and approached him. "May I?"

He smiled. "Well done, and yes you may."

She lifted her hands and completely undid the knot he'd created. "The knot you made was fine," she told him.

"It was imperfect," he insisted.

She gave him a questioning look.

"I can be a bit of a perfectionist at times."

"I hadn't noticed," she said, the faintest trace of sarcasm touching her voice as she lowered her eyes to his tie.

The smile remained on his face as she perfected the knot in his tie.

She stepped back and turned to look at his reflection.

He did the same and smoothed his tie down. "See? Perfect." He kissed the top of her head and tugged at each sleeve before turning and picking up his suit jacket.

"I should have made you breakfast," she fretted.

"I do the cooking, remember?" he reminded her, sliding his arms into the sleeves of the charcoal gray suit jacket. He squinted his eyes while studying his reflection. "I'm probably just going to grab something on the way, but feel free to make something for yourself, if you like." He reached for his wallet on the nightstand, but saw her collar sitting beside it. "I think you're forgetting something. Hair up."

She pulled her hair back. "I was just about to put that on," she claimed.

"Mmhm," he said softly as he secured the leather collar around her neck. He checked it for tightness. "Too tight?"

She shook her head. "No, Sir."

"Good." He hooked an index finger in the ring at the front of her collar and pulled her forward so he could kiss her long and deep. When he pulled back, he stroked her cheek affectionately and turned to grab his wallet.

Wringing her hands, she followed him out of the bedroom. "Didn't you say that I'd go to work with you today? It would be nice to get an idea of what my day-to-day will be like in the office. I wouldn't know what to do here."

"Today, I'm going to be slammed with work," he told her as he exited the bedroom. "I want to at least have *some* time to sit down with you and your manager on your first day. Today, I wouldn't have any time whatsoever for that. We've both been through a lot these past few days. So, relax. Enjoy a day without me breathing down your neck. Actually..." He slowed his steps as he neared the kitchen counter and opened his wallet. "What you should do is go to the salon. I can reach out for recommendations, or you can pick one of your own choosing." He withdrew several large bills from his wallet and pressed them into her hand.

"I should be able to find a salon on my own," she said quickly, shuddering to think which women he'd reach out to for salon recommendations.

"My briefcase. I need my briefcase. I'll be right back." He moved towards the staircase leading up to his home office.

The doorbell rang.

Destiny's forehead creased with worry.

André went to stand at the railing on the upper level. "Can you get the door for me?"

"The last time you asked me to do that, things didn't end so well," she grumbled.

"*Hesitation*," he said, dragging the word out.

"Yes, Sir!" she called back, fighting the urge to scowl. With her pulse racing, she moved towards the condo door. Before raising a hand to the doorknob, she closed her eyes and prayed that Reese wasn't on the other side of the door. She turned the doorknob and pulled the door open.

A short, older blonde sprite of a woman flurried into the condo, talking a mile a minute. "I know it's early and you probably have work, André, but you're not answering my text messages. You've left me no cho-" She stopped in mid-sentence when she realized that the person who'd opened the door was not André.

Destiny eyed the older woman, noting the similarities in facial features between her and André. They shared the same eye and nose shapes. The woman's mouth stretched into a wide smile and Destiny noted that they also shared the same smile.

The blonde woman raised both hands to cover her mouth. "Oh...oh, my."

"Hello," Destiny greeted. "My name is Destiny."

"I'm Mandy," the woman greeted, hurriedly extending a hand to Destiny. "Are you...are you the girl that Oscar was talking about?"

Confused, Destiny tilted her head to the side. "Oscar? The name sounds familiar, but..."

"Never mind that," Mandy said, with a wave of her hand. "Are you from D.C.?"

"I went to school there until recently," Destiny said.

Mandy clapped her hands happily. "And you...live here?"

Destiny didn't know how she was supposed to answer the question. "Uh..."

"Who was it?" André asked, rounding the corner. He halted his steps when he saw his mother. "Mom?"

"You weren't answering my text messages," Mandy said. "So, you gave me no choice but to hunt you down. André...who is this?"

"This is Destiny," André replied, his eyes darting over to Destiny. He approached his mother and gave her a warm embrace. "How are you feeling? Are you all right?"

"I feel fine," Mandy said, raising a forefinger to the bridge of her stylish prescription bifocals so she could slide them up her nose. "Is Destiny the girl from D.C.?"

He cleared his throat. "Mom."

"What? I'm not allowed to ask that?"

"Not to rush you," he said, "but I need to get to work. Is there something you needed? Something I need to do?"

"Your uncle Cal has been asking about you. He wants us all to have dinner this weekend. I kept trying to check with you to see if this weekend would work, but you weren't responding."

"I'm sorry about that. Things have been hectic on my end. Which day was he thinking? Saturday? Sunday?"

"Sunday," his mother responded.

Destiny looked between the two of them as they spoke. She couldn't help but smile at the energetic little woman, dressed in a chic white pantsuit with a mauve blouse.

"Sunday works," he said after checking the calendar app in his phone. "I promise I will call you today."

"I see," Mandy said, sending another glance Destiny's way.

"I really have to get going, Mom."

"You won't let me stay and talk to Destiny?" Mandy asked, looking at him over the top of her glasses.

He hesitated before responding.

Destiny spoke up. "There are some errands I have to take care of today," she told Mandy. "But I'm sure we'll get a chance to get to know each other." She looked to André for approval.

"I'm sure you will," he echoed, smiling appreciatively at her.

Mandy shifted her eyes between the two of them. She covered her mouth and squealed.

André rolled his eyes and placed an arm around his mother's shoulders. "All right, Mom. I will call you today to get the details about dinner on Sunday."

Mandy twisted around so she could look at Destiny, even though he was leading her towards the door. "Will Destiny be able to make it to dinner, too?"

"We will talk about that when I call, okay?"

"It was nice meeting you, Destiny!" his mother called over her shoulder.

"It was nice meeting you too, Mandy," Destiny said with a small wave.

At the door, André wrapped his mother up into a bear hug. "I love you," he whispered into her ear. "I know it seems like I'm pushing you out."

"*Literally*," his mother muttered.

"Only because I've been absent from work and I have a lot to catch up on," he insisted. "I will call you. I love you more than life itself. You know that, right?"

"I know that," she said, pulling back from the embrace. "I love you too. But if you don't call me..."

"I know," he said, reaching up and rubbing the back of his head.

She gave him a warning look, startlingly similar to the warning looks he gave Destiny when she was about to cross a line. The resemblance between the two of them was uncanny.

Once his mother was gone, he continued rubbing the back of his head. "Sorry about that," he said sheepishly.

"No apologies are necessary," Destiny told him. "She's adorable."

He walked up to her and wrapped his arms around her. "I'm glad you think so."

"You even look like her," Destiny commented.

"I get that a lot," he said, grinning.

She slid her arms around his waist. "So, I take it I won't be going to Sunday dinner."

"Actually, I want you to come."

Shock nearly knocked the wind out of her. "You do?"

"I wanted to talk to you about it without the pressure of my mom being here," he explained. "Things have gotten a little tense between us. It feels like we've overcome that. I didn't want to assume that you would be game to go with me…but yes. I'd like you to come with me."

Her brain tried to make sense of what dinner with his family meant - if anything. "I'd love to go," she said after the briefest pause.

He kissed the top of her head and stood there holding her for several minutes. "I have to go," he said, but didn't move to release her from his embrace.

Destiny didn't know her way around Mississauga. To her defense, she'd only been on a handful of trips around the city. It had been easy to conduct an internet search on local salons and read through the reviews but finding the salon proved to be a bit more difficult. Eventually she did find the salon, but only after getting turned around several times.

Even though Destiny had called to confirm availability, the salon was packed. Women were seated in the lounge area waiting their turn.

She signed in at the front desk and went to sit with the other ladies who were waiting to get their hair washed and styled. While waiting, she returned text messages from Carlos, Jasmine, and Candace, and sent a message to her mother to check in.

Carlos knew a bit about what Destiny had gotten herself into, but she couldn't tell him anything further about her relationship with André. Communicating with the rest of them felt odd. To them, she was a sweet, naïve girl getting her first big career break while dating one of the most well-known men in the Northern hemisphere. Meanwhile, just yesterday she was cuffed to some torture-device looking contraption. Even worse, she'd liked it. Just knowing some of the things she'd done and some of the things that had been done to her, made her feel slightly uneasy when talking to her parents *and* friends.

As always, Carlos wanted to know the deets. How was Canada? How was André? Had she started work yet? Had she allowed André to work on *her* yet? Was she a certified sex slave? She hedged the questions, which resulted in Carlos ringing her phone. Sighing, she stood up to find a spot where she could talk without bothering the other women in the lounge area. She walked towards the front door and brought the phone up to her ear. "Now isn't a good time, Carlos."

"I'm sure it's not," he retorted. "We barely talk these days, bitch."

She rolled her eyes but had to admit that she'd missed the sound of his voice. "I can't answer questions relating to André."

"I just need a yes or a no," Carlos told her. "I just need to know if there has been *any* progress with the whole... contractual arrangement thing."

"I can't tell you that," she said.

He was quiet for a moment. Then he said, "Just nod for yes or shake your head for no."

"What good is that going to do you?" she hissed at him.

"I'll be able to tell the difference through the phone," he insisted.

"Boy…you're talking nonsense. I'm hanging up now."

"Can you at least tell me if you're happy?" he asked quickly, before she had the chance to hang up.

She glanced towards the receptionist. The short, brown-skinned woman seated at the desk was staring back at her, shamelessly eavesdropping on the conversation.

She turned her back to the receptionist and faced the entrance door. Then she hesitated, pondering Carlos's question. *Was* she happy? Was it possible for her to be happy now, when just days ago she'd nearly walked away from this entire arrangement? She was well-taken care of, in the company of a man she loved. He loved her too, whether he was willing to admit that to himself. This weekend, she would get to meet his family. *Even though he is trying his best to show me how he feels about me, I don't know how I feel.*

"Hello? Earth to Destiny."

"I was thinking," she said defensively.

"You had to *think* about whether or not you're happy?" Carlos asked her, his voice laced with concern. "*Girl.*"

She sighed. "I'm happy," she responded.

"You sounded *ecstatic* just then."

"Things aren't perfect, but then again what relationship is?"

"Relationship?" he asked, perking up immediately. "So, it *is* a relationship?"

"I have to go, Carlos."

"That's all you're leaving me with?" he shrieked.

"I'll call you later, when I'm back at the condo," she promised, and ended the call before he could drag out the conversation any further. She returned to the lounge area and waited her turn.

Approximately a half an hour later, a heavyset woman with dark brown skin and an undeniable sense for edgy fashion appeared and called Destiny's name. The woman introduced herself as Julissa and asked what Destiny would like done with her hair. Destiny asked for a deep conditioning and stated that she wanted to keep her curls.

After the salon visit, Destiny stopped at a nearby Caribbean restaurant for lunch. She ordered shrimp roti with steamed vegetables and a side of fried plantains at the front counter and seated herself while waiting. Carlos was blowing up her text inbox.

"Brian, my man!" the cashier exclaimed in a thick, Jamaican accent.

Surprised at the outburst, Destiny raised her eyes from her cell phone.

A tall, Caucasian man wearing the finest in designer suits approached the counter. He had wavy, dark hair that was parted on the side. When he reached the counter, he proceeded to give the cashier a complicated-looking handshake. "What's up, brother?" he asked smoothly with a lazy grin. "Give me a minute...I don't know what I want to order."

"You always say the same thing," the average height, brown-skinned cashier said. "Then you always order the same thing. How is everything? It's been a while."

"Everything is good," the man named Brian answered, sliding a hand into the pocket of his suit pants. "I can't complain one bit. How about on your end?"

The cashier shrugged his shoulders. "I woke up this morning. I cannot complain."

"Hey - did you put your resumé in?" Brian asked him.

The cashier shook his head.

Brian shook a finger at him. "Khenan, what did I tell you? I can get you out of here and eventually into an office if you just work with me. Put in that resumé."

"I will, I will," Khenan promised.

"All right." Brian glanced at the menu posted above the counter. Then he turned and seemed to notice Destiny. His gaze lingered for a few moments before returning to the menu. "I'll take the jerk chicken with rice and peas."

Destiny lowered her eyes back to her phone.

Close to ten minutes later, one of the cooks called out, "Orders 476 and 477!"

Destiny rose from her booth and pocketed her cell phone. She walked over to the food pick-up area.

The tall, attractive man in the fine Italian suit reached the pick-up area only a moment after she did. He stood beside her, looking over both food trays. It was then that she noticed his eyes were the iciest shade of blue she'd ever seen. "I don't think I've seen you in here before, and I'm in here quite a bit."

"This is my first time here," she said, picking up her tray. She turned and headed towards her booth.

He grabbed his tray and in a few long strides, caught up to her. "My name's Brian," he greeted.

She set her tray down on the table and slid into the booth. "I heard."

He smiled. "I guess my and Khenan's voices carry."

"I was also being nosey," she admitted.

He laughed and gestured to the seat across from her. "Can I sit down?"

She hesitated. André was supposed to determine who she could and couldn't spend time with. That most likely meant she wasn't allowed to accept offers of sitting with young, attractive men. "I...should probably eat alone," she said, and the words felt awkward leaving her mouth.

"Ah, so you're married?" he asked her, pointedly lowering his eyes to her left hand.

She clasped her hands together. "No."

"But you're seeing someone," he pressed.

"I am," she confirmed.

He nodded. "I should have known. The pretty ones are always taken."

Her cheeks flushed. "It was nice meeting you, Brian."

"I didn't catch your name," he said.

"Because I didn't give it to you," she said, smiling.

He stared at her for a moment, then nodded again. "It was a pleasure meeting you." He started to walk away, then thought better of it and turned back to her. "If your boyfriend slips up and drops the ball, just let me know. Because I'll be there to catch it."

Destiny drove around before heading back to the condo. The streets of Mississauga led her into Toronto. The city was truly beautiful. Its architecture and culture were so vastly diverse. The people seemed generally pleasant and kind. Courteous. She wanted to explore more of the city but didn't have the faintest clue of where to go. Her knowledge of anything Toronto-related was quite limited, and she'd rather explore the city with someone who knew it well.

Pretty much the only person I know in town is André, she thought. *Hopefully once I start work, I can make some new friends.*

She returned to the condo and didn't know what to do with herself. There was only so much television a person could watch and only so much food she could eat. She resorted to snooping. It wasn't deliberate. Her intention was to walk into the bedroom to put her collar on. Upon entering the bedroom, she noticed that the closet door was open. She was curious to see how many pairs of jeans he owned, since she could count on one hand how many times she'd seen him wear them. Just a fleeting thought, the type of thought that a person usually let pass. Something to wonder and then dismiss. Only, she didn't let the thought pass.

His closet was a dream, a huge walk-in with built-in drawers and shelving. When a drawer was opened, it triggered a lighting system that illuminated the drawer's contents. The lights in each drawer flickered off when it was closed. When she opened the first narrow drawer, she was greeted with the sight of ties, sorted by color. When she opened the second, she found a collection of watches, displayed on their original watch stands.

"He is the most organized person I know," she said as she closed the watch drawer. She knelt to the floor to open the bottom drawer, which was larger than the drawers above it. This drawer, she'd never seen him open before.

The bottom drawer contained several boxes, varying in color. Crimson, red, and royal blue.

To open any of these boxes would be a violation of his privacy. Opening any of these boxes was probably an act that was punishable. And yet...

Pandora's three boxes called out to her. They asked her, *"Don't you want to know who you're living with? Don't you want to know who you've fallen in love with? Come on, you know you do. Open us."*

She sat down on the floor, Indian-style, and smoothed back her rejuvenated curls. She didn't want to take the boxes out of the drawer. He seemed so OCD that he would realize if the boxes were moved an inch to the right or left. She lifted the lid off the first box, which was crimson. A stack of opened envelopes was in the box. With furrowed brows, she reached in and grabbed the few envelopes that were on top of the stack. She opened the first envelope and withdrew the pieces of paper that were within.

Her heart thudded in her chest. Maybe it was because she knew this was wrong. Or maybe she knew that these boxes had the potential to change how she viewed the man she was currently living with. *You can stop right here, right now, and put the envelopes back in the box,* she told herself. *You haven't looked at anything yet. You are at a point where you can still walk away.*

Walking away would have been the smart thing to do, but she was overcome with curiosity. There were too many mysteries surrounding the man she was falling for, and she needed some of those questions answered. She started to read and covered her mouth with one hand after finishing the first letter. It was a love letter. From André to a woman. The letter was old; the paper was aged and already starting to yellow. But it was difficult imagining the passionate and heartfelt words on the page coming from him. He talked of love and marriage and children. He talked of wanting those things with the woman he was writing to in the letter. Her eyes filled with tears as she folded the piece of paper and shoved it back into the envelope.

This was another moment when she told herself she should just stop. Walk away with what she knew and leave the rest be. But after that first letter, she *couldn't*. She'd gotten a taste of a romantic André who believed in love and marriage and a possible happy life for himself. It was like a drug. She read the next letter, and the next. The letters went from happy and hopeful to angry, cold, and biting. It turns out his woman had cheated on him, for a very long period of time.

His heartache and pain jumped off the page. "*I'm a businessman now, but I will always first and foremost be a writer,*" he had told her the day she'd visited his office in D.C. He hadn't lied. He had an undeniable knack for arranging words in a way that evoked a strong response. The André on these pages was the same André who'd penned hundreds of hits. She clutched at her chest while reading, tears rolling down her cheeks. When she finished the last letter, she returned the envelopes to the crimson box and sat back, staring at the other two boxes through a veil of tears. Then she drew a forearm across her eyes and opened the black box.

At first, the items in the box seemed random. A tattered Jane Austen novel. A diamond stud earring. Just one. Its twin was missing from the box. A bottle of perfume. A princess-cut diamond ring. A compact mirror. Other odds and ends. These items belonged to a woman. Most likely *the* woman. She picked up the ring and slid it onto her ring finger. It was an engagement ring. Either he had proposed, or he was planning to. And instead of returning the ring, he'd kept it. Why? As some sort of morbid reminder?

She returned the ring to the box and placed the lid on top of the box. This time, she didn't hesitate with opening the third box. At this point, she just wanted to get it over with. Rip off the metaphorical Band-Aid, so to speak. She stared down at a collection of VHS tapes. Not DVDs.

VHS tapes. They were old. She pulled out two tapes from the box and looked at their labels. They were so old that the label ink was faded. The words were illegible.

Wondering what kind of footage she held in her hands, she stood and left the bedroom. She padded down the hall and into the living room, where she sat on the floor in front of the television. Upon opening the cabinet to the sleek, black entertainment center, she was surprised to find that he *did* own a VHS player. She placed one of the VHS tapes into the VHS player.

It took a minute for her to figure out how the television and VHS player worked together. After a bit of tinkering, the television screen flashed blue. Then the tape started playing.

A light-skinned kid wearing prescription glasses and an afro came into focus.

Destiny squinted her eyes. The kid was André. There was no mistaking it. Same downturned eyes, same grin.

"André, are you playing with the camera again?"

A short, blonde woman walked into the frame. Destiny covered her mouth with her hands when she realized that the woman was Mandy, his mother. Decades younger, but the curly blonde coif and Irish accent were unmistakable.

"I was going to rap and sing a little bit," young André said, adjusting the camera.

His mother raised her hands to her hips. "You didn't even finish your homework."

"Homework can wait, Mom. I'm going to be a star, just watch."

Mandy turned and spoke to someone who was out of the frame. "I blame *you* for putting these dreams into his head, you know."

A deep voice sounded from somewhere behind the camera. "What? He said he's going to be a star. I believe him. Let him go at it for a bit. He can do his homework in a little while. Right, André?"

"Thanks, Dad," young André said, beaming.

"What you *should* do is come over here and give me some sugar," the man off-camera told Mandy.

Mandy giggled and shook her head. "Behave." Still, she started to walk out of frame.

André disappeared out of frame and then the camera started moving. The camera turned and focused on Mandy as she walked over to a brown-skinned man with a handlebar moustache and a stylish pageboy cap on his head. The older man winked at the camera as Mandy sat on his lap and wrapped her arms around him.

Young André could be heard giggling behind the camera.

"All right, time for the camera to go off," Mandy said.

The picture cut to black. Then when a picture returned, the camera was focused and staring down a long hallway. No one was in frame, but loud voices could be heard. Shouting. Yelling. Accusations. Defenses. Ultimatums. A little bit of love and a little bit of hate, all intertwined to make for a heated argument.

Young André came into frame and his puppy dog eyes were teary. He turned his head and looked in the direction of the yelling. When he turned back to the camera, his cheeks were wet with tears.

Destiny wiped at her own tears in vain.

Again, the footage cut to black, and then there was a bunch of snowy white static.

She stared at the screen for several moments with tears running down her face, until she heard the door to the condo open.

19

"Hola? Hola, Señor Gaines?" The voice was high-pitched and thick with a Latin accent.

Destiny hurriedly wiped her eyes and exhaled with relief. André wasn't the person who'd walked through the door. It was the cleaning lady. What was her name? Francesca? Destiny turned off the television, ejected the VHS tape, and grabbed the tape she'd set on the floor. She stood up and brushed off the skirt of her dress just as a middle-aged Latina woman rounded the corner.

Francesca had dark brown hair pulled back into a ponytail. Her maid's uniform was pink and white, crisp and clean. She held her purse in her hands and looked at Destiny with wide eyes. "You are...you are Destiny, yes?"

Destiny nodded and went over to introduce herself. "I'm Destiny. Nice to meet you. Francesca, right?"

The woman smiled. "Yes. I will stay out of your way, I promise."

"You don't have to worry about that," Destiny said with a wave of her hand. Truth be told, she was desperate to socialize with someone other than André. She excused herself so she could return the VHS tapes to the closet.

I was so bratty with him and I dismissed the trauma that he has experienced. I even questioned if he was using it as an excuse to see other women. I pressured him to change who he is for me, without considering that he could really be hurting. Seeing those clips from his past helped her to realize just why he tried to convince himself that love wasn't real. Two meaningful relationships in his life, his parents' and his own, had crumbled as he bore witness. Both relationships had failed due to a betrayal of trust.

Later in life, he met a kinky stripper who was into BDSM. Some aspects of the BDSM lifestyle genuinely appealed to him, and he had demonstrated that. What had drawn him to the lifestyle was most likely the fact that a contract outlined each party's role in the relationship. A contract was a legally binding document. If a party failed to do what they were supposed to do, legal action could be taken. The contract periods were also short. If one of his women started messing up towards the end of the six-month period, she could easily be replaced. Simple. On the surface, it seemed that there were no pesky feelings or emotions to worry about. It sounded more like a business partnership than a relationship.

Until I came along, Destiny thought, reaching out and touching the closed drawer. She couldn't get the image of young André out of her mind. The sadness in his eyes had mirrored the sadness she'd seen in adult André. That same sadness was in his eyes as he struggled to communicate to her how much she meant to him. *Excluding the night he had me answer the door for Reese, he has gone out of his way to show me how important I am to him, and I respond by calling him a broken monster.*

She stood up, smoothed down the skirt of her dress and returned to the living room. Francesca was dusting and cleaning even though the room looked spotless. *Cleaning André's place must be the easiest job ever. He's a neat freak. There's hardly anything to clean.*

She sat on the living room couch and made small talk with Francesca. She was Dominican, had a husband, and three young children that she loved dearly.

"Which part of the city are you from?" Francesca asked her.

"I'm...from Arizona, actually," Destiny responded. "The United States."

Francesca's slender eyebrows shot up. "*Oh.* And you...you and Mr. Gaines..."

Destiny hesitated.

Francesca laughed and waved her hand in the air. "It's okay. I know."

Destiny lifted an eyebrow in interest. It made sense that someone had to clean and sanitize the playroom. With that considered, of course the maid knew about her boss's kinky habits. *Just how much do you know, Francesca?* she wondered. She didn't get a chance to ask the question out loud.

The condo door opened and closed, and a moment later André appeared in the living room, looking as debonair as ever. "Hello, Francesca."

Francesca turned and tilted her head towards him. "Hello, Mr. Gaines. How was your day?"

"Exhausting." He set his briefcase down beside the coffee table. "How was your day?"

"Not bad, *más o menos bien*," Francesca answered. "I am going to go finish up." She left the living room and headed towards the bedroom.

Destiny kept her eyes lowered.

"Good afternoon, Destiny."

"Good afternoon, Sir," she returned.

He leaned down and kissed her on the forehead. "Your hair is beautiful," he complimented while tugging a few of her springy curls.

"Thank you."

"You can look at me," he told her.

She hesitated before looking up. She was afraid that when she looked at him, she'd see the little boy she'd seen on the tape. But when she finally did raise her eyes, all she saw was André.

He swept the lapels of his suit jacket back and kneeled before her. "Are you okay?"

She stared into his eyes, remembering the words from the letter, and the events that had transpired on the VHS tape. *Are* you *okay?* she wanted to ask, feeling horrible about all the times she'd called him "messed up" and "broken." She nodded her head.

His forehead creased and he raised a hand to her cheek. "Are you sure?"

"I'm fine. Just...dying of boredom, I guess."

He smiled. "While I was at work today, I realized I've been a horrible tour guide. I haven't really shown you my city. We'll rectify that this weekend."

"You said that your day was exhausting?" she queried.

"Yeah, I had a co-worker rattling my ear off for half of the afternoon," he muttered, rolling his eyes. "I spent the last hour trying to play catch-up and failing. I missed out on a lot."

"I'm sorry," she apologized.

The crease in his brow deepened. He was starting to look concerned. "It's not your fault."

"I feel like it is." *Or maybe I feel guilty for digging through your stuff,* she thought.

He caressed her cheek and shook his head. "It will be fine. I'll catch up a bit this weekend. Monday, you'll come into work with me. You'll spend the morning with Human Resources and most of the afternoon getting to know your manager and your team."

"Sounds like a plan," she said, feeling nervousness set in. With all the craziness going on, she'd barely taken time to think about what working for Gaines Enterprises would be like, or whether she would get along with others in her department.

He bent his head down and rubbed the back of his neck.

"Take off your jacket and shirt and sit in front of me," she told him.

"Is that an order?" he joked.

"Please? Sir?"

He sighed, stood up, and removed his suit jacket. He laid the jacket on the armrest of the couch and unbuttoned his dress shirt. She watched as he peeled the dress shirt off but left his undershirt on.

"Take that off, too," she told him. Then added, as an afterthought, "Please, Sir."

He shook his head while reaching behind his head and grabbing the top of the tank top. He pulled it over his head and laid it on top of his suit jacket and dress shirt. "Better?" he asked.

She admired his physique. "Much." It felt like the temperature in the room had jumped up ten degrees.

"Can I sit down now? Or did you want me to take my pants off, too?"

"Don't tempt me," she said softly, already plagued with mental images of what he looked like with his pants off.

He was still shaking his head as he moved to sit down in front of her. She parted her legs to accommodate him and he leaned his back against the front of the couch, groaning.

She proceeded to give him a massage, starting with the tense knots around the base of his neck and moving down to his shoulder blades.

He raised his knees and rested his elbows on top of them. "That feels good," he said, tilting his head down. "You have magic hands."

"You're just now figuring that out?" she joked.

He laughed outright.

She continued to work out the stress knots in his neck and back.

"What did you do today?" he asked her.

Got my hair done, had lunch, met a hot guy but was a good submissive and rejected his offer to eat together, snooped through your stuff, you know...the norm. "Got my hair done, grabbed some lunch, drove around for a while, trying to familiarize myself with the city."

"How did that go?" he asked her.

"I got lost," she confessed. "A lot of the street signs are in French, and some of the streets split off from each other kind of weird."

"I probably should have warned you about that, yeah."

"Can you speak French?" she asked out of curiosity.

A fluent string of French flew from his mouth, and the language had never sounded more beautiful than in that moment.

"There is so much I still have to learn about you."

"Once you understand how the city is laid out, you will get lost a lot less often."

It took a moment for her to digest what he was saying. Hearing him speaking French had thrown her off. "I got lost on the way *to* the salon and on the way *back* from the salon."

"I'll show you around this weekend," he promised. "I can't have you getting lost. I know the city like the back of my hand, and I want you to as well."

She remained silent.

"That's all you did?" he asked.

"I came home and just relaxed, mostly. Kept Francesca company."

He nodded. "You should have your own home office." He was quiet for a few moments. "About that...the other condo unit..."

Her thumbs made circular motions at the spot where his neck connected to his shoulders.

"Were you still wanting to...I mean..." He peered at her out of the corner of his eye. "I don't know why I'm having such a hard time getting this out."

"You want to know if I still want to move into the other condo," she finished for him.

"Yes."

Because he'd been unable to finish the sentence, she knew that he wanted her to stay in this unit with him. A part of her wanted to do that - *especially* after the letters she'd read and the video she'd seen. Logic held her back from telling him that she would stay. That same logic said she deserved to have her own space, that it was quite early in their relationship for her to live with him. If he was still allowed to see other women, she at *least* didn't want to be there when it happened. "I think it would be best for me to move into the other condo."

He nodded as if he'd figured as much. "And the contract...you mentioned how it states that you only need to be available Friday through Sunday."

"I did." She knew what he was trying to ask. But even after the video she'd seen, the scorned woman in her wanted to see him struggle to get the words out.

"Are you still going to be available only Friday through Sunday?" he asked her.

She could see that his hands were fidgeting. Picking at each other. He was nervous, and that nervousness was endearing. An image of the little boy from the VHS tape appeared in her mind and she sighed. "If you need me during the week, let me know, and I'll see if I can oblige, Sir," she said.

He lifted a hand and covered one of her hands with his. "Thank you."

She closed her eyes and turned her head, trying to wipe the image from the VHS tape from her memory. When she was finished with the massage, he sat on the couch beside her and held her. She leaned against him, feeling both happiness and sadness at the same time.

Gaines Enterprises was just as intimidating the second time around. André introduced Destiny to a short, rotund lady named Margaret Stetson. She was a round burst of energy. Short, red hair, funky thick-framed glasses with a leopard-print design on them. She wore a black blazer, matching skirt, and a teal blouse.

The paperwork was never-ending. She had to complete federal and state tax paperwork. Margaret needed a copy of Destiny's identification.

"Mr. Gaines may have already explained this to you, but your employment will be based out of our offices in

Los Angeles," Margaret stated. "The documents will be forwarded to that office, and we will keep a copy of the documents here."

There was a thick employee handbook that Destiny had to take home and read. Then there were the new hire videos - the corny videos with notoriously horrible actors portraying stereotypical office situations.

André hadn't been exaggerating. Destiny's orientation lasted all morning. He rescued her for lunch. Instead of taking her to an offsite restaurant the way she'd expected, he showed her the company cafeterias. The building held a total of five large cafeterias.

"Each floor has a small break room," he explained as he showed her the first cafeteria, located on the ground floor. "But the larger cafeterias are scattered throughout the building on different floors. I wanted to make sure the majority of our employees could comfortably eat lunch onsite if preferred. In addition to the cafeterias, there are nice atrium areas and a lot of outdoor areas that can be used in the warmer months. We've done a pretty decent job. I don't hear many complaints coming through about the cafeterias."

She could understand why. In addition to being huge, the food selections were off the charts for a company cafeteria. There were vegetarian options and ethnic food choices offered - everything from soul food to hummus and pitas.

"As you can see, I don't really spare expenses when it comes to taking care of my staff," he told her as they entered the elevator. "They work hard for me. They are why this company is an industry titan. I could take the credit, and yes, I do deserve some of it. But they're the real stars, the real MVPs. I've worked with companies who didn't appreciate their employees and I always told myself that I would show my employees appreciation."

She couldn't help but be impressed.

He hit a button marked A, a level she hadn't yet seen. He informed her that the *A* stood for *Atrium.*

The elevator ascended and when the doors slid open, she moved out of the elevator. Tables and chairs were set up around a large, open space in the center. She walked over to a chest-high wall and looked out over the ledge. It was a long way down, but she was looking straight down to the ground floor lobby fountain.

He joined her side. "All of the floors have an open area like this. This is the only floor that also has a walking track mapped out, though."

A large glass skylight was above the open space. This level was right beneath the roof, on the uppermost floor. The flooring wrapped around the open space in the form of a hexagon. Greenery decorated the area, giving the cafeteria a garden feel. The food selection on this floor mirrored the selections of the cafeterias on the other two floors, which wasn't a surprise. "This is...so beautiful," she said, in awe.

"This is the most popular cafeteria out of all of them," he told her. "It tends to fill up pretty quick."

While they waited in line for food, whispers started. Women gave her pointed stares. Some would look away when Destiny returned their stares, while others boldly stared back. No doubt, they wanted to know who she was and why she was important enough to have lunch with the man who owned the company they were working for.

André wasn't helping. His hand was placed at her lower back, guiding her in whichever direction he wanted her to go. The intimacy of that alone would send a few tongues wagging.

"What do you do all day?" Destiny asked him curiously as they sat at a table with their lunches.

He grinned.

"I mean...I know you run a multimedia company, and you mentioned having a lot of meetings. But other than that, what do you do all day?"

He smoothed down his shimmering coral tie. "This company has several divisions: the record label, television and film production, and publishing," he explained. "My role is to make sure that each division operates efficiently. Most of my day is spent in meetings or on conference calls with the executives in charge of running each division. I'm very involved in A&R, very hands-on with the talent that is brought in through our doors. I tend to have a good eye and a good ear when it comes to new music artists - as does Oscar, who is still my right-hand man. When I'm not in meetings, on conference calls, or looking for new talent, I am reviewing reports that are submitted to me by department heads of each division. It is my job to look at the data and make sure they make sense. Sometimes I'm meeting with potential business partners or reviewing offers from companies wanting to do business with us. I do a lot of press for our company and host events. It takes a lot to keep this machine running."

"Wow," she breathed out.

"Eventually, I'll let you sit with me, so you can see it all in action," he told her, sectioning off a piece of his pasta dish. "You could be my sexy little secretary for a day. My first priority is to make sure that you're trained well for your job position."

"I'm familiar with public relations," she said.

"Your college instructors went over that field with you, did they?" he asked her with a smile.

She glared at him. "They did, actually."

He nodded, and the smile remained on his face.

"What? Do you know something I don't?" she asked him.

"We have our own way of doing things here," he told her. "You'll see what I'm talking about." He glanced at the sparkly watch looped around his wrist. "When we're done with lunch, I'll take you to meet your manager and make sure you're introduced to the team you'll be a part of."

Nervousness festered in the pit of her belly.

"They're a great team," he told her, sensing her nervousness. "There's nothing to worry about. You'll be fine."

She nodded and glanced around the cafeteria. Several faces were turned in their direction. With the attention they were getting, Destiny wasn't so sure that she didn't have anything to worry about.

They finished lunch and took the elevator to the thirty-fourth floor, which is where her office would be located. The office was bustling a bit more than the first day Destiny had visited. He led her down the long hall past rows of desks, turned and led the way to an office door. He knocked on the door. "This is your manager's office," he explained. "Great guy. Funny guy. You're going to love him."

The office door opened.

Destiny's eyes widened.

A tall, *familiar*-looking brunette man with piercing blue eyes looked down at her. Recognition lit up his eyes.

André told her, "Destiny, this is the manager I told you about, Brian Davies."

Shocking blue eyes? Check. Stylish, designer suit, complete with a sky blue tie that only made his eyes look even bluer? Check. Lazy grin? All across the board, check. "Oh, we've met," Brian said, leaning against the doorjamb while staring at Destiny.

André arched an eyebrow at Brian. "Oh, you have?" He turned to Destiny. "You've been making friends without telling me?"

"After the salon, I grabbed lunch from a restaurant that was close by," she told him. "He was there."

"The girl I told you about yesterday," Brian said, finally shifting his gaze from Destiny to André. "The one I met on my lunch break, remember?"

A muscle in André's jaw twitched. "Ah."

Destiny frowned in confusion. Brian *told* André about meeting her?

"The girl who had the boyfriend," Brian continued.

André stared hard at Brian.

Destiny wished that she could read his mind. There was a hard glint in his eyes that she'd only seen once - the night he'd fought Jordan. "Well...I guess the world is really that small," she said, trying to keep the mood light.

"You're telling me," André muttered. He said to Brian, "I want to make sure Destiny is introduced to the team. Get Zorica to train her."

Brian blinked. "Zorica? But...you said I was supposed to train her."

André shrugged nonchalantly. "I changed my mind. There are some projects I could use your feedback on."

Brian's entire demeanor changed. The lazy grin was wiped from his face and his expression turned serious. "I mean...if that's what you want."

"It is," André said, the look in his eyes leaving no room for argument.

Brian looked between André and Destiny. Realization dawned on him and he smacked his own forehead. "*You*, André? You're the boyfriend?"

André cleared his throat and pointedly glanced over his shoulder.

"I'm sorry...I'm sorry...come in," Brian said, stepping back and allowing them into his office. He closed the door once André and Destiny were inside. Then he turned to face them. "You two are dating?"

"What we're doing isn't your concern," André advised.

Brian's eyebrows shot up.

Destiny busied herself with checking out Brian's office. Not quite as large as André's, but still a lot larger than most. The furniture was modern-looking. A wall of windows behind the desk, shedding a ton of natural light into the room. Dark cabinetry housed a personal fridge.

"Destiny?"

She whipped her head back around. Both men were looking at her expectantly. "I'm...sorry. If you asked me something, I didn't hear the question."

"I asked if you're ready to meet the team," Brian repeated.

She nodded. "Yeah, sure."

The rest of the day was uneventful. The rest of the PR team was polite enough and let her know she could come to them with any questions. Zorica, a petite blonde with a Serbian accent, received the news that she would train Destiny and took it in stride.

On the ride home after work, André was quiet. That silence didn't let up once they returned to the condo. His nerves seemed to be wound tight, so Destiny gave him his space. After putting on her collar, she started reading the unnecessarily ginormous employee handbook while lying on the bed.

André came to stand in the doorway. He leaned against the doorframe and watched her read for a few minutes before speaking. "I keep telling HR we need to make the handbooks thinner. More concise."

"It's *extremely* wordy," she remarked, sitting up. "Are you mad at me? Did I do something?"

He shook his head. "No."

"You seem...unnerved."

"I didn't know you were the girl Brian was talking my ear off about yesterday," he said. "And now that I know, I don't like it. That's all."

"Oh."

"From now on, if someone hits on you, I want to know about it."

"I understand," she said.

He didn't bother to remind her to call him "Sir." With a heavy sigh, he joined her on the bed. "Maybe I should move you to a different department."

She frowned. "You don't have anything to worry about, with him. I-"

"It's not you I'm worried about," he assured her.

"You said he was nice and funny," she reminded him. "You said I'd like him."

"As a manager, he's great," André said. "I stand behind that. He's a skilled manager. He keeps the job fun and interesting. He makes it seem a lot less like work. But as a *man*..." He let the sentence trail off. "He's...persistent. And...intense. Once he sets his sights on something, he doesn't stop until he's gotten it."

Are you describing Brian or yourself? she wondered.

He saw the look in her eyes and shook his head. "I can have you moved to a different department. Or maybe even the publishing division."

"I can handle him," she told him. "I was introduced to the team today. I should just stick with the public relations department. If I moved to a different department now, it would look weird."

"You're challenging my authority and questioning my decisions."

"You're allowed to make decisions as long as it doesn't concern my career," she countered.

He leaned forward and rested his elbows on his knees. "I don't like this."

"I know you don't," she said, "but everything will be fine. He knows that we're together now, so he wouldn't try anything. You own the place."

"He was watching you while we were sitting at the table with the rest of the team," André mumbled.

Smiling at the jealous tone in his voice, she hooked her arms around his neck and hugged him from behind. "You don't have anything to worry about," she told him.

"Hmm," was all he said.

She rested her chin on his shoulder. "Should I worry about you and Bridgette?"

"You *know* you don't have to worry about Bridgette."

"And you should know you don't have to worry about Brian," she returned.

"You don't *know* him," André said firmly.

"Any unwanted advances could risk him his job, which I'm sure pays him very well," she said. "He wouldn't risk that."

He was quiet for a few minutes. "Maybe you can work in PR but have your office on my floor."

She pulled away from him and lowered her hands to her hips.

He laughed weakly. "That was a joke."

"The team seems solid," she commented, eager to change the subject. "They were very nice."

"They're good people," he said, sounding distracted. He was probably seriously considering moving her office to his floor.

She wrapped her arms around him again. "How about we relax tonight? Make dinner and watch a movie? Take a bath together? Fall asleep together?"

He stroked his jaw in contemplation.

"I mean...those are just suggestions, Sir," she said, catching herself.

"They're good suggestions," he said softly.

She scrambled off the bed. "Can I help cook? I miss cooking."

He smiled up at her. "You can help cook." He stood up and headed over to his closet. After changing into more comfortable loungewear, he left the bedroom.

She followed suit, swapping out her dress for a long pajama shirt. Before leaving the bedroom, she glanced towards the closet that held the explanations to why André was so guarded and possessive. A sad expression crossed her face before she turned off the light and closed the door to the bedroom.

The week thankfully went by without any André/Brian drama. André visited the PR department a lot more frequently than he needed to, and Brian kept his distance. Destiny's on the job training was to last for two weeks. Zorica alternated between reviewing training material and allowing Destiny to watch her work throughout the day.

Most of Destiny's job duties revolved around research. Her main mission as a public relations specialist was helping to protect the Gaines Enterprises brand. Keep tabs on articles and any mentions of the company. Contact entities whose reports or mentions were inaccurate and provide accurate information. The job sounded easy, but Zorica made sure to correct that first impression.

"You'd be surprised how many times we are mentioned in reports that have inaccurate information," she said, sitting at her desk with one slender leg crossed over the other. "You'd also be surprised at how difficult it can be to get into contact with the people in charge of printing the wrong information. We have to try our hardest to get information corrected, because some incorrect reports can have a damaging effect on our company's rep." Zorica explained that the job position Destiny was filling used to be her own. Zorica had been promoted and now her job duties consisted of creating press releases. "That makes me sound like I have more power than I actually do. Brian has to approve all of the press releases that I type up."

"Is someone talking about me?" Brian called out, breezing past them. "My ears are burning."

Zorica rolled her eyes. "He's quite a flirt. Watch out for him."

"I heard that," he called over his shoulder as he reached his office door.

Zorica shook her head. "He's nothing but trouble," she said laughing.

"So, he flirts with everyone?" Destiny asked, feeling relieved.

Zorica shrugged. "I wouldn't say *everyone*," she said. "He's selective. But he's very charming. The entire office has a crush on him. With men like Brian and André in the building, I don't know how any of the girls get *any* work done."

Tell me about it, Destiny thought.

Throughout the week, Destiny and André would wake up, sometimes make love as soon as they woke up, work out together, shower together, get dressed, and ride to work. Minus the occasional visits to her department, they spent the workday apart, then rode home together.

It surprised her that he didn't care if people knew they were involved. From what she'd seen on drama television shows, most executives at least made an attempt to hide their relationships with subordinates. André cared enough about discretion to make her sign an NDA before they started dating. Then why would he be okay with everyone in his office knowing that they had more than just a professional relationship? Just when she thought she was beginning to understand him, he always managed to do something that threw her for a loop.

Everyone was curious about their relationship. Women were quick to befriend her and quick to ask if she was seeing anyone. She hedged questions of that nature. Even though André wasn't afraid to show that she was under his wing, she didn't know how much she was allowed to say. For the sake of her own career, she also preferred for people to know as little as possible. The last thing she wanted was for people to assume that the only reason she had a job was because she was sleeping with the company owner.

On Saturday, André was true to his word and showed her around his city. He took her to the Royal Ontario Museum, the Art Gallery of Ontario, and the infamous CN tower, which he wanted to make sure she viewed at night. It looked magnificent and larger than life, blazing with bright-colored lights against the dark night sky.

The city was beautiful, and Destiny told him so.

"I've travelled the world a few times over," he said, his head tilted back as he gazed up at the CN tower. For once, he'd dressed casually in a black t-shirt, jeans, and boots. "There is no place like this city. I say that with confidence. There are cities that may have a few of its qualities. Maybe there is a city that is diverse or a city that has a collection of genuinely nice people. Maybe there is a city that is cultured and a city that is aesthetically beautiful. But a city that has all the above, *while* carrying the vibe that my city has...I haven't come across it yet. Not to say that this is the only great city there is. That would be a lie. But I don't know...there is something about this place, a trademark that makes it one-of-a-kind."

She smiled up at him. "The pride you have for this city is adorable."

He smiled back and tipped up her chin, staring down into her eyes. "The pride I have for this city is adorable..."

"Sir," she said before rising on her tiptoes and kissing him.

He enveloped her in an embrace and kissed her back.

They continued walking the streets of Toronto and passed a club with music wafting out of its doors. Destiny slowed her steps and stopped altogether, turning back in the direction of the club. It had been so long since she'd been inside of one.

André stopped and followed her gaze. "I'm guessing you want to go in."

"The music sounds amazing."

"Very bluesy," he commented. "Like the music I used to sing with my dad when I was a kid."

She tugged on his hand, trying to pull him towards the doors of the establishment.

He laughed. "All right, fine." He led the way back to the club, showed his identification to the door attendant and waited for Destiny to do the same.

The club was one large room, complete with a front stage that a live band was currently playing on. A dance floor area was in front of the stage, and tables were laid out behind the dance floor and on an upper level. The establishment was very classy, elegant.

Destiny wore a cute, little black dress, but felt a little out of place when she saw the more expensive dresses women in the club were wearing. André was even more underdressed than she was. It was a wonder he'd been let in, but then again, he was André Damian Gaines. He was no longer a rapper, but he was still the undisputed King of the Mississauga and Toronto areas. An establishment would be stupid to turn him away.

A short, balding man in a tuxedo walked past them and went to the front desk. "Antonio called in again. He's not going to make it tonight."

The man at the front desk rubbed his chin. "We can ask if anyone in the audience would like a chance to step into the spotlight," he suggested. "We can spin it. Make it an amateur night."

Destiny grabbed André's arm.

He gave a slight shake of his head.

Unable to hide her disappointment, she pouted at him.

"The audience didn't pay amateur night prices," the short, balding man grumbled. "We need to find a backup for him, stat. Antonio's been calling in more and more lately. We can't keep-" He'd turned his head while he was talking and stopped himself mid-sentence when he realized that Dré Gaines was standing in his club.

André returned the look.

"André." The man walked up to him. "I thought I recognized you."

"Joseph," André greeted.

Destiny glanced between the two of them. They knew each other?

"It's been how long?" the man named Joseph asked, clapping him on the upper arm.

André lowered his gaze to his arm with a frown. "Not long enough, apparently," he returned.

Joseph laughed. "You always cracked me up. Listen. You used to sing. And I know you know how to play the piano. I'm in a bind here."

"I don't entertain anymore," André reminded him.

"You'd be saving my ass," Joseph persisted, bringing his hands together in front of him in a begging gesture. "These people paid for a show. The band is great, but we're missing the pianist and vocalist. We need someone who can sing *and* play."

André's expression turned grim.

Destiny grabbed onto his arm again. "You would be amazing," she encouraged him.

He stared down at her. The look in his eyes softened after a few moments. He shifted his gaze over to Joseph. "You're going to owe me so big for this."

"Anything, anything, name it," Joseph said quickly, already looking relieved.

Destiny grinned.

"Don't smile too hard," André cautioned her. "You're going to owe me big after this, too."

André escorted Destiny to a booth and made sure she was situated before making his way towards the stage. He took long strides between rows of round tables until he reached the platform. Stairs were located to the left, but instead of turning in the direction of those stairs, he leapt onto the stage and rubbed sweaty hands on his jeans.

The band was still playing a bluesy tune as he moved behind the microphone stand. He turned on the mic and scanned the audience. "Hello. My name is André Damian Gaines. And I guess I'm singing for you all tonight."

There was a smattering of applause across the room, and chatter amongst the crowd. Confusion was quickly replaced with pleasant surprise.

André turned his back to the audience and walked over to the band. The band's music slowly faded out, then stopped altogether. André spoke to them, gesturing with his hands. The conversation between him and the band lasted several minutes.

Destiny's guess was that André was getting the band up to speed on his music, maybe asking them if they were familiar with any of his songs. The audience started talking amongst themselves, random conversation while waiting for André to take center stage again.

Destiny checked her text messages. She had two from Carlos and several from Candace. She typed in responses to them, but her fingers stilled on the screen of her phone when slow, hypnotic music started to play, heavy on synth.

André crossed the stage, grabbed the microphone stand, and moved it closer to the piano on the stage. The audience buzzed with heady anticipation as he adjusted the height of the microphone stand to compensate e for his sitting position at the piano. "We're almost there, just hold on for me," he said into the mic, his voice smooth and deep.

A few women in the audience squealed in response.

He smiled and turned back to the piano. The band continued to loop the beginning chords of the song while he prepared to perform. He flexed his fingers over the piano keys and leaned towards the microphone again. "It's been a while since I last performed, so be gentle with me. All right?"

More squeals from the ladies.

Destiny set her phone down on the table. A waiter approached and asked if she would like to put in a food and/or drink order. After minutes without a response, the waiter slunk away from the table.

André hummed into the microphone with his eyes closed.

Goosebumps rose along the length of Destiny's arms.

His fingers seduced the most beautiful music from the piano as he started to croon the words to one of his most popular ballads. His voice had the capability of a silkiness that caused tingles to run along the length of her spine.

When she glanced around at the other women in the audience, she could clearly see that his voice was causing reactions in them as well. Some women were fanning themselves off with their clutch purses.

His voice was deep, melodic, and all-around swoon-worthy. There were subtle changes to the arrangement of the song that he had to make, and those changes seemed effortless as he transitioned from one song into another.

His voice wasn't the only thing sending tingles down her spine. He had certain habits while singing. On higher notes, one eyebrow lifted in the sexiest way. He would pause, lick his lips, and turn his eyes to the audience while singing certain lines. A few times, he searched her out in the audience and maintained eye contact with her while his fingers stroked the ivory keys on the piano.

She gripped the edge of her seat and closed her eyes while listening to him. Towards the end of the song, he started throwing in adlibs. "Ohs," "whoas," and "yeahs" that were enough to make her melt. She crossed her legs tightly together.

There were moments in most women's lives when the man she was involved with exuded such raw sexiness, she thought, *Oh, he is going to* get *some tonight*. This...

This was one of those moments. In this moment, she was visualizing all the things she wanted to do to him. She bit her bottom lip while listening to him. There were parts in the song where his voice dipped even deeper.

His voice was simply enchanting. The screams from the women in the audience only gained in intensity. Some women were seated beside exasperated husbands, but even those husbands couldn't help but sway to the beat of the songs. The band kept their music understated and allowed André and the piano to have the spotlight. Each song blended into another and into another, until he'd performed enough songs to make a full set.

At one point, he stood up from the piano and moved the microphone stand back to the front of the stage. He adjusted the height of the stand again, stretching it taller. "How are you feeling?" After the applause died down, he hummed a tune into the mic. Despite how long it had been, he performed with such ease; he still knew how to command a stage and a crowd. "I have one more for you," he said, gesturing at the band with one hand.

The band eased into a different song.

"This is something that you haven't heard before, so again, be gentle with me."

The band looped the intro a couple of times until André took his cue and started singing.

"I'm broooooken…
Knew it before you said it,
And you won't let me forget it.
But you've awoken…
Desires I thought long gone,
Please don't do me wrong.
Because I trust you,
More than any other,
Sweetie, baby, lover."

At this point, he removed the mic from its stand and hopped down from the stage, working the room while humming. The tempo of the music shifted, and so did his flow as he started singing again:

"Oh…
Years ago, a girl shattered me,
Tried to mend the pieces
To the best of my ability…
When you called me broken,
it opened my eyes

To the fact I'm still healing,
I've just now realized.
You walked into my life
when I wasn't expecting you,
You're my beacon of light,
My role is protecting you.
I know it's not easy
Being with a man so complicated,
But be patient with me,
And I'll make you so glad you waited…
I said,
'I'll make you so glad you waited…'"

He paused, then reverted to the original tempo and flow of the beginning of the song. Still moving around the club floor, interacting with the enamored audience, he worked his way back to the stage as he started singing again.

"I'm broooooken…
Knew it before you said it,
And you won't let me forget it.
Baby, I trust you,
For you, I'd do anything,
Give me time to be your king.
Pleeeease be patient with me,
My beautiful Destiny.
I'll make you so glad you waited…
Trust that we are fated,
This is not to be debated,
I'll make you glad you waited…"

He hopped back onto the stage and returned the mic to its stand. Loud applause threatened to deafen everyone in the room. Even the annoyed husbands had to stand to their feet and clap their hands.

Destiny wiped at her eyes, standing up with the rest of the room.

André scratched his head and said, "That song is a bit of a work in progress, but thank you. It's been so long since I've been performed on a stage...it only makes sense that when I make my return to the stage, I do so in this great city." Extending an arm, he gestured appreciatively to the band. "You should really give the band a round of applause. I'm flattered they were familiar enough with my songs to be able to play them for you tonight. They had *no* notice and did an amazing job. Give them a hand."

More applause, more squeals, and a few whistles.

He closed his eyes and started humming again into the microphone. Then he wrapped both hands around the microphone and started to sing. When he opened his eyes, he was looking right at Destiny.

She stared back at him with a heated gaze.

A small smile curved his lips as he sang. After a few moments, he shifted his gaze to members in the audience. When the song ended, he stepped back from the mic and grinned. The band continued to play, and he bobbed his head to the music. Then he stepped forward and said into the mic, "I'm going to take a short break, then come back for another few songs, if you'll have me."

Applause echoed throughout the lounge.

André hopped down from the stage and walked through the center aisle. People stopped him to commend him on a job well done. A few asked him to snap photos with them. He obliged and resumed his slow approach to Destiny.

Beaming proudly, she met him halfway.

They met somewhere in the middle, wrapped their arms around each other, and held on tight. She stood on her tiptoes, grabbed his face in her hands, and kissed him.

He trembled in her arms, shaking with nervousness. But he kissed her back passionately and he didn't let go.

"You were amazing," she said into his ear. "You were *so* amazing. I told you that you would be, but you blew me away."

He pulled back so he could look down at her. The smile he flashed her was so boyish and charming, she couldn't help but feel an immense love for him.

The audience continued to vibe with André throughout the second part of the show and was extremely receptive. Some of the people in the audience sang along with him. It was amazing to watch. Most of the women in audience were bedecked in sparkling jewelry, but they were still ecstatic at music being sung to them by a man wearing a t-shirt and jeans. It was a statement as to just how talented he was. He didn't need pyrotechnics or choreographed dances. There wasn't a need for gimmicks and clownery. He could just stand there and sing, or sit at the piano and sing, and the crowd loved it. He soaked up all of the love the crowd was giving.

After the show, he was asked for his autograph by nearly everyone in attendance. He held up an index finger to Destiny, signaling that he would just be a minute. One minute stretched into thirty, but she didn't mind. This night was important for him. He itched to make music. He itched to perform again. It was in his blood; it was a part of him.

While certain aspects of the industry didn't jive well with him, his music - his voice - needed to be heard. There were generations of people who needed to hear what he had to say. He had to experience the audience embracing him so he'd know that if he did decide to take that leap and entertain again, his fanbase would welcome him back with open arms.

When he was finally able to tear himself away from the fans, old and new, he approached Destiny. "I feel like I've neglected you tonight. I'm sorry."

She shook her head. "You needed this. So, about the new song that you sang tonight…"

Flashing her a grin, he offered his arm. "It's not done, but you'll be the first to hear the finished version."

"It was beautiful. Why didn't you tell me that you're still writing music?" She leaned into him as they left the lounge. "Do you know how amazing you were?"

"You're inflating my ego," he warned, angling a look down at her. "And I didn't tell you that I was still writing music, because I wasn't sure whether or not it was even good. It has been a while. The song needs work. It needs structure. I wasn't expecting for that song to see the light of day. Being on that stage tonight and seeing you out in the audience though…In that moment, I wanted you to hear it in its raw form."

"I'm glad you let me hear it, and everyone *else* seemed to love it."

He laughed and shrugged one shoulder. "It felt good, being onstage again. Playing music. Using my voice."

"I'm so happy you did this."

He thought for a few moments and then said, "I'm glad you pushed me to." He leaned down and kissed the top of her head.

A buzzing sound came from his jacket.

His steps slowed as he reached inside his suit jacket pocket. He pulled out his cell phone, which vibrated in his hand, and held it up to his ear. "Hello? Mom - yeah. We scheduled for tomorrow."

They came to a street corner and he stopped walking. Attached to his arm, Destiny also stopped walking.

His brows furrowed. "Oh? Oh...well, no, I understand. Yeah. We can do it next Sunday. Would that work better? All right, for sure. Yeah." He hesitated and looked down at Destiny.

Her brows drew together. "What?"

"My mom says hello."

Destiny laughed. "Hello, Mandy!" she shouted into the phone.

André continued speaking into the phone. "Did you hear that? She says hi, too. I'll explain it to her. Yeah, yeah. I love you, too." He ended the call and repocketed his cell phone. "Dinner with the family is rescheduled for next weekend. Something with my uncle came up, and my mom is going to go over to help him."

"Okay," Destiny said, still clinging to his arm.

He started walking again, escorting her across the street and towards the lot where his car was parked.

"I guess we're going home now," Destiny said, a touch of sadness in her voice. Tonight was so amazing; she didn't want it to end.

"Not yet," he contradicted, as they moved through the parking lot. "There's one last thing I need to show you."

Half an hour later, they were parked in front of Gaines Enterprises. "You needed to show me the building we work in?" she asked, frowning at him.

He laughed and tugged her along with him.

She followed him to the front doors, which he had to open with a set of keys since the building was locked down for the night. They walked across the lobby. What could he possibly have planned that would take place in the office? After the looks they'd exchanged in the car, a few ideas came to mind, but this office building had to have security cameras installed.

While they were in the elevator, his phone buzzed again. He answered it, but his responses were brief. "Yeah. Five? All right. Thanks."

He was beginning to make her feel nervous. "You can't give me a hint as to what we're doing here?" she asked him finally, as the elevator climbed upwards.

His head tipped right, then left. Ultimately, he shook his head. "Nah. You're way too clever. If I gave you a hint, you'd figure it out."

The elevator doors opened to reveal the rooftop. A breeze swept inside the elevator cabin, ruffling her curls. He stepped out of the elevator. She timidly followed, expecting to see a dinner table set up somewhere, maybe. But there was nothing. The rooftop was completely barren.

He walked over to the ledge and stared down.

She stopped just behind him and wrapped her arms around herself.

He turned around and leaned his back against the ledge. "Tonight, I've been the happiest I've been in a long time. And I have you to thank for that."

"I'm glad you're happy," she told him earnestly.

"You're so perfect that it scares me sometimes."

Her heart fluttered in her chest. "That's how I feel about you."

A wry smile twisted his lips. "I'm not perfect. Far from it. Perfect would be a man who is ready to run off with you, get married, have children, and the dog, and the pretty house with the white picket fence."

Had he brought her here to break things off with her? "You at your worst is still better than any other man at his best," she said finally.

He pushed himself from against the ledge and closed the distance between them in three steps. "I'm nowhere near perfect, but whenever I'm around you, I want to be better. I want to *do* better. I want...I want to be the best man I can be, so I can be worthy of you."

Her breath caught in her throat. Where was all of this coming from? Was this because she'd pushed him to perform?

"There have been times when you didn't call me 'Sir,' as you should have. Times when you have spoken out of turn. Times that I *should* have punished you."

She broke eye contact and looked away.

He reached out and cradled her jaw in his hand. Then he tilted her face towards him. "I didn't punish you because that's who you are. Strong-willed. Opinionated. Wild. Stubborn. You're all of those things, which don't quite gel with the traits of a submissive. I don't say that to make you feel bad. Those characteristics make up who you are, and you are still perfect to me."

Her eyes welled up. The breeze picked up and a thunderous hum sounded in the distance.

"I saw you in the audience while I was performing, and I wanted to make you proud of me," he went on, smiling down at her. "I haven't wanted to make someone proud of me since..." He stopped himself and his smile faltered a bit. "I haven't wanted to make someone proud of me in a very long time. I looked out, and I saw you, and you *were* proud. Seeing that...*knowing* that...made me feel the happiest I have in *years*. After tonight, I realized that you're not just perfect. You're *everything* to me."

The thunderous humming sound drew nearer, but she barely noticed. She could only focus on the man who was pouring his heart out to her.

His brows slanted upwards. His hand was still cradling her chin as he asked her, "Do you understand...do you understand what I'm trying to tell you?"

She nodded her head, her eyes filled with happy tears. "I love you, too," she said.

He lowered his head and kissed her. They hugged each other. Her hair whipped around them as the thunderous humming noise drowned out all other sound.

She pulled back from the kiss and turned around to the sight of a helicopter landing on the helipad about thirty feet away from them.

"I've showed you one view of my city," he told her. "Now it's time for you to see another view of the city."

20

Brian leaned back in his chair, drumming his fingers on his desk. He stared up at the ceiling. *I'm stuck in the office on a Saturday night. I'm drinking Scotch as if that makes being stuck in the office any cooler. My friends are all out, or spending time with their families. Meanwhile, I'm here. Working. Drinking. Depressed as fuck.*

The past week, he'd spent working with André on that "special project" that was conjured out of nowhere. The minute André found out that Destiny was *the girl*, he'd jumped to action with this bogus ass project. What was the *special* project that needed Brian's finessing? Nothing but painful-to-read, eye-crossing reports. These boring, endless reports would have normally not even required his involvement. But what could he say? He couldn't tell the owner of the company, *"No, I'd rather spend the week working on my floor so I can scope out your girlfriend. Ever since the day I met her, I can't get her out of my mind. Because she is, without a doubt, the prettiest thing I've ever seen in my entire life. Not to mention, she's the first woman in years who has turned me down, boyfriend or not."*

A loud whirring sound cut into his thoughts and made him sit upright. He strained his ears, but he wasn't imagining the sound. The more time that passed, the louder the sound became. He stood up from his chair and walked over to the window. Was a jet plane passing?

He gazed out of the window, but a thought occurred to him. Gaines Enterprises had a company helicopter. That thought sent him jogging out of his office and down the hall leading to the front hall of the thirty-fourth floor. He didn't stop jogging until he reached the elevators. He pressed the button for the elevator. The elevator took its time in reaching him. "Come on, come on, come on," he muttered impatiently.

The elevator doors slid open and he stepped inside. He pressed the *R* button for the rooftop and waited, a bundle of nerves. He ran a hand through his dark brown hair, straightened his tie and suit jacket. The doors opened, and he saw a picture similar to the one he'd imagined on the way here: André and Destiny standing on the rooftop kissing while a helicopter was landing near them.

The elevator doors started to close again, and Brian's hand shot out to stop the doors from closing. He watched the two lovers kissing and felt a stabbing pain in his chest. He leaned his head against the elevator door and watched as the couple pulled back from the kiss.

Brian had known André for years. He'd been there when André had found out that his fiancé had cheated on him for the better part of their relationship. He and André had long talks about relationships and women.

Soon after André's failed engagement, he jumped on the casual relationship bandwagon. It had been quite heartbreaking to witness, actually. André, by nature, was a romantic. Witnessing him shutting off his emotions and becoming this...unfeeling playboy hadn't been easy.

Brian should be glad that his boss and friend had found a girl who made him want to feel again. A part of him *was* glad that André was starting to open his heart up again. But Brian couldn't help but wonder... *Why did the girl who walked in and changed André's life for the better have to be the girl that I wanted for myself?*

André helped Destiny into the helicopter, then climbed in himself. He pulled the helicopter door closed and sat in the seat beside her.

A gray-haired man in the pilot seat turned back and waved at them. "Hey, Mr. Gaines!"

"Destiny, this is Phil," André introduced as he started to strap her into her seat.

She lifted a hand. "Hi, Phil."

"Hi, Destiny," Phil called back. Even though he was yelling, his voice was barely audible over the sound of the helicopter blades that were cutting through the night air.

André positioned a headset on Destiny's head once she was strapped in. He leaned down and kissed her again while smoothing down the hair that had gone astray. Then he moved to strap himself into his own seat. He placed a headset on his head, then spoke into the microphone connected to the headset. "Without these headsets, you wouldn't be able to hear anything anyone was saying," he explained to her. "This is our company helicopter, if you couldn't tell by the 'GAINES ENTERPRISES' painted on the side. We're going to circle the city a few times. The skyline and lake are so beautiful at night."

"Make sure you're strapped in securely," Phil said into his own microphone. "In about thirty seconds, I'm taking this bird up into the sky."

André reached out, grabbed her hand, and caressed the back of it with his thumb.

"You are *so* getting some after this," she told him.

The grin he flashed her was all teeth.

"You were already going to get some after your club performance," she told him, and the tone of her voice was serious. "But what you said on the rooftop...and this..."

"Playroom?" he asked, keeping the sentence short since the pilot could hear their entire conversation.

Her eyes were locked on his as she said, "You can have whatever you want. You can do whatever you want."

He licked his lips and stroked his jaw. "Uh, Phil, we might have to skip the city tour. You might have to take us straight to my condo."

Phil laughed while adjusting some of the controls.

"You've got jokes," she teased him.

The sound of his chuckle seduced her ears through the headset earpiece. "Just remember that you said those words," he said. "Hold that thought for me."

The helicopter started to lift into the air.

André kept her hand in his, squeezing it on occasion.

She turned and gazed out of the window. The sky was dark, but a part of what made Toronto so beautiful at night were the buildings, lit up in an assortment of bright, pretty colors set against the perfect dark canvas. The helicopter circled around the city, then glided along the coast of Lake Ontario. Whenever she threw a glance André's way, he was looking at her. They were flying around a beautiful city at night, but the entire time, he'd had his eyes on her. "You're not looking out of the window."

"I've seen it already," he told her. "And its beauty pales in comparison to yours."

The smile Destiny gave André melted another layer of ice that had frozen around his heart. He lifted her hand to his lips and kissed her knuckles. *I don't know what the future holds for us, and I'm okay with that*. He knew what he would like it to hold, but he didn't dare start hoping for fairytale romances.

It was frightening. She was changing him, at his very core. Changing what he believed in, what kind of life he felt he wanted. She was breaking through the walls he'd put up to protect himself. It was comforting, knowing that someone loved him as much as she seemed to. But it was also scary, because he didn't know what he'd do if he ever lost her. Already, he couldn't imagine his life without her. He was at a point where he felt like he *needed* her. That was both overwhelming and fear-inducing.

His first urge had been to push her away. He'd invited another woman to his place, knowing that it would break

Destiny's heart. A part of him had even expected for her to walk away. Maybe that would have been best, best for him so he could return to his routine and best for her, so she could find a man that didn't have to work to be perfect for her.

But now, seeing the excitement, appreciation, and love in her eyes, he was glad that she hadn't walked away. If she had, he wouldn't have experienced this night. If she'd walked out of his life, he wouldn't have gotten up on that stage and performed. He wouldn't have shed his fears and expressed his feelings for her.

You have her, he thought. *You have her, and she's yours, and she's devoted to you. Now, all you have to do is keep her.*

She smiled the prettiest smile he'd ever seen in his life, an arresting smile that made his heart twitch.

He made a vow to himself, then and there, that he would do whatever it took to keep her. There was no denying it anymore. He loved her. He loved her more than life itself. He leaned his head back and closed his eyes. He felt her gently squeeze his hand and his heart expanded in his chest, growing to accommodate the love he felt for her. *Destiny is such a fitting name,* he thought, *because you are certainly my Destiny.*

TO BE CONTINUED…

Sneak preview loading...

Sneak Preview
of

Bound:

Broken Chains

Bound:
Broken Chains

Throughout André's and Destiny's relationship, she'd judged him quite harshly. She'd referred to him as *broken* or *messed up*, because she couldn't understand how he could be so sweet, loving, and affectionate while being so very emotionally unavailable. But the video and letters she'd found in his closet had shown her a side of André she hadn't seen before. That video and those letters shed an immeasurable amount of light into why André was the man he'd become.

She ran her fingers over the picture, overcome with sadness when she remembered the argument she'd seen on the videotape.

"You like this one?" Mandy asked her.

Destiny blinked and moved her hand away from the photo. "I do. I think...I think he looks adorable in this picture."

"This was a day I remember so clearly," Mandy said, closing her eyes. "He was just rapping. All day long, just rapping. I told him that he needed to do his homework, and his father-"

His father just let him keep rapping, Destiny thought, smiling wistfully.

Mandy drew back in shock. "How did you know that?"

Destiny nervously tucked strands of hair behind one ear. "How did I know what?"

"How did you know his father said he could keep rapping?" Mandy asked, glancing up at André. "Did you tell her about this day?"

André was staring at Destiny intensely, still swirling the wine in his glass. "I guess I must have," he said softly.

Destiny's cheeks reddened. *I wasn't just thinking. I was also speaking the words out loud. And now he knows.* She couldn't bring herself to meet his eyes. *Now he knows that you were rummaging through his things, and now he knows that you saw the tape.*

André was silent the entire car ride home. He still grabbed Destiny's hand and pulled it across the console. He pulled her hand into his lap and stroked the back of her hand with his thumb.

"Your mother was just as adorable as I remember," Destiny said.

"Mmm," he responded while driving.

"And she's a very good cook." Destiny was trying to get more than a "Mmm," out of him.

"I agree," he said.

That was it. He wasn't in the mood to talk, and she had a feeling she knew why.

They returned to the condo, where he dropped his car keys on the island counter in the kitchen. He removed his suit jacket and tossed it over the arm of the couch in the living room before collapsing on it.

She remained near the island counter in the kitchen, not knowing if he wanted her in the same room with him.

He stared up at the ceiling in silence. When he tilted his chin downward, their eyes locked. The look in his eyes was unreadable as he said, "I'm going to give you a set of instructions. I want you to listen to them very carefully. Understood?"

"Yes, Sir," she said softly, clasping her hands together to keep them from shaking.

"I want you to go into the bedroom. I want you to put on your collar. Are you with me so far?"

She nodded, her throat beginning to constrict. "Yes, Sir," she managed to get out.

He smiled, a smile that didn't quite reach his eyes. "Good. After you put on your collar, I want you to undress. Then, I want you to go into my closet."

The minute he said the word "closet," her chest grew tight.

"In my closet, there are a lot of drawers. I want you to go to the second group of drawers on the left side. I want you to open the bottom drawer." The expression on his face was calm, but his voice had a sharp edge to it. "There are three boxes in this drawer. I want you to take all of them out. I want you to bring them out here and set them on the coffee table. Do you have any questions about the instructions I have given you?"

He knows. He knows and he is going to punish you. She opened her mouth to speak. She wanted to apologize to him. Apologize for snooping through his personal effects without asking. Apologize for not telling him that she had sooner. Apologize that he had to find out she'd gone through his things on a special night they were spending with his mother and his family. They'd had a great time with his family, but now that night would forever be stained with this moment.

The expression on his face was stoic. "Did you have a question?"

No...I just wanted to say that I'm sorry. I'm sorry for not being honest with you. I'm sorry for being nosey. I didn't mean to do anything that would make you distrust me. The words were right there on her tongue, but she couldn't get them out. She was afraid to speak. She hung her head down, frustrated with herself. "No, Sir."

"Please do as you have been told," he said, finally breaking eye contact with her and walking to the far end of the living room.

She chewed on her bottom lip and walked to the master bedroom. Once in the bedroom, she closed the door behind her and pressed her back flat against the it. Panic started to set in. *He has come so far in trusting me, and I've fucked all of that up with one huge mistake.*

On the day she'd searched through his drawers, she hadn't expected to find a videotape dating all the way back to his childhood. She expected to find maybe a little black book. Something trivial that would still give more insight about him. He was a mysterious, fascinating man. She had wanted to know more about him. She had wanted help in understanding who he was, as a man.

I wanted to feel closer to him, she thought now, leaning against the bedroom door. There was no telling what kind of punishment he was going to inflict on her. Possibilities flooded her mind, and she had to push those thoughts out of her head. For all she knew, he could be timing how long it took for her to return. How long should it take for her to put a collar on and bring out three boxes?

She heard a door open and turned to face the bedroom door. As quietly as possible, she eased the door open and peered out into the hallway.

The door to the playroom was open.

She blinked, swallowed, and closed the door. *Take a deep breath, girl. He loves you and he would never hurt you, not really. He'll punish you for snooping through his shit. After this, his trust in you might be on shaky ground, but everything will be okay. First things first, I might want to actually follow his orders instead of hiding in here all night.* She took a deep breath. After collecting herself, she walked over to the nightstand. Her thoughts were all over the place as she gathered her hair over one shoulder, picked up the black leather collar, and buckled it around her neck.

Moving towards the mirror, she reached a hand behind her back and started to drag down the zipper on the dress. As she allowed the dress to fall to the floor, she tried to think of what she was going to tell him. How does one apologize for nosing through someone's family drama? Everything she came up with sounded lame, even to her.

She groaned in frustration, staring at her reflection. A curvy, pretty, black girl with sunkissed medium brown skin, almond-shaped eyes, a cute nose, and full lips stared back at her. *Why did you have to open that damned drawer?* she asked herself. *And when you saw the boxes that were in it, why did you have to open them?*

The sound of a door closing reached her ears. He'd grabbed whatever torture device he intended on using and was probably on his way back to the living room, where he would carry out whatever punishment he deemed fit for her disregard of his privacy.

She hurriedly removed her undergarments and carried her clothes to the hamper. Then, she walked over to the closet and opened the door.

There were benefits to being the head of a corporation worth nearly a billion dollars: this closet was one of them. Insanely spacious, especially for a condo unit. High-tech to the max. When she stepped inside, lights flickered on, detecting her movement. She padded over to the column of drawers - a familiar column of drawers that she'd stood in front of weeks ago, on a day when André had gone to work. She dropped to her knees, remembering the letters he had written to a former fiancé who'd cheated on him. The letters started off as love letters but had quickly become something else. He still had the ring he'd given to that woman, a beautiful diamond ring. Then there was the videotape...

She closed her eyes, trying to push the memories to the back of her mind. *Follow the instructions you were given, Destiny. You're taking too long in here.* With quick movements, she opened the drawer, removed the boxes from it, and carried them out of the bedroom.

When she returned to the living room, André was seated on the couch. A flogger, a whip, a long chain, and a paddle rested on the couch beside him. He didn't speak, and he didn't have to. The orders he'd given her had been precise. She should know what to do next.

She placed each box on the coffee table, then stood with her head bowed.

"On your knees," he said softly.

More words leapt to her mind. Explanations. Words of apology, of regret. Words that would at *least* give him an idea of why she'd done what she'd done. But she couldn't speak any of them. Her throat grew tighter and tighter, to the point where it was difficult for her to breathe and swallow, much less speak. Unable to get the words out, she wordlessly obeyed his order and lowered down to her knees.

"Look at me," he instructed.

She lifted teary eyes.

He held her gaze for a long time. "I'm going to ask you a question. I want you to be very honest with me when you respond. Do you understand?"

I'm so sorry, André. I didn't mean to disrespect you. I just wanted to understand you. "Yes, Sir," was all she said.

He tilted his head towards the three boxes. "Have you seen these three boxes before?"

The question was so simple. Had she seen these three boxes before? The boxes were crimson, black, and royal blue. They each varied in size. The crimson box was the box that held the beautifully written letters. All the letters, including the angry ones, were written in a such a poetic way. She could feel his pain, feel just how intense his heartache had been. Even though his heart was broken, she could feel how much he longed for the woman who'd done him wrong.

The black box held random items. A Jane Austen novel, a ring, perfume, other odds and ends. Paired with the letters in the crimson box, those seemingly random items told a story. Those items in the black box were keepsakes, items that reminded him of the fiancé who'd broken his heart. And the royal blue box...

She closed her eyes, feeling tears coming on. The blue box had the videotapes in it. The question he had asked was so simple, and yet she was having the most difficult time coming up with an answer that gave justification to her actions.

"Are you going to make me repeat myself?" he asked softly.

Tears shimmered in her eyes, causing her vision to go blurry. She didn't want to disappoint him. It had taken so long to get him to trust her. *But he already knows the answer to the question,* she thought. *He is asking only as a courtesy - in the off chance he's wrong.* "Yes, I have seen these boxes before, Sir," she said, her voice shaky.

A muscle in his jaw twitched. Otherwise, he remained still. "Have you seen what is in these boxes?" he asked.

A lone tear slid down her cheek as she nodded her head.

"I need a verbal response from you," he said, his voice still soft and deceptively calm.

"Yes, I have seen what is in the boxes, Sir," she responded.

He closed his eyes and turned his head to the side.

She lowered her eyes and another tear fell. "I'm sorry," she said.

"Don't speak," he told her, his words clipped. With his hands clenched into fists, he rose from the couch. His body was tense with agitation as he grabbed a long, heavy chain from the couch.

More tears fell and she wiped at them with her hands.

"I'm very disappointed in you," he said, kneeling beside her. He hooked an index finger in the ring at the front of her collar. He tugged on the ring, pulling her face closer to him. Then, he lifted the chain and connected it to the D-shaped ring. He tugged on the chain to make sure it was secure.

It's not just a chain, she realized. *It's a leash. He has me on a leash right now, like I'm some kind of dog.* She risked a look up at him.

For the first time since she'd made the slip-up at his mother's house, he allowed emotion and intensity to show on his face. "I want to be able to trust you," he said slowly.

"You *can.*"

He closed his eyes. "I said, 'Don't speak.'"

"But you have to know how sorry I am," she said, the teardrops turning into steady streams of tears. "I wasn't being nosey for the sake of being nosey. I just wanted to understand you better. Now, I feel like I do. I'm sorry I didn't tell you. I didn't want you to be angry, when...when I'm glad I saw what I saw. If I hadn't..."

He narrowed his eyes at her. "If you hadn't, then what? You wouldn't be here right now? You would have walked out on me?" His voice sounded dangerous, like he was close to the point of losing control.

She pursed her lips shut.

He wound the chain around his hand, yanking her face closer to his. "Answer the question."

"I don't know," she said in a tiny voice. "When I found those boxes, you and I were going through a rough time."

Releasing the leash abruptly, he stood up. He turned his back to her and ran a hand over his head.

Please try to understand where I'm coming from. Don't hate me for what I did, please.

"You can't...you can't go through my things without permission," he said emphatically. "You can't continue speaking when I tell you not to. You are being extremely disobedient. I'm trying..." He paused, shaking his head. "I'm trying to be lenient with you, and you're making it impossible."

"You can't understand why I wanted to know more about you?" she asked him quietly.

"Whether I understand the reason, you are disobeying specific orders that I've given you. You are *disrespecting* me. I cannot tolerate disrespect, Destiny. No matter *who* you are. No matter how much I lo-" He stopped himself and turned around.

Hope sprang into her heart and she hated herself for it.

He walked over to her, bent at the waist, and picked up the end of the leash. "Follow me," he said, and started to walk across the living room.

She started to stand.

"On your hands and knees," he called over his shoulder.

She lowered back down on her hands and knees as the slack in the leash decreased. His grip started to tug at the collar, forcing her forward. She started to crawl behind him. The curtains over the tall, floor-to-ceiling windows were drawn open. She rarely saw them closed. His condo unit had a view of a gorgeous, Olympic-sized pool with no neighboring condo building in sight, but she still felt like she was on display. She followed him to an ivory chaise lounge and stopped just short of it.

He tugged on the leash, yanking on her collar. "Up."

She crawled onto the chaise lounge.

"Bend over it," he instructed.

Memories of being spanked and flogged sprang to her mind.

"Don't make me repeat myself," he cautioned.

She bent over the back of the lounge chair, ass-up.

He walked around the lounge chair and touched her hair gently. His fingers dug around in her hair and one by one, he removed the hairpins that were holding the chignon in place. When her hair fell around her shoulders, he walked away. A minute later, she heard his voice. "Stay there. Just like that."

She couldn't see him, couldn't see what he was doing. If she had to guess, she'd guess that he was returning to the couch where he was keeping his toys. Wiping at her tears again, she stared out the window.

She was still staring out the window when he came up behind her. She saw his reflection, saw him staring down at her. He allowed some of the items to drop to the floor but held up the paddle. His fingers ran over its smooth, wooden handle. "Because this is a real punishment, and not play, this *will* hurt," he warned. "For you to learn your lesson, it has to."

"I understand, Sir," she said sadly, feeling a slight tug on the leash. He was gripping the end of the leash again. Leash in one hand, paddle in the other. Closing her eyes, she gripped the back of the chaise lounge, preparing herself for the pain.

He spanked her with the paddle. *Hard*. So hard, she screamed. So hard, her eyes fluttered open without her even meaning them to. So hard, she gripped the back of the chaise lounge until her fingers hurt. He didn't stop. The hits were back-to-back, pain on top of pain. From the look on his face, it wasn't something he was enjoying. He didn't take pleasure out of having to punish her. It was something he felt that he needed to do.

Her ass cheeks were beginning to sting. Tears streamed down her cheeks. She cried out that she was sorry. She cried out that she would never go through his things again. She made promises that she would try not to disappoint him ever again. But he didn't let up. He continued to hit her. She had tried to prepare herself for the pain, for what the paddle would feel like. But he was relentless. There *was* no preparing for his wrath.

25 Years Ago...

"I saw the way you looked at her!"

"I wasn't looking at her in any special way, Mandy."

"And you're lying to me!" There was a brief thump sound, most likely the sound of something being thrown. "Is she the woman you're calling late at night? Is she the woman you're seeing when you're on the road? Look at me!"

Young André stood in the hallway entrance, gripping his toy microphone in his hands. He didn't understand what his father could have done to make his mother sound so angry. Moms and dads loved each other. They weren't supposed to argue and fight. André held the microphone to his chest while he listened. Another thump, and this time the thump was loud. The sound nearly made him jump out of his skin. He turned and ran, but didn't know where to run to.

There was a coat closet at the far end of the living room, near the front door of the small house. André ran to it, threw open the door, and slid inside, the bottoms of his footie pajamas lacking any kind of friction when rubbing up against the hardwood floor. He closed the door and hunkered down inside of the closet, breathing heavily.

Even from inside of the closet, he heard the yelling. He dropped the microphone and covered his ears with both hands, shutting his eyes. Trying to shut out the sounds of yelling, trying to shut the world out. His toy microphone spun around in a circle on the floor for a full minute. By the time the microphone stopped, so had the yelling.

When André's eyes fully adjusted to the dark, he could see that the top end of the microphone was pointed at the door. He grabbed the door handle, turned the doorknob and slowly pushed the door open. Timidly, he poked his head out.

His father was storming down the hall with a suitcase.

Alarmed, André pushed the door all the way open and rushed out with his eyes wide. "Dad!"

His father hesitated, a guilty look entering his eyes.

His mother came tearing down the hall. "You're just going to leave?"

His father stared at him and raised a fist to his heart.

With more tears forming in his eyes, André lifted his fist to his own heart, mirroring his father's sign of affection.

André held the flogger up in the air. A fine sheen of sweat graced his forehead. He heard soft whimpering and shook his head, clearing his old childhood memories. He raised his eyes to his reflection in the window. His reflection appeared to be a crazed individual. Haunted, wide eyes, entire body taught, veins straining against his skin.

Destiny's rear end was red. Completely red. Slash marks from the flogger made lasting imprints on her skin. Her skin hadn't broken, thank God. But she was crying, clinging to the back of the chaise lounge with her head bowed. Her back was covered in sweat. Her arms and legs were quivering.

His grip on the flogger loosened and the flogger fell to the floor. How many times had he hit her with it? When had he picked up the flogger? He couldn't remember. Fear seized him, and he stood there quietly, not knowing what to do. His first urge was to gather her up and hold her. Massage her until she felt better. Carry her to the bathtub and bathe her. Spoil her. Even though he wanted to do those things, he couldn't. Giving a submissive a reward right after a punishment was essentially sending mixed signals.

Inwardly cringing at the sight of the red marks on her backside, he took a step back. "Your punishment has been carried out. You may go to the guest room."

Lately, she'd started sleeping in her own condo when she had to work the next day. Even though it was a Sunday night, he'd taken her punishment too far and wanted to make sure she was okay. She didn't question it, but she also didn't move from her spot.

"Did you hear me?"

She didn't respond.

"Destiny."

She sniffled and lifted her head so she could stare at his reflection in the window. Then, she slowly turned her head and angled a look at him over her shoulder. Tears still streaming down her cheeks, her nose running. Her hair a wild mess - still beautiful, but she looked like an untamed lion. And her eyes. Those large eyes that he couldn't get enough of, had so many emotions in them. Love. Hate. Fury. Confusion. Sadness.

His heart clenched when he saw the look in her eyes.

She straightened, releasing her hold on the back of the lounge chair. After carefully placing one foot on the floor, she winced in pain.

Pain that you caused her, he thought.

Pain that she deserved, his subconscious countered. *She went through your belongings without permission. That is a sign of disrespect. A complete disregard for your privacy.*

But you didn't open up to her, he thought. *How else was she supposed to learn about the events that have shaped you?*

She could have asked, his subconscious reasoned. *She felt free enough to speak her mind on other topics. Why not that one?*

It's just a closet. A closet with drawers. And the drawer she happened to open just had a set of three boxes in it. How could you punish her for checking to see what was inside? Did she really deserve for her ass to be beaten to the point where it's completely red?

She stood before him, her tear-filled eyes reflecting the last emotion that had been buried beneath the rest. Hurt. Her eyes asked him, *"How could you do this to me? How could you do this to me if you love me?"*

He blinked back at her, trying very hard to maintain his composure. Trying hard not to break down while she was standing in front of him. "You may go to your room," he repeated.

She stared at him for another beat. Then, she turned and walked out of the living room. The chain leash dragged behind her, making a loud rattling sound on his expensive hardwood floor. A moment later, he heard the guest bedroom door open, then click closed.

"Fuck!"

Destiny nearly jumped out of her chair. The exclamation was *that* loud. With her nerves rattled, she stood and walked out of her office. The main floor was dark; the lights were turned off to reserve energy. All the cubicles she passed were empty. The EXIT signs cast a soft, red glow over the office. The door to Brian's office was closed, so she knocked.

"Yeah?"

"Can I come in?"

He hesitated before answering. He hesitated for so long that she thought he wasn't *going* to answer. She was nearly to the point of returning to her own office when he said again, "Yeah."

She opened the door and peered inside.

He stood with both hands braced on the top of the desk. His suit jacket was draped across the back of his chair. A glass sat on top of his desk, and she doubted that the amber liquid in it was juice of any kind.

With her brows drawn together, she entered the office, linking her hands together. "Are you okay?"

"Yeah," he said without lifting his face to look at her.

She walked closer to his desk, trying to get a better look at his face. "Did something happen?"

When he looked up at her, his face was flushed. His face being that shade of beet red made his eyes appear even bluer than they did normally. "The media got a hold of some of our financial records. Records like that are kept confidential. So, if they got a hold of it..."

She gasped. "You have a leak in the office."

He nodded and lifted his glass. "Yeah. We've got a leak," he said shortly before taking a long swig.

She eyed the glass with concern and crossed the room, going to stand next to him. "It's going to be all right," she assured him. "We'll figure something out. We-"

"So you're an optimist?" he asked, cutting her off. "A journalist who's an optimist? That's a first."

From where she stood, she could smell the liquor on his breath. "How long have you been drinking?"

"Not long," he lied, and took another swig.

She reached out and grabbed the glass from his hand. "You don't need this. Everything *will* be fine."

"You only say that because you're naïve," he said. "The situation just went from bad to *worse*. With the documents they have, they'll make us out to look like *liars*. Okay, Destiny? So yes. We all came together and made this very pretty statement to release to the press. And we released it. But guess what? We might as well have stayed silent because the documents they have make that statement look like a *lie*. The public won't trust any statement we release now." He snatched his glass from her.

"What is drinking going to do to solve the problem?" she asked him, genuinely curious.

"Drinking makes me feel like my life is a little less shitty," he responded without pause.

"Your life? Shitty?" She turned her head and surveyed his office. The sheer size of it...the only larger office she'd seen belonged to André. "You work for an amazing company. You have a great job. The team loves you."

He nodded slowly. "I have a great job. A great career. You're right." His eyes lowered to the liquor in the glass. "I have a lot of money. A killer wardrobe. A badass car. Several badass cars, actually. I am grateful for my career and how far I have come, but I work all the time. When I go home, no one is there waiting for me. I have this *amazing* house. It's beautiful, but it's *empty*. I have these amazing things, but no one to share them with. Which... kind of makes those amazing things quite worthless."

He was treading on territory that was difficult for her to coach him through. "I'm sure you will meet someone one day," she assured him.

"I already have," he said, and his voice strained.

"Brian..."

"I know." He gave her a tragic smile.

"I'm sure you'll meet someone else," she said, trying to keep her voice upbeat. "Someone who makes me pale in comparison."

He shook his head sadly. "No one is going to compare to you."

She took a deep breath and looked away from him.

He lifted a hand to her cheek.

She flinched away from him. "You can't do that," she hissed at him.

He returned to staring down at the top of his desk.

André wanted to move me to a completely different department because he felt like something would jump off if I stayed in Brian's department. I told André that he had nothing to worry about and then this happens. She turned her back to him and covered her face with her hands. "Why are you doing this?"

"I don't know why I did that. I'm sorry."

Her mind was racing. "André told me that if anyone hits on me, I have to tell him about it. But...I can't tell him about this. It's *you*. We both *work* with you."

"I know," he said, his voice thick with intoxication.

"And even beyond that, the company is in crisis. If I *did* tell him, and he fired you, then the company would be defenseless. We'd have to find a replacement for you. Meanwhile, Palmer, his minions, and the press would have a field day tearing Gaines Enterprises to shreds." She closed her eyes. "Why did you *do* that?"

"Because every time I see you, I want to touch you. It's just you and me here, so I wanted..." He stopped himself.

"I don't know. I'm drunk. Let's just sum it up to I'm drunk. Would that make things easier for you?"

"For *me*?" she shrieked. "Brian, I'm trying to help you keep your fucking *job*."

He ran a hand across his forehead. "I'm sorry."

Her heart broke a little for him. *What is it with men having the ability to put on this brave front for the world while being so broken?* It took her a moment to remember that it wasn't just men. When her ex, Jordan, had cheated on her, she'd put on a brave front, too. She had issues with trust and wanted nothing to do with guys. Internally, she was a mess for quite a few months. She had to take time and work on that, but while she worked on it, she kept a brave face on. Just because she was torn apart on the inside, didn't mean she had to ruin everyone else's good time. With a sigh, she reached out to give his back a pat. She rubbed up and down his back. "It's going to be okay," she promised him. "If you want to talk about anything, I'm here. I can even be a wingman and score you some hot dates."

He chuckled. "My wingman? Hot dates?" he repeated, laughing.

"Don't underestimate me," she told him in a mock-defensive tone. "I'm the best wingman you could ever ask for."

"I would never underestimate you," he said, his voice low. "I'm horrible for putting you in such a compromising position with your boyfriend, who also happens to be my superior. There's just this one thing, though." His gaze gravitated to her lips.

Her voice shook as she took a step backward. "Brian, don't."

He straightened his posture, turned, and easily closed the distance between them. He raised his hand to cup her cheek and looked her in the eyes before lowering his head and gently kissing her on the lips.

ABOUT THE AUTHOR

Shiloh Starr was born in Waco, Texas, and raised in Zion, Illinois. She has been writing short stories ever since she was a child and has been writing novels ever since junior high school. She currently writes in the genres of horror fiction, young adult horror, science fiction/fantasy, and romance. In addition to the *Bound* series, she has written young adult horror series *Hidden Treasures,* a paranormal series called *BloodLust*, and a romance novel titled *Open Book*. The first novel in a romance series titled *Fireworks* is the next project that will be released by the author.

Her books can be found at: www.sandstarr.com

www.ingramcontent.com/pod-product-compliance
Lightning Source LLC
Chambersburg PA
CBHW021120260626
47169CB00005B/1366